Helen was standing in front of me, swaying sexily.
'I've got to change,' she said. 'You can help. Undo
these buttons, will you?'

The material of her blouse was silky and slippery
beneath my clumsy fingers.

'Don't you just love the feel of it? I love it next to
my skin. Could you pull it out of my skirt?'

I did so and the blouse opened, revealing a deep
red slip edged with black lace.

'Do you like it?' she asked, fondling the material.
'It's so soft. Go on, stroke it.'

She pushed her bosom at me and I tentatively put
out my hand. She took hold of it and placed it on the
full firm mounds of her breasts.

'There, Nick, what do you think of that? . . .'

The Blue Lantern

Nick Bancroft

HEADLINE
DELTA

Copyright © 1993 Nick Bancroft

The right of Nick Bancroft to be identified as the Author of
the Work has been asserted by him in accordance with the
Copyright, Designs and Patents Act 1988.

First published in 1993
by HEADLINE BOOK PUBLISHING

A HEADLINE DELTA paperback

10 9 8 7 6 5 4 3

ISBN 0 7472 3966 5

Typeset by
Letterpart Limited, Reigate, Surrey

Printed and bound in Great Britain by
Cox & Wyman Ltd, Reading, Berkshire

HEADLINE BOOK PUBLISHING
A division of Hodder Headline PLC
338 Euston Road
London NW1 3BH

The Blue Lantern

1. Serendipity with Helen

Helen. I was unbelievably lucky to have Helen as the first woman I made love to in a full sexual sense. As I'd say now, having lived in Canada for the last thirty-odd years, she was my first lay. And what a lay! I was a late starter by today's standards, twenty-one and as naive as hell, back then in England almost three years after the end of the war. Apart from a few furtive fumbles I was still green but you have to remember that trying to get sexual favours out of a woman then was like asking her to commit suicide. Most women held off, expecting you to marry them before they gave out. But Helen was not like that.

I was living on my own in London at the time in a poky second-floor flat in an old house that was falling apart. It had escaped the bombing but only just – it had suffered from the effects of blast and so was very shaky: plaster fell off the ceiling all the time, a couple of windows had cracks in them, floorboards were loose.

Altogether it was a miserable hole and, to add to my misery, I hated my job. I was the lowest of the low, a clerk in an income-tax office. I had just been transferred from Manchester where I'd spent the first twenty years of my life. My mother had died when I was fifteen and my father moved in a sloppy, blowsy woman I didn't like. So when I was given the chance to work in London I jumped at it.

I was often broke and depressed in those first few months. My flat was ratty, with decrepit, second-hand furniture, and often I had no money to keep the small gas-fire lit. Sometimes I just took to wandering the streets and some evenings I'd meet one or two prostitutes who thought I was fair game for them. And so I was and once or twice I was tempted, especially when I was approached by a really pretty girl who was about my age and probably just starting in the game. She was almost shy when she asked me if I wanted a good time. I'm sure she would have given me a very good time but as usual I had no money. So I just had to live with my sexual frustrations.

What kept me going was the theatre. The little money I had when I lived in Manchester was spent going to see plays, usually try-outs, at the big old Opera House. So in London I used to go to the theatre whenever I could afford to, and that worked out at least once a week, going straight from work to queue up for a cheap seat in the gods.

And that's how I met Helen.

I met her by chance – I literally bumped into her in a theatre bar during an intermission, making her spill her drink onto her blouse. I thought she'd yell at me but she just stood there stroking her blouse where there was a damp patch, smiling at me. 'Not to worry. This stuff doesn't stain. You wouldn't believe what's been spilled on this.' She gave me her smile again, showing white, even teeth in a large mouth she'd made the most of with a deep-red lipstick. She looked at me out of large brown eyes, her face framed by wavy brown hair that fell to just above her shoulders. Then she turned back to the man she was with, leaned into him and whispered something in his ear. They both laughed and of course I thought they were laughing at me.

Later I bumped into her again after the show in another bar just round the corner from the theatre. I'd just had a quick pint and was ready to go and catch my bus home. Coming out of the Gents I guess I was staring around and I bumped straight into Helen again.

'Sorry,' I said.

'It's you again. Habit of yours, is it, banging into people?'

'No. I just wasn't looking . . .'

'Is this your way of trying to chat me up? Or are you just looking around to see who else you fancy?'

After a pause, she said, 'Well, are you?'

'What?'

'Trying to chat me up?' Then she put her hand on my shoulder. 'Don't worry. I don't mind.' And she pressed her hand a little harder. 'Wait a minute.'

She leaned around to whisper to that man she'd been with in the theatre bar, then she turned back to me. 'Gerry here is looking for young men like you.'

I wondered what she was up to.

'Oh, he's not like that! Far from it!' She laughed. 'Maybe you could work for him.'

I didn't know what to think but I made my mind up quickly when she said, 'I bet I've made you miss your last bus. Why don't you let me drive you home and I'll tell you the kind of thing Gerry'd want you to do?'

Well, whatever the work was, I knew I'd be crazy to turn down a ride with this great-looking woman, so I nodded my head. She said a quick word to Gerry, then she linked her arm in mine and we walked out of the pub to her car.

Cars were still scarce in England then, so when she

stopped at a low-slung sporty job I was very impressed
– as I was with her legs when she slid in, her skirt
riding up high. She leaned across to open the door on
the other side for me, smiling up at me, then saying,
'Get in, as the actress said to the bishop.'

She didn't ask me where I lived, just drove, a bit too
fast in the traffic. While she was driving, she told me
about Gerry's business. 'It's a bit shady. Import business. Brings in things people want but can't get too
easily these days. You know, Scotch, French wine,
high-fashion clothes, lingerie with this new stuff,
nylon, and silk. You should see what the French are
making with nylon. Like this.' And she pulled up her
skirt to show me her leg sheathed in a nylon stocking.
'What d'you think?'

'Terrific,' I said, staring at her leg. She laughed. 'I
didn't mean that, but thank you all the same. I meant
the job. For Gerry. People pay a lot for the stuff he
brings in so he pays well. He needs reliable delivery
men, young men who look like butter wouldn't melt in
their mouths. Like you. He trusts my judgement and
when I saw you I thought you'd be the right kind of
person. Unless you're stuck on the job you've got.
How'd you like to work for Gerry . . . and me?' I
couldn't resist her smile when she asked me, so I said I
would.

'Good. Now we can relax,' and she put her foot
down. She still hadn't asked me where I lived and she
was driving in a different direction but I didn't say
anything. I just wanted to stay sitting next to this
woman with the flashy legs and the great smile.

Then it started to rain. 'Dammit! And me without an
umbrella. Well, not far to go now.' Soon she pulled up
to park on a side street with large brick houses. She

4

pointed at one of them. 'That's mine . . . well, the top floor's mine. Come on in for a drink. We'll have to make a dash for it. Here, help me off with this, will you?'

She started to take her jacket off, a form-fitting grey velvet coat. I put my arm round her shoulder to help slip her arm out. As she did that, she leaned against me and I caught a smell of heady perfume.

'Nice smell,' I said.

'Gerry brought it in. I love French things, don't you? This jacket. You wouldn't find velvet like that in England. Trouble is, rain falls on it, makes spots and it won't come off.' She folded the jacket with the silky lining outside. 'Right. Let's go.'

'But what about your blouse?' I started to take my jacket off. 'Put this round your shoulders.'

'I'm alright. I told you, you can spill anything on it. Nothing stains.'

Helen's place consisted of three large rooms, her living room furnished with a comfortable deep-seated sofa, two cosy armchairs and a plush carpet. She waved me in, said, 'Take a pew. I'll just go and hang this up,' and shook out her velvet jacket. As she disappeared through another door I caught a glimpse of the bedroom. When Helen came back, she went over to a small buffet and took out a bottle of Scotch, holding it up to me. 'Gerry's. The best. Want one?'

'I'm really just a beer drinker.'

'Come on. One little snort of this will do you the world of good. Relax. Take your coat off. Put your feet up.' She poured a hefty slug into one glass. 'There.'

'Aren't you having one?'

'Well, I've had a fair amount tonight. When I get a bit squiffy, I'm never sure what I'll get up to.' She smiled. 'But I guess a nightcap'll hit the right spot.' She poured herself one, then slowly swayed over to the sofa where I was sitting. She stood in front of me. 'You know, that rain. Got me quite wet. Maybe I'd better go and change.'

'Here, I'll take the glasses.'

'That's alright,' she said, then still holding them, she stretched her arms out wide. 'But you can help me.'

I stood up and she moved a step closer to me. 'Undo these buttons for me, will you?'

I'd never had a woman willingly offering to let me undo her buttons before so I must have hesitated.

'Go ahead. It's alright.' I fumbled my way nervously. 'Careful, Nick.' The material of her blouse was silky and slippery. 'Don't you just love the feel of it? So soft. I love it next to my skin, I hate to take it off but it's really quite wet. Could you hitch it out of my skirt?'

The blouse opened as I did that revealing a deep red slip edged with black lace. I'd seen nothing like that before so I stared at it.'

'You like that? Didn't I tell you Gerry knew the best stuff to bring in? It's that new nylon. Feels great.' She handed me a glass and then she began to stroke the material of her slip. 'So soft. Just feel it.'

She pushed her breasts at me a little and I put my hand just under them.

'Go on. Stroke it. Nice, eh?' I was very tentatively stroking my hand across the material by her ribcage.

Then she took my hand and held it in front of her face. 'Nice hands you've got, Nick. You shouldn't have had so much trouble unfastening the buttons. 'Course, there's a knack to it. Need to make your hands a little slippery and smooth.'

She lifted my hand to her mouth, licked a fingertip then sucked my finger into her mouth. Slowly pulling it out, she then licked her way down the length of the next finger, her tongue warm and soft in the space between the fingers, moving up the next finger, till she took both fingers into her mouth. She was doing this slowly, deliberately, delicately and I was getting excited, stiff in my pants, ready to burst out. Then she worked on my thumb and, as she slid it out of her mouth, she said quietly, 'You know what they say about the thumb? Tells you a lot about a person . . . well, about a certain part of a person.'

She sucked it into her mouth wetly, then out. 'You've got a very good thumb, Nick.'

Then she said, 'Now try this,' extending her arm for me to undo the button at the wrist and, strange to say, I did it quickly. 'There. What did I tell you? You're a fast learner, Nick. Now the other one,' holding out her other sleeve for me to deal with. 'Thanks. Better take it off now,' and she walked away from me with a seductive sway, beginning to slide the blouse off her shoulders, disappearing into the bedroom.

I thought that would be the end of it, a woman like Helen, maybe twenty-five, twenty-six having a little fun with a young kid. I expected her to come out of the bedroom wrapped up in a dressing gown. But no, when she reappeared she hadn't covered herself at all. She came over to me and reached across to an end-table.

'Forgot my drink,' she said, picking it up and sipping it, touching her fingers delicately at her mouth. She looked down at herself, at the lacy slip covering her breasts. 'It's so nice, I hate covering it up.'

She drank again and again put her hand at her

mouth. 'You know what they say about a man's thumb, what it tells you? They say that about a woman's mouth. Is that what you've found, Nick?'

I didn't know what to say but I didn't have to say anything, for she licked her fingers and stepped up to me and very deftly undid one of my shirt buttons, then quickly another, then another.

'See how easy it is?'

And soon she had them all unfastened, running her fingers down inside my shirt till she touched the waistband of my trousers. That made me jump a little because I was straining big and hard inside my trousers. I stepped back but she held on to me and stayed with me. 'One handed,' she whispered.

Then she leaned across me, putting her glass down on the table. 'See how two hands can do it,' pulling my shirt out of the waistband, then her hands were at my fly, undoing one button at a time with each hand. They were now close to my cock, brushing it a little but only as if it was part of undoing my fly. She made no attempt to deliberately touch me there. I suppose I could have thrust myself against her hands but I didn't want to spoil anything she was doing, perhaps even make her stop. I decided to let her do what she wanted – and besides, I was enjoying the tease.

Soon she had my belt undone and my trousers were slipping down. It was obvious that she could see how my cock was sticking up stiffly but she still ignored it.

'That's how it's done, Nick. Now it's your turn.' She turned sideways to me, pushed me gently back to sit on the sofa and pointed at the large button holding her skirt at the waist. 'Just one. Bet you can do it in a jiffy.' She took my hand, sucked three fingers deep into her mouth. 'Try that.' And the button was undone quickly. 'Good boy.'

She wriggled and the skirt fell to her ankles. She stepped out of it, threw it to one side and then swayed in front of me. 'Didn't I tell you the French make great undies?' And she did look terrifically sexy swaying back and forward in her red slip with the black-laced edges. 'Feels great to wear it.'

She took my hand and placed it on her thigh. 'Feel that. So soft and silky, isn't it?' I stroked her thigh, and, leaning forward, my cock was pushing hard, trying to thrust out of my underpants.

'You don't look too comfy like that, Nick.' She bent down, slid my trousers down, quickly pulled my shoes off, then the trousers. 'Something in the way here,' she said as she reached for my underpants, pulling the elastic so that she uncovered my cock, not touching it, sliding the pants down and off. 'There. And wasn't I right? You do have a very good thumb, Nick.'

She sat next to me, eased me back and her face came over mine, her wide-open mouth on mine, her tongue slipping into my mouth. She began to slide her tongue in and out and, as she did this, her hand was on my cock. Her thumb and finger were at the base and, in rhythm with her tongue in my mouth, she moved finger and thumb up and down the length of my cock, flickering fingers at the fat head, stroking in circles round the foreskin. I was still stroking her thigh but she pulled one hand to her breast. 'Two hands are better than one,' and with that her other hand snaked into my crotch, cupping my balls, squeezing the thick stem at the base of my cock while her other hand stroked.

Then she took her hand from my cock, licked her

fingers. 'Good for other things, not just buttons,' and suddenly my cock was squirming deliciously in wet, creamy fingers till I thought its stiffness would burst out of its skin and I felt one finger playing with the slit of my cock, as if it was trying to entice come to leak out. And a little did ooze out and that finger rubbed the sticky cream all round the knob head till I thought my cock would break apart in a tingling explosion.

By now I had moved my hand under her slip, stroking up her thigh and, as I touched that thin strip of silk of her panties that covered her quim, she let out a little gasp. The silk was really wet and my finger probed and rubbed all around, prising the silk back, feeling how wet her slit was. She began to circle her hips round and round as if she was turning on my fingers stroking her. My balls were beginning to ache, feeling full of come but her hand was steadily stroking and squeezing. Her fingers were slowly rising and falling along the length of my cock as if she were trying to pull out a great flood of come – it was still oozing out and her fingers were hot and sticky with it, slippery on the stiffness.

My other hand was pushing off the straps of her slip and her bra till her round breasts came free. I began to play with her nipples and they became hard, sticking out. She whispered, 'my nips are getting as hard as your dick.' Saying that seemed to get her started for she came out with an incredible monologue. This was new to me, a woman saying all these extraordinary sexy things – there we were, my fingers wet with her cunt juice, my mouth sucking her breasts, her hands all over my cock and balls and this stream of words in my ear.

'Lick my nips. Wet. Your cock's wet. Such a comey kid you are. A cocky boy. My creamy cunt. Nick, Nick,

10

with his big prick. Such fat balls. This is so fucky. Wait to spurt out. Cover me with come. Sucking and fucking. Hard fat cock. Cock and come. Suck and fuck. Your fingers are fucky.' Then as she talked she slid down and put my cock on one breast, then the other. 'Your big fat cock is crying with come. Come on my breasts, drown my breasts with come. Nick's prick, come, come.'

Now she was sliding my cock between the warm round softness of her breasts. And she went on talking as my cock rubbed over her breasts, sometimes sticking up, and she pressed her tongue out to touch the very tip between the words she was saying till I couldn't stand it any longer. I had wanted to make sure I fucked her, though I knew that as soon as I touched that silky cream of her quim all the come would surge out in a great jet, but I couldn't resist the words she was saying, 'Come, Nick, come cock, prick's coming, flood my tits, flood me, come on, come on, come, he's coming, coming, come, Nick, cock come.'

And come I did. The first spurt, released with a great flying jet, might have gone halfway across the room but her hands were right at the tip of my cock, catching the come, letting it leak through her fingers. I felt it warm on my fingers, rubbing it on her breasts. Her fingers were covering all the length of my cock with come, juice slipping through her fingers while she pulled at my cock as if she wanted to milk the last drop of come out till I was drained. And we lay there, sticky with come and my cock slowly lost its stiffness though still fat and silky in Helen's hands.

'Sorry,' I said. 'I shouldn't have . . .'

'Nothing to apologize for.'

'I couldn't wait.'

11

'I know.' She leaned down to kiss the tip of my prick. 'Such a lovely prick for Nick. Like your thumb. A thumb full of come.'

'But what about you?'

'I loved it. I just love it when you squirt out like that. All over me. And we've got the rest of the night. You young kids with your big cocks. He'll be sticking up again in no time.' Then she pulled her slip up and reached for her panties. 'Got my blouse wet but you made my panties wetter. Feel how wet they are.' And she took my hand and placed it on the soaking silk. 'Just leave it there. Gently, gently.'

And so we lay there, my fingers squirming round in her quim inside her panties, her fingers coaxing my prick from its limpness until she made me stiff again.

As we were stroking each other she was telling me a little bit more about Gerry's business, how he'd give me things to deliver, sometimes Helen driving me, other odd jobs, steering clear of the police. 'Don't panic. Gerry's very careful. Just keep your eyes open, that's all.' And we kept right on stroking and snuggling but as if we were just talking business, as if we were paying no attention to cock and cunt and breasts, till eventually Helen began to talk about how a young man's cock soon comes back to life, how it made fucking so much better because the second coming took a longer time, how she liked to relax feeling the come drying on her, smelling it around her, made her feel sexy again, how she liked to keep her fingers on a cock waiting to make it stiff again, 'ready to be its own fucking machine again,' and of course all this talk and her insistent fingers aroused me again. 'Well, look what's happening,' she said. 'The poor thing wants to go to work again.'

She got up from the sofa and peeled off her slip. She looked enticingly sexy in her panties, garter belt, stockings and high heels — and she knew it, strutting around in front of me for a while. I felt my cock begin to twitch. 'Your cock can go to work for me, and you think about working for Gerry, though I think all your brain's between your legs right now.'

She came over to where I was sitting, put one foot up on the sofa, put her hand on my shoulder, then brought her other foot up. She was standing over me, straddling me, my prick pointing up at her. She looked down and said. 'Poor thing. So big and long but not quite long enough to reach up here.' She smiled down at me, opening her cunt lips with her two hands. 'Don't worry. My sweet lips'll come down to it.'

She bent her knees and her slit was at eye level. Her fingers were still pulling at her quim, pushing the silk of her panties to one side. 'You get what you see,' she said, moving her pelvis closer to my face.

I reached up to pull her panties down but I had to stop when I had them halfway down her thighs for her legs were open. I put my fingers on that triangle of dark hair, letting one of my fingers slide along her slit. She looked down at me, then bent her knees a little more to make herself comfortable on my fingers, making sure my finger rode up and down her clit. Then she began to rotate her pelvis. 'I'm getting really wet,' she said. And my fingers were slipping around inside her squirmy moistness.

Then, leaning one hand hard on my shoulder, she pulled her panties down to her ankles. She shook one foot out, then raised the other leg her panties were hooked on. This made her cunt open wider around my fingers. She slipped off the panties, and then hooked one leg on my shoulder, steadying herself with her hand on my other shoulder. Her quim was right next to my face and I watched my fingers moving in and out, round and round in her glistening wetness. My other hand gripped her buttocks, one finger manoeuvering towards the crack of her arse. My cock was straining upward, wanting to be fondled by her hands, but she couldn't reach down and she was too involved in turning her cunt round, well oiled now on the axle of my hand, my fingers going in and out like a piston.

'You're making me horny, Nick.' Slowly she sank down, taking her leg from my shoulder, bearing down on my fingers, kneeling over me, hovering her quim over my cock. Then she gently reached for my prick and led it to those juicy lips of her cunt, rubbing it along her clit, moaning as she did. My two hands were now holding the cheeks of her bum and she moved up and down, teasing the head of my cock with her cunt, touching its tip, then raising herself, then down a little further, letting my prick probe in a fraction more each time. I was hot and stiff as an iron rod, wanting to push right inside her.

Then she got tired of the tease. 'Put it right in. I want to feel your big fat cock inside me.' She sat herself on my cock, her legs now wide open, up in the air by my shoulders, still circling herself as my cock probed inside. I could not move much, just thrusting up as she wriggled her cunt around my prick, like sliding into thick, warm cream with twitches like little electric shocks as she held onto my thick cock, holding it still while she tweaked me, and I felt shudders along its length, twinges and tingles, tightening, then relaxing. All I could think of was my cock being covered in such a slippery tingling sensation. And gradually it was as if all of me was inside her and my whole body was full of come that wanted to surge out through my prick into her.

All at once we were into a new slow rhythm of fucking as she adjusted to me, as I tried to sink in and out. She raised up so my cock almost came out, letting the lips of her cunt tickle the head of my cock, drawing the skin wetly back, then she sank down on it and it was like diving in slow motion into a pool of warm oil, the tip of my cock sliding deliciously against soft walls inside her.

Helen began to whimper, I was sweating and grunting with the effort. 'Fucky man,' she whispered. 'Keep fucking like that. I want to come. Make me come. Now. Now.'

And nothing could stop us now. Everything was all focused in cock and cunt – all squirmy and moist and sloppy, Helen's mouth as wet as her quim, on my mouth, sucking at my lips, my cock reaching inside her as I grabbed her shoulders to pull her down as far as I could. My balls banged against her and it was as if she wanted them inside her as well. I felt huge inside her, almost as if my prick was stiff and big enough to reach so far up inside her it would stand like a backbone and the head of my cock would be tickling her throat – but it was my tongue flicking at her tongue, going in deeper trying to lick at her throat. Helen was writhing and gasping, though her mouth was wide open on mine, her noises spilling with her saliva dribbling all around.

And suddenly my cock split open with a great gush of wet hotness, splattering it inside her. Helen flung her head back and moaned loud, jiggling faster on my spurting cock, still thick and hard, and it felt as if come was gushing like an oil strike, would go on spurting, filling Helen who was clinging hard onto me, her nails digging into my back, her legs now hooked on my shoulders holding me in tight as she pushed down on me.

So that was it, my first fuck. I really struck lucky, especially when I thought I'd botched it by coming all over her breasts first. But she seemed to like to feel all that sticky come on her, rubbing it round her nipples, licking it off her fingers, making my cock all slippery with it. I think maybe it made her feel horny as hell and she was on tenterhooks waiting for my prick to stiffen again as she kept thinking about fucking with me. That's why I think she liked to come out with all her talk, her words so horny and making her feel randy, and making me feel ready to go at her again. And all that made me feel comfortable with her, as if we could do anything. Anything we decided to do would be alright with her. She liked calling things by those names and while at first I was shocked by her talk, I soon liked it because it certainly made me feel as horny as she was.

I learned fast with Helen. Of course I worked for Gerry because that meant I could keep seeing Helen and I had a fantastic four or five weeks with her. But Gerry kept me busy and soon Helen moved away from me – I suspect Gerry used her to recruit others though she told me that she didn't always find the recruits as interesting as me. I began to see her less often but in a way I didn't mind because Gerry always had a few women hanging around and I discovered one or two were very amenable, so what I learned from Helen came in handy for me with those others.

Helen and I fucked again that first night. About five

in the morning, I felt her big sloppy mouth almost devouring my lips and teeth and tongue, eating at me but very softly while her hands were expertly coaxing my cock up to hardness. I responded very quickly though I think I was very deeply asleep. I guess I felt flattered that she'd come out of sleep and wanted my cock again. This time it happened quickly. I turned to her, stroking her cunt, discovering she was already velvety moist. Then her voice in my ear: 'Quickie. Nick's quick prick.' And she pulled me inside her and it was fast banging, all over in two minutes, but beautifully explosive. We both fell back to sleep quickly.

Then a little later we were at it again and after that I don't think I could have managed it once more, though Helen went around after we'd got up, teasing me, flashing her fingers at my crotch, telling me she wanted that stiff cock again. 'Aren't you English?' she said. 'A stiff upper lip and a hard cock.' I was feeling sore, and worn out but as relaxed as I'd ever been. A word I learned later seemed to fit the bill to describe that marvellous night I spent with Helen, that first long encounter and all the other times with her – seren-dipitous. The dictionary defines 'serendipity' as 'an aptitude for making desirable discoveries by accident.' And Helen was certainly a desirable discovery – seren-dipitous indeed!

2. The Nurse and The Blue Lantern

After Helen had worked me over so thoroughly, I slept deeply till about ten thirty that morning. Of course, that meant I missed work but I was only an office junior, a job I'd always considered temporary till I could go to university. It paid enough for me to live poorly so Helen's place – her classy clothing, her sexy lingerie – were all calculated to make me fed up with the measly amount of money I earned.

You can imagine how I felt that morning after such an exciting time with this attractive woman who was now wandering around in a flimsy peignoir that floated open as she moved. She took a delight in swirling around me, serving me tea as she waltzed around, sipping at her cup. Once she put it down and headed to the bathroom, coming out with a bottle of pills. She tossed two or three of them into her mouth, swilling them down with tea. She saw me watching her and laughed. 'Don't worry, Nick. I haven't got a headache. I'm not making any excuses. The only ache I have is down here,' and she touched her pubic mound suggestively. 'And I know just the thing that will cure that.'

She swayed over to me and put her hand on my crotch, beginning to slide her fingers over my cock. I must have flinched – it was still delicious to feel her working me up to a state of semi-arousal but I was feeling sore. My cock had been really busy with Helen. 'Oops! Better be careful. Don't want you out of commission. I still have some plans for you.'

As she sat down on my knee her peignoir swirled out wide and she wrapped it around my shoulder, cuddling close to me while one hand snaked inside my underpants to my balls which she let rest on her cupped palm. 'There! I'll be able to tell by the weight in them when they're ready again.' She was gently massaging my bare back with the silky material of her peignoir. My cock, sore as it was, was twitching, flicking against her wrist as her finger reached right under my balls. She whispered in my ear, 'I'll soon have you feeling right as rain. I've got something good for what ails you. Just relax.'

We sat for a while. She seemed to enjoy teasing me, her hand inside my underpants not quite touching my cock, now stiff and hard but slightly sore, playing with my balls, her other hand sliding silk across my back, whispering, 'Isn't that nice and soft? Remind you of anything like it that's nice and soft? Something you can slide right into? Silky and creamy,' and she tweaked my balls enticingly.

Then she began to ask me a little about myself, what I worked at, what I was going to do with my life.

'It doesn't sound as if you'd mind giving your job up. You'd be much better off if you worked for Gerry. Besides, I'd see more of you if you did. And I do mean more of you!'

Her fingers searched out the head of my cock and her fingertip played exquisitely around the stretched-back skin. I shuddered a little at her touch.

'I can see that gets to you.' She laughed a little. 'Not bad for a well-brought-up Catholic girl, wouldn't you say? Would you believe I was a goody-two-shoes? When I was a girl, I'd have to invent things to confess each week.' She laughed. 'I wouldn't have to invent anything these days.'

Her fingers slid gently along the whole length of my cock, up and down slowly. As she caressed me, she said softly, 'Forgive me, father. I can't keep my hands off prick. I like to put it right inside me.' She giggled. 'But I don't need to ask forgiveness, do I? It's too nice, isn't it?'

She stroked me gently, making sure not to make me more sore – though what she was doing was a delicious mix, it made me feel extraordinarily sexy but there was an occasional twinge of pain. I twitched a little when I felt those little strikes of pain and then her fingers would become even more gentle, almost like a healing touch.

'Mind you, once I got to be about sixteen, I was beginning to feel really randy and the more I used to hear about flesh and the devil in church, the more I wanted to sample it. I became a real terror. I'd sit in the back pews in church and feel up any boy sitting next to me. I'd put a prayer book over his crotch and sneak my hand under it. I think the news got around fast because there was always a scuffle on Sunday mornings as all the boys would try to be the lucky one to sit next to me. And some of them couldn't wait. They'd cream their pants almost as soon as I touched them. Damp patches showing on their trousers. And some of it got on my gloves. I loved it. I was a real flirt.' She stopped and looked straight at me. Then her hand was suddenly more insistent and I felt very sore. I tried not to flinch because I didn't want her to take her hand away. 'I'll have to do something about that. Can't let a little soreness get in the way.'

She went on to tell me how later she'd trained as a nurse. 'All those medical students! I went wild for a time. But once you've been round bodies day after day, it sort of puts you off. That's what nursing does to you. You see all shapes and sizes, fat and thin, blood and guts, dirt, so you lose interest. A lot of the regular doctors could see I was interested in what they wanted, so it was fun for a time. Some of the patients as well, but I got disgusted with myself eventually. It got boring, believe it or not. I kept wanting there to be something special, someone special. Then along came Gerry.' She gave my cock a delicious squeeze. 'You can tell I'm not bored now, right?

'Gerry was a patient, he'd come in to have his appendix out. He was always kidding around with all the nurses. I wondered just how many of them he got into bed in the few days he was there. Still, he seemed to take a special interest in me and the second time I was in bed with him, he asked me if I wanted to work for him. He could see I was bored and I obviously liked other things! He said he wouldn't work me too hard, there'd be good pay, lots of laughs. At first I thought he wanted to set me up in the game but he just laughed when I told him that. 'You deserve better than that, kid,' he said. 'Just be my Girl Friday, that's all.' Well, I was flattered because Gerry always sounded so classy, so sophisticated. You know, he's been to good schools and all that. His family has plenty of money and I suspect he bought his way out of going in the army.

'So eventually I gave up nursing. I liked being with Gerry. Sometimes he'd spend the night with me but I wasn't really his steady girlfriend, he likes women from his own class. But he set me up here, paid for my clothes, taught me how to act like those women who hung around him. All I had to do was run a few errands, watch the staff in the restaurant, that kind of thing. I thought there'd be a catch in it but so far there hasn't been. He even let me have the car. Oh, I see Gerry with some of his seedy friends. I know he may be into a few big rackets but I keep my nose out of that. I just do my job. He never tells me much about what's going on, about the juicy pies he's got his fingers in – and speaking of fingers in pies,' and here she took my hand and placed it on her quim, 'I know you've got a sweet tooth.' She laughed. 'But it isn't exactly your teeth I want to taste it. Just stick your big fat knife in there so you can cut yourself a nice slice.'

And her hand was covering my cock till it began to swell up more. My fingers stroked around her and she wriggled to make herself more comfortable so her slippery wetness let my fingers sink in a little deeper. She murmured, 'Little Jack Horner. Horny in your corner. Isn't that plummy? And yummy? What a good boy you are.' She stopped talking, her head leaning on my shoulder, eyes closed while she savoured my fingers circling round her soft moist lips.

'Well, anyway, I make deliveries, keep my eyes open for Gerry, find him people I like the look of. He trusts me, so when I saw you last night . . .'

'Just why did you pick me up last night?'

'I wouldn't call it picking you up. After all you were the one who bumped into me.'

'D'you do it often?'

'You jealous? You don't have to be. You'll see. There's always plenty of other women hanging around Gerry – they'll take care of you even when I'm busy. And I don't mind that. I'm on the look-out for Gerry.

Well, and for me as well. I look for someone who's fed
up with what he's doing. They're the ones useful for
Gerry. When I saw you looking at me at the theatre, I
thought, why not? The kid looks nice. Looks like butter
wouldn't melt in his mouth and I bet he's bone-hard
just looking at me. And Gerry was getting himself
pissed. He'd be no use to me then and I was feeling
randy so, being the tease I am, look what happened. I
just guessed you'd be the type. I mentioned it to Gerry
the first time you bumped into me and he said I could
give it a try. Then I thought I'd lost you till you
bumped into me again in the pub. Luck, meeting you
by chance like that. Nothing chancy about this,
though.' She was talking about my cock, now standing
fully awake and firm in her hand. 'This can bump into
me any time.'

She began to push my pants down but then the
phone rang. 'Damn!' She went to answer it and when
she came back, she was pouting a little. 'Too bad. Just
when I was getting interested. That was Gerry. Wants
me to take you to see him. For lunch. So we'll just have
to save this till later,' she said, patting my hard-on
briefly, squeezing my balls. 'I don't have a thing on this
afternoon, if you know what I mean, and I'm sure you
don't, so, after lunch, you can come back here if you
like.'

Helen drove me back to my place for a change of
clothes. She pulled a face when she saw my rat-hole.
'My God, Nick! We'll have to get you out of here. Better
stay with me till Gerry can find you a place.'

When she drove me to the restaurant to see Gerry,
she dropped me off and said, 'He'll tell you what he
wants you to do. I'm not coming in – men's talk. But
come back and see me after lunch.' She revved the

engine and, as she pulled away, she fondled her breasts with one hand, looking back at me quickly. I watched the car drive away and then realized that I had only the vaguest idea where she lived and I didn't know her address.

The restaurant was called the Blue Lantern, a 'tarted-up' place, as a friend of mine would have described it. 'Kidneys for breakfast, plus-fours and pass the marmalade, darling,' he'd have said. The walls were papered in a deep red flock pattern, the tables discreetly placed apart with starched white tablecloths and wine bottles covered in masses of wax which had dripped down from the candles stuck in them. Even for lunch, the maitre d' was in a dinner jacket and the waitresses, most of them attractively nubile, were in traditional maid's uniforms.

But somehow it all seemed on the verge of sliding away into tattiness. No work had been done on the place, certainly nothing since the beginning of the war and nothing since the end of it, either. The walls had patches of discoloration even one or two bad splotches. The tablecloths were threadbare, some of them too flimsy to take the starch so they looked grey and frayed.

A few people were eating but it wasn't crowded. Most of them looked either grim or distinctly unhappy, caused maybe by their jobs or the food on their plates. The whole place looked like the foyer of a brothel collapsing into seediness and, from what Helen had mentioned about Gerry, I wouldn't have been surprised if the maitre d' hadn't led me into the back room where an overweight and blowsy woman would be waiting for me. As it happens I wasn't too far wrong in my surmise and I discovered that the back rooms, where everything really happened, had certainly been kept in good repair.

I saw Gerry sitting on his own so I walked over to his table. He looked up at me with a quizzical look, then grinned. 'You're Helen's young man?' I nodded. He grinned again. 'Treated you well, did she?'

'Very well.'

'What do you call yourself?'

'Nicholas . . .'

'Say no more. Don't need to know your surname. Keep things simple. The less we know, the less other people know, right?'

'Whatever you say.'

'Order something to eat. Whatever you fancy.'

The words were pleasant enough but there was a kind of peremptory edge to Gerry's voice, sounding like one of those who spoke with a precise and clipped upper-class accent, a voice that gave the orders and expected to be obeyed without question. I was something in awe of those people. I always suspected they had money and looked down on someone like me.

'Helen tell you much?'

'Not much.'

'That's my girl. Well, she wouldn't would she? Liked her, did you?'

'Very nice.'

'Very nice? You can do better than that, can't you? Good-looking woman like Helen. Going out of her way for you. She did go out of her way for you, didn't she? She didn't have to do that, you know. But I could tell last night she'd taken a fancy to you. I'd have been surprised if you hadn't turned up here today.' He grinned again. 'I saw you giving the place the once-over when you came in. A bit run-down, I know. But

26

all the real action takes place in the back. Private club. Have to be a member to get in there. If you work for me, you'll be a member.'

He paused and scrutinized me. I half expected he'd take out one of those eyeglasses jewellers use, screw it in his eye and peer hard at me to see if I was the genuine article. 'I suppose you want to know what you'll be doing for me if I take you on. It's a pretty loose group I run. I just try to help people get a few of the things they deserve and of course that means that we get a few of the things we deserve.' He went on in this vague way for some time and I wasn't sure I was getting the drift but eventually he hinted at the idea that he had certain contacts – 'at home and abroad,' he said – and, after the long years of the war, people deserved to enjoy themselves a bit. 'So I provide goods and services, the sort of things a bit difficult to come by these days. Mind you, I have to go about it carefully and quietly and sort of sideways.' He grinned as if he liked the idea of being a crab. 'So why shouldn't we spread a little happiness around?'

By now it was obvious he was talking about black-market deals and as almost everyone was into this in their own small way – making deals, exchanging ration coupons, paying a little more to buy more than the ration you were entitled to – I wasn't particularly bothered by this, even though I was suspicious of someone like Gerry with his cool, almost sardonic voice.

By the time we'd finished eating, Gerry had convinced me to give up my job so I could work full-time for him, but he didn't really explain exactly what I'd be doing.

'Not to worry, old man. Nothing too difficult. Delicate sometimes, you know.' He winked at me. 'And mum's the word.' He laid one finger on his mouth. 'And it's best if we don't see each other too much. Work through Helen.' He winked at me again. 'I'm sure you won't mind that, will you? We can keep in touch through her. So you just keep in touch with her, if you know what I mean.' He leaned over to me with his hand slipping inside his jacket. 'You'll like keeping in touch with her, eh?' There was a leer in his voice.

I was finding this very disconcerting. First of all, I was to do some kind of work for Gerry without really knowing what it was; secondly, I'd been seduced by an attractive woman as part of a plan for me to meet Gerry in order for me to do this unknown work; and thirdly, here was Gerry suggesting I keep on seeing Helen though, in a way, she was Gerry's woman.

Then Gerry pulled out a big, fat wallet and gave me a slim wad of notes. 'Here. This'll keep you going for a bit. Go and grab a taxi. Back to Helen's.' I must have looked puzzled. 'Well, that's Helen for you. Reckons everyone knows where she lives.' He scribbled on a scrap of paper and gave it to me. 'There you go, old son.' He stood up – the interview was over. He folded his newspaper under his arm. 'Must be off. No rest for the wicked.'

'But,' I stammered, 'what am I supposed to do?'

'Helen'll let you know. Nothing too complicated.' He slapped me lightly on the shoulder. 'Off you go. Helen's waiting for you, I'm sure.' He gave a quick bark of a laugh and turned away, walking to the back of the restaurant. I stood there watching him saunter away. I looked at the banknotes in my hand, fanning them out limply. They were five-pound notes, something I had rarely had before. Thirty-five quid, a small fortune for someone like me. And on top of them the scrap of paper with Helen's address. I memorized it, shoved the paper and the notes into my pocket and walked out of the restaurant like a jaunty tap dancer. I'd pushed any scruples I may have had to the back of my mind. That money in my pocket helped. Things were definitely looking up. I went to the nearest taxi stand, clambered aboard, lounged back and gave the driver Helen's address.

At first I thought I was at the wrong place for when I rang the bell, the door was opened by a nurse in uniform. After a couple of seconds I recognized that it was Helen.

'Ah, you've come for your appointment. Well, the doctor's not in but I'm sure I can take care of you.' She pulled me in, crushing me against her starched uniform. I didn't quite know what to make of her. She was looking vibrant, bright-eyed, a smile playing around her luscious red lips.

'Here, let me take your coat.' She slipped it off my shoulders and draped it over a chair. 'Well, we don't have to wait for the doctor. I think we can proceed with the examination. Let's see here,' and her fingers were loosening my tie, then undoing my shirt, pulling it out of the waistband of my trousers. Her hands began to slide across my chest, pinching one of my nipples, then the other. 'You're certainly in good physical condition. We'll soon have you back in shape, I'm sure.'

She unbuckled my belt, deftly sliding my trousers down. 'Step out of them, please. Now for your underpants.' By now, of course, I was beginning to stand upright, especially when she put one hand under my balls and took my cock in her other hand.

She leaned down as she pulled the foreskin away from my cock-head. 'Certainly nothing much wrong with that.' She held my cock between two fingers and I began to swell more. She stooped a little lower, 'Ah, yes, I can see. It is a little red. Of course, they usually are red, aren't they, especially at the end there?' She put a gentle fingertip on the slit of my cock. 'Does that hurt?' I shook my head. 'Let's see about this.' She looped her finger and thumb around my fatness and slowly rode them down the length which was pulsing like mad. 'There. That's not too bad, is it?'

Her finger and thumb were pulling up my thick stiffness now. It was an exquisite touch but a little painful when the skin folded over my cock-head. 'That's a little sore, is it?' I nodded. 'Usually it's a little more sore when you pull down like this,' and her fingertips rolled the skin back and down. My cock-head really felt swollen but she kept her fingers pulling down, one finger flicking at the strip of skin that holds the foreskin. She pulled down slowly and I was certain that all the skin would be peeled away and all I'd have was a fat, red, very raw and tender cock stripped of its outer skin. But somehow I didn't want her to stop. 'I think I see the problem here and I have the very thing for it. Just wait there.'

She walked very briskly into the bathroom and while she was there, I bent down to remove my shoes and socks. I felt a little silly standing there naked with a long red prong sticking out in front of me but I just stayed there, waiting for her to come back. She returned holding a large jar from which she'd already removed the lid.

'A spot of cream in the right place will do the trick.' She scooped a big dollop out of the jar and gently scraped it onto my cock. 'Very soothing, isn't it?' She took another scoop and massaged my balls with it, her fingers moving towards the crack of my arse. She kept massaging, holding the jar in her other hand. 'We have to cover the whole area,' and with that, her hand moved to slather the cream all over my cock. Her hand was now working systematically, my cock squirming in the slippery ointment. Helen was now standing quite close to me. 'We have to make sure we cover all the painful spots. Would you hold the jar for me, please?' She gave me the jar to hold and then both her hands were sliding and slithering cream all over my cock and balls. 'It's beginning to feel better already, I'm sure.' I was squirming in and out of her fingers like a stiff eel. I was not sure how long I could take it before I let loose with my own cream.

'You know, this is your own fault, doing all those naughty things last night. A pity you have to suffer for it, though, but you should try not to spill yourself. The way you spurted out all over my breasts. You know, all that wet made me sore there. Maybe I should put some ointment there as well.' She moved one hand as if to undo the buttons on her uniform. 'Silly me! My fingers are all greasy. Mustn't stain my uniform. Would you help me, please?' She thrust her chest at me and so with my free hand I unbuttoned her uniform. 'You're getting very good at that,' she said as she shrugged it off her shoulders. She was wearing nothing underneath. 'You have the ointment. Could you put some on, please?' So I took a small scoop. 'Start at the nipple and work it all around.'

So we stood there, she rubbing and stroking my slippery cock while my fingers circled round first one nipple, then with more ointment on the other. She moaned a little as I did this and her hands became even busier on me. 'In between, remember? You put yourself in between. Must have made it sore there.' So I lathered her with the cream between her breasts. I put the jar down and now I had two hands to rove over and between her breasts. They felt deliciously soft and slippery just as my cock did as her hands probed all the different surfaces, all the tight skin around my balls, slowly working me towards my shooting out my jism. 'Careful now,' she whispered.

She knelt down and took my cock to let the tip touch each nipple in turn. Then she rolled it over her creamy breasts till finally she placed it between them, squashing them against the hardness, and I began to fit into a rhythm, one of her hands touching the tip of it as I rode up and down, her other hand constantly playing with my balls. 'I hear come has medicinal properties. So make me better. Squirt it all over me. Keep going, Nick, then keep coming. Come, come!'

Eventually, that's what I did, splatting it all over her neck, then moving down to spill some on her breasts as her fingers moved to rub it onto her nipples, round and round.

The rest of that afternoon and evening Helen and I became a couple of grease monkeys. We used that ointment and Helen got some of her other creams, body-rub oil, jellies and face creams and we spread it all over us in all the nooks and crannies. She smoothed it along the crack of my arse and her fingers slid in there, one probing deep inside, wiggling around, pressing deep, her other hand full of some jelly massaged around my cock. At the same time I put a handful of cream on her quim and my fingers worked it round and round the lips, a finger straying inside, another revolving around her clitoris till she was squirming with delight, yelling in orgasmic pleasure. I wondered what her landlady who lived on the floor below made of all the bellowing, shrieking and squealing that erupted from us – but maybe she'd heard it all before from others with Helen.

I suppose that day was the first time I discovered all the sensual delights of the body, not just my genitals but other places – oil spilled around toes, Helen's tongue probing into my ear, then licking around the lobe while she whispered a throaty monologue of sexual phrases, her hands everywhere, guiding mine into the places on her body that gave her the squealing shudders. What an education that was! If I was a little sore when we began, I was almost untouchable by the time we fell to sleep exhausted.

It had been an extraordinary thirty-six hours for me since I'd met Helen. I'd still been a naive and innocent young man of twenty-one the day before, someone who had blundered his way through a few mainly unsatisfactory sexual encounters and now in a short space of time Helen had introduced me to an enormous variety of sensual pleasures, leading me on, showing me how to prolong and magnify the shivering delights of the body. As I was falling asleep that night, I felt I'd sampled almost everything there was in sex and my education in these matters was virtually complete. But over the next few months I was to discover just how wrong I was. I was about to learn a lot more.

3. Driving and Dancing

I wouldn't like to give you the impression that all my days and nights were completely filled with sexual exploits. I was working for Gerry and he kept sending me out delivering packages, sometimes with Helen, sometimes on my own by taxi. Still there were distinct advantages to working for Gerry. It enabled me every now and again to meet some of the young women who worked for him in the restaurant and, more particularly, in the private members' club he ran in the back rooms. Two or three evenings a week he ran gambling there and once a week or so he put on a dinner dance and that usually developed into something like an orgy. The businessmen came with their tarts and mistresses and they'd sit, have dinner and a few drinks, all very sedate, relatively quiet. A quartet played romantic music and the couples danced. But later on in the small hours the music began to swing, became a little more bluesy, and soon some of the men's hands were gripping their partner's arse seductively and worming their way inside the woman's dress to grope her breasts. And eventually those hands began to slide up the women's skirts. So I'd see the women hanging onto their men, skirts hiked up to their waists with the men fondling them. One or two couples would be off at the side, moving rhythmically as the men ploughed into the women. Gerry had one or two flats upstairs he let out for sexual assignations so some couples drifted away to indulge themselves upstairs.

While I've called it an orgy, that might be a little inaccurate. It wasn't as if there was group sex, with everybody stripping off and milling around. Occasionally four people would be together but on the whole it was all very low-key. Still, for me when I saw this happening, it appeared to be pretty natural. At the same time it made me feel very randy so I began to realize that sexual indulgence was nothing to be ashamed of. I learned that it was a real part of everyone's life, not something to be kept secret and considered a little unnatural. At Gerry's it had the look of a well-behaved rite. Everyone knew Gerry wouldn't stand any nonsense and he had a couple of bouncers just in case any trouble arose — which it rarely did.

Gerry put his trust in one man who was capable of looking after problems for him in the club. His name was Benny, a boxer in his younger days, a classy light heavyweight. Back then everybody thought Benny would fight himself into the big time but soon after he reached thirty I learned that he'd been beaten severely a couple of times, so he quit. He still kept himself in shape but not like in his fight days. The men who came to the club liked to listen to Benny talking about his glory days in the ring, watching his battered face light up when he remembered his best fights. And some of the women liked him to talk as well, finding a romantic aura around this man though his squashed face and shambling gait was not something that made him attractive to women. And the way he talked in his slow, mumbling way suggested that his brains had been scrambled to some extent. But nearly everyone liked him, knew he could still take on anyone who caused trouble. He had the reputation of being a boxer who in his day could move like lightning, keeping out of harm's way, and while he didn't pack a lot of punching power, they say he could sometimes unleash a perfect right hook. So everyone knew Benny was someone to be reckoned with if any rough-house broke out.

The first time I was at one of those dances and saw the couples beginning to paw at each other, going off into dimly lit corners, pulling clothing off to get at each other, I was very surprised. The dances I'd been to, while you tried to dance really close, getting smoochy, you certainly could never try what went on at the club. So I wondered what everybody else would make of it. But the bouncers just lounged around, apparently paying little attention, Benny was behind the bar talking to the bartender, the waitresses were going about their business, clearing dishes from tables, carrying trays into the kitchen, unconcerned with what was going on, though one or two smirked at each other, raising their eyebrows. Others smiled and winked at me, even giving a slinky sway to their walk as they passed me.

Gerry obviously had an eye for young women – all his waitresses were nubile delights. He dressed them in short-skirted outfits with a long row of buttons down the front. Most of them – there were six or seven of them – kept the top couple of buttons undone so they showed a good deal when they leaned over the customers. I'm sure that earned them good tips: some of the men stuffed pound notes in the front of their dresses, letting their hands stray around

inside. They patted arses, slid their hands along
legs, and the waitresses flirted outrageously with
them but always moved quickly away from those
wandering hands because it was one of the un-
written rules of the club that the men were not to touch
the girls too much and the girls were expected, at
least while they were on duty, to remain somehow
aloof.

I didn't see any of them going upstairs with anyone
– after all the men brought their own women – but
when I looked back on this later, I had no doubt that
those waitresses wouldn't have minded joining in the
dancing if asked, and would have been ready for
anything that transpired afterwards. After all, Gerry
and Benny were flexible about the way the club was
run and provided they had finished their work, the
waitresses' time was their own. So those couple of
waitresses who'd winked their way past me were
inviting me into something, I suppose; I mean, I was a
personable young man and they must have known I
was some kind of personal assistant to Gerry. I never
took up their offers then, though I had some dealings
with one called Dorothy a little later. During that first
week or so I was just overwhelmed by Helen with
whom I was staying. I was flattered by all her attention
and I was enjoying myself with her hugely.

But I was still confusing all that sexual attention
with a kind of love. I hadn't yet reached that stage of
thinking of sex as an open commodity, something that
was in the very atmosphere of the club, something that
one could take or leave without any real compunction,
there simply for everyone's enjoyment. However, I
soon got over my scruples, if that's what they were,
and managed in those few months I was working for

Gerry to educate myself to all the possibilities around
me.

The other evenings at the club were given over to
strippers. You have to remember that this was very
unusual in England at that time. No public nudity was
allowed except in so-called 'tableaux'. Those were
staged poses and the naked girls were not allowed to
move. That's what the Windmill Theatre became
famous for, chorus girls posing naked but not moving.

But Gerry's club was very different. It was private
and barred to the general public. So the stripping there
was complete and the strippers certainly moved! And
it was real striptease, not the stripping that goes on in
most strip bars these days. It was altogether more
seductive, more subtly sexy. Of course, I'd heard about
striptease but never seen it, except in some American
movies, though those scenes never revealed much and
always stopped short of any real revelation. Still, it
made me feel randy to watch those American films in
which women took off their clothes, so when I found
out Gerry ran a strip club on three evenings I made
sure I went to see the girls in action.

The strippers were good. One I liked especially, as
did most of the men. She was the favourite and really
gave herself to the audience. Her name was Judy, with
full firm breasts, tall, with terrific legs, cropped blonde
hair and a pretty face, though up close you could see
she was probably a hard case. She usually performed
in a black skin-tight evening gown with a long slit
almost up to her waist and she was an expert in
showing a lot of leg, elegantly shaped by the highest
heels I had ever seen on shoes. She'd peel her clothes
off very slowly, dancing around eventually in just
black stockings and a garter belt, acting coy about

removing her bra, strutting about in her garter belt. She took a long time doing her act and it was obvious she was enticing almost every man in the place, but nobody got close to her. Nobody, that is, except Frank Bledsoe, who began hanging around the club more and more. It was rumoured he was some kind of gangster, an unusual tough guy in England then – thin moustache, glaring cold eyes, tight-curled black hair and a camel-hair coat he usually draped over his shoulders. He was always accompanied by his bodyguard, a big ex-wrestler called Christoff, broad-shouldered thick, overly blond hair, with a perpetual sneer on his face. People suspected that Bledsoe was into some heavy illegal activities at the time – running a string of whores whom he kept in line because he fed them drugs, and he was big in the drug trade as well. Not many people liked him.

I wondered why Gerry tolerated him in the club. He was there most of the nights I was and I heard he was in on other occasions as well. I also heard he had brought Judy to one or two of the dances, and he'd brought Christoff with him too. I once heard Benny suggest that the three of them – Bledsoe, Judy and Christoff – were getting up to all kinds of weird things together. So why did Gerry let Bledsoe run with one of his strippers? I don't know. I thought he would fire Judy at any time. Then I began to think maybe Judy was running with Bledsoe because Gerry wanted her to find out what he was up to. But Bledsoe was a greasy con-man so he'd be wise to that. Maybe he was looking into Gerry's operation, ready to turn Gerry over to the police so he could take over.

Nobody understood what was going on and certainly the way Judy fawned all over Bledsoe, the way she always managed to work her way to Bledsoe's table when she was down to her panties, the way she sashayed around him coyly letting him almost finger her panties, pull at the elastic, pretending she didn't want him to but pushing her pelvis out, circling it round and round right in his face, seemed to suggest she was enjoying handing out her favours to him.

Those were my evenings at the club, those evenings I didn't stay home romping with Helen. Sometimes she went out. I always presumed she was with Gerry, having a good time or doing some job for him. Occasionally I'd see her at the club with Gerry. She'd pass around like a hostess, joking with the customers and she'd pay absolutely no attention to me. She never explained why she ignored me on those occasions and I never asked. I don't know what kind of an answer I would have been given for I soon discovered that she was very unpredictable. I could never tell the kind of mood she was in, though we still had great times together. She'd take a couple of drinks, swallow some pills and she'd take off into some fabulously sexy ideas she wanted to try out. Sometimes, however, she could be phenomenally bitchy. I found that out when I went with her on jobs in the first two weeks.

I began to watch her when we were delivering. Sometimes she'd sit in an intricately patterned chair and a finger would pick at a thread, unravelling it, snapping it off, scuffing the weave and this all done surreptitiously. Twice she spilled tea onto richly tapestried rugs. I saw her go out of her way to kick a small, spindly leg of a table, not breaking it but leaving a livid scratch on it. She would sometimes make the person we were delivering packages to squirm as much as possible, haggling about the price, and then fingering the notes carefully, almost gingerly, as if they were somehow unclean or as if she felt she hadn't been given the right amount. She sprinkled cigarette ash on chairs, she ground her high heels sharply into polished hardwood floors. Once she nudged a fine china teapot off a table, smashing it to smithereens. She wreaked some small havoc at almost every place we visited.

And yet that nasty mood of hers would not always continue when we got back to her place. More often than not it made her nearly manic and she'd run me ragged sexually. Sometimes the nastiness held and there was nothing I could do for her. She resorted to Scotch, downing two or three quickly and then she would throw pills into the back of her throat savagely. When she started to drink, I usually left her and went down to the club. That's how I found out what was actually going on there.

In the car when she was driving and the nasty mood hit her, she changed gear ferociously, often grinding the gears mercilessly, then letting rip with a formidable vocabulary of swear words. Sometimes she took a swig from a flask she kept in the glove compartment and then her driving became even more reckless than usual.

But she wasn't in her nasty moods that often and I could put up with them most of the time because of the delights she gave me with her body. She really knew how to fire me up and, in turn, I soon learned how I could drive her wild. She was one of those women who obviously liked to show how sexual she was. She loved to show off, and when she was out with me she'd touch me and pat me, show lots of leg, smirk dirtily at me quite openly and I think that was just to make all the men seeing this envious of me because she was giving me her favours. Sometimes she would act like this in the car. It would embarrass me but usually, besides being embarrassed, I'd be excited by her behaviour.

Once, going on a delivery, we were driving through the centre of town in heavy traffic. I thought she was turning nasty, honking at other cars, leaning out of the window to shout obscenities, banging the wheel in frustration, fiddling with the frill of her high-necked blouse as if she felt it was strangling her. She kept tugging at it and suddenly it ripped completely open. Somehow she released her bra so she was driving naked from the waist up. She coasted to a stop at the traffic lights, rolled the window down and yelled across to the driver of the car standing next to her. His eyes were popping out of his head at the sight of Helen's breasts.

'Just look at this boy!' she yelled. 'Can't keep his hands off me. Can't wait to get home to feel me up. You can't see but he's got his dick out. Waving it around. Wants me to toss him off and he'll shoot it all over my tits.' She leaned over to me, put her arm round my shoulder and pulled my head onto her breasts. 'He's always wanting to suck them!' The light changed but the next car didn't move. The driver was too busy staring at us. Helen laughed, put her foot down and drove away fast. She went on driving like that, flaunting her breasts as she swerved past car after car. I'm sure we nearly caused quite a few accidents.

Another time the engine sputtered and coughed and the car jumped in crazy jitters. 'Damn it!' Helen jumped out, lifted the hood and looked in. 'Looks like a leaky radiator hose. Got anything I can wrap around it?' I flourished my handkerchief at her but she shook her head. Then she stood close to the car, her hands rummaging under her skirt. I peered out and saw she was taking her panties off. She shook them at me. 'Nylon's good for leaks!' She laughed. 'They're used to getting wet!' She went to the bonnet again, looking as if she was wrapping the panties round the leak. When she clambered back into the car she said, 'That should hold it for a bit.' And off she drove into the steady traffic, the engine purring smoothly.

'If some randy man was travelling with me, he'd start taking advantage of me. Sitting here driving, wearing no panties and this skirt one of those wrap-around jobs. Hardly holds together. I'm always afraid it'll fly open every time I sneeze.' And she gave a mock sneeze and I think one of her hands had sneaked off the wheel because her skirt flew open. Her hands were now firmly gripping the wheel. 'Wouldn't be a thing I could do about it if he wanted to feel me up. Have to keep both my hands on the wheel in this kind of traffic.' And so of course, after that suggestion, I leaned over and began to stroke her.

She shifted her legs – I wasn't sure, given what was happening, whether she'd be able to brake quickly if she ran into trouble. She kept her hands on the wheel while my fingers rubbed her, feeling the juice begin to slip around my fingers. She sighed and gasped a little, murmuring, 'You impudent boy! Fancy thinking of doing this to me!' And I kept on prodding my finger in and out, slowly, then quickening a little. I finger-fucked her all the way home where she stopped the car with such force I nearly went through the windscreen. She leaned against me, whispering in my ear, 'You randy bastard! I'm all sticky and wet. You'd better come in and do the job properly!' She virtually hauled me out of the car, grabbing her skirt around her with one hand, the other pinching my arm, pulling me in through the door and staggering up stairs with me in tow.

I sometimes wondered afterwards whether she had faked that jerking and sputtering of the engine just as an excuse to be in the car with no panties on, knowing she could make me a suggestion that I wouldn't be able to resist.

When we drove up to Lincolnshire on our way to an out-of-the-way village on some job she was doing for Gerry, she did something quite dangerous but very exciting. While we were driving, Helen was talking away, telling me I should learn to drive. 'Cars are good for getting sex. You could borrow this car and take out one of those waitresses I see you eyeing at the club. Plenty of room in the back to lie her down and have your way with her, as they say.'

She kept on saying how easy it was to learn to drive, showing me the steps of changing gear, using the clutch, the accelerator, the brake pedal. Every time she did something, she explained what she was doing till I got fed up with her constant explanations. Eventually I became angry with her and told her to shut up. She started to yell back at me, complaining that if I had any decency I'd learn to drive so she didn't have to do all the driving.

'It would be a great help to me and I'm only trying to make sure it'll be easy for you to learn. But no. All you can do is shout at me, as if I don't know what I'm doing. You must think I'm a terrible driver. Maybe you think you can do better.'

By this time we'd pulled off the main road and were cruising along a country lane with high hedges on each side. She pulled the car over onto the grass verge and climbed out, slamming the door behind her. 'Alright, clever dick! Move over and drive yourself.' I protested I didn't know how, didn't have a licence. 'What does that matter? No one around here's going to stop and ask for your licence. I've told you how this thing works. You think you're such a smartass. Mr Big Brains going to university! Well, let's see you do it then. Get behind the wheel!'

I'd seen Helen in these intimidating moods before and I'd never been able to deal with her. Usually I just left her to get over them on her own but here we were, out in the wilds of Lincolnshire. After arguing for a while and getting nowhere with her, I decided to try to drive. I had some idea about the mechanisms and so I thought if I just puttered along very slowly, maybe in time Helen would come to her senses.

But it didn't turn out that way. At first Helen kept looking at me with a vague sneer on her face, telling me when to change gear, not to ride the brake, to ease the speed up a little before the engine died on me and after a time I began to relax a little though my hands clenched the wheel tightly and I stared resolutely ahead.

Then I felt her fingers on my knee, beginning to move slowly up my thigh. 'Helen! Don't do that! Please!'

'Keep your eyes on the road, your hands on the wheel, and drive!'

'I'll have to stop the car if you . . .'

'If I what? You're just the driver. You do what you're supposed to do and don't worry about me.' A finger or two flicked very close to the swollen bulge in my trousers. 'Besides, I haven't heard you complaining when I've started to do this before.'

'Yes, but this is different!'

'So enjoy the difference!' Her hands were busy with my fly buttons. 'You always like this, Nick,' her fingers burrowing inside, tickling at my stiff cock.

'Not now!'

'This'll make you relax.' Her fingers were maddeningly just touching the skin round my cock-head, rolling it back, stroking the exposed crown. Her other hand was delving inside my trousers, pulling my underpants aside, lifting my cock out, that hand lingering under my balls. 'There! Isn't that better?'

And in a strange way I almost felt like settling back to enjoy the expert caresses of her hands. I wasn't quite relaxed but, trying to concentrate on the road ahead while I was feeling those sexy sensations from her hands, I was feeling more excited than usual.

'Your prick's throbbing like crazy, Nick. Such a hot cock. Didn't I tell you you'd feel better?' As she leaned over me, one of her elbows was pressing down on my knee and so my foot was pushing down on the accelerator. 'You're going faster, aren't you? You like it faster? Faster, but not too fast.' And her hand was jerking my cock up and down in steady strokes, my balls squirming under the pressure of her hand.

'Helen! Please! Be careful!'

'Don't worry. I'll be careful. Don't want you to run out of oil too soon, do we? I'll look after your gear shift.' She manipulated me with her fingers round and round, her fingers more devastating than ever. I spilled

out a little spunky liquid and she squeezed and
touched the wetness with her fingertips and spread it
all over my cock-head.

'Please, Helen, what if a car comes!' My driving was
very erratic by now.

'Well, you'll just have to come as well, won't you?'
Her hands kept on with this incredible stroking so that
I could think of nothing but my cock and how exquisite the feeling was. Be damned to the car and the
driving! If we crashed, what a delicious way to go,
going and coming at the same time. Why I didn't think
of stopping the car, I don't know. I suppose I was too
caught up with the feel of Helen's hands on me,
making my cock feel stronger and longer and fatter
than it had ever felt before. So hard and thick – her
hands seemed almost too small to hold it and I felt as if
it was going to burst at the seams, spray out more and
more jism than it seemed possible to contain in my
cock.

The car was careering down the country lane. If
another car came, we'd have been sure to have had a
head-on-collision. But I was on a collision course of
my own and it was my cock that was driving me. I
couldn't stop Helen so the least I could do was still try
to steer the car. I wanted to come, my cock was so
swollen and somewhere in the back of my mind
must have been the idea that if we got it over with,
then we'd be out of danger from my driving. Helen
kept working at me and then she began one of her
monologues.

'Come on, baby! Let's drive! Fast and hot. No
braking. Keep going till you come. You want to come,
don't you, Nick? Come and come. Spill it out for me.
Such a hard prick. Nick's prick is slick and thick.' The

words went on and on, her hands were insistent, pulling, rubbing, stroking, my cock slathered in oozings, her hands wet and slippery on me and she led me on, ready to burst and I did, in great spasms, and I splashed all over the panel, saw the come dribbling down the speedometer, the petrol gauge. 'You're certainly not running on empty,' she said, keeping her sticky hands caressing my cock. I was shuddering all over and leaned back, took my foot off the accelerator and let the car shudder to a stop along with me.

'What a terrific drive, Nick. We were really steaming along, weren't we?' She patted my cock. 'Your gear shift is really responsive to the lightest touch.'

Eventually she got out of the car, walked round and had me clamber over the gear shift into the passenger seat where I lay back, my cock a little limper but making me feel extraordinarily relaxed and satisfied. 'First lesson's over, Nick. You're a quick learner. I'll guarantee the next lessons'll be even better.'

As I sat next to her those following few minutes, I wondered what on earth she could dream up for the next lessons! That first one had driven along a razor edge of danger and excitement and I couldn't make my mind up whether I'd really like her to give me more lessons like that the next time we went driving. But after we'd done our business in the village, with Helen dealing with some ragged old man in very strict and peremptory terms, she drove back to town very fast, speaking very little, paying almost no attention to me, springing quickly out of the car at her place and making a quick dash upstairs for the bottle of Scotch.

And that's how Helen was in those first days I got to know her, 'up and down like a bottle of pop' as my mum used to say about people like her. When I'd beaten a hasty retreat from one of her moods, I found some consolation down at the club watching the strippers. If it was a gambling evening, then I'd spend some time talking to Benny or with any of the waitresses who weren't busy.

I particularly liked one called Dorothy, a very pert and perky number, not too buxom, not too tall, but just a bubbly package, always smiling, tossing her strawberry-blonde hair back and letting it fall in a wide arc across her shoulders. She often came to stand by me when Judy was stripping, whispering every now and again, things like: 'she's good', 'she knows what she's doing'. 'All the men here would like to get into her pants', 'look at her aiming it all at just one man – if she can reach him, she knows she's got all of 'em.' So I was able to spend pleasant relaxing evenings at the club. And my time was pretty well my own except when Gerry sent me out with Helen or on my own to do a job.

One evening Helen was busy getting herself ready to go out early. She told me she was meeting Gerry and I was to come on to the club later. 'Gerry wants to talk to you. Later on. Sounds important to me. Better make sure you're on time. Gerry doesn't like hanging about waiting for somebody.' Then off she went. I didn't find it strange, her going off early like that. She took the car of course but I had money now to take a taxi. I pottered around Helen's place for a time, then I decided to go down to the club. I'd be there in plenty of time so I could have a beer or two, watch the strippers till Gerry and Helen arrived.

Judy was doing her usual great job, seductive, sultry, coming on to the men sitting at the tables,

especially if they had a woman with them. Judy egged
them on and then she worked her way over to Frank
Bledsoe's table. As the spotlight fell on Bledsoe's table,
I was surprised to see Helen sitting between Bledsoe
and his thug, Christoff. Judy obviously didn't like
Helen being there and the final part of her strip was
especially provocative, Judy pushing herself close to
Bledsoe, sliding out of her tiny panties, thrusting her
pelvis close to him, then trailing the panties round his
neck as a finish. Then she flounced away quickly,
sweeping up her silk dressing-gown at the side of the
stage. Bledsoe half stood up as if to go after her but
Helen laid a restraining hand on him, shaking her head
at the same time.

I was puzzled to see Helen with Bledsoe, particularly as she had told me she was meeting Gerry. She
was cosying up to him so I thought maybe Gerry had
put her up to it. After all, someone like Benny would
surely let Gerry know what was happening, though
Bledsoe's table was off to the side with only very
subdued lighting so Helen was probably not very
conspicuous. I didn't think she had seen me as I was
standing in the shadows at the back of the club talking to Dorothy who was between me and Bledsoe's
table.

'Seemed a bit upset tonight, wouldn't you say?'
Dorothy said. 'Seeing her man – or should I say men,
with that Christoff snot there as well – with another
woman. Still, you shouldn't let it get to you when
you're dancing. You've just got to let it flow along,
maybe dance yourself up to another man and really
come on. Make sure he gets a good stand, if you know
what I mean, show the other one what he's really
missing. That's the way I'd do it, anyhow, and I bet I

51

could be as good as Judy.' She laid a hand on my arm. 'I'd better go and sell some drinks now Judy's finished. Will you be around later?'

'Yes. I have to see Gerry when he comes in.'

'See you later then.'

When Gerry came in, late, he walked straight into the back, into his office, I supposed, and I saw Helen follow him quickly. It was that time at night, early morning really, when a lot of the men had left but Phyllis, the last stripper, was doing a nicely cosy and dreamy strip, the music moody. Dorothy had come over to join me as she'd finished for the evening. 'She doesn't come on strong, does she? But at this time of night, who'd want anyone to come on strong in here?' I nodded and Dorothy gave me a knowing look.

'You've been watching these girls closely.'

'Well, that's what you're supposed to do with strippers, watch 'em closely. That's what all the men do in here.'

'Yes, but that's different. Why are you studying them? That's what it looks as if you're doing.'

'Well, maybe I am.' She paused. 'You notice how the best ones all have a character they work out of?'

'What d'you mean?'

'Take Judy, for instance. She's the sophisticated lady who likes to show off while acting as if she's not quite sure she should be doing it. She's putting it on – you know Judy's not really like that off-stage.'

I didn't, I'd never talked to Judy, but you could see that while she danced for Bledsoe, she was somehow different when she sat with him.

'And just look at Phyllis now. Not too many left to watch. She's a slow teaser but you know she's a

52

no-nonsense girl. Straightforward but sexy. Gives you what you want at the right time.'

Dorothy was right. Phyllis was into a slow strut now, walking round the floor in just a garter belt and stockings, her arm sliding along the backs of chairs not quite touching the shoulders of the men sitting in them, strutting away seductively, a quick look back at each man she passed, shaking her hair out.

'I didn't know you were studying all this, Dorothy.'

She laughed. 'Certainly I've been studying. And I have a few ideas of my own. After all, I don't want to stay a waitress all my life. I have my own character worked out.' She laughed again. 'Bet you'd never guess what it is.' I shook my head. 'You might be surprised.'

'Probably.'

The club was beginning to close down. Phyllis had finished. The musicians were packing their instruments away, the few men left were putting coats on, straggling away. And still Gerry hadn't talked to me. He was in his office with Helen – or maybe he'd taken her to one of the flats upstairs, maybe he was grilling her about Bledsoe. Dorothy went over to help Benny close the bar. I just sat at a table nursing my last beer.

Then Gerry came out on his own, a slow swagger across to me, till he was standing looking down at me. I didn't know whether I should stand – sometimes I even felt as if I should salute him! But then he sat in a chair opposite me. 'Glad you could drop in, kid.' He made it sound as if I was the one who had decided to come, and not him who had asked me to see him. 'Keeping busy?' I nodded. 'Enjoying the work?' I nodded again. 'Helen tells me you're doing well.' So maybe they'd been talking about me in the office this evening.

'Well, there's a job going at the Great Asian Tea Company. You might like it. A nice, clean-cut young man like you. They'll like you there. Anyhow, I've got an interview there for you. Work in the office first of all, do a few odd jobs, promote you to tea-taster after a bit. How d'you fancy that?' I didn't know what to say. Was Gerry getting rid of me? What had I done he didn't like? Was Helen telling him something just to spite me? What was going on?

'Not to worry, old son. Don't need to take the job if you don't want it. But I'd like you to go for the interview. Old Gibbons, he's the boss there, fussy old soul, so dress nicely. You have a decent suit?' I nodded. 'You'll hit it off with Gibbons, I'm sure. Just be polite. Deferential. He's so proud of what he's set up there, he'll want to give you the whole works. Show you around. Where he gets his teas from, the chests all stamped with the names. Assam. Darjeeling. The best teas. Not the blends. Special teas. Course, he won't show you round himself. He'll let his secretary do that. Miss Nicholson. Margery. Nice girl. She always keeps an eye out for what's shipped in. Takes care of the bills of lading as well. Very useful, she is. Nice girl, as I say. Comes on a bit snooty at first but she's alright once you get to know her. So pay no attention if she comes on with the snooty bit. She likes to crack on she's a cut above the average. Doesn't fancy getting mixed up with the common lot. But she's alright. And a very nice pair of . . .'

Gerry looked at me, his hands in front of him as if he was going to shape some nice curves. But he went on after he laughed, 'Nice pair of eyes. Real sharp they are. She'll know what to show you when she takes you round the place, the cellars where they keep the tea. So when she shows you the chests with Assam and Darjeeling and Souchong, make a special note of them, will you? Fix 'em in your mind. Might care to make a drawing of exactly where they are in the cellar. I mean, not right then and there. When you get home. Draw the chests, where they are, especially in relation to the stairs. They have these stairs that go up and there's a kind of trapdoor. It opens out onto the yard at the back, well, more like the side really. Margery knows when the stuff's in but she hasn't got a head for knowing exactly where they store the chests. She knows they're in there. So, you know me. I like to know a bit more than that. Everything ship-shape. That's how I like it.'

He stood up and leaned across to pat me on the shoulder. 'I know I can rely on you. Come and see me after the interview. Give my best to Margery. Oh, and don't mention my name to old Gibbons. Wouldn't want him to know I fixed the interview for you. But you might find a way of letting Margery know that I arranged it. Helen'll tell you when the interview is.'

He looked towards the door he'd come through and as if on cue Helen came out and joined Gerry. 'Time for beddy-byes,' Gerry said. 'Getting late. Make sure the door's locked when you leave. Helen's running me home. You got enough to take a cab?' He dropped two five-pound notes on the table. 'Better see that Dorothy gets home as well. Lives with her mum somewhere, I think. So long, kid.'

He waltzed Helen away – she looked back at me giving me a smile and a tiny shrug. I watched her walk out of the club with Gerry, uncertain about her, her dealings with Bledsoe, her dealings with Gerry, and just where I stood in all that.

I turned around to find an opened bottle of beer on

the table. 'I took it before Benny closed up.' It was Dorothy who had sat down across from me. 'Well, here we are. Drink up.'

'Aren't you having one?' I asked her. She shook her head. 'I'm not a great drinker. Try to keep my head clear. Besides, I thought I'd show you something while you're drinking your beer. I've seen you with Gerry so maybe you can tell him about it.'

'About what?'

'You'll see.' She stood up, climbed onto the stage, went across and switched on a few footlights, quite low, in blues and reds. 'You'll have to imagine the spot following me. And the music. I'll hum a bit but I'm no great shakes at singing. But I think you'll like my other shakes. Ready?'

I didn't really know what she was up to. She was at the side of the stage where the lightboard was. Then she came out. She was still in her short-skirted waitress dress though she'd undone a few of the buttons on the bodice. She was carrying a tray and she moved sinuously across and then down to my table where she placed the tray. 'Stretch your legs out. Make yourself comfortable.' There was a a fat, long French roll of bread on the tray, together with a slim but long cheroot and a box of matches. 'Smoke, sir?'

'I don't smoke. Well, sometimes I have a cigar at Christmas.'

'Maybe this is early Christmas and, anyhow, who knows what present you get till you unwrap it? And I think you'll want to smoke specially when you see what present I've got for you.' She was murmuring this very quietly, leaning down to me, the collar of her dress falling open so I could see plenty of cleavage. She didn't seem to have a bra on. 'Remember what I

told you about strippers, how they play out a character, different to what they really are. Well, I thought,
how'd it be if *I* did it? What character would I play?
Maybe I wouldn't be different, just be what I am, a
waitress, only more so. Serve up a hot menu. Like this.'

She began to sway her hips slowly, her voice
humming a soft but bluesy tune, her arms waving
languorously, bowing her head low, her long hair
falling down and then swirling it back as her head
came up. She circled round my chair, close, almost
brushing against me and when she came in front of me
again, she had undone one or two more buttons. She
kept up her seductive undulations but stopped humming. 'What d'you think?' she whispered.

'Very nice.'

'Of course I'd be up on stage first of all but I'm giving
you a closer look. In any case the other girls do come
down into the crowd, don't they, dancing round the
tables. Well, I serve something up for the men, like the
beer I brought you. And this bread.' She picked up the
long loaf and began to fondle it in her hands. 'I know
waitresses aren't supposed to touch the food but this is
different, right?'

She was now poking the end of the loaf inside her
open dress, beginning to hum again, dancing slowly,
the bread stick inside her dress, rubbing it in and out,
one hand undoing more buttons till she managed to
pull the top away from her shoulders. Then she was
working the bread between her breasts, still humming
till the bread stuck up between her breasts, reaching
up near her mouth. She stuck her tongue out as if she
was going to lick the end of the roll.

'We're not supposed to eat the food either. But I bet
the men are wishing I would. Put my lips on it and it'd

remind them of something else.' Then the end of the
loaf was circling round one of her nipples, sinking
across her stomach, down and down, resting at her
pelvis as she thrust herself around it suggestively.
Needless to say, I had the equivalent of the bread stick
standing up stiffly in my trousers.

Dorothy was slinking around me, bending so her
breasts were near my face. 'Like a little bite?' I nodded
and tried to take her nipple in my teeth but she moved
back. 'Not so fast. I want to make sure your appetite's
worked up.' The loaf was now lying just above her
knee and she was sliding it under her skirt which was
hiked higher so she showed a good deal of leg. 'D'you
like what I'm serving up? Most strippers do their
dancing like this – fix on one man in the audience as if
what they're doing is just meant for him. A stripper
knows if she can reach him, she's getting the attention
of all the others. After all, it's for the whole audience
she's dancing.'

By then her other hand had raised her skirt high so I
could see the bread roll nudging at her panties. She
hummed huskily as she pushed the roll as if it was
trying to pry inside the elastic. She was also unfastening the waist of her skirt and suddenly she was
swinging around and the dress fell away.

'Of course, there's always one way to see if you're
having an effect on a man. 'She swayed in closer to me,
the roll still between her legs, 'The crust's really hard,
just the way I like it.'

Her arm snaked out and very carefully, as if she
didn't want to touch me, she began to unfasten my fly
buttons, opening my trousers. Naturally she saw the
great bulge in my underpants. 'I can see you like my
dancing.'

She went on dancing, rubbing and stroking different parts of her body with the roll, between her legs, turning round and bending down so it poked at the cheeks of her arse, sliding along the crack, edging into the tight elastic of her panties there. 'I could make a meal of this,' she murmured.

I was constantly surprised at how the women I'd met through Gerry liked to talk. I'd always thought women didn't like anything to do with sex, that you always had to sneak up on them unaware. And that was the problem – how can you sneak up on a woman when you're holding her for just a kiss and she can feel a thick knob begin to swell against her? In my younger days I even used to try to put my prick where she wouldn't feel it, as if we both would be embarrassed by it, as if she'd know exactly what was on my mind – and of course she did know that but I thought it was something she found distasteful. I began to learn differently as I grew older and now at Gerry's it was clearly in the open, just as it was obvious to Dorothy right at that moment.

She went on humming, stepping around, working the roll up, stroking it near her mouth, rubbing a little at the end, then down to massage her breasts, then around across her stomach so she could lie the whole length of it along her pubic mound, one hand stretching her panty elastic wide and very slowly the tip of the roll disappeared inside. Her hand pulled at her panties and slid them down. As she bent to remove them from her ankles, the roll nudged at the top of her legs, between, pushing through, in and out.

'Must be careful not to make crumbs or break it.' She danced forward and lifted the waistband of my underpants and my cock sprang out and up. She still hadn't touched me. 'I won't be able to do this if I do the dance at the club when it's a strippers' night of course.'

My knob was straining up. I just sat and watched it twitch as Dorothy writhed around the bread roll. 'Usually you have a drink when you're eating,' she said as she danced towards the table and took the bottle of beer. She slid the long neck of the bottle into her mouth, not drinking, clogging the opening with her tongue. She sucked on it, letting it edge to her lips, then pushing it deeply inside. The beer was frothy inside the bottle and when she pulled it out of her mouth, the creamy liquid seeped out. 'My! Look what's spilling out. Mustn't let it dribble all over.' Her long tongue flicked out and licked up and down the bottle and of course that set me imagining how her mouth might work on me and that started me twitching even more!

She passed the bottle to me. 'Have a little taste.' I put my mouth at the neck of the bottle, remembering her mouth on it, then felt a little beer slip into my mouth. 'Take your time,' she cooed. 'Better to drink it slowly.'

She had put the bread roll on the table and was rotating her hips in long, undulating motions as I sipped the beer. 'I need a drink.'

I proffered the bottle to her, up towards her mouth.

'No, here.' She pushed herself slightly sideways, sank down a little. One breast was close to my face. She put the opening of the bottle over her nipple, turning it round and round, humming sexily. Of course I was thinking of my mouth on the bottle and just where the bottle was then.

I was throbbing quite heavily as Dorothy continued her movements with her hand slowly circling the bottle at her nipple. She pulled it away, a little foam now glistening on her breast. She handed the bottle to me. 'Taste.'

At first I thought she meant for me to lick the beer from her breast but the way she had given me the bottle suggested she wanted me to drink from it. 'Suck on it.'

I drank, then she took the bottle back, pushing it onto her other nipple, and we did this for a little while, me drinking, she wetting her nipples from the bottle, little runlets dropping down her breasts. By now my mouth was tingling from the beer and with the idea of drinking from the bottle which had been pressed onto her breasts. But each time I moved towards her, my mouth slightly open as if I would try to lick at her nipples, she danced away. 'Not allowed. Rule of the club. No real touching.'

Soon her breasts were bubbly and wet, shining in the subdued lighting. Then she put the bottle on the table and put one hand over my mouth. 'You've had enough to drink. Now it's time for an after-dinner smoke.'

She took the long cheroot in her fingers, manipulating it gently as if it was a long, thin cock. She let her tongue run its length before she pushed it carefully between my lips. Then she took the matchbox, took one out and again her fingers moved on it as if it was a dwarf prick, her fingers trying to coax it up to be big and stiff. 'I'll fire you up.'

But I was already fired up and I think Dorothy already knew that. She struck the match and I puffed on the cheroot. 'Smoke it, Nick. Make it nice and red-hot. Red at the end. Puff it up.'

Dorothy was still doing this lazy dance round me and I was puffing smokily on the cheroot. She was using the bottle again, this time insinuating it between the top of her legs, a finger over the top so the beer wouldn't spill. She stroked it back and forth across her pubic mound, shaking the bottle a little till she let some thick foam spew out. That creamy liquid stuck in little streams on her triangle of hair. Then she said, 'Just look how wet I am! Maybe I should heat myself up again. Are you hot enough?' She meant the cigar but she also meant me as well.

She took the cheroot out of my mouth, saying, 'You need a stand to put your cigar on – another stand different to the one you've got!' I wasn't quite sure what she meant about a stand for the cigar but she was right about my stand – I was really swollen to a large, long erection.

She held the cheroot out at arm's length and her other hand went to her mouth. She wiped the inner side of her lips onto her fingertips, they were very wet, almost dribbling with juice. Her fingers moved to a breast and the tips rubbed the wetness round the nipple and across the breast just above the nipple. She kept sucking on her fingers and then made that part of her breast slippery with her saliva till I could see it shiny with moisture. Then she reached her other arm over and very carefully rolled the middle of the cheroot along the slipperiness. She let the cheroot rest along the top of her breast, checking it for balance there, letting the red-hot end jut out from her skin. And of course the end I had smoked at jutted out on the other side.

She cautiously lowered her fingers from the cheroot. The wetness, together with the stickiness of the foam she had spilled on her breast earlier mixed with her saliva to make the skin very sticky so the cheroot lay across her breast on its own, a thin curl of smoke rising up making a grey haze round her hair, coloured by the red and blue of the lights.

She leaned towards me, keeping her back straight, turning slightly sideways. The end of the cheroot was close to my mouth. 'Smoke. Take a slow drag. Careful. Don't burn me.' I began to raise my hand to steady the cheroot but she said, 'Remember the rules – no touching. Just smoke.'

So I gently put my lips to the cheroot and drew on it. It was a sweet smoke, my mouth so close to her breast and I was careful not to drag on it unsteadily in case I caused the cigar to shift and roll onto her. I wanted to reach up and stroke her there but I was afraid I'd disturb the cheroot and so burn Dorothy's breast. I suppose she knew she could trust me and I remembered how she'd said a stripper, if she was really good, was always in control.

Finally she took the cheroot away, ground it out in an ashtray, and the dance was over.

'I need a drink after that.' She took a long swig from the bottle and flopped down in a chair at the table next to me. And there I was again, sitting next to a naked lady, my knob sticking up in front of me, still very stiff, both of us sitting there as if it was the most natural thing in the world for us to be doing.

'Well, what d'you think?' she asked me.

I glanced down at myself. 'Terrific. Look there. You can tell it had the desired effect on me.'

'I'll have to take it a little more . . .' she paused, then went on, 'sedately if I do it in the club but I wanted to pull a few stops out for you.'

'You certainly did that.'

'Well, I don't suppose the men in the club will be

sitting with all that hanging out when I dance so I'll just have to guess how it's going over.'

'I can vouch for it. You'll drive 'em crazy.'

'D'you think I could sell it to Gerry?'

'I'm sure you could.'

'Would you ask him for me?'

'Sure, if you think it'll do any good.'

'Well, you've seen it now. You can tell him how impressed you were.' She looked across at me and smiled. 'And I can see it's made a lasting impression on you.' Then she stood up. 'I'd better clear up.' I wondered if I should make some kind of move but I couldn't really tell if she expected me to because she became very business-like. She swigged the last of the beer, took the bottle, the ashtray, the bread roll and then walked over to retrieve her dress. She dumped the debris behind the bar, and slipped quickly into her dress. 'You ready to go?' she asked. 'Do you want to call for a taxi?'

I put myself together stuffing myself, a little more droopy now but still showing signs of interest, into my pants. I went over to the phone – taxis were always available when you gave the club name for the drivers knew there would be plenty of money in tips. While I was doing that, Dorothy was checking that all the doors at the back were locked. Then she went up on stage and turned off the lights. One small light was still on over the door which led into the front. In that very dim light Dorothy walked slowly across to me where I was waiting at the door. When she stood next to me, she kissed me lightly on the cheek. 'Thanks for watching,' she said.

'Entirely my pleasure.'

She looked questioningly at me. 'Surely not *entirely*

your pleasure.' She shrugged. 'Sorry about the club rules.'

We walked out through the restaurant, making sure we locked the outside door. While we stood waiting for the taxi in the doorway, Dorothy cuddled up close to me, giving me little pecks and squeezes almost like promissory notes and I wondered when I'd be able to collect them. Then, in the taxi, after she had given the driver her address – 'I'd invite you in but my mum always waits up to see that I get home safely' – she settled cosily next to me and almost before we had started to drive away, her hands were suddenly alive at my crotch and after that evening of course I soon leapt to attention down there.

She pulled my cock out, whispering, 'Taxis don't have rules.' Her hands were both gentle and strong, tickling and teasing, then fast and urgent. I was too surprised to do much more than lean back and let her continue. After all, she'd done nothing in the club when she was stripped, claiming the club rules stopped her from doing anything with me, so I had a vague feeling that maybe she was simply a cockteaser though the way she talked to me hadn't really suggested that. Now here she was, her hands full of my hardness, cushioning my balls, stroking, coaxing, rubbing, fingering, pulling and pushing at me. 'Couldn't let you go home with a case of lover's balls,' she murmured. She licked her fingers and spread the wetness round my cock-head and I was reminded of the things she had indicated with her mouth during her dance.

The driver drove on oblivious, I think, to what was going on in the back seat, though he must have found out the next morning for Dorothy brought me on and on during that short ride to her house till I came fully over the edge, shooting out a great load through her fingers and some of it spurted out and dripped from her fingers onto the upholstery. She timed it perfectly, with the same kind of control she had exhibited as a dancer. Just as she knew how to time the length of each portion of her dance, so she knew the ways to string me along, exciting my cock towards a climax, holding her strokes back, gentle, then urging me on, persuasive, firm, then firmer till I had to let go.

I discovered that she just had time to wipe herself dry, licking the moisture off her hands, and smiling at me as she cleaned her hands then with her handkerchief. She gave me a pat, tucked my cock inside my pants, then sat up straight and said, 'Here, driver, please.' The taxi stopped, Dorothy kissed me briefly, saying, 'Goodnight, Nick, and thanks again '

'Thank you.' She opened the door, slid across the seat, managing to show her shapely legs. 'Rules are meant to be broken sometimes so who knows?' She winked at me and said goodnight again.

I watched her walk to the terraced house where she lived with her mother. I swear she was moving in that slow, seductive fashion of her dance because she knew I'd be watching – another promissory note, I suppose. Then she turned and waved and disappeared inside. I gave the driver Helen's address.

She wasn't at home when I arrived. I was thankful for that; after what I had been through with Dorothy that evening I wasn't in the mood for her incessant sexual demands, however pleasurable she made them. And it was equally possible she could be in one of her nasty moods. So I went to bed, hoping I'd be asleep before Helen came back. Soon I had sunk into a deep sleep and when I woke in the morning I had a vague memory of a dream in which I sat naked eating a meal while both Helen and Dorothy served me, offering sexual favours.

4. Time for Tea

I never expected to be out on a date with Margery
Nicholson, not after the day I'd seen her at the interview at the Great Asian Tea Company. But there I was,
sitting in the Gaumont with her, and in one of those
double seats. Gerry had been right — Margery Nicholson fancied she was some superior being, showing me
around the tea company, explaining some things to me
though some of the explanations I didn't need. Her
whole attitude was patronising, even condescending,
though every now and again she gave hints she was
sometimes a different kind of person. Still it was a
shock to me when Helen came back from seeing Gerry
and said, 'That snobby secretary, what's-her-name,
Nicholson, well, Gerry told me you're to meet her to
take her to the pictures this Tuesday. I don't know
what gets into these young tarts, snob that she is,
thinks she's better than the rest of us but not above
wheedling round Gerry to get a free evening out.
Anyhow, Gerry says you're to meet her at the Gaumont
on the Kilburn Road, next Tuesday for the first house.'
I found it strange sitting next to Margery Nicholson
in the dark on the back row in a double seat. Our thighs
were touching occasionally; in fact, it seemed to me
that she pushed her thigh hard against mine though
maybe she was just shifting in her seat. It certainly
wasn't a situation I thought I'd be in after I'd spent

time with her when I'd been interviewed by Mr Gibbons.

Gibbons himself was like a character out of Dickens, complete with pince-nez, a starched collar, a conservative brown suit, tight brown boots and a hail-fellow-well-met manner. He was perched on a high stool next to a counter dirty with spilled tea.

'I don't like to keep myself locked away in an office. I'd rather be out here. Used to be a tea-taster myself so I like to stay where the action is.' He waved his arms to indicate the dreadful clutter on counters all around the walls. They were covered with teapots and urns, a lot of cups with no handles like tiny chamber pots, some with some vile-looking brown liquid in them. The counters were scratched and stained with water-marks and dark splotches. 'Now, my Miss Nicholson, general secretary, she really runs the place though she's only been here a month or so. Runs a tight ship, she does. Likes to keep herself to herself so I let her have the office. She burrows away in there like some kind of mole.'

Whatever you might want to say about Margery Nicholson, you wouldn't really imagine her as a mole. She was one of those English girls who give a first impression of being unapproachable, a little off-putting. She was just this side of being plump with quite a large bust, high set, in a blouse buttoned at the neck. There was something a little military about her, something a little larger than normal. Though her mouth was not big, her lips were full and she drew attention to them by shaping them with heavy, dark-red lipstick. Her hair was just a little too tightly curled, though immaculately in place. Her pencil skirt was just a little tight and revealed her sturdily shapely thighs. She was wearing high heels and so her legs and the whole shape of her from the rear were something to behold as I walked behind her. She walked purposefully, straight-backed, hobbled just a little by her skirt, her stockings rubbing together with that shimmery-whispery sound. She was wearing nylon stockings and that was a give-away that she was one of Gerry's women. Altogether Margery Nicholson came across as someone a little aloof but a woman who was holding in, and sometimes not quite holding in, a kind of lusciousness.

I mentioned Gerry's name to her when I first met her in the small reception office. 'Oh, one of his lot, are you? Fancy you're the bee's knees, I suppose. What makes you think you'll be able to do this job? I could do it blindfold but I'm only a woman so, of course, they don't think about offering the job to me. And those layabouts from Gerry. I've seen too many of 'em to be impressed. Cocky little snots, most of 'em. Well, let's take you along to see Mr Prissy Gibbons then.'

The interview was a breeze, almost as if Gibbons was determined to give me the job. I didn't tell him I was thinking of going on to university soon. I tried to make it sound as if all I'd ever wanted to do was work in a tea company so I could learn all about tea.

'Very satisfactory,' Gibbons said to conclude, rubbing his hands together. 'Your school reports look good. I'll need a couple of references, of course.' I told him I'd send them to him soon. He got down from his stool and shook my hand. 'I'll let Miss Nicholson show you around. Knows all there is to know about how this place runs.'

When she came out of her office, Margery nodded her head towards a long corridor, turned and strode away. I followed her and, as I've said, I liked the view from behind. She wasn't wearing one of the 'new look' longer skirts so I enjoyed the way the material clung round her buttocks which she moved with a decided sway. We went through a door to a set of narrow stairs leading into a large cellar. Two or three nondescript men in brown work-coats were wheeling plywood chests about on small carts. Two were working at a long counter measuring and weighing, then scooping tea leaves into one-pound packages.

'We're just managing to get the better teas now. Look!' She pointed to a large untidy pile of chests with hieroglyphics stamped on them. 'That lot's Golden Nepal. First shipment we've had for a long time. Because of the war.' She placed a finely manicured hand with dark-red nails on the top of one chest.

That was an ultimate sign of sophistication for me then, coloured nails. Most of the girls I'd known used clear polish, if they used any at all. Colour was supposed to be tarty but Margery Nicholson, in everything about her appearance, gave no impression of being a tart. She was very carefully dressed, well-tailored, neat and she kept herself slightly remote from the workers in the cellar just to show that her position in the company was a better one than theirs. When I saw women well-dressed like Margery, I always tried to imagine them rumpled, in a hot steamy situation, their reserve and their neatness coming apart, dishevelled, looking forward to letting a man undo them till they were ready and waiting, panting. I didn't quite see Margery in those terms but I did wonder briefly whether she had a boyfriend and whether he had ever managed to get her unglued. It was difficult to imagine and yet there was a sneaking sense that, yes, Margery might just let herself go sometime. But the way she was showing me around then was not conducive to thinking about her like that.

'India,' she said, as if I didn't know where Nepal was. 'Same as Darjeeling.' We walked through an aisle with chests on either side of us, and I was frantically trying to memorize the names, some written in English, some in that hieroglyphic script though Margery told me the names of those.

When we came to the back wall of the cellar, I noticed stairs leading up to a double trapdoor. Margery peered down some side alleys. 'Some Soochong in there. Don't understand why people fancy that so much. Tastes like burnt rags to me. Now there's something to drink.' She pointed to a big bulk of chests. 'Yunnan. China tea, but not the green. Black. Lovely to drink. Very expensive, that is. Wish I could afford it.'

'I've never tasted it. Never even heard of it.'

She looked at me somewhat disdainfully. 'I didn't expect you would have heard of it.' She turned and stepped decisively ahead of me. 'That's it. Come on. I can't spend all day showing you around. Some of us have work to do. And I know Gerry's errand boys – try and keep you talking. Think they're so clever, you're going to fall all over them and before you know it, they've already got you in bed! Fat chance!'

We came back to the narrow stairs and she started up them. I hesitated a little so I was well placed to have a good look at her legs under her skirt. She was wearing a lacy slip (something from Gerry, I thought) but I didn't see much more than that as her skirt was too tight. She turned around at the top and gave a brief smile, well, more like a toothy sneer. 'Sight for sore eyes, was it? Well, you can put your eyes back in your head. You're just as bad as that lot down there, all running to the bottom of the stairs when I'm coming up. Juvenile fatheads! As if they'd never seen a woman's legs before.'

I didn't know what to say. After all, I had been staring up her legs and she knew it. Maybe she was some kind of cockteaser, or at least one of those women who would let you have a little peek but only to let you know what you were missing – you'd never get a chance to handle the goods. 'I bet they don't often get a chance to get a load of legs as nice as yours,' I ventured.

She tutted. 'Well, there's a compliment. Think you're hot stuff with the ladies, do you? I'm not surprised you're one of Gerry's boys. But I've found it's mostly all talk with them, most of 'em, anyhow. Run a mile if they thought anything'd come of their talk.' That had the sound of a woman sure of herself with men. She wouldn't be taken in by sweet words, would be looking for something more substantial than talk. But at least it also sounded as if the aloofness might break down on occasions.

I thought of that as I sat next to her on the back row of the cinema, that push with her thigh on mine. Was she interested? Or was she simply out to prove she could handle anything I might try so the message was: don't try anything? In fact, when she'd led me to sit on the back row, and when we had sat down in the double seat, she turned to me and whispered, 'Don't get any ideas. It's my eyes. I don't like to be too close to the screen.' But that didn't mean she had to choose the very back row, and then, ten minutes or so later, she pushed against me with her thigh.

Originally I thought I wouldn't enjoy this date with her and I was only there with her because Gerry had told me to go. I waited outside the cinema for her and she arrived at exactly five to seven – the film started at seven. I said hello but she merely nodded at me. She was looking good in a tailored dress with bright gold buttons all the way down the front, the collar wide in a V, emphasizing her large-ish breasts. The skirt was still fairly narrow though not so narrow as the skirt she had worn at the office. Her hair was combed out, fluffed around her head. She looked good.

I'd decided that, if she persisted in her superior attitude, I'd simply enjoy the feature film, see her home and then I'd go on to the club as it was a strippers' night. I presumed Gerry wanted to treat her to the date as a reward for what she had done for him at the tea company when she showed me around – the information I had gathered that afternoon I had spilled out to Gerry the next day.

So I settled in to watch the picture till I felt Margery's thigh pressing mine. A few minutes later she slumped down a little and that caused her to lean against me harder, scrunching my arm tighter into me. I lifted it away and didn't quite know where to put it to make myself comfortable. It seemed sort of natural to move it over the back of the seat and as I did that, Margery shifted her head so that it leaned on my shoulder. I tentatively laid my hand on her shoulder, my fingers stretching out, feeling the warmth of her body through her dress and my fingertips just touching the start of the plumpness at the top of her breast.

She looked up at me and I thought she'd come out with some snide remark and tell me to take my hand away. What she said in her usual ambiguous tone was,

'Don't get too fresh!' What was I to make of that? Did it
mean she didn't mind me being 'fresh' as long as I
wasn't 'too' fresh? Anyhow, she sat there leaning into
me and I kept my arm around her.

After a while I tried to manoeuvre my fingers down
a little to fondle more of her breast but I found it
awkward and she said, 'You trying to make yourself
more comfy?' Then she began to fiddle with the jacket
she had laid across her lap and by the time she had
settled it to her liking, her elbow was somehow
propped against my upper thigh. The movement of
that elbow was quite provocatively close to my groin
though I wasn't sure whether she was deliberately
trying to be provocative – her eyes stared resolutely
ahead at the screen. I didn't want to move as she had
obviously made herself comfortable.

In fact, with that elbow and part of her arm along my
thigh and her elbow nudging into my groin, I became
partly aroused. I wondered if she actually felt me
swelling up with her elbow there. Every so often I
moved my fingers across the top of her breast, very
slowly as I didn't want to draw attention to the
stroking. She said nothing and I began to get the feeling
that though we were both looking at the screen as if the
action there was too absorbing for us to be involved in
anything else, it might be that something else was
hovering around in both our minds.

Well, it certainly was hovering around in mine but I
didn't really know about Margery. She hadn't rebuffed
me but I really hadn't done anything too forward to
warrant one of her off-putting remarks. So I supposed
she maybe knew where I might want to be heading and
she got a kick out of knowing that I wanted to head that
way but she was ignoring me and would call a halt to

anything she didn't want to happen. At least that seemed to be the ambiguous way she was behaving.

Then she moved again, easing down in her seat a little. My other arm was sort of limply crossed over my chest but I didn't attempt to move it because it might cause her to move again and I did still have my arm around her, my fingers in their slow, trickling way were stroking her breast and her arm and elbow were digging more into my thigh and groin. By now my hard-on had increased and, as she slid down a little, her other breast pressed gently against my hand in its awkward position on my chest. At the same time this movement of hers somehow forced her elbow further up and in and she seemed to be moving it slowly round, prodding well into my crotch.

With other women I'd been with I'd have taken this as a deliberate invitation and slid my hand inside their blouse or dress. But I was still unsure about Margery — was she unconscious of all this? Just getting herself comfortable while she watched the screen? In those first few days I had suddenly been thrown into Helen's bold ways so I didn't have to make any decisions in that regard because Helen always made herself eminently clear. But now with Margery's ambiguity I was thrown back to all that fumbling uncertainty I'd encountered with girls in my adolescence. Should I proceed? Was that what Margery expected? But I frankly couldn't make up my mind.

We sat like that, her elbow in my groin obviously aware of my erection, my arm around her, fingers loitering across the top of her breast, the knuckles on my other hand pressing lightly into her other breast. Every now and then her elbow rotated slightly, almost as if she was trying to feel out the length of my shaft with it. So I started to push in with my knuckles savouring the soft and yielding curves of her breast as I applied a little pressure. So there we were, in a sense feeling each other up but with bony parts, not really with palms or fingers, and both of us were doing it as if it really wasn't happening.

We stayed like that till the end of the picture and we walked out in the crowd without talking, not holding hands. I helped her on with her jacket outside, making small talk – how I'd enjoyed the picture, how nice it had been to see her again, how pleased I'd been when Gerry had arranged the date for us.

'Oh, Gerry didn't arrange it. I did.'

'Really?'

'Don't sound so surprised. You didn't come on that strong like some of Gerry's other fly boys. You didn't seem to be the smart-alec type, not like the others Gerry sends around.'

'You've been working for Gerry for some time then?'

'Yes. He gets me jobs and I return the favour for him. I've been dogsbody in a tobacco company . . .'

'I wouldn't call your body anything like a dog's.'

'Go on with you! You and your compliments. Anyhow, I was stock control clerk for a liquor place. Did orders for a dress shop, even got me to go over to France a couple of times. Had to stop though. The ferry made me seasick.' I couldn't imagine Margery ever losing control over herself to let herself get seasick. 'Gerry sends some of his boys around to check me out and of course I check a few things out for Gerry. And those boys, they think they can check me out for themselves. Most of 'em are daft. Full of themselves. So you were different. Didn't really check me out, though you did try to get an eyeful of my legs. I forgave you though when you said you liked them.'

'Well, yes I did like them . . . I mean, I do like them.'

'First off, I thought you were having me on but you looked sort of shy when you said it, just like a proper gentleman. So I thought I wouldn't mind going to the pictures with you. And you weren't quite a proper gentleman but at least I didn't have to slap you away. I wondered how you'd behave. Now I know.'

'You mean, sitting in the back row was a sort of test?'

'You could call it that if you want. But it turned out quite cosy, didn't it?'

She surprised me again. I realised that she had known all along what was going on back there in the cinema, leaning into me, probing me with her elbow. So if she engineered all that, what did she expect me to do now? Was she inviting me to respond in the same way? I decided, as she was the one testing me, I'd let her go on with her test – I was interested in what she might try. 'Well, whatever your test was, I'm glad you asked for the date.'

'Don't get yourself into a tizzy about it. Or flatter yourself because I asked for the date. I just suggested it to Gerry, sort of in passing.' So she was off again, backing away as if she didn't want her snooty poise to collapse.

We were strolling away from the cinema. She had linked arms with me and we talked comfortably enough, so I suggested we go for a drink. 'Oh, we couldn't do that,' she said. I took this to mean the evening was over for her so I said I'd see her to her bus or ride home with her.

'No need for that,' she said, shaking her head. I must have looked puzzled as if the date was strange because she wanted it to end, at least that's what I thought she meant but she went on, 'We haven't finished yet.'

She pulled on my arm, hurrying me up a little. We turned off the Kilburn High Road down a side street with small terraced houses, some gaps in between where bombs had dropped, past a corner tobacconist with headlines scrawled in black on a sheet of paper jammed into the stand for the *Evening Standard* till we came to the last shop in the street, a greengrocer's with big letters in white paint across the window: 'Bananas tomorrow. Open at 8 sharp.'

I was sure I hadn't been in this area before. I wondered if Margery lived somewhere near and that's why we'd gone to that particular cinema. She turned another corner and it was beginning to be like a maze to me. I couldn't make her out – this didn't seem the kind of district she would live in, or even know, given the kind of haughtiness she often affected. Then after another ten minutes of twisting and turning down different roads, we were on a street that looked vaguely familiar to me.

We were walking past another row of shops and when we came to a double-fronted one, she stopped and yanked me into the deep doorway. She let go of me and leaned back into the corner by the door. She smiled at me, a genuine smile this time, not her usual snide sneer. 'Come in out of the light,' she said, reaching an arm out to pull me to her. She put her arms around my neck and, very unexpectedly, she reached up to kiss me, a deep open-mouthed kiss, her tongue squirming into my mouth. I felt her teeth hard against mine.

Her lips were very moist, the inner sides slippery, and she was gently pushing her body against me. Of course, though I was surprised, I responded, fitting myself against her, pressing her into the corner, my hands trying to find the buttons on her jacket so I could ease my hands inside and perhaps fiddle with the buttons on her dress, though we were locked so closely together I found it impossible to do any unfastening. I looped my arms around her more tightly and we held a kiss for a long time, my tongue now loosely circling inside her mouth. I could feel the sharp edges of her teeth and she began to close them gently, her lips holding onto my tongue and she began to suck, drawing my tongue inside, further and further till I felt the tip would soon be tickling her tonsils. Her sucking was so fierce I thought she might unlatch my tongue from its root. This ferocious and sudden embrace and the long kiss was certainly exciting and my penis, rock-hard, was jammed against her where her pelvis seemed to be urging me to ram it strongly onto her.

Then she pulled away from me quickly, pushing me back. 'Steady on!' she said though not in a discouraging tone. She still seemed to want to be in control, wanted things on her own terms, appearing as if she liked to indulge but then turning away – her damned ambiguity again! 'Can't get too frantic yet.' I noticed the 'yet' – was that another indication she would pursue this later? Maybe, after all, she was the same as Helen and Dorothy in spite of her constant tipping of the balance, first one way, then the other. She did keep shying away as if she wanted to remain distant from what was happening even as she was enjoying it. Still, she did have an inviting smile on her face.

'Wait for the copper,' she said.

I didn't know what on earth she was talking about and the look on my face must have shown it.

'Don't you know where you are?' she asked me though again I didn't know what this place had to do with what we were doing in the doorway. I shook my head. She sidled past me from her corner, then pulled me after her till we were almost out of the doorway. She gestured with her arm and, about fifty yards up the street, on the corner, I could just make out the large letters across the front of a building: Great Asian Tea Company.

'Why d'you think Gerry got us together this evening?' I thought it was just a simple date, asked for by Margery and worked out through Gerry. 'We're on point.'

She lounged back into the corner and beckoned me back so we were soon cuddled together again. She went on to explain, obviously thinking I was following the drift of the conversation. 'We could have just met here at about nine thirty. That's what I always did with the others. And that's all that mattered to Gerry. But I thought the picture before'd be a nice idea and it's a fairly easy walk here.' She looked at her wristwatch. 'Should be along in about five minutes or so, Gerry says.'

'Who? And what's all this about being on point?'

She sighed. 'I was forgetting. You haven't done this before, have you? Not like the others. They always liked being on point with me. Give themselves a cheap thrill but I always kept it strictly business. Mind you, you can't fake it really. You have to make it look real. But as soon as the cop had gone, I'd give 'em a swift knee in the groin. That smartened them up!'

I still couldn't understand what she was driving at. 'On point?' I asked again.

'Look out. Keep your eyes peeled for the rozzers.'

82

The slang word sounded slightly shocking coming from her. 'Cops have regular beats. This one here comes up this street around nine thirty, checking no one's around trying to break in, making sure all the doors and windows are locked and haven't been tampered with. He checks out a few more streets up there.' She nodded her head sideways in the direction of the tea company. 'Crosses over and round the corner and down a few more streets, doubling back down there.' She nodded in the other direction. 'Takes him around an hour or so unless something holds him up. So you know there's going to be no cops around here for fifty minutes or so. Plenty of time to get up to any kind of mischief you fancy.'

At first, when she said that, I thought she was inviting me into randy mischief and we could get started once the copper had gone past. But then it dawned on me why we were in this particular doorway near the Great Asian Tea Company. Margery knew when the expensive teas had come in, and I'd given Gerry the lowdown on just where those chests of tea were in the cellar. This was obviously one of the ways Gerry got some of his supplies. Margery had done jobs for Gerry before; the places where she had worked were all associated with the items Gerry dealt with: tobacco, liquor, dresses and lingerie. Something was about to happen at the tea company and Margery and I were the look-outs for it.

'I get it!' I said. I felt quite excited about it, if a little apprehensive.

'Keep your voice down.'

But I still wasn't quite sure why I'd been brought into this. Why did I need to be there with Margery? 'Why two of us?' I asked Margery.

'One person hanging about, man or woman, well, a copper's going to smell a rat. It'll look as if he's up to no good, mooching around on his own. But a couple in a doorway, he's used to that, a place where they can have a quiet snog. A copper'll move 'em on maybe but he won't think they're up to anything else, too interested in what they're doing, he thinks. So we've got to play it up but we've got to keep a look-out as well, in case he comes back or someone else comes around and notices and calls the cops. I found it easy to do the look-out with others.' Her smile brightened. 'So don't get yourself too worked up just yet.'

'Just yet,' she had said!

'The copper's not here yet but maybe we should have a bit of a try.' She pulled me in closer and then moved us as if we were in a slow, smoochy dance so we could see out into the street. Then she snuggled up tight and we were cheek to cheek.

'I can see down the street from here.' I could feel her warm breath at my ear. 'Can you check up the other way?'

I could see along the street but her pelvis was squashing against me so I knew I was going to find it difficult to concentrate on keeping my eyes skinned under those circumstances. And then she began to lick my ear, her tongue inside and she mumbled, 'You still watching?'

'Yes,' I whispered though I am sure she knew I was really thinking of other things because my cock was stiff and fat against her.

'You'll do,' she said, then broke away from me, shuffling back into the corner. 'Is your wallet handy?'

I nodded but again I didn't know why she'd mentioned it. She put her hand out. 'Let's see it.'

84

I briefly thought that somehow this was all a set-up and she was simply going to steal my money – as it happens Gerry had just paid me and there were a few fivers in the wallet. Still, I passed it to her. She stroked her other hand hard across the surface as it lay on her palm. 'You boys are all the same. I can feel that hard round ring in there.' She flipped it open and pulled out a couple of French letters I had stuffed in there.

She was the first woman I'd met through Gerry who seemed worried about contraception. Helen never bothered and it hadn't arisen with Dorothy. I always carried Durex in those hideous maroon-purple enve-lopes but I hadn't ever really used one. I'd been in a couple of spots where I had fumbled one on, tearing at the packet, then messing about so much rolling it on that the woman had cooled down considerably and I never got anywhere with her. It was a relief being with Helen. I supposed, being a nurse, she had taken care of the problem.

Margery held onto the two packages when she gave me my wallet back. They'd been in the wallet a fair amount of time and the envelopes looked creased and dog-eared. 'You always expecting to use these?'

I nodded. 'I'm a good boy scout – you know, be prepared.'

'Well, I just didn't want you fiddling around with one of these with me.' I wondered if she had taken care of the problem herself like Helen or whether it was simply a warning not to try anything with her. She stuffed the French letters in her jacket pocket. 'In case you're wondering, it's a bit nippy to take my knickers off.' She patted her pocket. 'These are safe with me for the time being.'

Ambiguous Margery! I wondered whether this was

all part of her wanting to be in control. Maybe she'd
take her knickers off inside so I thought about taking
her home afterwards. Or maybe it was all a no-no.
Then she stepped to the edge of the doorway and
glanced down the street. 'There's a torch flashing
around down there. I'll bet that's him. Stupid, giving
the game away to any burglar, him shining his torch
about like that.' She came back inside the doorway.
'Well, we'd better get ready for him.'

Deliberately and matter-of-factly, she undid the buttons on her jacket, pulling it open. Then she started on
her dress, opening it wide down to the waist, showing
a white slip with a lacy band across the top – one from
Gerry, I imagined. I must have been gaping at her, for
she said, 'We've got to make it look real. Not that I
want to give him too much of an eyeful when he shines
his torch in here. That's what he'll do. He's got to find
us going at it. So come on over here!'

My hands reached out for her as I stepped closer but
she stopped me again. 'And let me do all the talking.
And try not to look at him. Keep your face in shadow.
We don't want him putting two and two together later.
So we don't want to give him the chance to identify us.
I'll give him a bit of sweet talk. We can act shy, upset
we've been discovered. Well, let's get on with it then!'

She pulled me to her, her arms firm around me, her
mouth sloppily open on mine and she began her hard
sucking at my tongue again. I accommodated my body
to hers, pushing a knee between her legs which opened
easily as I moved it in and up, hoping it would push
her dress up a little. She responded by adjusting
herself so she could obviously feel my quick-growing
erection.

We stayed like that a while and I began to push

harder at her, trying to get my cock where it would be knocking up against her quim. I switched round a little, one of my hands slowly sliding up through the opening at her waist until I could feel the silkiness of her slip. I placed my palm over her breast and stroked, letting two of my fingers pinch her nipple gently. It felt big and hard even through her slip and bra.

One of her hands was now on my buttocks, fingers probing into the crack of my arse as if she was going to push along and under so she could feel my balls tight inside my scrotum. She was also using that hand to push me onto her, then back, then onto her again as if she wanted to feel my cock doing those regular strokes even though we were still muffled in our clothes. She let my tongue go but her mouth took up the same rhythms as her hand on my arse so my tongue seemed to be fucking her mouth which was as wetly slippery as I imagined her quim would be, feeling my long, thick shaft slamming slowly into her dress, thinking of it bursting through her slip, her knickers, as she called them.

I was getting carried away with this, my fingers inside her slip now, moving the hem up, my other hand fidgeting at her breast attempting to push the slip aside and her bra. I was so intent on these manoeuvres that it came as a shock when bright light flooded the doorway.

'What's going on here, then?'

Margery pushed me away and I tried to look sideways into the light. Then I looked at Margery. She was clutching her dress to close it with one hand, brushing at her skirt with the other. 'Oh, you gave us such a fright, sergeant.'

'Constable, miss, just constable.'

'I'm so embarrassed. I've never been caught doing . . . I mean . . . could you lower the light, constable, please? I'm all . . . in a fluster.' She was fumbling with her dress buttons, fastening them, then patting her hair.

'This isn't allowed, miss. Public indecency. You could finish up in court.'

'Oh, constable, you wouldn't do that to me, would you? My poor mum would die of shock.' Then she nodded at me. 'And what about him? You see, his wife doesn't know anything about . . . oops!' She acted as if she was blushing. Then she mumbled at me. 'I'm sorry. I shouldn't have . . .'

'I'll let you off with a warning this time.'

'Thanks so much, constable. It's not that we're really doing anything wrong. We don't see each other often and we've no place to go. My mum's at home and he can't get away so it's very difficult.'

'Well, we're not supposed to let this happen. Suppose someone was to come along . . .'

'Well, we thought this was a quiet place.' She giggled coquettishly. 'We didn't want to shock anyone, did we, George?'

I stammered, 'No, no, not at all.'

'You'll have to move along.'

'Of course. We understand, don't we, George?' Margery by now had buttoned herself up, holding her jacket closely around her and had even turned up the collar. 'I just need a minute or two to get myself straight. And you too, George. Just look at you.' She leaned down and brushed at my trousers, deliberately giving my crotch a quick touch. She probably felt I was still half-aroused. The constable turned his torch off.

'Well, you hurry up now.'

'Won't take a jiffy.'

'And don't let me catch you around here again. I'd have to charge you then. Goodnight, miss. Don't be too long now!'

'We won't, honest.'

The policeman started to trundle his bike up the street, clicking his torch on every now and again, moving up the street slowly. 'Nitwit!' Margery said, then leaned into me to give me a big kiss. 'Good boy!' I grabbed at her again.

'Hold on! We'd better get out of here in case he looks back and sees we're still in here. Don't want him thinking anything suspicious. Let's just dawdle behind him so he can see us if he turns round.'

We began to stroll lazily along. 'Put your arm around me. Look interested.' I *was* interested and was frantically thinking how I could continue with Margery. But she was walking on, up to the street corner, then crossing, walking on past some shops, watching the policeman wheeling his bike till he turned the corner at the end of the street. As soon as he'd disappeared, Margery pulled me into a shop doorway. I noticed we were opposite the Great Asian Tea Company.

She pushed me into the corner. 'Wait there!' she said as she stepped onto the pavement. She ran up the street and I peered out to watch her. At the corner she flattened herself against the wall and carefully poked her head around the corner. Then she reached into her handbag and there was a sudden flash of light. She backed away from the corner and there was another flash, then another and she came scurrying back to me.

She stood at the edge of the doorway, looking out. 'Come on, you slowcoaches,' she muttered. I stood by her and she put her hand on me to stop me from stepping out. After a minute or two, a light brightened the street.

'Keep it down!' she hissed into the night and, as if she'd been heard, the light dimmed. I heard the low purr of a car engine. Margery grabbed my hand. 'Come on,' she said and she began to run as best she could in her high heels.

We crossed the street and huddled against the wall of the tea company. Then I saw a large van pull round the corner and Margery stepped out into the van's lights and waved for it to stop. A little man climbed out and Margery ran to meet him. She turned her head and hoarsely shouted, 'Nick!' When I joined them, the two of them were conversing in animated whispers till Margery pointed round the corner, then moved off, pulling me with her, the little man following.

We came to trapdoors set in the side of a wall like a coal chute. I recognized those doors as those I'd seen at the end of the cellar.

Margery was rooting inside her handbag while the little man in his dark sweater and jacket bounced impatiently up and down. 'We haven't got all night, you know!' he snapped.

'Keep your hair on. I've got it here somewhere.' Margery pulled a key out and pushing it hard into the lock at the centre of the doors, turned it with a loud clicking and rattling.

'Don't make such a racket!' the little man said nastily.

'It's not my fault if it grinds like that.'

'You just keep to your own grinding, little Miss Tight Arse. I've had some of your nonsense before. Get the doors open.' The man strode back to the van and pounded on the side. Margery yelled at him, 'D'you want to wake up the whole bloody neighbourhood?'

'Shut your trap.'

'Here, Nick, help me with these.' She was struggling with the doors but they were too heavy for her. I pulled and swung them open. Behind me came the man and three others, all dressed in dark clothes. 'Move your arse out of the way!' the little man said and pushed Margery roughly to one side.

'Keep your hands to yourself!' Margery grated at him.

'We've got to get on. Don't have much time.' The man jerked his head at the other three. 'You go on in. I'll pull the van closer.' He ran back to the vehicle as the men clambered through the doors and down the stairs. We stood to the side and Margery waved the van in closer. The man came back and said, 'You two beat it. We can handle this now.'

Margery sniggered, then said, 'I hope so. After your last cock-up.'

'Whose fault was that? You got too stuck into other things. Not watching out properly. Didn't give us much time to clear out.'

'You took too long.'

'You were too busy letting some dink feel you up.'

'I was not!'

The little man grinned. 'I know what gets into you when you come on these jobs. Mind you, I wouldn't mind being one of them who gets into you.'

'Wouldn't you just! Well, no deal for you. You just do your job and I'll do mine.'

By this time one of the men was backing up the stairs holding a tea chest, another man helping him from below. A voice from the cellar floated up to us.

'Stop gassing, Harry. Let's move this stuff.'

'Right!' Harry turned to Margery. 'Get out of it then. You know Gerry doesn't want you hanging around us.' He went to the stairs. 'And keep your eyes open this time.'

Margery began to walk away and I followed her. The little man called after me. 'Hey, son. You too. Watch out. Don't just think about rogering her. And watch out for her. Regular terror for dick, she is. So you'll really be able to whack it to her. That's what I hear. She ain't just the little miss high and mighty as she cracks on to be.'

Margery snapped back at him, 'You just think everybody's mind's as filthy as yours.' She took my arm and said to me, 'Pay no attention to him. What does he know, the little squirt?'

A shout came from behind us. 'Don't forget to lock up after us!'

'I know, I know!' Margery called back.

We kept on walking and crossed the street. There was a grocer's on the other corner which Margery pointed at. 'There! That's where I thought we'd hole up! We can see all the streets from there.'

Soon we were in the doorway. 'We'll hang on here. It should only take them about half an hour if they get a move on.' She pulled her torch from her handbag and put it down on a low ledge. 'Keep it handy to flash at them if anyone turns up.'

Then she turned to me. 'Now, how d'you fancy a bit of public indecency?' Again she was opening her jacket, undoing her dress, this time right the way to the hem, holding it open.

Of course I stepped to her and away we went, mouth on mouth, sucking in, tongues sliding in and out, my hands stroking the smoothness of her slip, getting under it, raising it, feeling it silky on the back of my hands, her hands on my buttocks again, rocking me against her, my cock very upstanding, still inside my pants but I knew I'd be able to loosen it out when I felt the time was right. I curled one hand round to feel the swell of Margery's buttocks, one hand picking at the elastic of her knickers, trying to finger my way inside.

'Not too indecent,' she whispered and for a moment I thought she was going to back away again though her hand was very insistent on my arse, making me prod at her. She was sucking hard on my tongue, one hand stroking the back of my neck. My finger was running under the elastic, edging towards her pubic mound, while my other hand was loosening my fly, grabbing my cock out. She felt it touch the top of her thigh and let out a gasp as she sucked harder on my tongue.

Her knickers were snug and tight against her so there was no way I could push my fat cock inside under the elastic. And it didn't appear as if I was going to be able to pull them off or even ease them down a little. In a way Margery was acting the way she had acted in the cinema, as if she was paying no attention to what I was doing down there, or even to what she was doing, with her mouth full of a soft moisture and relentlessly sucking my tongue.

Every now and again she pulled slightly away from me – I suppose she was looking around, checking if anyone was on the streets. I certainly wasn't doing that. I was too busy thinking of a way to get into Margery's knickers, especially after I heard the little man hint that Margery was not as prim and proper as she tried to act. She was breathing heavily and rubbing herself seductively against me.

Still, the best I could do was place my cock just at her slit, rubbing my cock-head against the silky band of her knickers covering her quim. I pushed and her legs opened a little. I pushed harder inside, my two hands now groping at her breasts, my mouth slavering on hers.

I was incredibly hot now even though I had concluded that this was as far as Margery would let things go. It reminded me a little of that dangerous drive I'd had with Helen, the way then I knew I was in danger but how that danger made me more excited. I knew now, though I suppose the idea was buried somewhat, that I was in some danger as I was an accomplice in a robbery, part of the gang acting as look-out though I was not quite sure what I would do if anyone suddenly appeared on the scene.

Somehow I was not too disturbed within myself for being an accomplice. I rationalized it by telling myself I was an unwitting accomplice. I had had no idea when I went out that evening I'd be participating in a robbery and Margery had led me on till all I could think about was how I could work at breaking down her resistance. Then I was running with her, out of the doorway, then meeting the other man, opening doors for the gang. The little man had been so obstreperous, I didn't feel I could have refused and walked away from Margery in those circumstances. Anyhow, there was no doubt my adrenalin was high and this pumping at Margery, my cock nudging at her quim, felt extraordinarily sexy.

I kept pushing at that silky band, sliding my whole length slowly in, Margery closing her legs hard on my cock, sucking my tongue deep, then letting me slide it wetly to her lips as my cock almost painfully dragged its length against her, the head knocking at her clit till I pushed deeply in again.

Years later we used to call this 'dry humping' but that's not often the case. It certainly wasn't the case with Margery, for she was certainly not dry. That silky band of material covering her slit was almost swampy with her juices. In fact, she breathed in my ear, 'I'm indecently wet!' My cock, feeling all that juice and with my tongue so slathered in Margery's mouth, I knew would soon let loose its own juice, shooting it along that slit, spout a stream under and onto her slip at the back, especially when Margery somehow had her hand at the back waiting to touch my cock-head with her fingers, sliding the slip around it, tweaking it with that soft silk as if her fingers wouldn't let go, her legs holding on tight and my cock finding it hard to withdraw.

I knew I couldn't last much longer as she was increasingly squeezing and touching me, helping me on till I sensed we were both heading to that last surge and I drove on and into her till I couldn't hold it any longer. As I felt the first sprinkle emerge, I touched it to the silky band on her slit. She yelped a little and then as the rest gushed out, I battered my way along, making the tops of her legs creamily wet so my slide was easier and the juice spread along the whole length of my thick shaft as I let fly. Margery's fingers must have felt that jet of come spreading onto her slip at the back and she grasped my cock in the wetness of the silk, wanting to milk more out, squeezing my cock-head, letting it bang into her palm.

I rested there a minute or two, Margery's fingers still working at me almost absentmindedly as she was looking over my shoulder keeping watch. She moved to flick her tongue along my lips, flicking it briefly in and out. I was in that usual state of seeming to be bathing in a warm and sunny wetness. She held onto me, whispering, 'Don't forget to keep looking.' Then she pulled away from me, began to rearrange her clothing, buttoning up, while I did the same. She was also peering out and eventually I heard an engine start, lights flashed on, then off. Margery turned back to me and said, 'All done.' I presumed she meant the robbery had been successfully completed but then she added, stretching a hand out to touch my crotch, 'How does it feel to be indecent?' Without giving me time to answer, she went on, 'Come on. Got to close up.' We hurried across the street and Margery locked the doors. And soon we were back in that maze of side streets. 'How d'you like being on point?' she asked me.

'It was great. Thanks for letting me do it with you.'

'I can't say you're much good at it.' Was she doing her see-saw act again? I thought she'd enjoyed what we were doing. She must have sensed what I was thinking. 'I mean the look-out stuff.'

'Well, I didn't see you doing much of that. And anyhow there wasn't anything to look out for.'

'That's what you think. Too stuck into something else, weren't you?' She grinned at me.

'Why not? Nothing much going on out there.'

'You've got a lot to learn. Didn't you see anything?'

'Can't say I did.'

'Didn't you see the old geezer taking his mongrel for a walk?'

'No.'

'The la-di-da woman and her poodle?'

'No.'

'Just as well the copper didn't come back. You

wouldn't have seen him either. Fat lot of good you'd have been warning the others.' I really didn't know how she'd seen what was going on. Of course, I didn't really know whether she wasn't just making it all up.

'I don't know how you do it,' I said. ' You seemed so . . . involved with what we were . . .'

'Oh, I was.' She squeezed my arm. 'But I still do my job. Don't listen to Harry. I know what I'm doing.' I had to agree with that though not in quite the terms she was thinking of. 'I was a bit worried about those two kids just three doors down from us. But they stayed put. I guess they were only doing what we were doing!'

'How did you know any of those people wouldn't cause any trouble? I mean, seeing the van and all that.'

'You get to know. Most of 'em round here, they don't want anything to do with the rozzers. They wouldn't want to land anyone in trouble. Unless it was someone's house being robbed.'

'But how d'you know?'

'Well, they're just taking their dogs for a walk. And those kids had other things on their minds. Probably didn't even see the van. And how would they know anything was going on? Just a van loading stuff. Working late, they'd think. You just get a feel for it. But someone stopping, taking an interest, wondering what's going on, they go round to the cop shop. But most of 'em couldn't care less. You've got to watch out for gawkers.'

'Fancy you seeing all that and me just doing . . .'

She laughed. 'Just doing what was very nice. And I don't get too . . . distracted doing the watching, I mean.' She grabbed my arm more tightly as we walked. 'I'm all squishy down there. Nice and juicy.' Then she rummaged in her pocket. 'You can have these back now,' she said passing me the Durex. 'From what it feels like down there, I'm not sure they'd be able to hold it all! You're a really spunky man, Nick. You know, when I'm sitting on the bus, I'll feel all that, trickling down, going cold and sticky. And I'll think about who spilled it there!' She smiled up at me. 'Fancy me sitting there on the bus, sitting in it! I've a good mind to give the game away! Someone sits next to me, I'm going to tell them. Make your ears burn! I'll tell 'em I don't believe in the milk of human kindness because I'm sitting in the cream of public indecency.'

She didn't want me to see her home. 'Enough for one night, Nick.' So I just took her to her bus stop. I didn't ask her for another date. After all, she was one of Gerry's girls so I was sure I'd see her again. And, anyhow, she'd arranged this first date and, if she'd really enjoyed it, I supposed she'd contact me through Gerry again.

No one ever mentioned the robbery to me and I didn't see any report about it in the papers. I suppose it was a relatively small crime and it certainly didn't have any sensational trappings. Still, I looked forward to being a point man again, Margery and me as a team, or even with some other delectable girl Gerry had recruited. Whoever or whatever it or she was, I knew I'd always be ahead on points.

5. 'Go See Margo'

'Go see Margo for me.' Gerry's voice floated huskily across the stiff-starched tablecloth at the Blue Lantern where he conducted most of his business. He liked to act out some weird approximation of an American tough guy though he was never able to sustain the part for very long. I'd been working for Gerry for just over a month now, delivering letters ('You can't trust the post,' Gerry told me) and parcels, and making visits to pick up notes to take back to Gerry. Once he sent me down to a small village in the middle of nowhere, with houses straggling down one main street and just outside, in the middle of large fields, landing strips and abandoned Nissen huts used by the airforce during the war. I couldn't figure out why Gerry would have dealings with anyone in such an out-of-the-way place, especially with the almost toothless, scraggy-haired man I delivered a letter to.

Gerry never told me much about his business. 'What you don't know won't get you in trouble. Won't be able to tell the cops anything if they nab you.' I was still very naive and I believed that the police would not come after me simply for making deliveries. And besides the good pay Gerry gave me, there were other perks. Like Helen. And Margery.

When Gerry asked me to see Margo, I expected it

would be the usual delivery job so I asked him what I had to take with me.

'Nothing, old sport.' Gerry grinned. 'Except yourself. Margo likes fresh-faced youngsters like you. Give her a treat, you will, not like the dogsbodies she usually has to put up with.' He pulled out his wallet and slid out a fat wad of five pound notes, passing the money to me. 'That's the usual for Margo.' Then he pulled out more notes and handed those to me. 'See if you need these extra.'

I must have looked puzzled at being given all this money so Gerry went on, 'Margo's been with me a couple of years now. Came in with me straight after the war. I helped her get on to her feet,' adding, after a pause, 'mostly by lying on her back. She's pretty much out of the game now, just helps me out running that side of the business. But she's a clever bitch and I've been wondering for some time now if she isn't skimming off the top. Collecting more than she should and keeping it for herself. Getting a bit too big for her boots, she is. So that's where you come in.'

'What do I do?'

'It's like this, old son. I usually send a few clients her way to buy stuff from her and I hint that she or some other girl is "available". You know what I mean.' Gerry grinned widely. 'Well, I've told her you'll be going round to visit her tomorrow and I said you'd like her to be "available". That first batch of fivers, that's what she gets. But see if she tries to hike the price or suggests you can buy Scotch from her – see if she's charging over the odds. Let her know you're carrying plenty of cash. See what she goes for. But don't give in too easy. See how hard she pushes to grab the extra from you. Like I say, she's a clever bitch, but she's a real talker and if she likes you, and I think she'll really like you, she might spout a lot. Just keep your ears open. Maybe I'm wrong. Maybe she isn't the thieving bitch I think she is. Well, no harm done to check her out. And you'll have a good time. She can be a real charmer. And don't mention you work for me. That way she'll talk more. Just tell her we met here some lunchtime and we got to talking and one thing led to another . . . She knows how these things happen. She's expecting you around noon tomorrow.' He slipped me three more fivers. 'Take a taxi.' He scribbled on a scrap of paper which he then handed to me. 'Here's Margo's address.'

Margo lived in a good part of town, one of the districts that had missed much of the bombing, though her house was a little isolated: the houses along one side of the street had been hit and so were empty now, and her house had a front garden surrounded by a hedge of high bushes and one tall elm tree in front of the window. It was a large Victorian house and when I reached the front door I was faced with a large, leaded panel of bevelled glass stained with bright colours. I rang the bell and after a few seconds I saw through the glass a shape moving towards me. When the door opened I was greeted by a stunning young woman dressed in the traditional clothes of a maid – black dress, a small white apron, a frill of lace in her hair, black stockings, high heels. For a moment I thought this was Margo – I'd heard enough about the fantasies some men had about maids and Margo was dressed up that way for me. But this gorgeous maid simply stood in the doorway, looking at me with a questioning look.

'I'm here to see Margo,' I stammered. She swung the

door wide and with a small wave she invited me in. Closing the door behind me, she walked ahead of me down the hall and when she came to a door on her left, she opened it for me and waved me in. She closed the door and I heard her click-clacking her way towards the back of the house. I was tempted to go back to the hall to peek out at her walking away, her slim figure swaying on her finely shaped legs, the black seams of her stockings showing them off. But I decided to wait where I was, so I sat down on a comfortable high-backed chair with curved wooden legs and delicately carved arms.

It was the most sumptuous room I had ever been in – heavy velvet curtains partly drawn across the large window covered by a film of white, a high fireplace with a large, mirrored overmantle, a sofa matching the chair I was sitting in, a deep and plush armchair, and three end-tables which looked too fragile to be holding the three brass lamps on them. The carpet was Indian, richly patterned in blues and greens. I briefly wondered if Gerry had had this shipped out with his chests of tea. I was not used to these kinds of furnishings so I felt a little uneasy. It made me think that if this is how Margo liked to live, she would probably be one of those snooty, upper-class English women, remote, beautiful maybe, but convinced she was superior to everyone else. How wrong I was.

When she glided into the room, my immediate impression was one of colour. She was wearing a dark green dress which, while not tight-fitting, outlined her shapely figure. Her hair was dark copper and fell past her shoulders. She was younger than I thought she'd be, probably in her mid-thirties. She moved gracefully to me on high heels, a tall, striking woman. I noticed her eyes were green and as she held out her hand to me she smiled, her dark red mouth opening to reveal perfectly even, dazzling white teeth.

'You must be Nick.' Her hand felt soft though she gave mine a little tight grip before sliding her fingers away across my palm. Then she signalled me to sit down and she sat on the sofa opposite me, crossing her splendid legs. 'Teresa tried to tell me you were different from the others who come here but her English isn't that good and I know only a little Italian. She's only been here a couple of weeks and she's very shy so she doesn't talk much. But she's been a great help since she's been here.' She smiled at me again. 'So how did you meet Gerry?'

I told her I had met him through my boss who had sent me to close a business deal with Gerry. I'd had lunch with him and he mentioned how he knew some women. 'He mentioned you in particular.'

'How nice of him to send me such a personable young man. But you don't look the type who needs to come to see me.' She gave me a questioning look which quickly changed into a smile. 'Still, I'm glad you did. I'm sure I'll be able to accommodate you . . . with whatever you may like. I suppose Gerry explained about . . .'

I stood up, moving over to her as I pulled out my wallet, making sure she could see it jammed with notes. I peeled off the requisite number and handed the money to her.

'Oh, I didn't mean you to . . . You needn't have worried about that just yet.'

But she still took the money from me and counted it before she put it on the table next to her. 'You're well organized, I see. Exactly the right amount.' Then she added after a short pause, 'Under normal circumstances, that is.'

She patted the cushion next to her. 'Why don't you sit here?' She reached to the table and rang a small bell standing there. 'I usually like to do the civilized thing before we get . . . sidetracked into something else. Teresa will bring us some tea so we can talk and get to know each other a little. No need to rush things. I'm free the whole afternoon.' She gave me her astonishing smile again. 'Though I suppose Gerry explained that if we go over the time, well, maybe you could see your way to offering a little extra.' The smile remained on her face but her expression was obviously framing this as a question.

'Gerry didn't mention anything like that, just what I've already . . .' and I pointed to the notes on the table.

'Well, Gerry's got so much on his mind, maybe he just forgot to tell you.'

I started to stand up. 'If it's too . . . inconvenient . . . I mean, I had no idea I'd have to . . .' But she pressed her hand on my thigh and left it there.

'Oh, don't be silly. I hope you don't think I was trying to suggest you weren't welcome here. I'm sure we can come to some mutual agreement. It's just that, well, my head's been full of Teresa. My expenses are a little more than they have been, you see. Teresa has no money and I feel responsible for her. She's the niece of a friend of mine and I promised I'd look after her. Gerry doesn't know about her. And I know what he'd tell me to do with Teresa.'

The door opened. 'And here she is, with our tea.' Teresa was carrying a silver tray with an elegant silver teapot and two fine China cups and saucers, milk and sugar.

'Let's not spoil our afternoon, Nick. Here, Teresa, set it down here.' She indicated a low table to one side of the sofa. 'That'll be all for now, Teresa. And remember, I don't want to be disturbed at all . . . unless I ring for something, of course.'

Teresa curtseyed a little and left the room. 'I hope she understood that. We wouldn't want her coming in at the wrong time, would we? She's led such a sheltered life I'm not sure what she'd do if she came in on anything . . . untoward.' She smiled again. 'And she's so shy. She'd probably never get over it.'

Margo poured tea for us and as we sipped at it she asked me a few questions – where I'd been to school, where I'd worked, what I was going to do with my life. While she made all this sound like a simple, genteel conversation, I had the impression that she was probing me, almost as if she knew I wasn't quite what I said I was. She made a few sly digs at Gerry, about how he was in control and called all the shots.

'He doesn't know about Teresa, doesn't understand how my expenses have gone up.' Then she leaned towards me. 'Now I usually have to ask for a little something for the maid.' She was now resting her fingers along my inner thigh.

I hesitated a little before I replied, 'Well, I didn't come here to see the maid.'

'Of course. But she's a part of the house now, so perhaps . . .' She left her sentence unfinished, looking me straight in the face, but I shook my head slightly. She shrugged. 'I understand you didn't expect to have to . . . but it's . . . a special circumstance. And I don't want Gerry to get his hands on Teresa. And I'd be very grateful.' She stood up in front of me and smoothed her dress around her waist so that her breasts were outlined curvaceously. 'I could do some very special things for you.'

I smiled up at her. 'Gerry told me you were very special anyhow. And you know Gerry. He'd ask me how things went and he'd find out about anything extra. I'm no good at lying so it might get you in trouble.'

She was almost pouting now but she managed to turn the pout into a smile. 'And I can't afford to get his back up. After all, he does give me a few supplies to make life a little easier for me. I can show you.' She gave me her hand. 'Are you ready?' I took her hand, stood up and she led me out of the room and up the stairs.

The bedroom was elegant – it had a large brass bedstead with a lacy flounce turned back to show red satin sheets and brightly white and big-stuffed pillows. Against one wall was a large wardrobe with a full-length mirror-door. Margo pulled the door open to reveal a row of slots which she reached into, pulling out an emerald slip and panties. 'This is the kind of thing Gerry supplies me with.'

She held the slip in front of her, holding it at the waist to show how it fitted, then flung it onto the bed. 'Or maybe you just like these on their own.' She put the panties against her. 'There's lots more.' She drew out a white half-slip in filmy silk, holding it up for me to see. 'Just think what that would do for a woman. Of course, Gerry charges me a lot for these sometimes – they're not all presents. But I think they're worth it. Don't you think they're worth it?'

The white silk flew onto the bed and now she was strutting towards me with some dark-blue panties in her hand. She stood close to me. 'So good to feel something this silky next to you. Feel.' I touched them briefly and then she placed the panties at my crotch, moving them up to stroke my face with them. 'Isn't that what you boys are always saying – I'd like to get into her pants?'

Her hand slipped onto the back of my neck and I felt that soft silkiness there as her mouth moved gently onto mine. This was so enticing I began to respond by pushing my lips hard on hers, my tongue trying to push into her mouth but she backed away a little. I thought this was going to develop into another request for an extra gift of cash but she whispered, 'Don't rush at it, Nick. Let me show you.'

She came back to me, the silk in her hand slippery on my cheek, at my ear, my neck while her mouth was sweetly wet on mine, her tongue flicking inside my mouth, at my inner lips before probing inside further. Then she said so quietly I hardly was able to hear the words. 'I love a long tongue, all smooth and wet, going in and out. Lovely to slide around . . . before we get to the hard stuff,' and by now she was moving her pelvis close against me. The hand holding the panties moved to my mouth. 'Taste how sweet they are. Think about where I wear them. Make them wet with your lips. Creamy panties.'

My mouth was sloppy and I sucked on the material till she snatched it away, going back to the wardrobe to pull out more lingerie, flinging each piece onto the bed, a whole array of brightly coloured slips, panties, bras, garter belts: light blue, yellow, pink, black, red. As she threw them she said, 'Make yourself comfortable, Nick. Take your jacket off, and that tie.' She took the jacket from me, patting the pocket where my wallet was. 'Now go over and choose something you'd like to see modelled.'

I chose a rich red slip and panties, edged with intricate lace that showed a high cut which would make them fall enticingly high on the thigh. I put them on the rail at the foot of the bed. 'So you're a red man. Interesting. It's not a colour that quite suits me. But we'll model them anyway.'

She strolled past me to a sash hanging by the head of the bed and pulled it. Then she came to me, linked arms with me and walked to an armchair which she pushed me into. 'Relax. And watch.'

She perched on the arm of the chair, one arm snaking round my neck, the other ever so slowly working its way up my thigh towards my crotch. 'Red. I bet I know what's red as well.' Her hand was now pressing against the bulge in my trousers. 'Red and already nice and hard.'

Her hand began to unbutton my shirt and her fingers then stroked my skin gently. 'We'll just sit here and get comfy. I've rung for Teresa. These Italian girls are so . . . unquestioning. D'you know that's what Gerry does? Brings girls over from Italy, Malta, sometimes France. He doesn't have papers for them but he arranges for them to come here and marry their boy-friends. Of course they really don't have boyfriends here. Gerry arranges that too. Marries them off to people he knows – they get a nice ten-day honeymoon spree with the girl. Getting married means they're English so they can't be sent back. Gerry puts them to work for a year or so then they're on their own. They're happy to be here, away from their bombed-out towns. There's food here and they earn money, then they get free – well, some of them stay at it, of course. This friend of mine heard about the scheme and asked me to arrange for Teresa to come over. But I didn't want Gerry in on it so I brought Teresa over myself. She's really happy here. Such a sweet nature. And helpful. She'll do anything I say.'

Her mouth was at my ear and these words were sprinkled with little licks, her tongue smoothing all the contours and crannies, the tip of her tongue sliding right inside. 'But she's very expensive. That's why I have to ask for maid service extra. I don't want to have to turn to Gerry for help. I wouldn't like him to get his hands on her.'

There was a knock on the door. 'Come in,' Margo said. It was Teresa who stood shyly just inside the door till Margo waved her in. 'You needn't be bashful, Teresa. And we certainly don't need you to be the maid right now. We'll just be friends.'

She went to Teresa and unfastened her apron and took the lace cap out of her hair, taking some pins out as well so that her hair fell in long black tresses down to her shoulders. 'There. That's better.'

Teresa was standing as if she didn't quite know how to take this.

'It's alright, pet,' said Margo. Then she turned to me. 'Of course she only knows a few words of English. But she'll be alright. Fancy spending ten days with her on a honeymoon! There's lots of Teresas out there just waiting to come over here. A good racket to get into, eh, Nick? Think of all the perks – you could choose any of them for yourself.'

She took Teresa's hand to lead her to the bed, turning her to stand and face me sitting in the chair. Margo passed her the lingerie I had chosen.

Her face lit up when she realized she was being

given the slip and panties as a present. Then she began to move but Margo laid her hand on Teresa's arm. 'We should see if they fit you.'

Teresa looked puzzled.

'Oh dear, I'm not sure she knows what we're talking about.' She gestured to show that she wanted Teresa to put the slip and panties on but Teresa became flustered, tilted her head shyly, looked down at her feet.

'Oh, we can't go on with you being so shy. Nothing to worry about here.' She unbuttoned Teresa's dress at the top but immediately Teresa's hands flew up to draw it close around her. She began to shake her head, staring at me.

'He's a friend. Nothing to worry about. See, I don't mind.' Margo stepped towards me and with some captivating swaying moves she began to unbutton her dress. When she had finished, she said, 'Nothing to it,' and she swung around, the dress flying open to reveal black panties, garter belt, bra. Then she pointed at Teresa, shrugging off her dress and coming to sit next to me again.

Slowly, fumblingly, Teresa unfastened her dress and almost in time with Teresa, Margo unfastened my fly buttons, whispering, 'Fair's fair. Everybody's buttons have to be the same,' and her fingers found their way inside. Teresa swung around just as Margo had done – she was wearing a full white slip. And again, just like Margo, she let the dress fall from her shoulders. Margo's hand was now stroking my balls, letting them rest in her palm, fingers flickering up my stiff stem. Of course, after this striptease by two women I was incredibly hard.

Then Margo whispered, 'Remember what we said about getting into a girl's pants.' She got me out of the armchair by pulling me up by my cock, her other hand pushing my trousers down, my shirt off. 'Let's see if you can get into Teresa's pants.'

'But she's . . .'

'She won't be shy now. Look what she can see.' And she grasped my cock in both hands. 'She'll soon lose her shyness seeing this up close.' As the two of us walked towards Teresa, she was staring, or so it seemed to me, at my cock, with Margo's hand on it. Margo used her other hand to lift the lacy hem of Teresa's slip and drew my cock inside it, laying it on Teresa's thigh. Her skin felt warm and soft and Margo was pressing the silky slip against my cock. She stepped back a little and said, 'Let's see if he can find his own way up there.'

I nudged my cock further up, Teresa pressing herself against me, the slip clinging to us tightly. Margo came to us and lifted the slip higher so that it bunched up around Teresa's waist. Then she went to the wardrobe to swing the door open so Teresa and I were reflected in it.

She adjusted the mirror, saying, 'Are you in yet? I can't see.' Teresa was now clinging to me, her breath hot on the side of my face so I stroked one hand up her thigh, my finger lifting the edge of her panties aside so that I could slide my cock in, feeling the warmth of her and the slight scratch of her pubic hair. She began to whimper huskily and tried pressing herself closer.

Margo came back to us. 'Oh, you understand that alright, don't you?' She then pressed herself against my back. I felt her breasts squash against my shoulder blades, the warmth of her thighs spreading along the backs of my thighs, her hands lightly sneaking round to massage my groin.

'A male sandwich,' she said and laughed. And yes, there I was sandwiched between two women with my cock sandwiched between silky nylon and the soft flesh of Teresa, my hands now caressing the round curves of Teresa's buttocks, fingers slipping inside the panties there. This mixture of being egged on by one woman and the effect this was having on the other woman was very arousing and I could feel my prick straining and throbbing inside Teresa's panties, all of me enclosed inside soft flesh.

'This is lovely, Nick.' Margo murmured, 'But don't get carried away. We haven't even begun the modelling yet.' She grabbed my shoulders and pulled me away from Teresa, still standing behind me, her hands now folding around my cock smoothly, rolling the skin back so the fat head swelled out under her tickling fingertips. I made to turn around but she held me in place with a little more pressure on my cock. Then one hand lifted from me to point to the bed where the lingerie I had chosen was draped.

'Teresa!' Teresa understood. In a flickering shimmer of white she peeled her slip off, standing in her white panties and bra, the slip held loosely in her hand.

'Here!' Margo said and Teresa tossed the slip to her who then draped it as a soft skin over and down my shoulders. The feel of it reminded me of the lush velvet touch of the panties Teresa was now tantalisingly drawing down her black-stockinged legs, stepping out of them, holding them delicately. Margo reached out a hand and Teresa stepped to her to give her the lacy garment.

Margo hung the panties by the elastic on my cock saying, 'Here's the nearest hook to hang them,' stroking the silkiness along my length and under my balls. That made me shiver all over and my cock twitch. 'Can't keep you out of a girl's panties.'

Teresa had now pulled on the red panties, bending to take the half slip from the bed. She was now more in the spirit of things for she bent low to the bed, showing off the enticing globes of her arse covered by the red nylon and lace.

Margo then turned me around and pushed my cock inside her black panties, one hand cupping my balls with Teresa's silk, the other smoothing the silk of her panties along my stiffness nestling against her skin. Her mouth pressed onto mine, her tongue flicking along the inside of my lips, against my tongue so I was now feeling I was immersed in slipperiness, all velvety and wet-silk, with Teresa's slip slipping down my back.

Still holding me in place against her, Margo moved me to the bed and, with a little push, sprawled me on it. She climbed beside me and began an incredible massage – the lingerie she had flung on the bed now became a maddeningly erotic trail of soft slippery touches all over me. She moved the silks slowly up my legs, lingering them up my inner thighs, into that delicious slit between my balls and arse, another hand deftly sliding off her own panties which she used as a gentle smoothness on my chest up to my face, whispering, 'All wet for you. All creamy with my honey.'

She took my hand and carefully led it up her thigh till my fingertips were touching her juicy lips there. She began to move round and round on my fingertips and I could feel her getting more moist. By now she was bending over me, letting her long, dark-copper hair brush across my cock. It felt as soft and tickly and teasing as all that nylon she had stroked me with.

While she was doing this, she suddenly stopped, her hair fanned out from my cock and down my thighs. She looked up at me through this tangle of hair. 'You like this?' she asked. I nodded. 'Plenty more if we cut out Gerry and go it on our own.'

I was amazed that she could still be thinking like that right in the middle of what we were doing. I was too shocked to reply. In any case I couldn't figure out why she wanted to latch onto me and I wasn't sure just how she could get out of Gerry's clutches. And I was a little frightened of Gerry and what he might do. 'Wouldn't you like to help me?' Then all words were silenced as her mouth closed around my cock.

That was the first time I'd been sucked – it was not as common in those days as it is now. Helen would do almost anything sexual but not that. And that first time with Margo, in fact, any time, is difficult to describe – that exquisite sensation of feeling such liquid lips, such tonguing. Margo also knew how to use firm fingers pulling at the skin of my prick, her mouth almost letting go, her lips kissing the slit where come was ready to spurt out, one finger circling that ring of skin, her tongue flicking at it and at that thin strip of skin till she took the head into her mouth and the inside of her lips rubbing, mouth opening wider, swallowing me inside, deep inside, one hand gathering silk to smooth over my thighs as she sucked and licked, a hand down right at the root of my cock, so stiff and hard and yet so gently sucked inside that warm fluid mouth.

She did all kinds of variations on this for a time but her fingers could obviously sense the pulse of my cock quickening and I was feeling an unbearable ache in my balls to let go. Her mouth drew slowly up my cock, her lips resting just at the tip.

'There,' she said and her fingers slid up my slippery cock as if she wanted to ease come out of it. And some did spill out so she smoothed it with her fingertips around my cock-head. By now I was tingling all over, wondering why I wasn't exploding. The whole length of my prick felt brimming with come.

'Careful,' she muttered, then she licked her finger-tips. 'Delicious. Taste yourself.' The tip of her tongue flicked slowly to lift a little creamy drop and then her face came up to mine, her tongue licking the inside of my lips and through this loose slippery kiss she was mumbling, 'My tongue's your prick, your mouth's my quim.' Then into that slobbery sucking and licking and probing she put two fingers, moving them in and out of my mouth.

Helen had taught me a good deal in the time I'd been with her. I'd been innocent till I met her. If there'd been no Helen, I'd have shot off with Margo on my first penetration – as the tip of my cock felt the lusciously smooth lips of her cunt, such wet and honeyed sliding like liquid round my cock head, pushing in deeper, slowly, feeling I was growing longer and fatter and stiffer.

Margo seemed able to gauge exactly when she should stop taking me in further, when to stop squirm-ing, when to relax the grip of those soft muscles, pulling me inside her till I thought my come must burst forth. But then she relaxed me and took my cock out, rubbing the head along her slippery lips, letting the come mix with her slithery juices there. Then she pushed it back in, hooking her feet on my buttocks to press me inside. Again and again she drew me on as if she was ready for my cock to open in a flood of come and soon her rhythm became more insistent, and her breathing quickened, and I heard an occasional low grunt in her throat. She thrust her breasts up to my mouth and I slathered them wetly, nibbling at one nipple, then the other.

Her hand reached down to hold my balls, squeezing them gently, then holding them to squash them, trying to cram them inside, cock and balls together. And then it was all hard riding and I couldn't stop the croaks and gasps spilling out of my throat. She rolled me over and, on top now, she pulled herself right to the tip of my prick, then plunged down, up, down, until I sensed we would ride on now, the squishy slapping of our bodies accompanying our motions. We were driving ourselves to the edge, then back, then driving on, my cock inside her and out, her triangle of hair and wetness thrusting up to take me in again till there was no holding back. Come poured out of me, slithering and sticky, inside and around Margo's cunt as she thrashed on sucking me back in to finish her off, arching her back, shuddering, till she finally flopped on top of me.

Afterwards, Margo was playful with me, taking my limp cock to rub it where come was dribbling out of her, sucking my tongue into her mouth, fingers in the juice before she put them inside my mouth. It was only when we were lying back relaxed that I noticed Teresa was still in the room. She had been watching! She was lolling in the armchair, the red slip high on her thighs – and she was smiling at us!

Margo began again about Gerry and how she could run the operation herself. I wondered why she wasn't more concerned about Teresa after what she had said about her being so naive. But there she sat, smiling, showing lots of shapely leg so I supposed she hadn't been done any harm watching Margo and me.

Margo was saying how I'd be an ideal partner for her in the business. 'You look so young and innocent. Nobody'd suspect you. You and Teresa both.' Teresa giggled almost as if she understood what we were saying though she may simply have been responding to Margo's playful ways with me.

'Tell you what,' Margo said. 'I'll tell you what I know about Gerry's operation and you can spill it all to the cops. You don't need to give your name. Just phone them. Then they'll pull Gerry in and it's all clear for us. What d'you say?' Her hands were coaxing my cock towards hardness again.

'I couldn't do that. My boss is a friend of Gerry's. He'd try and find out who made the call.'

'They'd never find out it was you.'

Margo rolled away, stood up, went to the wardrobe and put on a dressing gown. 'You don't know what you're missing, kid. We just had a great time in bed. Put up a bit of that cash you've got stuffed in your wallet to get us rolling and we'd be a going concern, with lots more of this, me and Teresa. Good times with the two of us.'

Teresa was still smiling. Margo picked up my jacket and patted the pocket where my wallet was. Then she threw the jacket onto the bed and moved next to Teresa who was lying deeper in the chair, the slip riding up to her waist, the panties frilly at the top of her thigh.

'I'll leave you to think about it. Come on, Teresa!' Margo swept out of the room. Teresa blew me a little fingertip kiss and then left.

I was still surprised how tenacious Margo had been. After I had had such a great time with her I found it difficult to think that Gerry was right, that she was nothing but a cold-hearted bitch, just after the money. I puzzled about this as I put my clothes back on. Then I heard the doorbell ringing. Another client, maybe. So I finished dressing quickly, a man's voice and Margo's rising to me though I couldn't distinguish any words. I wondered if Margo was going through the same process with him, Teresa bringing in the tea, Margo asking for more money for maid-service. I still couldn't quite believe that Margo was as calculating as that.

When I was dressed I wondered if I was simply supposed to go downstairs and leave, though I needed a taxi.

But the problem was solved for me. One or two of the stairs creaked as I walked down so when I reached the hall, the door of Margo's living room opened. Margo stood at the door. 'No need to creep out like that.' She smiled her brilliant smile. 'Come on in. There's a friend of mine I'd like you to meet.'

I felt embarrassed to go into the room and meet this other client. Maybe he'd turned up unexpectedly – I remembered that Margo had said she was free for the afternoon. It made me feel uneasy – there I was, just come down after fucking with Margo, and now Margo wanted to introduce me to this client who'd know what I'd been doing there and who was going to be doing the same thing, and we'd sit around and chit-chat. Still, I didn't see any way round it. I decided I'd go in, say hello, mouth a few pleasantries, ask Margo to call me a taxi and leave. So I walked past Margo into the room ready to put a brave face on it. Imagine my surprise when I discovered the man in there was Gerry.

'Well, there you are, old sport. Margo's been telling

me you've been getting on like a house on fire!' They both laughed good-naturedly, though I suspected that in some way they were also laughing at me. 'Didn't I tell you Margo was something special?'

He'd actually told me she was a bitch so I didn't know what he was getting at.

'He's quite special himself. Knows how to make a lady happy,' Margo said.

'That's Helen's doing, I'd guess,' Gerry said.

Margo came over to me and kissed me on the cheek. 'Oh, don't sell him short, Gerry.'

I couldn't understand what Gerry was doing there. Was he checking up on Margo himself even though he'd sent me to check her out? Then I began to wonder if he was checking up on me, worried about me going in with Margo. I began to sweat a little – I was a little frightened of Gerry.

'Don't look so worried, old son. What have you been doing with him, Margo? Fair wore him out, I shouldn't wonder.'

'Don't tease him any more, Gerry.'

'Yes, well, I suppose you've been teasing him yourself, haven't you?'

I wasn't really catching the drift of this conversation till Gerry turned to Margo. 'Tell him what we've been up to.' For a moment I thought Gerry was one of those voyeurs and wanted a full description of what Margo and I had been doing or even that they'd had a camera installed to film everything.

'We've been a little unfair with you, Nick,' she said.

'We've just been checking you out, Margo and me,' Gerry added.

'All I told you about smuggling in the girls, that was true. We do it together. Gerry arranges the trips in and then I take care of the girls.'

'So this was all a put-up job worked out between you?' I turned to Gerry. 'And what you told me about Margo being a . . .'

'A bitch?' Margo and Gerry laughed 'No. Well, not much of one.'

'But I still don't see what this has to do with me.'

'Well, it's like this. The operation's got a bit worrying. The last lot I brought over, the man in charge of the girls — why, the bastard ran off with one of 'em. She probably fucked him blind all across Europe so's he couldn't see what he was doing.'

'And they took a couple of the other girls as well,' Margo went on. 'Can't run a business like that where you can't trust anyone.'

'I'll show 'em when I catch up with 'em. I've got a few leads.'

'But if the cops get their hands on them, who knows what he'll say to save his skin?'

'And I can't let that happen again. So that's where you come in, kid.' Then Margo came over to me again and patted my crotch. 'After today, I found out that you're a nice man to fuck, Nick, but you're not one who thinks with his cock.' She looked across at Gerry. 'You wouldn't believe how I was putting it to him, but he never budged. Held on tight to what you told him.'

Gerry walked over to the table by the sofa, picked up the money I'd paid Margo and brought it over to me. 'Here. It's yours. I know how Margo can tease your brains out, and your cock, so I'm sure we can certainly let you do the job we have in mind for you.'

'Those Italian and Maltese ladies won't get round him. A tough nut to crack.'

'Depends who's doing the cracking. How's about me

cracking his nuts?' It was Teresa talking. She'd just come into the room, waltzing in, untying the sash of her dressing gown to reveal she was still wearing the red half-slip I'd chosen. She slid it up her thigh to reveal that she was also still wearing the panties. 'What about a crack at this, Nick?'

'You know English?' I said.

'Sure I do.'

'You're not Italian?'

'Born and raised right here. Just helping Margo out. But I tell you, watching you two going at it made me want to climb on the bed with you. I'm still randy as hell.' She sashayed over to me. 'How about it, Nick?'

'I'm still not sure I understand what's going on.' I mumbled.

'Well, you've been in my pants once today. How about doing it again?'

'Hold on, Teresa.' Gerry said. 'You've been doing well for me, Nick, and after today, well, I can see you're the man I'm looking for. We've got seven girls waiting over in Malta. Usually we bring 'em across by train to the Channel, then ship 'em across. This time I've got hold of a plane.' It began to dawn on me now why Gerry had sent me down to that isolated village with the old airforce landing strips. 'And you'll go over there and be in charge. And I guess no one'll be able to run off in mid-air. Those girls are all yours till you bring 'em safe and sound here to Margo. So, feel free to fuck 'em blind on the way if you want. Might be fun fucking in mid-air.'

'Who cares about mid air? My room's just one flight up. Come on, Nick.'

So it turned out to be Malta soon, but right then it was Teresa one flight up. I put the money Gerry had given me into my wallet, took Teresa's hand, leading her out of the room and up the stairs. As we reached the top, Margo shouted after us, 'And there's no charge for maid service, Nick!'

6. Teresa

I heard nothing more about Malta in the next few days and I began to think maybe the plans had all fallen through. I'd been doing the usual errands for Gerry, sometimes on my own, sometimes with Helen. She was getting more manic, her driving more reckless and the evenings I spent with her, while still very enjoyable, were becoming more demanding. She wanted everything stronger and longer, wanted me to recover quickly so we could start again and soon I felt I wanted to get out of her clutches for a time. Helen still treated me well, she was terrifically sexy but things were growing a little crazy.

So I was glad when she announced that I was to report to the club one evening. Gerry had something important to tell me. Immediately I thought about Malta. I was a little scared about that whole business. I'd never been in a plane and it was an undercover operation, illegal as well. But I was looking forward to it oddly enough; it would give me another kind of excitement after Helen's continuous demands. I wasn't satiated with sex — what young man in his early twenties is ever satiated with sex? Besides, Helen and Margo had given me samples I would never forget. And then there was Teresa, she was more my age but I thought I'd disappointed her on the one occasion I'd been with her. I'd been given a good going-over by

Margo – with a little help from Teresa on the side – but when Teresa had invited me upstairs that afternoon I hadn't really recovered from Margo's ministrations though Teresa herself had not complained.

I went to the club. It was a gambling night, roulette and blackjack mainly. I went over to the bar to talk to Benny, then after a while the door at the back of the bar opened and out walked Teresa.

'Why, hello!' she said when she saw me.

'Hello. I didn't expect to see you here.'

'Well, I usually work at Margo's, as you know.' She smiled. 'We've spent the last few days putting the rooms in order for the girls from Malta. They'll be staying with us the first week or so. We're all ready. But where are the girls?'

I shrugged. 'I'm meeting Gerry tonight. Maybe he'll let me know.'

'Things are pretty slack at Margo's right now so she sent me to help Benny out, you know, stock control, count the bottles, tell Gerry what we need, count the take. Give Benny a chance to chat up the clients, keep his eyes on things.' In fact, Benny by now had gone over to one of the tables and was talking and laughing with the men playing cards there. 'And when Benny's doing that, it gives me a chance to socialize with a client.'

Teresa looked stunning, wearing a dress in a bright floral design, full-skirted but snug at the waist and in the bodice so that it showed off her breasts. The dress was sleeveless and her arms looked pale and slender.

'You look better out of your maid's uniform.'

'Well, it's a change.' She smiled openly at me. 'You too. If I'm not mistaken, you liked me out of the maid's uniform that afternoon.'

'I certainly did.'

'How come you never came back to see me? I thought you liked it at Margo's.'

'I did. Very much. But I've been busy.'

'I'll bet you have – I hear you've been staying at Helen's. She's kept your hands full, I'm sure.'

'We've been running errands for Gerry.'

'Among other things, I bet. You have to watch out for Helen. She's a tricky lady.' She paused. 'Anyhow, that doesn't mean you couldn't come and see us.'

'I didn't think I could just barge into Margo's without so much as a . . .'

'I'm sure Margo would love to see you again. She doesn't often get young men like you coming around. And from where I was sitting, it looked as if you were enjoying yourself.'

'I certainly was.'

'And I enjoyed the bit I contributed . . . I thought you liked that part.'

'You know, afterwards, when we . . . I mean . . . upstairs, I didn't exactly . . .'

'Well, maybe not like what you and Margo got up to but it was nice and cuddly.' She paused again. 'I was beginning to think you didn't like me.'

'On the contrary.'

'Well, in that case . . .' She patted my hand on the bar. 'I'll be right back. Don't go away.'

She walked out from behind the bar and I watched her. Her walk was as I remembered it at Margo's, very seductive. Some girls have no idea how to walk, they are slovenly, but Teresa knew exactly how to move – a little swivel from the waist, a comfortable stride, letting her skirt somehow cling to the back of her thighs, her back very straight – I'm sure those watching her approach their table liked the way she moved and, of course, they were getting a good eyeful of her shapely breasts as well. And that's what I saw as she made her way back to me. She had been to talk to Benny at the table. She didn't go back behind the bar but stood next to me, quite close, her bare arm touching my jacket sleeve, her perfume floating around us.

'I'm glad you came in tonight. It's not very busy, Benny said he can spare me for now. So what are we waiting for?'

She took me by the hand and led me through the door at the back of the bar. 'Since I've been working here, Gerry has let me stay in one of his flats.'

She was going ahead of me up the stairs and I was given a good look at her legs, the full skirt swirling around them with a glimpse of the lacy hem of a black underskirt. 'It's too late to go back to Margo's. In any case, this is really convenient.'

The flat was just a large room with two doors at the back. I imagined these would lead to a bathroom and a kitchen, for the large room had everything else: a large bed with pink satin sheets, a deep armchair, a small sofa, a table with a wireless on it, a standard lamp in one corner. Though it had quite a lot of furniture, it didn't look cramped because where the wall behind the bed met a side wall was a large, long mirror and it reflected everything in the room, making it look twice as big.

'Like it?' She spread her arms and twirled around slowly. Her skirt flew out and I admired her legs again and the seductive-looking lace on her underskirt. Then she flopped into the armchair, the skirt folding across her thighs. 'Not bad, is it? Actually I'm glad to be away from Margo.'

She looked up at me. 'Well, don't just stand there. Make yourself at home. Sit down.'

I sat on the sofa looking across at Teresa, lazily relaxed in her chair. 'Why's that?'

'What?'

'Why d'you want to be away from Margo?'

'Oh well, I mean, I really like Margo. She's always looked out for me, never let Gerry get his hands on me. But she's a very clever lady and I think she's up to something.'

'You mean, all that stuff about me supposed to be testing her, maybe there was something in it?'

'Possibly. She's been with Gerry a long time, right from the beginning, knows all the ins and outs of the business. And she's always run the girl side. She's been in the game since she was quite young and this is a good deal she's making here. She can pick and choose who she wants to go with, special clients.' She smiled at me. 'Like you.'

'How did you get to know Margo?'

'She was a friend of my aunt's. I lived with my aunt when I was just a kid. My mum and dad were killed in an air-raid, you see. I don't know, maybe my mum was in the game on the side. And my aunt I think, but I was a bit dim when I was younger. I was fourteen, fifteen then and didn't really know what was happening. They used to pack me off into the tube shelter. Both my mum and my aunt never came down themselves till later. I think they were probably having it off with the air-raid wardens or any soldiers they met in the pubs.'

She stood up, brushing her dress straight. 'Want a drink? Ever had champagne?'

I shook my head. 'Well, you're in for a treat. Champagne doesn't go to your head. The bubbles always make you feel light and airy and . . . you know. I'll just nip down and get a bottle. It's on ice in the bar. French champagne. Another of Gerry's French connections. And I could see from what you got up to at Margo's, you like things French. Like this.' She smoothed her dress from her knee, up her thigh to show the black underskirt.

'Yes. I noticed that before.'

'I was hoping you would. Lovely, isn't it?'

'Especially on you.'

'Why, thank you. You deserve a drink for a compliment like that.'

Soon we were both relaxed, sitting on the sofa, sipping champagne. I'd taken off my jacket and Teresa was in the corner of the sofa, her legs stretched across my thighs while I stroked that silky grain of her nylons.

She told me that when she was about seventeen, Margo had taken her under her wing. 'I used to be her maid.' I must have looked puzzled. 'Well, not really. I'd dress up for the part when Margo brought a man back to the flat in Soho. She was good, was Margo. She'd go to work on the man, he'd be all hot and bothered, then she'd ask him for money for maid service. And she nearly always got it. I didn't have to do anything. The man usually just wanted me out of the way so he could get on with it with Margo. I often got a fiver. Men are so thick, especially when they can't wait to stick it in you.'

She snuggled down a little, moved her legs up my thighs so one of them pressed against where I was already half-stiff. She didn't make it obvious but I am sure she knew what she was doing. And the way she talked! That was part of it, not like Helen's sexy monologue, though I soon learned Teresa liked to talk sexy. Her voice was quiet, a bit throaty, she was often ready to laugh and she made me feel comfortable, as if what she was talking about was the most natural thing in the world – which I suppose it is.

'So me being the maid when you came to Margo's was like old times for us. That's why Margo tried that old pitch about maid service. Mind you, that time I'd really have liked to join in.'

'Well, you did.'

'Not as much as I'd have liked to. I don't know whether you noticed but I was feeling real randy when I was stripping off for you and then there you were, inside my panties. God, I wanted to grab you right then and put you inside me. But I was under strict instructions from Margo and when she gives instructions, you'd better do what she says. Best not to get on the wrong side of her.' She leaned up a little and pulled me down to speak very quietly in my ear. 'I'm glad I could talk to you before you went to Malta. I just wanted to warn you.'

'Warn me? About what?'

'I don't know what Margo's up to but just watch your step.' She leaned back again and sipped at her glass. 'Anyhow, when Margo started with Gerry, naturally I went along with her. So here I am – and here you are. Cheers!' She raised her glass in a toast.

'What did you mean about Helen?'

'Helen? Haven't you noticed? You've probably learned she's a real sexpot with anyone she likes – and I bet she likes you! But she's also a big boozer. She can drink a lot of men under the table. Tell me, has she been taking her aspirin while you've been there? That's not aspirin, you know. She still has her medical connections. Seems as if she needs some kind of a boost every now and again. I'm sure she treats you right, but watch out. You never know which way she's going to jump.'

Teresa drained her glass and reached down for the bottle at the side of the sofa. It was empty. 'Well, I could go and get another but you know what they say. Too much and you can wilt.' She looked straight at me. 'And I wouldn't want you to wilt now I've found you again!'

She wrinkled her nose at me and smiled broadly. 'You just don't know what to make of me, right? You must have thought I was pretty stupid at first, that day with Margo. Me acting as if I didn't know how to talk.' She laughed. 'That's a real laugh. I really like to talk. You know, a lot of the pleasure comes out of talking about it, thinking about it just before you do what you talk about. A lot goes on in your head, not quite fantasies but pretty close. Imagining what it'll be like. Anticipation. I don't know about you but I get a real kick out of talking and thinking about what's going to happen. Do you?'

She pressed her leg hard against my crotch and she could feel how hard I was there. 'I can feel you're anticipating quite a lot. I tell you, I started to antici-pate as soon as I saw you in the bar. One of those magic moments. That's what I call them. Those times when you just know something great is going to happen with somebody. There's all kinds of moments like that.'

She was sliding the calf of her leg slowly against my stiff cock. 'Half the fun's thinking about what it's going to be like, talking about it before or on the way. Magic moments – the first kiss getting you started, the first time you touch his cock, the first time his fingers fumble around with your bra, then he's sliding your pants down and you know what he's really thinking about and you're thinking the same thing. You're on the same wave-length. Anticipation.'

She cocked her head on one side. 'I bet a lot's going on inside that head of yours right now and I can feel it's making you randy.' She pushed her leg hard against me. 'Am I making any sense?'

I nodded though I was a little baffled by the way Teresa was talking so openly. Then all of a sudden she stood up, stayed by the sofa looking down at me. I must have looked startled.

'You see? You're way ahead of me. Slow down that head of yours. Enjoy the anticipation.' She put her hand out to me and when I took it, she pulled me to my feet, holding on, moving me close to her. 'Let's see if I can touch what's in your head right now.'

She took my face between her hands and then her mouth rested on mine gently as slowly her tongue reached onto the inside of my lips. My mouth opened, her lips softly moist, her tongue slipping just a little into my mouth and I tried to pull her to me and put my arms around her. But she stepped back.

'Hold on. We're still at the anticipation stage.' Abruptly she turned away and walked in that slinkily seductive fashion away from me. 'Just stay there and watch.'

She waved her arm and I saw two reflections of her in the mirror. She was undoing the button at the top of her dress, unbuckling the belt at her waist, quickly drawing a zipper down, her hand pushing the dress from her shoulders. It fell down at her feet and she stepped out of it, all this with her back to me though I could see her from a different angle as well because of the mirror.

She turned to face me, smiling. 'Well, I've stepped one step out of anticipation. How about you, Nick?' She raised her arms towards me and I walked over to her. Her hands came to my shoulders and her mouth again was moistly against mine. She let her tongue slide around my lips slowly, round and round as if she was savouring something particularly tasty and, as she did this, she managed to sigh out a few words buzzing them against my lips. 'Wet. Slippery. Sweet Nick. Anticipate.'

Then she pressed herself to me. My arms went around her. I could feel her warm breath at my ear, her hair tickling my cheek, her hands, after she had taken mine in hers and placed them on her buttocks, were firm on my back. 'Feel the silk,' she whispered and my hands were stroking around the soft texture of her black half-slip. 'So soft. Just like I'm feeling.'

We stayed like that for a while, our legs so placed that she was thrusting against me and my erection was moving against her and in spite of the barrier of my trousers, I had the sense of the silkiness of her slip because of my hands on her buttocks.

Then she began to unbutton my shirt and soon had it off, her fingers playing around my chest, pinching my nipples. 'Like mine. Hard.' She bent to suck them, nibbling a little. My hands were working at her slip, trying to raise it a little, thinking to get my hands under it but she murmured, 'Not so fast. There's plenty of time. Anticipate. Watch me.'

Her hand moved to my chin and she pushed it so I was looking in the mirror again. I watched my own hands spreading and smoothing along the black slip, her buttocks revolving as she pushed against me, her tongue sliding from one nipple to the other.

And then again she stopped and turned away from me. 'Take the weight off my feet. You stay there.' She walked to the armchair and pushed it so that it was reflected across the angle of the mirror. She sat in the chair and beckoned me over to her. She was sitting with the slip slightly above her knees, the nylon stretched tight across her thighs. She reached up to me and pulled me down to her knees. 'Time for a little taste.'

She took my head to her knees, easing it between her thighs. Then my head was under the black and I could see little though I was making a moist trail with my tongue first on one thigh, then the other. Her hands were now stroking the slip around my head and, as I explored further, I could feel the delicate lace tickling my shoulders. I kissed the thin band of material of her panties where it covered her slit. 'Lovely lips. Taste me.'

I felt her lean back in her chair and in the almost-dark under there, I could sense her only as a musky smell, with the pressure of her hands fondling the back of my neck with her slip. 'In the dark. Secret. But I see you. In the mirror.'

I had never done this before. For someone to put his head under a woman's skirt to taste her was always considered very exotic in those days, very uncommon but exciting to think about – anticipation, and here I was doing it! And I still considered myself a relative innocent in sexual matters (but learning fast), invited into that secret spot to put my mouth there.

For one absurd moment I imagined myself like one of those old photographers with a black cloth over his head, focusing a clear image. I had only a fuzzy image but I sensed a warmth, a vaguely salty smell.

By now I had a hand following my mouth. I was running a finger along the thin silk that was tight against her slit and I began to feel that nylon moistening. I must have been doing something right for Teresa was letting out little yelps and occasional words. 'Yes. There. Touchy-touchy. Gently. Please.'

In fact, Teresa's running commentary was very instructive and helped me to cotton on to what I was supposed to be doing. 'Inside. Pull. Now in. Ah! Yes!' My finger was now sinking into slippery softness so I began to move it in and out. 'Slowly.' Then when my finger strayed outside, I touched a place that made her shudder even more — I had discovered her clitoris and so I made it squirm under my finger. Teresa shifted herself for the full benefit of my stroking, shuddering sighing. 'Yes. Yes.'

How to describe that wriggling little tail of flesh, its taste, its feel? Slithery under my tongue, never catching it still, thinly syrupy, a little sweet but more salty. My finger was probing deeply inside her while I licked. Then I held her clit between my lips trying to flick my tongue at the same time. That was driving her into more spasmodic jerks of her body, her voice now huskier, more breathless and with my mouth filled with her moistness, my tongue slippery, my finger with a creamy softness round it, I was feeling very excited.

'Beautiful. Careful. Push in. Deep. More.' So then I inserted two fingers, in and out, reaching in deep, then slowly withdrawing to the very opening of her quim, touching her clit slightly before I plunged in again.

Now her legs were resting on my shoulders so my

head was tightly between her thighs. I was so excited, my prick felt tremendously hard, thick and strong. I still had my trousers on and so I was stuck inside. My head was trapped between Teresa's thighs and my cock was straining to burst out. I was feeling the need for some release. But it was Teresa who got the release.

As I pumped my fingers in and out, her words gave way to small moans, intakes of breath and suddenly I felt something give way. All that slipperiness and softness around my fingers widened and Teresa loosed a strange exhalation from her quim sounding like a small fart but because I knew where it was coming from, it excited me and I moved my fingers faster and deeper. Her pelvis was thrusting down on my fingers and also gripping me hard. She gave a long, husky shout, not too loud, her whole body quivering. She had come to orgasm – and again that was a first for me and of course it deepened my own pleasure. I felt her relax as she sighed.

Her hands held my head still. 'Slow down now.' Then she began to wriggle, lifted up her hips, her hands now no longer on my head and for a moment I didn't know what was happening – not that I cared much for I was in a trance under her slip, my fingers and tongue bathed in her juices there as I worked on her with a slow, deliberate rhythm. Then I felt nylon sliding down my back. She pushed at my shoulder so my arm came away from under her slip and, with her legs on my shoulders, she somehow manoeuvred the slip over my shoulders, then down. So now I was wearing it. She gently moved my head from between her legs which she brought down, stood up and pulled me to my feet.

I felt a little foolish: there I was, still in my trousers

but with a black half-slip over them, standing in front of Teresa who looked ravishing now in just black panties, bra and stockings. She reached behind her to undo her bra, flinging it aside. Her breasts were not very big but beautifully round, nipples standing up so her breasts looked like twin symmetrical cones, firm, inviting my hands to stroke them. She stooped down and both her hands quickly rose under the slip, my belt soon undone, my fly buttons ripped open with one quick snatch, then trousers and underpants pulled down, over my feet, tossed away. My cock sprang up and out, the cock-head feeling a delicious touch of silkiness against the slip.

'You're a soft touch,' Teresa said. I looked at myself in the mirror – the slip was stretched tight where my cock stuck out. With an almost imperceptible touch Teresa placed her fingertips on the nylon where the end of my cock prodded out: such gentleness on a cock that felt so hard and strong. Then both her hands gathered nylon and rubbed it over my balls while her fingers slithered along the length of my cock. The nylon came over my length, then two fingers started at the top, stroking with maddening slowness down, taking the folded-back skin, pulling it down, another finger playing with that strip of skin holding it to the slit at the top. I didn't know how long I could last but, again, Teresa was ahead of me.

'Don't get my slip wet. You've already made my panties wet.'

Then she deliberately and gradually stroked my cock, sometimes one hand looping round to rub my arse, pushing the nylon into the crack, sometimes her fingers snaking under my balls, the fingertips touching my arsehole. Time and again she brought me almost to the finishing point; indeed, I oozed a little. She touched the small damp spot on the slip with one fingertip, then raised it to her mouth to lick it, then kissed me sloppily, whispering as she drew her mouth away, 'You've tasted me. Now you've tasted yourself.'

Teresa kept on with her massaging with the nylon. 'Anticipation. Think what will happen when I slide this off you.' Then she grabbed my cock and balls with both hands, pushing a lot of nylon around them.

After that marvellous massage in silky lingerie that Margo had given me and now with Teresa's lingering fingers on the nylon holding my cock, it was the start of my life-long fascination with lingerie, not simply seeing women wearing it, undressing to reveal all that silkiness they are wearing, thinking of my hands stroking it, thinking of me rubbing myself against it, pushing my cock into it, under it, reminding me of all that juiciness I will soon slip inside – I suppose I was learning all the things Teresa was saying about anticipation.

We stayed standing by the bed for a time while Teresa took me through a series of strokings and touchings inside her slip, her hands sometimes draping it all over me, sometimes sending it shivery along my back down to my arse, pulling it between my legs to squash it against my balls, then burying my long prick in soft, shimmering touches.

Teresa was certainly an expert in assessing just how long to continue: she often brought me to the verge of spilling into the nylon. My cock felt rigid and fat, as if it would brim over. Various drops leaked out and Teresa's hands made me tingle with great expectations of release but she kept me shuddering, gasping, groaning right at the edge till she uncovered my cock and, clasping it in one hand, she led me by my throbbing member to the bed.

'Lie back there, sweetie,' she said. 'Feel those silky sheets. Keep your eyes on the mirror. I'm going to let you see how I can make you feel even more randy.' And she did. Teresa instructed me in the delights of oral sex, still something novel for me though Margo's mouth had given me extraordinary pleasure. Teresa knew that – she'd been watching – but right now she seemed determined to prove to me that Margo's mouth and tongue were far behind what she knew and at the same time, between the exquisite attentions she gave me, she persisted with her running commentary.

She sprawled next to me. I could see her face veiled with stray hair, her hands in place on my thighs and then she said huskily, 'Look at you. Standing up so straight. Just waiting for me. Now watch him disappear.' She leaned up a little, her lips met my cockhead, slowly opened and unbelievably I watched my whole length enter her mouth. Slowly, slowly, down, down, till all of it was somehow surrounded by a warm wetness.

I was nudging against the inside of Teresa's mouth, moving so slightly, and then coming up, the inside of her lips gently slippery, somehow quite tight as she sucked up to my cock-head, letting her sweet mouth rest before that easy slide down again, full inside her moist mouth. And while she was doing this mouth massage which felt as if I was being bathed in warm oil, her hands were softly draping her slip on my upper thighs, reaching the nylon under my balls, squeezing them.

I just lay there, excited both by the attentions of her mouth and hands and by the fact of seeing how carefully and cleverly she swallowed my cock. Seeing myself so expertly handled was an added pleasure. With her mouth just near the end of my cock – I could feel her breath fluttering around me there – she said, 'There's more to it than just lips and tongue. Hands to touch the wet.'

With that, two of her fingers ran circular motions around my foreskin, pulling it back and the tip of her tongue circled with the fingers, keeping everything wet and slippery, the inside of her lips then taking over while her whole hand grasped my hard length, stroking up and down. Her tongue became sloppy at my cock-head and then she went down the whole length again. 'Little rests are nice.' Her voice floated up to me from down there as she drew the slip in a handful round my cock, pulling it slowly till it covered me, trailing down to my thighs.

Then her lips were nuzzling at my pubic hair with my cock entirely in her mouth. I could feel the back of her throat touching the tip. Her hands were caressing my balls, gripping the root of my cock hard as she let it slide slowly out, her tongue flickering all around, whispering, 'Mouth, lips, tongue . . . and teeth,' and her mouth came down on me again. As she sucked up, her teeth nipped ever so gently at that pulled skin, then at the rim of my cock-head, then the needling sharpness of her teeth along the cock-head itself, then out before plunging down again. Several times she did this, and it was excruciatingly exciting.

For me, this sucking and licking is almost as good as fucking if it's done properly and I soon discovered that Teresa did it properly. When I looked back I realized that Margo's mouth was splendidly luscious but she was mainly interested in making sure I knew just how good she was. It was as if she was simply out to prove that she could tip me beyond myself whenever she wanted to. While that was part of what Teresa did as well, I really felt that Teresa loved to do this and she knew exactly how to heighten the sensations with every part of her mouth, together with her hands.

She licked all the skin round my cock-head, slow, then fast, sloppily, then just skating her tongue around, then her teeth, nipping, harder, then almost biting, till I was quivering all over, struggling with myself, wondering whether I should let myself go – it would be such a gorgeous release – or hold on and let Teresa drive me to more and more ecstatic edges. I loved to feel her dribbling saliva all over my cock, then plunge down to take the whole length inside. Then she sucked at my balls while both her hands rubbed the wetness all over my cock, first slowly, then faster and faster till I thought my jism would fly out onto her or into her mouth in a great flood. But she always sensed that moment and stopped, pulling her mouth away to watch as a little come oozed out. She would flick her tongue at that droplet, then smear it over my cock-head.

'Now let's watch you disappear inside me,' and she rolled onto her back, stretching her legs wide, pulling me to her by my cock. With her finger and thumb on me, she wagged my cock at her clit, rubbing it there, gasping a little. Then she pushed my cock down till it touched the opening of her juicy cunt and miraculously, as if I was sliding into a velvety-moist tunnel – the sides of it pressing softly, tight yet loosely stroking, strongly engaging every part – I slid slowly inside.

'In. In deeper. Just look at us.' And I watched myself pumping between her thighs, seeing my cock glistening shiny-wet when it pulled out, wanting to drive it deeper. With Teresa's legs round my waist, she exerted pressure to roll us over. She was on her knees, her arse high, and my prick was caught tightly, almost having to force its way in but, once in, that delicious moisture took it over, little flutterings along its length.

Teresa's backside took up the rhythm, riding me, taking more and more of me inside, then out, not letting me escape, but almost, then plunging me in deeper. We both knew this could not last long. My cock was tingling, come tantalizingly at the tip, ready to burst, and Teresa was panting hard, a gruff litany of groans and shouts getting louder till she said through clenched teeth, 'Now. Come now.'

And my cock opened the floodgates. Teresa had moved so I was just outside her quim. Her hand snaked round to hold my cock as it poured out its cream and it was as if she was painting the lips of her quim with it and then her clit. I could feel my cock in her hand, her finger touching the slit as it spurted out, her touch adding more tingling sensations so I felt as if my cock was flying away in squirming, moist ecstasy, rubbing itself in a soft grip and squishing around in exquisite, damp, almost swampy depths.

Teresa's fingers were oiled with jism, my cock slithered around them, still prodding at the lips of her quim, her other hand spreading her slip round my arse, folding it down the backs of my thighs. Those moments of release I still remember as high excitement, added to which was the sight of our two bodies wriggling around, working at each other, Teresa's face alight with fulfilled desire, mine with a tough scowl of happiness on it.

And the coming down from that zenith was also

terrifically sexy, an ending that was in itself exciting but it also set a seal on the great pleasure of mutual indulgence. Teresa rolled away from me and lay on her back next to me. She panted out, 'Kiss me.' I leaned over to her face but she said, as she squirmed my cock against her, 'No. Down there.'

I switched around to where her hand had stayed in the warm squish of juices and I licked and sucked at her, tasting my own come and her body's oily sleekness. Then I felt the slippery openness of her mouth on my cock again, tasting the skin bathed in those same juices, an indescribable drowning in pure moist sensation.

Then somehow we closed our love-making with our two open mouths sloppy with our juices mixing together, tasting that stew of saltiness and sweetness, the undeniable musk of total togetherness.

I dropped off to sleep, my final recollection the reflection in the mirror of bodies covered with sweat, closely held together, faces hidden in hair. It could have been just one body lying there, satisfied with sweetness and peace.

Then about an hour or so later there was a discreet knock at the door. It was Benny who said through the door, 'Gerry's here. You'd better come down, Nick.' And that's when I was told the flight was on in three days' time. I'd be off to Malta, if the weather held, by the end of the week.

7. Tea with Mrs Courtney

'Listen, kid, don't get any big ideas.' The chauffeur had leaned back soon after I had climbed into the Austin Princess saloon car, sliding back the glass dividing driver from passenger. 'You might have heard a few tales out of school about these upper-class bints fooling around with the butler and the gardener, well, Mrs Courtney ain't like that. I mean, she might be dying for it – her husband's been away in Germany for months now. He's in the army. But the missus doesn't show any of us the time of day.'

I settled back to enjoy the ride out into the country. I didn't know quite what to expect. I'd been to visit Mrs Courtney five days before just as a messenger delivering parcels, with Helen who had been in one of her bitchy moods and treated Mrs Courtney badly. She almost threw the packages at her though I put mine down carefully – I think there was a carton of Scotch. Helen deliberately scraped her muddy high heels clean on the expensive carpeting. I'd felt sorry for Mrs Courtney because she seemed such a nice person though I'd been brought up as a child of working class parents to see people like her as snobs who always put on superior airs. Helen had teased her about the price, refusing to give her the goods till Mrs Courtney was almost begging her for them.

And now here I was, taking more parcels to her, on

my own this time. 'Well, you made a hit with that snotty-nosed Courtney woman, Nick,' Helen told me. 'She's sending a car round for you – I suppose Gerry's letting her have extra petrol. Those upper-class bastards always stick together. Anyhow she wants you to make the next delivery. Specially asked for you. On your own, not with me.'

I could understand why Mrs Courtney didn't want Helen there again after the way she'd behaved before but I didn't make any more of her request to see me on my own. So I was simply going to enjoy riding out to her place, making my delivery, then come back to Helen's and hope she was going to be in a better mood than she had been for the last two or three days.

When I arrived the door was opened by a maid, quite a nice-looking pert girl and I had a flash of memory about Teresa at Margo's. I wondered if I was being set up again for some kind of enticing episode. The maid showed me into a spacious room I hadn't been in on the previous visit. It just seemed too big to me, the carpet too plush, the furniture too thickly padded, the upholstery just too splendid in its design of large pink flowers entwined with green sprigs. It all made me feel uncomfortable. I perched on the edge of a large armchair, springing to my feet when Mrs Courtney came into the room – she was one of those imposing women who you felt deserved almost subservient attention. I don't want to make her sound too much like an authority figure but it was obvious that she had been brought up to expect people's undivided interest as a matter of course.

She swirled into the room in a full skirt of peacock blue and a silk blouse of white with full sleeves, the collar falling away to reveal her slender neck. The blouse opened quite low but fitted firmly to outline her breasts. She walked towards me, extending her hand. I didn't know whether to shake it or kiss it – she seemed almost like royalty. But I did neither for she moved a little closer and placed her long, slender, exquisitely manicured hand on my sleeve. 'So good of you to come. Please sit down.' She waved her arm to indicate the chair I had been sitting on and she turned around and with an elegant walk went over to a long ottoman.

'Nick, isn't it? Is that short for Nicholas? I always think one should use a person's full name, don't you? After all, that's the name you were given, not the short form.' I nodded though I actually didn't mind being called Nick but this woman had such an agreeable, if imposing presence that I felt I could go along with anything she suggested.

'Well, Nicholas, I'm so glad you could come. I hope I haven't taken you away from other business. It's quite a way out here, the least I could do was send you my car.' I nodded again. 'Do you always work with that woman you came with last time? She seemed to take an instant dislike to me. Horrid woman.'

'Helen's not bad.'

'Does she treat you well? I hope she's not always so bad-tempered. Perhaps she treats you better. I hope so.' She smiled.

'It's just that Helen thinks people like you are snobs.' I blushed a little. 'I mean, she thinks you've got all this,' I vaguely swept my hand to indicate the room and all it contained, 'without doing any work for it.'

'Well, I don't imagine her life is particularly hard. You don't think that about us, do you?' I shook my head. 'Good. You looked an eminently sensible and nice boy.'

She looked around and saw the parcels on a side table where I'd put them when I came in. She reached into a pocket at the side of the skirt and pulled out a small handful of notes so I went over to her and took them from her. She looked up at me with a smile and patted the cushion next to her.

'Sit down here next to me. You're in no rush to leave, I hope.'

I sat next to her and she edged a little closer to me though I didn't think she was coming on to me, just making herself comfortable. 'Tell me about yourself, Nicholas.'

Then she turned to look at me, her eyes wide and a smile on her large mouth, stroking her coppery hair back from her face. 'You look so nice, bright-eyed and bushy-tailed,' smiling again, then saying 'Are you bushy-tailed?' I think I blushed. 'Never mind . . . for now,' and she patted me briefly on the knee. 'How did you get involved with that horrible woman and this black market business?'

I told her briefly about my working in income tax so working for Gerry was a relief from that. 'And I hope to go to university next year. They wouldn't take me this year. All the men getting demobilized get first choice.'

'I see. There are still plenty of them left in the army. Like my husband. He's over in Germany. He only gets back to see me every three or four months. I wonder sometimes why he doesn't come on leave more often. Makes me think maybe he's carrying on with one of his cute ATS girls. Is that possible, d'you think?'

'I'm sure I don't know.'

'Come now. Don't be shy. There must be some reason. Just look at me. Though I say it myself, I'm still attractive.'

'Yes, you are.'

'That's very sweet of you. You know, sometimes, it seems to me, women can be too attractive. It puts some men off. They think that a woman who is good-looking is unapproachable, wouldn't be interested in doing the usual things men are interested in. Well, that's not true. Women like to do the same things. And it's just too bad if you have to wait around too long to do those things if your husband can't be bothered.'

I found the conversation drifting in an odd direction. She seemed almost to be gazing into space as she said all this till she shook herself a little and patted me on the knee again.

'Please forgive me. Perhaps I shocked you. Maybe you think I shouldn't talk like that. And I shouldn't burden you with my troubles. But I miss being with a man.' She stood up and put her hand out to me. I took it and she helped me up next to her.

'Well, perhaps it's better to call a spade a spade.' Then she smiled again. 'Though frankly I'm glad to say I don't have anything to do with a spade. I have a gardener to do that kind of donkey work. A bit of an old dodderer but he gets the job done. Let me show you.'

She was still holding my hand in hers, it was soft and warm. She gave me a little squeeze, turned away from me as she dropped my hand and walked ahead of me, swaying in an attractive manner. I admired the way she moved, her skirt folding around her legs as she sauntered languorously on her high heels. Her trim ankles were showing as I followed her through double doors into a conservatory with large, flowering potted plants and small trees with a spread of large leaves.

'I call this my Garden of Eden. I can hide away from

everyone and everything. I give strict orders not to be disturbed when I come in here.' She went ahead around one of the trees, leaning against it, looking back at me. Then she reached up and pulled one of the flexible branches across her body, a large leaf hanging down from her waist covering her upper thighs. 'Just like Eve.' She sighed a brief sigh.

'The trouble is, there's no Adam. Sometimes I feel like Lady Chatterley but what good would that do? I told you, my gardener's pretty decrepit.' Then she moved away from the tree and stood by a plant which had large yellow flowers shaped like long tubes with the ends of the petals curling open. She held one gently in two fingers and softly stroked those curling petals, leaning over to smell it. 'Lovely scent. Come and smell it.'

I strolled over to her, put my nose to the flower and smelled a heady perfume. Mrs Courtney placed a hand on the back of my head, pressing me a little closer to the flower, the pressure of her hand keeping me there.

'It's a tropical plant. I've forgotten its name. Some tribe or other worships it. The people there claim its smell is an aphrodisiac.'

She let my head go. I was no longer bending over the flower. I watched her as she rather dreamily took the flower in one hand and rubbed her fingers caressingly up and down the petals.

'It's lovely to touch as well. As smooth as velvet. I love to have my hands smell of the flower. Delicious.' Some of the perfume was being released in the air around us and I could still smell that sweet but musky scent, 'Such a lovely smell. And feel. I can certainly understand why a plant like this would give that tribe ideas. Just look at the shape of it,' and her fingers were massaging the flower till finally she snapped the stem and held it in her hand. 'I thought we'd have tea.'

She walked away to a white wrought-iron table with a fresh white tablecloth on it. She rang a small bell and it seemed almost immediately the maid appeared carrying a tray with a silver teapot, a plate of small cakes, napkins and plates which she set on the table. 'That will be all, Emily, thank you.' Mrs Courtney began to pour tea into exquisitely delicate china cups. 'Come and sit down.'

As I sank into the soft cushion on the seat of one of the wrought-iron chairs, Mrs Courtney came round to me and flapped open a serviette. 'You'll have one of these sinfully sweet confections?' she asked me, nodding to the plate of cakes.

She leaned over to place the serviette on my lap, smoothing it over my thighs. I could have almost sworn her fingers lingered a little longer than necessary as they brushed the serviette flat on my lap. Her hand produced an automatic reaction from me and it was possible Mrs Courtney felt my semi-arousal. She smiled down at me, a knowing smile.

'I know young men like you have insatiable appetites. Well, go ahead.' Then she picked up the flower she had brought to the table and placed it at the side of my plate. She moved her chair a little closer to mine, offering the plate of cakes with one hand, the other lying gently on the flower, her fingers splayed along it. 'What are you going to study at university, Nicholas?'

'I'm interested in literature.'

'Are you? Do you read all these risqué books, like *Lady Chatterley's Lover*?'

'I've heard about it but I haven't read it.'

'Oh, but you should. Absolutely fascinating. Maybe

you'd like to borrow my copy.' She held the flower so
the end of the stem rested on the table and the flower
stood erect. 'I was reminded of it when we were talking
about the garden in here. These flowers. You may have
heard there's a scene when Lady Chatterley drapes
flowers on the gardener.' She held the stem with one
hand while her other hand was stroking the long petals
up and down. 'Hangs them on him. You know where I
mean.'

I blushed.

'Oh, silly me! I've embarrassed you again. I'd forgotten you're still quite young. And still shy.' She
touched me briefly on the thigh. 'No need to feel
embarrassed with me, Nicholas. I hope we're going to
be friends. I know I'm a little older than you but it's so
nice to find someone I can talk to about books. All my
husband's interested in is his golf and his infernal
cricket. I'm not sure that bats and balls are all there is
to life, are you?'

When she said 'bats and balls' she added just a little
of a knowing tone to her voice and she turned to me
with a kind of twinkle in her eye. That made me feel a
little uneasy again and, as I was taking a bite of cake at
the time, I made a botch of it and a little cream squirted
out at the side of my mouth. I reached down for my
serviette to wipe it but Mrs Courtney laid her hand on
mine, pressing down quite hard on my lap. 'Let me.'

Her hand came up to my face. 'You can probably
still smell the flower on my fingers. Smell.' Her warm
fingers were resting just by my nose and I sniffed,
catching a strong whiff of that heady perfume. Her
fingers wandered along the top of my upper lip,
tickling and gently stroking till they reached the corner
of my mouth. A finger touched the drop of cream,

lifted it away and then her finger moved to the centre of my mouth. 'Open. Can't waste cream these days.'

Her finger slid into my mouth very slowly, entering deeper and deeper, then pulling out, the moist finger-tip smoothing across my lips. 'There. You could probably taste the scent of the flower as well.'

Her hand went back to pick up the flower on the table. She held it erect again. 'You know, though I like to think all those ideas about love potions and such are so much nonsense, I think that tribe might have been right – about this flower, I mean. Don't you think so?' She laid the flower down and her hand strayed onto my lap, ostensibly to smooth it flat but it seemed to me she was really feeling my erection which had now grown firmer since she had poked her finger in my mouth and had stroked the flower again in such a suggestive manner.

She waved her other hand across the table and said, 'More tea? Cake? They're delicious. I could go on eating them but I have to watch my figure. But don't let me stop you. Have another. Please take it.' She held the plate of cakes up to me but her hand was a little unsteady – I thought maybe she was too interested in what her other hand had found in my lap though what happened next was something she contrived, I suspected.

The plate of cakes tilted and one fell off onto the floor between her chair and mine, rolled a little and stopped just under the table.

'How clumsy of me!' she said, bending down, then stooping to pick it up. I thought this was rather odd; surely she could have called the maid in to clean it up. But no, there she was almost under the table, her head and shoulders under the tablecloth. Then I felt fingers quickly moving up my thigh under my serviette and beginning to unfasten my fly buttons. The fingers reached inside, probing to release my stiff cock from my underpants. Then her fingers covered it with my serviette before she emerged and sat back in her chair.

I looked down – my serviette was like a tent with my cock acting as the central pole. I didn't know whether to bunch up the serviette to cover myself more, whether to ignore it or whether now to take the initiative though I was still uncertain whether this attractive, rather aristocratic woman was teasing me, simply having fun as a revenge for the way Helen had treated her on the last visit.

Mrs Courtney deposited the dropped cake on the table and lifted the flower to her nose. Her lips and tongue nudged against the petals and then she said quietly, 'No need to be shy with me, Nicholas, though I've noticed that certain parts of you are not shy.' That was really the first time she had said anything direct about what was happening though some of her earlier remarks had obviously pointed in that direction.

She slowly drew the serviette from my lap. 'Maybe it is a little shy – look! How charming! That whole top part is blushing but what a beautifully shiny blush!' One hand was now trailing inside my fly, fingers leisurely tracing the outline of my balls. 'Perhaps we'd better cover that blush so we don't see how shy he is!'

Very slowly she brought the flower down and slid it carefully over my stiffness. I could feel the sepals inside pushing against the stretched skin of my cock-head like soft needles and I twitched and throbbed as the petals folded round me, slightly wet from her tongue. She pushed till the curl of the petals brushed against my pubic hair and her fingertips began a maddeningly gradual touching up and down my cock, the velvet texture of the fragile flower felt delicious. Her other hand was busy searching out the very root of my cock, her palm cupping my balls, her fingers reaching back to the very edge of the crack of my arse.

'There, there,' she whispered. 'You mustn't be shy. No need to blush though it's such a bright and beautiful red. All things bright and beautiful!'

She was now concentrating on moving her hand all over the flower until I felt she had found the very centre of my whole nervous system. She eventually drew the flower up my whole length, then off, holding it up to her mouth.

'The scent's disappearing. It must have rubbed off.' Her head came down, hair falling in tickling trickles onto my cock. She tossed her hair back, her nose close to me and she began to touch my cock almost imperceptibly with her nose, first right by the slit, then little by little down, the tip of her tongue flicking a wet streak along the whole length. 'It tastes good as well,' she murmured.

Remember, to feel a woman's mouth on me was still a new sensation and I began to be afraid I would shoot off too quickly, streaming jism into Mrs Courtney's hair. At that time I always felt a little embarrassed about coming, about spilling all that creamy but sticky liquid onto or into a woman. I suppose it was my memory of when I used to masturbate – at first come is warm and slippery but it soon turns cold and sticky and I thought women wouldn't like the feel of it.

Teresa was setting me straight about all of this. She told me that most women love to feel wet and sticky, they like to feel themselves getting moist around a man's fingers, they like their fingers to feel those first drops of come oozing out. I was beginning to realize that women like the feeling of power they have, because they know when they get a man to a certain point he will do almost anything for them. Once they have their hands full of cock, they know their touches will make a man want to spurt out anywhere. Though most men have been conditioned to believe that a woman wants to experience those great hot streams inside her, she'll take it anywhere, on her hands, her breasts, her stomach, her thighs and he's happy to feel it pumping out anywhere too. That also gives a man a sense of power because at a certain point a woman will do anything to make a man come, to make him squirt it out.

So Teresa was already teaching me that a woman will take it anywhere, sometimes in odd places, in her ear, up her nose, over her eyes – 'a sexual fog', Teresa called that – in a little stream falling down the crack of her arse. Teresa was still not sure how many women actually wanted a man to come in their mouths. 'Some women just love to feel that squirt into their mouths, hard on the back of their throats, covering the roof of their mouth, tasting it all over, almost spilling onto their lips so they like to swallow it. I think most women like a big, thick, throbbing cock in their mouth but quite a lot only like to suck it till they can feel the come's ready to fly – I can feel that in you, Nick, that big vein in your cock is beating away like mad and the tip of your cock, it's like I can feel pins and needles in my mouth – well, then they take it out just in time and it spurts out onto their breasts and neck. They love to get hold of that squirming prick, all hot and slippery, watch the come pouring out, feel it showering onto them. Sometimes they like to let it surge all over their face though some women don't like it there.'

Teresa knew what she was talking about. I'd discovered she was an expert in these matters and she certainly practised what she preached. But she insisted I let her know when I was about to come – sometimes I didn't manage to tell and she was always happy to keep sucking hard at those times, milking the come out of me – so she would gobble away till I surged deep into her mouth. I asked her why she wanted to know when I was going to come. Why did it matter if she was going to take it in her mouth? She said she wanted to make sure she didn't take it out of her mouth to lick it at that time because there was no guarantee where the uncontrollable pumpings would spray

'Don't get me wrong,' she said. 'I love the taste of come, I love to put my fingers on the slit when come's pouring out, that's a real turn-on for me and it drives a man crazy – he thinks his cock's just bursting with come and I'm swimming my fingers through it. And I don't mind feeling those hot gushes hitting me on the face, just like the first drops of rain in a shower. But if I get it on my face, chances are some of it's going to squirt up into my hair. And that I don't like. I mean, I love the feel of come on me and you can't really feel it in your hair. But most of all I don't like it in my hair because it dries very fast and it makes tangles and knots and I can never get them out without a lot of hard pulling. So,' she'd say, when she was talking like that, 'come and give me a drink or a hot shower.'

I didn't know just how Mrs Courtney felt about this so I let her stay with her head there, her hair all around, stroking and caressing with her hands, her mouth, lovely soft ministrations. Then she suddenly stopped and for one fleeting moment I thought this was just a tease taken to an extreme. She stood up and I thought she'd laugh at me and tell me to leave. But instead she said, 'That tribe really knew what that flower can do.'

She picked up the flower again and closed her mouth around it without crushing it while she walked over to the tree with the large leaves. 'They must have used these for clothing,' she mumbled as she kept the flower at her mouth. She pressed a large leaf against her breasts. 'Perfect fit.'

She let go of the leaf, then quickly slipped off her blouse, pulling the straps of her slip over her shoulders, reaching to her back to unfasten her bra, lowering herself behind a small bush, then standing up with a large leaf against her breasts. She drew the flower from her mouth nibbling the ends of the petals without tearing them. 'The leaf's as silky as my blouse.'

She pressed the leaf against her so I could see the shape of her breasts.

'And it's a little juicy, makes me a little damp. Good for the skin, I suppose.' She was massaging the leaf on her skin. 'This leaf has its own fresh scent.' And she beckoned me to her.

I felt somewhat ridiculous walking towards her with my cock pointing out and up in front of me, sticking out of my trousers. When I was standing in front of her, she pulled the leaf across her breasts and down, then, putting her hand at the back of my head, she pulled my head down to her breasts.

'Smell,' she sighed and carefully moved her breasts around my face. 'Taste.' And she thrust a nipple at my mouth.

I flicked out my tongue, circling the little bumps

around the nipple, then taking it between my lips and into my mouth. By now her hands were at work again on my cock and balls as she wrapped the leaf around them. I felt a slightly sticky juice on me and again Mrs Courtney bent down to smell the leaf-juice, tasting it with her tongue, her open mouth closing around my cock-head, her lips peeling back my foreskin, settling further down the length. The leaf was gone now and her hand was busy stretching, pulling, stroking as her mouth moved its moisture down and around, her fingers pushing my trousers down so her lips could suck first one ball, then the other, till with a gasp she took them both into her mouth, her fingers rubbing the sticky juice and her own mouth-wetness all over my cock.

I thought I'd soon be providing my own supply of juicy wetness for my cock was twitching, feeling as if it was filling with a full head of steam, ready to spurt out with come, slippery onto her fingers. But she stopped and again I half-expected she would laugh at me, leading me on so far and then leaving me.

She stood up, smiling and looking directly at my cock. She reached across her waist and unfastened a catch, pulling the skirt open with one sweep of her arm. It fell away and she then drew her slip down. She stood there in just her panties and high heels. Stooping to pick up the flower she tugged her panties down, stepping out of them. She pushed the petals of the flower between her legs, spreading the petals out. 'There's a little scent left,' she muttered.

I knelt down, my nose resting in her hair down there, smelling a faint perfume mingling with her slightly sweaty, slightly musky scent. My tongue slid onto her clitoris, down to the wet lips of her quim as she shifted her feet, opening her legs wider to accommodate my licking and sucking. She was struggling with my jacket, taking it off, then my shirt, then she was pulling me up and with one great push she had my trousers and underpants off.

She was holding me close now and my cock was rubbing all over her slit, her hand guiding it, the flower still between her legs. 'Mix up all the juices,' she said, straining herself upwards, nuzzling her slit onto my cock-head and slowly letting my cock penetrate her little by little.

Now her hands were on my buttocks, pushing me hard against her, then relaxing till my cock edged almost fully out. Then her hands pushed again and she manipulated me in and out until in an extraordinary gush, an explosive spurting out from my cock, I covered the lips of her cunt with hot come and she rammed me into her again.

Afterwards she picked more leaves, more flowers, wiping them around my cock, then held them to her nose, rubbing the juices on her breasts and between her legs, stooping down to lick my still semi-erect cock every now and again. 'Getting the last drop,' she said, till I began to think I might come again.

After a few minutes she stopped and became almost business-like, slipping on her blouse and skirt acting as a well-mannered hostess as if nothing had happened between us. I struggled back into my clothes.

'I'm glad you could come.' She put her hand to her mouth, then laughed. 'Come to deliver the parcels, I mean, not . . . the other. I think you could tell I was glad about that! You too, I think.' I nodded. She smiled and held out her hand. This time I kissed it and I could still smell the scent of the flower mixed with a little of my salty smell.

'I hope you'll come again,' she said and again there was that faintly humorous tone when she spoke. 'Next time perhaps we won't be so formal, now that we seem to have got to know each other.'

'I'd like that very much, Mrs Courtney.'

'Well, if we're going to be more informal, you'd better stop calling me Mrs Courtney. You can call me Phillipa. I suppose that would be Phil for short, if I believed in shortening names, that is. Maybe this time, for once because I'd like to say something like "I hope you enjoyed having your fill!" ' Again that sly comic edge was in her voice and at that point I enjoyed the joke without blushing. In fact, I don't think I blushed again when she asked me to make deliveries over the next few weeks – and each time I went back I did have my Phil.

8. The Maltese Connection

Malta. The Mediterranean. My mind was full of romantic images which allayed my fears about flying and about being involved in the illegal enterprise of bringing foreigners in to become British citizens. I began to feel that Gerry's business was much bigger than I had at first imagined and not simply a fly-by-night black-market operation, though that was certainly a part of it, considering all those deliveries I'd made of booze, cigarettes, lingerie, dresses and tea. And while I'd been told that Gerry had the right connections – in France, for instance, where he could get the lingerie and stockings – it was now obvious to me that Gerry also collected his goods by means of robberies.

Gerry remained a shadowy figure to me for I worked through his intermediaries. Even on the evening with Margery, I hadn't really seen much of the robbery taking place. But that was Gerry's way. He never let any of his people know too much of what was going on. We all knew bits and pieces but no one seemed to know the whole picture, maybe Helen and Margo knew more than anyone else. I was also beginning to realize that Helen was unreliable; I'd seen her cosying up to Bledsoe at the club so I knew I would have to go carefully with her.

And the club? What did I really know about it?

What was it a cover for? There was the gambling, the dances, and I thought the restaurant was legitimate enough. The stripping was obviously a good source of revenue but what other things were going on? What shady deals were struck there?

I knew Gerry was into prostitution. Teresa had told me enough about that, though it was a cut above the usual streetwalking racket. Margo looked after a call-girl service and her house was some kind of high-class brothel. And now I was to become involved in bringing in women who would become part of that side of Gerry's business. You only had to look at Margo to realize that it was very lucrative and that was why Gerry was prepared to take the risk of running an illegal immigration operation, even hiring a plane this time to fly new ladies in.

So I was going to be an accomplice in that illegal immigration. I knew it could land me in real trouble with the police but because my knowledge of Gerry's enterprises was so limited, I convinced myself that the authorities would see me as a mere pawn. At least, that's how I rationalized my participation in these ventures and, in any case, my involvement in these activities beyond the law carried with them a great deal of excitement. Even that ridiculous deception of the policeman with Margery had set my heart racing though part of that came from the way Margery treated me. I certainly didn't want to give up my job with Gerry now I'd been thrown into that devastatingly hectic sexual arena with Helen, Margo, Teresa and Margery. And I didn't want to give up my occasional visits to Mrs Courtney either.

So the flight to Malta took on a lot of romantic aspects which stopped me from really getting myself too scared. Malta wasn't exactly the Riviera but I kept thinking about all that sun, those passionate Latin types, the beach life and me being in charge of what would probably be a group of ravishingly beautiful young ladies who knew what kind of life they were heading into — well, what red-blooded twenty-two-year-old male would throw away that kind of opportunity?

And yes, I was twenty-two. In fact, my birthday was the day before I was due to fly to Malta. I remembered my twenty-first birthday, that key date into manhood, and what a staid affair it had been: I'd simply got drunk with some friends. It never entered my mind then that within a year my life would open up into free-ranging sexual adventures with amenable and attractive women. I had left behind me all of that fighting with young women I'd had to do to make them come across, always failing, always miserable afterwards for my failures at seduction. Now I didn't even have to try: these ladies just seemed to fall into my lap.

So in my mind Malta was part of that whole set-up of raunchy, free-for-all sexual behaviour and I was able to bury my fear of flying under that sense of feeling how lucky I'd been to fall into this new style of life.

Because of the war I'd never been out of the country. And even if there'd been no war I'm sure I wouldn't have been able to travel because I had never earned enough money. But my dull English upbringing had inculcated in me the idea that anything European was necessarily wicked and inviting. So I was looking forward to my trip to Malta, an island steeped in mysterious romantic lore for me. It had been a British outpost during the war, bombed and battered, the population virtually at the mercy of the enemy but holding on. To reward that population, the government, in a rare gesture of thanks and appreciation, had awarded the island the George Cross, the highest British civilian medal for heroism. I'd heard so much about the air raids and bombardments, and the way the people had lived deep in caves, that I'd built up an idealized picture of people living on the edge of death and the threat of invasion for years. I was reminded in a strange way of the persecution of the early Christians and their lives in the catacombs. And of course Malta had that other connotation of the Crusades, its function as headquarters of the Knights Templar.

All this added up to a romantic vision of beautiful damsels in distress, in fear of their lives, and somehow I imagined myself as a knight in shining armour rescuing these delectable beauties from dark and mouldy caves. I didn't think of their lives ahead as call-girls after their rescue from Malta.

As it happened I spent much of my twenty-second birthday with another delectable damsel, Teresa, who I had been seeing more often than I was Helen (who was more involved in doing business at the club – I'd frequently see her with Bledsoe and wonder what was going on between them). Teresa was spending more time at the club as Margo had little for her to do at her place and they were waiting for the Maltese operation to be completed. So Teresa was working at the club, still living in the flat there, and I stayed with her often.

She was just as ravishingly sexual as she had been in my first real encounter with her, perhaps more so, for she was a relentless experimenter. She was not like Helen, though, who would pursue her sexual tricks so ferociously that I'd often feel depleted in the end even though the experience was always extravagantly enjoyable. Teresa knew just how to drive me to incredible edges and peaks, stringing me out but always choosing the right moment to let go and bringing me to a shuddering climax. She taught me how to keep her strung out at the pitch of orgasm and to know I was doing that to her made it all the more exciting for me, especially as she would talk and whisper and shout and encourage with her running commentaries.

Sometimes when I was at that ecstatic point when I knew a great surge of jism would spurt out, she would pull my cock out of her, hold it at the root with her fingers circling my balls while her other hand smoothed my cock-head. 'Let me see it fly out,' she'd whisper to me and of course I was ready to oblige, her fingers in the cream as it shot out and up. 'I like it inside me but sometimes it's more exciting to watch it, and feel it hot on my fingers, flying way up, splattering all over the place, not hiding inside me, just a secret between us.'

I suppose she was something of an exhibitionist and she made full use of those mirrors. Sometimes she'd position herself so she could see us as she pulled my cock out and let it rest on the lips of her quim and make me cover those lips with come. She loved to see it dribble all around there, taking my fingers to stroke them in that sticky flood till she went crazy with orgasmic pleasure again. Sometimes she wanted me to come in her mouth, and it was delicious to feel her slippery kisses, her swallowing, her letting the come cover her lips, her mouth full of that white-grey liquid. She'd lean over and kiss me with that sticky mouth, her tongue licking the come into my mouth. Then she'd push my head down to make me suck and lick her cunt, my mouth tasting my own jism and hers as I kissed her there.

Sometimes in the middle of the night, when we were lying spoon-fashion, she'd thrust her buttocks at me, so my limp cock would nestle in the crack of her arse and I wouldn't stay limp for long. She never wanted me to penetrate there but she loved to slide her crack along my large shaft. She'd reach her fingers down, curl the skin away from my cock-head very gently and massage it into the lips of her vagina till I felt them become juicy, her fingers wet on me as well, as she gave little yelps and moans. She'd do that till she reached orgasm though sometimes she pulled me right inside and we had a slow on-our-sides fuck. And then she liked me to push really deep inside her. She would get marvellously juicy, leaking all over the bedsheets, muttering, 'I can feel how fat your cock-head is up there. Fat and thick. Push more. More! Harder!'

And then there would be no stopping me. I'd feel that pulse rising up my length and I would flood inside her, and my cock would thrash in and out bathed in that slathery-slippery moistness, fast and deep, till I rolled away from her and she'd hold my cock, stroking maddeningly at my engorged shaft. Often I thought it would split apart until finally it grew less stiff.

In the evenings and nights I spent with Teresa, I kept thinking that we'd run the widest gamut of sexual congress possible but I was constantly amazed how she always managed to find something new. It may have been just a small, additional refinement to something we'd done before but she always made it seem new and fresh. She played tricks with her lingerie, stuffing the nylon right inside the crack of my arse, then drawing it out in an excruciatingly lingering way, bucking against me, draining me, the silk then trickled up and down my backbone till I felt it would dissolve, me left gasping as Teresa now smoothed the nylon slip over my arse. Then she did wonderful stripteases for me, giving me close-up views of herself in those mirrors near the bed. And all of this was done in a completely relaxed fashion, different from the some-times spasmodic, hectic sessions Helen drove me through – though she too reverted every now and again to that delicious slowness she had led me through the first time I had been with her.

I remember one particular idea Teresa introduced on that night of my birthday, in fact it was about six in the morning when the two of us had just woken up. We had both slept deeply after an evening and night of Teresa's especially inventive sexual acts. We were lying on our backs close together, my arm under her neck and reaching down to fondle her breast. She nestled her head closer into my shoulder. 'Since you're going off to Malta and I'll bet you'll be getting all those women in a to-do in the plane, maybe I should show something to make you remember me.'

She gave me a juicy kiss on my cheek and threw the bedclothes back. She noticed my cock was already standing at attention a little. 'Well, look at him,' she said. 'He's all ready for something.' She leaned down to my stomach, her hand kneading my balls, her lips placing another juicy kiss to lubricate the tip of my cock. 'There. All set. But you have to roll over.'

I hesitated, my hesitation mixed with disappoint-ment because that meant I'd be on my stomach and Teresa wouldn't be able to do her special massaging. 'It's alright,' she said, but I still hesitated. I suppose, like most men, I didn't like turning my back and so be unable to see what was happening. Teresa of course noticed my hesitation, for she went on, 'You'll be able to see in the mirror.'

But I still didn't roll over, there was a vague sense of distrust in me, maybe something to do with the idea that this was more like a position assumed in a homosexual encounter. I even very briefly wondered whether Teresa had a dildo and was going to use it on me.

'I'm not going to hurt you or do anything you don't want me to do. Honest. You're really going to like this. I always know what you like, don't I?'

I nodded.

'Well, then,' she said, giving my shoulder a little heave. 'Come on. Roll over.'

So I did.

'Put your arse up just a little.'

That worried me again so I turned my head to watch Teresa reflected in the mirror. She was kneeling beside me and I watched as her arm snaked out, then under my body to hold my cock in a firm grasp. 'See. It's only so I can hold you.' She squeezed my cock. 'And you know how much I like to hold you – and how much you like me to hold you.'

Then her other hand began to stroke my arse, round and round, fingers sliding slowly along the crack. 'Now I'm going to show you your very dark and secret place.' As usual, the sound of her voice telling me what she was going to do, though this time I didn't really know what she meant, made me excited. She felt my cock twitch in her grasp. 'Didn't I tell you you'd like it?'

Her fingers were very slowly drawing their enticing gentleness along the crack of my arse, down, pressing along, not in, but as if they were making their way back to feel under my balls. 'The most secret, the darkest and oh-so-nice-to-touch place.'

Still her fingers were crawling along. 'I'm nearly there.' One finger reached my arsehole, circled it, round and round. 'Nearly found it. Such a little secret place.'

Then suddenly she touched me and I felt as if the whole of my backbone would flame out in a warm glow, my balls seemed washed over with syrupy liquid, my cock swelling fatter, pushing into Teresa's hand. It made me feel as if I wanted to fuck but, in an unusual way, it made me feel almost as if I wanted to be fucked, not by a penis but to be taken into a lubricious quim, lubricated with moist lotions, a deluge of softness and sweetness. I wanted to stay like that, suffused with a warmth all around my pelvis, my arse, up my back, round to my stomach, spreading wider and wider.

'Your little secret place. So small. So wrinkled. I'm going to smooth it out.' It was difficult for me to know just where her fingers were stroking so gently because whatever she had touched opened outwards to flood me with a sense of being immersed in a long act of fucking, both giving and receiving at the same time. 'Such a lovely dark place. But it isn't a secret now. I've found it. You've found it.' Then she bent down to me there. 'Time for me to lick it.'

I was trying to discover just what Teresa had found in me that gave me this extraordinary sensation. I concentrated and what I could figure from the way she bent her head down and the position of her arm was that she was massaging a small piece of flesh that stretched from my arsehole to the back of my scrotum.

Later, I examined myself to see that spot, so secretly hidden, though now I would never forget for Teresa's tongue was juicing it, one finger straying around, till I seemed drenched in a soft spongy layer of velvet, her tongue smooth and satiny lapping there and then, very gently but easily, one of her fingers probed my arsehole. I thought I would never like that but now, with my secret spot so thoroughly alive to touch, with her other hand so regularly and insistently stroking my cock, that finger in my arse, prodding in and out (especially in) reached up and across as if it was probing through me, stretching to tickle my cock and balls from the inside.

All of this is a very inadequate way to describe Teresa's exquisite fingers on my secret dark place but all I know is that, much as I had enjoyed all the ways Teresa had touched me and stroked me, this was the most deliciously exquisite, driving me to dangle inside a dewy layer. Layer upon layer, in fact, a sexual pleasure unknown to me before. Somehow, in my assurance of being male, Teresa had unlocked something else in me without losing that hard, driving maleness.

'It's my secret now,' she said. 'We can keep on sharing it.' And on and on her finger moved inside me, her fingers and mouth on my secret spot and I was melting away, one large pool of pure drenching sensation and I wanted her to keep doing everything but I also wanted to come and I knew I would spew out streams of it, probably more than I had ever released before. And Teresa knew she was bringing me to that, both her hands and her mouth working now to bring me out of this immersion into hot, liquid release. Then she was ready, rolling me onto my back to hold both her hands on my cock as I watched the jets of jism spurt out with great force, most of it splashing onto her breasts, some dribbles on her hands, rubbing one finger now along my balls and down to find the secret place still juicy from her mouth. She lay next to me, holding my head against her warm, sticky breasts. 'It's our secret now,' she murmured.

I left Teresa about ten that morning to go back to my place. I was no longer living with Helen and I wasn't seeing that much of her, apart from some occasional deliveries. She was always off on some job, at least, that's what she told me. I began to make my own deliveries by taxi and most weeks Mrs Courtney would send her car round for me so I could deliver goods to her and spend time with her.

My new flat was similar to Helen's, the top floor of an old Victorian house. I suspected Gerry had several of these houses as places of assignment for his call-girls. Certainly my flat was decorated in a flowery, brothel-like manner but it was plush and comfortable.

Helen was to drive me to Lincolnshire that afternoon. The flight to Malta was planned for early evening, providing the weather held. Gerry had written out a few instructions for me and had sent them, together with a fat envelope stuffed with money, with Helen. I was to deal with a man called Joe and Gerry warned me in his note that Joe would try to hold out for more money before he handed the women over to me. Gerry thought there would be seven but he sent some spare cash in case Joe had rounded up some more who wanted to come. 'But don't let Joe deal you out of all the other money! Remember Margo!' He was reminding me of that afternoon with Margo when she had tried to wangle money out of me. I suppose

Gerry thought that if I could hold out against Margo, I should certainly be able to manage Joe. Gerry added a P.S. 'Wrap up well. It gets cold up there. But maybe the ladies will help you to keep warm on the way back.'

So I put on my light tweed suit and I had a thick scarf and heavy overcoat. That hardly seemed the right clothing to take on a trip to the sunny Mediterranean so I took my briefcase stuffed with a swimming costume just in case I managed to go to a beach to take a dip. I was still clinging to my romantic ideas though Helen gave me a bitchy laugh when I told her.

'You'll be in and out fast, Nick. It's not a place you want to hang around long. Make sure the clowns who are doing the flying start the refuelling as soon as you land. You go and grab the girls and get out of there quick. You don't want the local gendarmes breathing down your neck. If any problems crop up, don't hang around trying to solve them. Get out of there!'

Helen was in one of her snappy moods and she drove me fast and furious without talking very much and fortunately she didn't try any of her other tricks either. That gave me time to think about the errand I was on. I was still not quite sure just how illegal this was. After all, Malta was still a British possession so I wasn't quite sure why it was that Gerry had to smuggle them in. I think there were still tight restrictions on just how many people they were allowing into the country and I suppose one of the ways he was getting round that was to marry them off as if they were coming in as war brides. Maybe he had false papers for them so he didn't want to bring them in officially, this way nobody could trace them and he could run the women as part of the call-girl service without a problem. And some of them might be foreigners in any case.

As usual, Gerry hadn't explained much about the operation. I wondered if the women knew exactly what they were getting into and I was a bit queasy about being a delivery boy in the flesh market but Gerry had assured me that they'd have a better life in England. In one of his rare moments of confidence, Gerry had told me, 'Just remember, old son. Malta was a port of call for the navy. And you know what sailors go looking for when they're in port. These girls know what's what, believe me. And they're grateful to be getting away from Malta and being bombed to blazes. Most of 'em lived lousy lives there.'

The beginning of the trip was not very auspicious. Helen drove out to an abandoned airstrip and even the car, driving along it, jounced and bumped ominously on the cracked and weedy surface. I wondered how the plane would manage to take off. I had visions of the wheels puncturing in the potholes, the plane slewing round, broken-winged and bursting into flames.

My visions stayed with me when I saw the two-engined plane, painted in that drab wartime camouflage – was it war surplus? Had it been ripped up by too many bombing runs? I walked around it while Helen was joking, then haggling with the two-man crew. I saw a few tears in the fabric, some rivets looked loose, wires here and there looked rusty.

It turned out that the two men, Dennis and Reg – they didn't give me any surnames – were old RAF types and their conversation was liberally spattered with RAF slang. Once they'd been paid off by Helen who waved cheerily to me as she drove off, Dennis and Reg strolled over.

'First flight, laddie?' Dennis asked me. I nodded. 'Not to worry. Good old crate.'

He pounded on the fuselage – dust flew and a few bits dropped off. He turned to Reg. 'Hey, remember that last run to Hamburg?'

Reg laughed, then said, 'Christ, yes! I thought we were really going for a Burton that night.'

Dennis patted the side of the plane again, almost as if it was a dog. 'She's holding up well.' He looked up. 'How's the ceiling, Reg?'

'We'll do it.' Reg sounded a little dubious but I wondered if they were just having some fun with me. 'Got to keep low anyhow. Under the radar.' He leaned towards me. 'And cross the coast when it's dark.' Then to Dennis he said, 'Hope I can see my bloody way in when we get there.'

'I'll get you in.'

'Oh Christ! Dennis the ace navigator. I'm surprised he can guide his dick into an open cunt. And how d'you know the instruments are any good?'

'Checked 'em out yesterday. Should work, most of 'em. Unless the gremlins come along for the ride.'

They both laughed though it didn't do anything for my confidence when I listened to the way they talked. Helen was right when she called them clowns, I thought. But soon they became serious, walking round the plane to inspect it, fingering certain parts, Reg pulling at the wing flaps, and finally Dennis pulling the blocks away from the wheels. Reg zipped up his flying jacket and clambered into the plane, giving Dennis a jaunty thumbs-up when he was sitting in the cockpit. 'All aboard!' he yelled out of his window. Dennis returned the thumbs-up, saying, 'Wizard prang!' If it hadn't been for the ramshackle runway and the battered look of the plane, it reminded me of all those films I'd seen about bombing runs, with Dennis and Reg as devil-may-care air aces.

Dennis turned round in the doorway and stretched out his hand to help haul me inside. Then he reached back to close the door. 'Locked in, cap'n!' he yelled. Reg grinned back and shouted, 'Welcome aboard the Hindenburg!' I could have done without the comic repartee as my confidence in the flight had not been bolstered when I saw the inside of the plane. It looked cavernous, a wide aisle running the length of it up to the cockpit. Dennis waltzed along it and suddenly disappeared to the side. I followed him and discovered he had a little cubby hole with an overhead light and a small ledge containing an intricate map, ruler, set square and compass; some dials were set in a row just above him. I sat down on one of the hard benches running along both sides of the fuselage and I wondered if this had been a plane for paratroopers. I looked down to see if I could see any bomb doors under my feet but the floor seemed solid enough.

'Well, kick her in, Reg.' A great shudder shook the plane as one engine turned over but didn't catch. 'Got the elastic wound tight enough, Reg?'

'Tight as virgin cunt. Pinched it from Sally's knickers.' Then an engine broke into a roar as I felt a terrible shaking down the whole length of the plane. 'There she goes!' Reg shouted.

'That's only one!'

'The other's a dream.'

'Let's hope it isn't a wet dream!' That set them both into gales of laughter but then I felt another tremendous shake run through me from the bench and I was deafened by an unholy noise. At least it drowned out any further inane conversation from Reg and Dennis.

Soon the plane was lurching and banging along the runway, setting my teeth on edge, making me feel as if my bones would fly out of their joints. Then with a sudden heave we were airborne and even above the roar of the engines I heard Reg let out a whoop of delight. 'She's a good old gal!'

The two men were silent for a time, severe in their looks as they worked at setting the plane's course. It was as if they were actually hauling the plane up by sheer physical force. I looked ahead as the plane speared through filmy clouds at first, then heavy blankets of white till, after a while, we broke through the cloud cover and levelled out into a world purpled by the setting sun. 'Tally ho!' Reg shouted back to us.

The plane wasn't as noisy now and except for an occasional dip and drop when we hit air pockets, the flight was relatively uneventful. Dennis and Reg reminisced about the war, ignoring me for the most part till Reg blasted at me, 'No longer a virgin, eh?' This was a sudden change of topic, I thought, till he went on, 'First flight, I mean. Nothing to it.'

'Just like your first shag. Bit scary, scared you'll shoot your load too soon. And maybe you do but after that, it's as if you've been shagging all your life. As the man says, nothing to it. Whip your dick out, start the props, take off and away you go!'

'Speaking of shagging, what about that lady with you? Does she? I mean, do you get your nooky there?' I grinned. 'I thought so. You can always tell, the way they talk, coming on a bit. Knows a thing or two, she does. And no budging her on the money bit. She says we'll get extra pay because these women . . . well, maybe we can collect from them on the way back, if you know what I mean.'

I shrugged. 'I don't know. Maybe they'll be scared of flying.'

'Dennis and me, we'll teach 'em how to fly!'

'Too true! Got to pass the time somehow.'

'Right-o! This bloody thing flies itself. Maybe those bints'd like to handle my joystick!'

Dennis laughed and added, 'They can cross my co-ordinates any time!' They went on in this jocular manner for some time and I sat back to enjoy the flight. Nothing untoward happened so I felt safe flying through the darkness. But it was cold and I had to sit hunched into myself, pulling my overcoat tightly around me.

'I can see you're in need of a bit of hot stuff,' Dennis blurted at me.

'Aren't we all?' Reg shouted back to us.

Eventually they became serious again as we approached Malta. I was up with Reg peering ahead into the dark. He gradually pushed the nose down into the pitch black. 'Shit!' he muttered. 'I hope we don't go slam bang into a bloody mountain!'

'Trust your old Dennis. I can always find the right hole to slide into.' And just then the plane began to rock from side to side. 'Upstream air pockets. Blasted things.'

'What d'you expect when you're riding in between two mountains?'

'I hope to Christ you've got us fixed right.'

'A piece of cake, Reg. You see any lights yet?'

'Not a bloody one!'

'They said they'd have a few flares out but can't show too much.'

The plane was see-sawing a little wildly and the engines sounded uneven. 'I'm taking her down, Dennis, and I'd better damn well see something soon or I'll be up your flaming arse!'

'We're fine. You just keep rocking her in, Reg.'

'Flares up ahead. Jesus! Nearly flopped right down on them!' There was an almighty bump and for a moment I thought we had crashed, skidding to a stop while the plane fell apart around us. But we rattled and bounced and jiggled, the engines letting loose terrifying roars till we finally slowed, then stopped, Reg cutting the engines. 'Wizard prang!' he roared.

'Here, lad,' Dennis said when he opened the door for me. 'You just take a shufti out there. See everything's alright.' Reg was staggering out of his seat and down the aisle. 'Hey, and listen,' Dennis went on, laying a hand on my shoulder. 'Get your business done toot sweet. Load the bints on quickly. We'll be refuelling. Then we blast out of here. We've got to make it over the coast before it's too light, then nobody's any the wiser. Understand?'

Lines of a few feeble flares stretched in front of me at the end of which I saw a dilapidated Nissen hut with one small light shining over the door. There was no one in sight; I was surprised no one had watched us come in. I hoped everything was in order and the women were already there so we wouldn't have to wait around for them. As I neared the hut, the door opened and a small but wide-shouldered man stepped out. When he saw me approaching, he held up his hand like a traffic policeman. I stopped and he said loudly, 'Gerry?'

'No. Nick.'

'Nick?'

'Yes. From Gerry. You Joe?'

He nodded and prodded himself in the stomach. 'Joe. Yes.'

I reached into my inside pocket and pulled out the fat envelope, waving it in front of him. He made a quick snatch at it but I moved back a little. 'No,' I said. 'The girls.' He flicked his head sideways at the door, then we both stood still a moment. 'The girls?' I said again, and made as if to stuff the envelope back in my pocket. He gave me an expansive smile, spread his arms out wide as if he was going to embrace me but he turned to show me into the hut. Behind me I could hear the whine of an engine and I turned round to see a small tanker travelling towards the plane with Dennis and Reg waiting at the side of the plane.

Joe opened the door for me and I stepped inside. One bare bulb was hanging down at the centre so not much light spread into the corners of the hut. At the far end two small groups were standing, huddling together, with small suitcases and carrier bags on the floor around them. Their heads all lifted to stare out of the shadows when they heard the door open.

Joe made a big, florid gesture towards the two groups of women. 'The girls,' he said. 'Beautiful!' His gesture changed into a short bow. Then he straightened up, his arm shooting out with his palm extended flat in front of me. I slapped the envelope into his hand, strode past him to go over to the girls. They all stared at me as I approached, some shifting their feet uneasily, one or two with anxious looks on their faces, one or two smiling tentatively.

Three women were off to one side, dominated by a tall slender woman on high heels, a ratty fur coat swinging open to show her slim figure encased tightly

179

in a red-and-white striped dress. She grinned at me. The other two stayed close to her, two blondes, a little brassy but attractive in an obvious, almost bold way, standing there in tightly belted raincoats. Just looking at them, I thought that those three were probably already well into the business, perhaps bar girls for visiting sailors or even ready for tourists who were beginning to trickle back into Malta. I nodded at them briefly and the tall woman slowly sized me up, her eyes drifting up the length of my body. Then she turned away, so I stepped over to the other group.

At first I thought they were a collection of drab women, a little like overgrown schoolgirls assembled for a school trip. I wondered whether they would fit into Gerry's scheme of things. They certainly all looked as if they would lead better lives once they had been smartened up by Margo but, for now, they looked a little threadbare, a little bedraggled, a little thin, a little frightened. I thought I'd better at least try to reassure them and convince them I wasn't an ogre so I moved to one of them, a smallish young woman, quite buxom, in a short jacket over a thin cotton dress of washed-out pink. Her face, pretty without being particularly striking and devoid of make-up, brightened when I said, 'Hello,' and smiled. She smiled back and I could see she had large bright brown eyes that gave her a soft look. She almost curtseyed and said, 'Lisa.'

That first exchange put the rest of the group more at ease and I went round to each one, saying hello and in turn they each spoke their names: 'Irena', 'Maria', 'Helga', 'Frankie' (a short form of Francesca, I discovered later).

I seemed to break the ice with this group but I wasn't quite sure what I could do about the other three.

I was saved from doing anything about it because the tall slender one swaggered over to me, gave me a brilliant smile and said, 'Hi. I'm Carmella. I speak English a little. The Yanks. In Italy.'

Her hand felt soft in mine and, as she withdrew it, she let it linger smoothly on my palm. 'Nice boy. Nice hands.' She leaned in to whisper to me, 'Soft like pussy. You like?' That was the first time I had heard that word but the way she said it, the way her hand stroked mine, I knew exactly what she meant. Of course I nodded back to her and said, 'Yes,' and she winked. She was establishing, I thought, that she, and the two with her, knew what they were about. I found out that Carmella certainly knew the ropes and she never would let anyone push her around. Eventually she helped me round the others together so we could board them on the plane without too much fuss. That took a little time as I tried to explain how I'd like everyone out of there and on the plane.

I felt a tap on my shoulder. It was Joe who began to shake the money in my face, muttering in broken English that it was not enough. He'd been promised more, he indicated, flinging his arms about dramatically. All the women were staring at us, and I suppose they were wondering whether their flight to freedom, if that's what they considered it to be, was suddenly going to be cancelled.

I tried to placate Joe but he became more voluble, spouting Italian now with just a few English words. I pulled out my wallet and explained as best I could that the money I'd given him was for seven women and I was willing to pay more as there were eight. But Joe went on, a slightly demented, florid man like a marionette whose strings were being pulled violently and spasmodically. I showed him some banknotes but he simply kept on talking, his voice increasing in volume. I knew I had to take charge or the women might refuse to get on the plane for me.

Then I felt the money removed from my hand. It was Carmella. 'Joe!' she said sharply. 'The nice man has the money. How much?' She thrust the banknotes at me like a hand of cards and I slipped out what I considered was a fair extra payment and handed the notes to Joe. He looked exasperated and was about to explode into another tirade when Carmella bawled, 'Enough!' Then her other hand reached down and grabbed his crotch hard. 'OK?' she said in a tough voice. Joe began to squirm and said in a whimper, 'OK, OK!'

Carmella eventually let go of him, dusting her hands together as if she was ridding them of something unclean. She turned to me. 'Yes?' I nodded. 'You take us to fly now.'

She peeled off one of the notes and stuffed it down the front of her dress. 'We go, yes?' Then she patted her breasts and smoothed her dress down outlining her formidable thighs. She poked two fingers into her cleavage to rearrange the note. 'Want it back?' She smiled. 'Some time, yes?'

'Yes,' I said. 'But now we have to go on the plane.'

'My hands not like this . . .' She gestured a tight squeeze. 'I like more . . .' and she fluttered her hands and held one as if she were jerking it slowly and softly up and down.

She went back to her two friends and the trio shepherded the other five who began to potter about, nervously picking up cases, fastening coats, straightening hair. Joe was off to one side, counting his money. The girls dribbled towards the door, Carmella urging them on from behind while I led the way. As I opened the door, and the first ones stepped out into the hot, humid air, I heard Reg's voice, 'This way for the poontang express!'

Carmella at my side said, 'Poontang! Means pussy, yes?'

'I think so.'

She pointed at Reg and Dennis. 'Yankee?'

'No. English. Like me.'

'English like pussy, poontang, OK? Jolly good show, what?' she added in an attempt at an English accent. I was beginning to like Carmella. She had a sense of humour, she knew what she was up to, and she'd helped me with Joe so that reconciled me somewhat to the job I was doing, making it less distasteful. She could obviously take care of herself and she was in the process of taking care of the others. She reminded me a bit of Margo, a little earthier perhaps, and I wondered how Margo would react to her. But that was not my problem. My problem was getting my cargo back to England, and I was wondering how Reg and Dennis were going to manage that.

They were larking about, lifting the girls through the door of the plane, squeezing them, patting them, making rude gestures, laughing, joking with each other but most of the girls were looking solemn, even woebegone.

The night was black with only a few stars and the flares threw only a flickering light so the scene was a little macabre. Somehow I could tell that we had landed in a narrow cleft between two mountains and even in the darkness they loomed over us. I suppose this had been chosen as the landing site as it would be virtually impossible for anyone to guess a plane was

flying in there. We had made it in but I was worried
that we would find it difficult to take off and manage to
lift sufficiently quickly to avoid crashing into the side
of a mountain.

Not that Dennis and Reg seemed concerned. Their
spirits were high – I imagined that the thought of
travelling for hours with young women aboard made
them almost jocularly ecstatic. But I was certainly not
ecstatic about our prospects and the scene inside the
plane was not calculated to make me more sanguine.

Carmella and her two friends were sitting close up
to the front near Dennis' cubbyhole and I hoped their
presence wouldn't distract him from his job. Reg
kicked the props into action with a deafening roar from
the engines. The other five sat huddled together on the
opposite bench, looking abject and apprehensive,
clinging to each other when the engines thundered
into life and the plane shook as though it was going to
rattle itself to pieces. Reg wheeled it round to line it up
on the runway. Then he opened up the throttle. It's
probable I'd have heard the five women screaming if it
hadn't been for the engines roaring. Even Carmella and
her friends were staring across at us with wide-open
eyes and furrowed foreheads.

Suddenly Reg let everything rip. We battered along
the airstrip faster and faster till a sickening lurch lifted
us. It didn't seem to me that the plane was going to
remain aloft but maybe Reg was aiming for a small gap,
keeping the plane low till we had cleared the two steep
sides of the mountain. Then gradually Reg hauled the
plane up higher till it felt as if we were literally
breaking the pull of gravity, the plane lead-heavy and
struggling till there came a moment almost as if the
plane had been tied to a piece of elastic, stretching it

tighter and tighter till it snapped and we were free in the air. Reg and Dennis obliged us with great yelps of delight and Carmella and her friends broke into huge grins. The other five relaxed a little but their faces were still creased with looks close to alarm. As we rose higher and the temperature in the plane dropped, it became really chilly. The five scrunched themselves together in a vain effort to keep themselves warm and Carmella pulled her patchy fur coat around herself. I sat apart from the others, my hands deep in my overcoat pockets and pulling the material close for warmth.

We levelled off and I could see Reg and Dennis relax. They merely had to keep a steady course for a few hours now. Dennis crawled out of his cubbyhole and sat on the floor near Carmella and her two friends. Reg leaned back in his seat, glancing back at Dennis and the women, his hands only lightly on the control stick. Dennis moved to lean against Carmella's legs and she looked down and smiled a little, managing to look both sympathetic and slightly contemptuous at the same time.

A minute or two later Carmella stood up, causing Dennis to fall sideways. She strolled down the aisle to me and put her hand on my cheek. It felt icy. 'Cold,' she said. 'Need to put it on something hot!' She nodded towards the others. 'Look. All cold.'

The five sitting together had their arms round each other in a desperate attempt to keep themselves warm by body heat.

'Very unhappy. Find hot for my hands.'

I couldn't think of anything to say or do. My face and head were feeling the cold though my overcoat was managing to ward off the effects of the altitude.

'We could dance,' Carmella said, then strolled down the aisle like a model. She swung her moth-eaten coat open as she turned, letting it swish over Dennis. She came back down the aisle and for a moment I actually thought she was going to do a strip to warm us up though I knew that she was really too cold to do that. She swayed seductively down the aisle towards me, one hand fingering the front of her dress, possibly to remind me that she had stuffed the banknote there. Then her other hand pulled at her skirt, raising it to show me a good length of thigh before she swung her coat back over it, swirled round and began her stroll back to Dennis. There she circled round his back, reached her hand down his neck, her fingers sliding inside his fur-collared flying jacket. He beamed and Carmella yelled out, 'Make my hand warm.'

She leaned forward further, her other arm stretching down to unzip the jacket and insert itself inside his shirt. 'Hot,' she said as she settled down behind Dennis, her hands inside his clothing moving along his chest and stomach.

'Hot stuff!' Dennis shouted up to Reg who was grinning as he watched.

The two women friends of Carmella's stood and waltzed their way up to Reg. He put his free arm round the waist of one and the other squeezed behind his seat to his other side. I couldn't see much of what was happening but it was obvious that they were following Carmella's example and soon had their hands inside Reg's clothes, snuggling very close to him.

Then the first girl I'd spoken to, Lisa, stood up and approached me putting her hand to my cheek. She had watched Carmella. Her hand was freezing. She sat next to me and put her hand inside my overcoat pocket, gripping my own hand there. Helga came and sat on the other side of me and did the same thing. Then Frankie came over, crouched in front of me, carefully undid one of the overcoat buttons and slid her hand inside. The other two left across from us hugged each other tightly for warmth.

Soon I felt cold hands burrowing inside my coat from all angles, searching for warmth. One hand moved to my shirt, snuggled under it and gradually it felt less cold as fingers spread like a fan across my stomach. Frankie's hand was at my thighs which I clasped together so her hand would feel their warmth though I must admit that was making me feel warmer around my crotch, especially as the hands in my pocket were pushing in deeper, prodding at my groin.

The vibration of the plane gave me a pleasant tingle and I was being lulled into a doze though those hands sliding inside my clothes were enough to keep me awake. At times the three women sitting with me whispered to each other though I couldn't understand them. Occasionally they giggled and, after a time, a hand under my shirt was fingering the waistband of my underpants, another hand had one finger pushing between the buttons of my fly, someone unbuckled my belt, a hand was at my back and had somehow wormed its way down to my arse, crawling its way to probe the crack. The hand was now inside my underpants, warm and getting warmer as it cupped my balls.

I couldn't tell whose hands were doing these things but I was at the mercy of them as if they were the slippery sliding tentacles of an octopus. For a long time fingers touched and prodded and probed. With my overcoat now open Frankie pressed herself into my thighs as a hand sought out my cock which had grown and hardened under this flickeringly incessant attention. Different fingers flicked and fussed over my balls, one finger traced the roundness of my cock-head, a finger and thumb circled the fat base, three fingers moved up and down the length.

Eventually my hands found their way inside the women's dresses, pressing inside, feeling a breast here, a thigh there, a calf, a nipple, easing further inside to find warm wetness and I'm sure Dennis was involved in the same way with Carmella and Reg would be keeping the plane on a steady course, I hoped, while his two women helped him along and his free hand strayed into their warm places.

The hands kept stroking me, fingering at the tender skin, rolling it back, a fingertip ran round and round the head, a palm pressed the shaft, a finger poised at the slit sometimes, waggling it open. Fingers curled round my thickness, my balls were fondled, my cock swelled harder. The pressure of those hands was finely tuned, sensitive to what was happening to my cock, listening to my sighs, following me when I shifted to make a hand more comfortable. Their bodies pressed in closer to me, my hands wandering inside their clothes till I found first one quim, then another, fingers inside a double creaminess. The girls were whimpering, giggling, gasping. I was beginning to pant, to know that those hands would pull me along to orgasm and finally I gushed out. I'm sure I spurted onto all those hands which kept up their stroking in a wet and slippery way, my cock squirming about in all those fingers till the hot come cooled. The women still kept their hands there but huddled closer to me.

And so we flew back, a throbbing machine of groping and feeling, keeping ourselves warm in the best way. So the time passed and as we neared the coast of England, we rearranged ourselves and sat quietly till we landed.

Then we all stood up at once and I soon found myself in the middle of a soft scrum of eight women, with Carmella leading my fingers down her cleavage and the others gripping me by my shoulders, round my waist, fondling my buttocks, all of us trying to move together down the aisle and out into the dawn light of Lincolnshire.

9. Punch and Judy

'What did you think of the fight last Sunday?' Teresa asked me. I was lying on the bed in her flat at the Blue Lantern – we found we could spend time together there without too many people knowing about it.

'It was alright but I don't go much on boxing.'

'No?' Teresa said. 'I love to see two men fighting. All those lovely muscles.' She leaned over and gave my crotch a squeeze.

'They don't use that kind of muscle in boxing.'

'No, but you can think about it when you see those two men in their shorts and their muscles bulging out.' She looked down at me. 'You've got a pretty fair bulge down there, I'd say.'

'I'd rather use this than try to bash someone's brains out. Boxing's not for me. Still, I liked the way it ended. I didn't know what Benny was going to do, then all of a sudden, wham!'

Teresa laughed. 'It couldn't have happened to a more suitable person!'

'Weren't you surprised?'

'I was at the time. But last night at the club Benny told me how it happened. Made a whole lot of sense then.'

'So what did he tell you?'

'First he told me how it all started. Bledsoe was in the club one night, a few weeks back. He had that big

ape Christoff with him. Judy was flinging herself at
him, dancing him a big come-on. You know, that
woman can be a real pain. Thinks she's the only one
with a great body, the only one who can dance like
that. I can do what she does just as good as her.' Teresa
rolled from the bed and stood at the foot of it, slowly
swinging her hips, lifting her hair high off her head,
pushing out her breasts, fingering a button on her
dress, then sliding the hem of her skirt up to show her
shapely leg.

'Hey, you don't have to convince me. That's terrific.'

'Maybe I should do this on stage.'

'Just save it for me.'

She leaned over the rail at the foot of the bed. 'Well,
anyhow,' she went on, 'that night Judy's making this
play at Bledsoe and you know how Benny gets when
he thinks there's maybe trouble brewing. So he's
watching Judy and that lug Christoff goes for him.'

'Why?'

'Christoff claims Benny's coming on to Judy. Well,
you know how Benny goes when he's upset, the way
his eyes go. Looks sort of shifty. It doesn't mean
anything, everyone knows that. He's been cut around
there so many times in his fights, he doesn't even
know himself what his eyes are doing. And in any
case, with that face of his, so beaten up, how could
anyone think he could make a play for a dish like
Judy? I mean, I like Benny but let's face it, his face
looks as if it's been chewed up in a meat grinder. I
think this Christoff's just after Benny, maybe putting
on some show for Judy, this big man talking tough to
what he thinks is some played-out old boxer. Bledsoe
tells him to stop throwing his weight around but
Christoff keeps at it. Then Benny starts into him, says if

he doesn't stop, he'll throw him out. Christoff says Benny couldn't throw a mouse out of a hole. That gets Benny's goat and he squares off at Christoff. Bledsoe steps in then and says if they want to fight, he'll arrange a proper fight. He'll pay Gerry for the use of the club, set up a proper boxing ring and they can fight it out some Sunday afternoon. So that's how they set up the fight.'

'So why does Bledsoe do this?'

'I don't know. Maybe he wants to bet on his man Christoff, make some money. Maybe he's trying to impress Judy, you know, getting two guys to beat each other up for her. I mean, Bledsoe thinks Christoff is some big bruiser but you can tell he knows nothing about boxing. Not like Benny. I mean, what I understand is Benny was pretty good in his day, so when Gerry hears about this he agrees. He thinks he can make some money as well. And so do all the others who come to the club. They're putting their money on Benny.'

'That's what I would have done if I was a gambler, bet on Benny. Christoff's just a big ox with no brains.'

'So Benny starts to train, doing road work, he even set up a punching bag in the back and you can see he's setting himself up pretty good. The bets are piling up on Benny — most of the men around here, well, they think this is about Judy. They like to watch her do her strip, she looks good and most of them'd like to get to her but it looks as if she's just making a play for Bledsoe and most of them don't like him. And Benny's beginning to look really sharp.'

'I didn't know this was happening around here. I just thought it was some grudge match.'

'It was, in a way, but I guess it also seems to be some

kind of fight between Bledsoe and Gerry. They're both laying heavy bets on their man. So it's all set for the big fight, and the Saturday night some of the men make sure Benny gets back to his place early. He says he's just going to do some loosening up exercises, nothing too heavy. Then he'll get to bed early, all primed up for the big fight. But it doesn't work out that way.'

'What happened?'

'What Benny tells me is this, as far as I can gather. You know how he talks like his tongue's all glued up or something. Anyhow, there he is in his place, ready for bed, wearing a pair of his old boxing shorts for luck, he says, and there's a knock at his door. He opens it up and there's Judy. He says she looks scared and she pushes right past him, closes the door behind her, leans against it as if she thinks someone's going to come charging in after her. She's got on this fur coat — there's a rumour that Bledsoe bought it for her. She turns away from the door and asks Benny to look out to make sure no one's followed her. He can't see anyone outside so she relaxes a bit. 'I just had to come and see you,' she says, 'but don't let on to anyone.' She tells him she's heard Benny was a great fighter — seems she always followed the fights. 'So I had to come and tell you. I came straight from the club, just as soon as I'd done my strip. I just put a few things on and got out of there.'

I knew Teresa liked talking, playing parts and she was really enjoying this. I could see she was acting out all the roles, standing there like Judy, wide-eyed and sort of terrified. Teresa took up the story again. 'She tells Benny that Bledsoe has laid out a lot of money on Christoff and now he's worried because he can see that Benny is in great shape. So he's got this plan. If he sees

Christoff being beaten up by Benny, he's hired some-one to get to Benny's bucket in his corner. He's going to slip something in the water, then when they wipe Benny's face off between rounds, this stuff will get in his eyes and he won't be able to see and Christoff'll just be able to bang away at Benny.'

'But why is Judy telling Benny all this? I thought she was in thick with Bledsoe. After all, if Bledsoe wins, some of that money's going to pass on to Judy.'

'Well, Judy convinces him she really likes boxing and she hates anyone who tries to do the dirt. She likes a good, clean fight. Doesn't matter who wins, so long as it's a good fight. That's going to appeal to Benny. Then she goes on about how she likes watching the fights. 'I love to see boxers going at it,' she says, 'sweating it out, all muscles, dressed in those shiny shorts.' And then she makes her first move, according to Benny. She reaches out and touches the shorts he's wearing. 'I love the feel of them,' she says. Benny tells me she starts rubbing around, her fingers going up his thigh, round the back, stealing up to his arse. Her other hand's tugging at the waistband and sort of stroking his stomach. Benny says he tries to move away because it's giving him a hard-on – Benny's shy when he's telling me this but I know what he's talking about. I bet he's sticking out at the front of his shorts.'

'Just like me now.' While Teresa had been telling me this, she'd come round the bed and begun to do what she said Judy had been doing to Benny. Her hand gripped my thigh high and she pushed under, resting it on my arse while her other hand brushed up my crotch slowly, stopping at the waistband of my trousers. She pulled sharply and all the buttons of my fly were undone. 'Benny only had his shorts on,' she said and she tugged my trousers down and off. 'Just like you now.'

'And me sticking up like this, just like Benny.'

'Judy starts to stroke all over his shorts, not actually touching this big erection he's got, but damn near, Benny told me.' And Teresa's hands were doing the same kind of thing, her fingers edging up the top of my thigh under my underpants, maddeningly near my balls without touching them and her other hand was sneaking down from my stomach nearly flicking at my cock.

'Benny tries to get rid of her, saying she should be getting back to do her strip. "I just finished," she says. "I don't go on for a couple of hours. In any case one of the other girls will take over for me if I'm not back. Anyhow, I'm ready to go on just as soon as I get back."' Teresa clambered off the bed and unbelted her dress, unsnapping the fasteners.

'Then Judy swings open her coat,' she said, swinging around and letting her dress fly open. She was wearing those red panties I'd first seen her in, a red bra, black stockings and a garter belt. 'Underneath her coat Judy's wearing her strip stuff, not the evening gown but her low-cut bra with her tits nearly falling out and some lace-patterned stockings fastened to a garter belt, her heels showing off her long legs and skimpy panties. She swirls around, her coat flying out and Benny can see all this and then she lets it fall from her shoulders.' Teresa let her dress fall to the floor. 'Like the outfit?'

'You look great,' I said.

'No, I mean that's what Judy asks Benny, about her strip outfit. And much as I don't like her, I must say she looks good in it.'

'So do you – in what you're wearing.'

'Thank you.' She curtseyed and began to walk and sway seductively away from the bed, wiggling her arse, giving me a fetching grin over her shoulder, then turning back to the side of the bed. 'Judy starts to strut up to Benny and she says, "I like boxing so much, I've been thinking of working out a routine, with me wearing boxing shorts, shorts like yours, Benny." Then she hooks both hands in the waistband and starts trying to pull them down.' Teresa leaned over and kissed the tip of my cock through my underpants. 'Judy didn't do that to Benny. She just tried to wrestle his shorts off. And he told me he had this big hard-on . . .'

I gripped my cock and flourished it at her. 'Just like me,' I said.

'I can see. It's looking good. I'll deal with that later. But Benny's thinking he doesn't want Judy dealing with his. He's got the fight the next afternoon and all the people he knows in the club have got money on him so he holds onto his shorts. But her hands start creeping around and she's fingering his back down near the crack of his arse. And her hands are all over his shorts, saying "I love the feel of this satin. It's smoother than mine. Feel for yourself." She takes Benny's hand and puts it on those skimpy panties and she starts to push her mound into Benny's palm. "Check it out, Benny. It isn't as silky, is it?" '

Teresa knelt on the bed, took my hand and placed it on her panties. I put my hand on her crotch and pushed a finger inside the nylon. I felt her moistness and I slowly stroked my finger inside her silky slit, deeper and deeper. She began to rotate her hips round my finger inside her. While I was doing this, she went on with her story.

'Judy asks Benny what he thinks about when he sees her stripping in the club. "Would you like me to strip for you now?" ' she says. Teresa did a final rotation around my finger, then crawled off the bed.

'Benny's standing up close to Judy.' Teresa signalled me to get off the bed, so I stood close to her, my cock sticking out so far in front of me that it was almost touching her. 'Judy goes over to the wireless, finds some music and off she goes, dancing real close to Benny and soon she's unlatching her bra and her big bosom's right in front of Benny's face. By this time, he tells me, he's sweating like mad.'

And so was I because Teresa had taken off her bra. She was fondling her breasts, stroking her nipples which soon were jutting out.

'Then Judy put her hands round Benny's neck and pulled his face into her bosom, squashing him against her tits, her nipples right by his mouth so he can't avoid sucking one of them, at least that's what Benny said.'

Teresa pulled my face into her breasts and I began to nuzzle at them, licking one, then the other, liking the rubbery feel of her nipples in my mouth, as I made them slippery with saliva, taking little nips at them with my teeth.

Teresa's voice sounded a little breathless as she went on with her story about Benny. 'Judy starts to pull at Benny's waistband again and pulls his shorts down. She gets them past his knees so she's bending down there and Benny says he's nearly going crazy because he can feel her hair all over his dick, soft but spiky, scratching at him till she lifts her head back and she's staring straight at his thick prong, letting it poke into her eyes, stroking down her nose. Benny's slavering all over the place when he's telling me this, his eyes bugging out because then he tells me that she took him all the way into her mouth! Can you imagine? He's trying to keep his mind on the fight while this woman's sucking him.'

As she was saying this, she pulled my underpants down, kneeling in front of me. She bent forward, slowly her lips opened and she took my cock deep into her mouth. I could feel the back of her throat touching the tip of my cock. Then her hands were caressing my balls, gripping the root of my cock hard as she let it slide slowly out, or not quite out. Her lips held my cock-head, her tongue flickering all around it. Of course she couldn't go on with her story as her mouth was busy on my cock for a few minutes. When she finally let me slide out of her mouth, she kept her hands gently stroking her mouth-moisture all around my cock.

'You can imagine Benny's problem, trying to keep his mind on the fight . . .'

'When a woman's doing that to you, it's difficult to keep your mind on anything else.'

'Exactly. That's what Benny said, telling me how Judy's caressing every inch of his cock with her tongue and mouth, taking his balls in, till he says he can't resist and he starts to fuck her mouth. That's how he described it. He said he wants to get it over with so he won't wear himself out too much before the fight. But he's also thinking he's enjoying this too much with this terrific woman – he'll never get another chance like this. By now he's right on the edge but Judy won't let him go. She starts to rub him all over her breasts and finally, Benny can't believe this, he is now fucking her breasts, right between them, with Judy pressing them against him and when he shoves up hard, she flicks her tongue out and licks the tip of his cock. Benny's going crazy, Judy's got him all hot, and there he is on the edge again but Judy stands up, puts her hands on him and guides him between her legs. She's still got her panties on and he's rubbing against them. He can feel that they're silky and wet and he's banging away at her, wants to get into her but can't, till she whispers, "Pull them off." So he does and he's doing what he thought he'd never do, sliding in and out of this great-looking woman and she seems to be enjoying it as well. Benny told me she was crying out, saying things like "Punch me! Give me your haymaker!" Then she pushes him onto his old sofa and sits on top of him, riding him till he rolls her over and pounds away so he can finish off. Her legs are up on his shoulders and he's deep in her. She's almost scream-ing and he keeps driving himself on till he lets every-thing go. Benny says he felt emptied out so he collapses as if he's just fought ten hard rounds.'

While Teresa was telling me this, I was doing some of the things she talked about. I drew her panties off and began a slow massage of her quim and soon she was drenching my hand. Her voice became a little shaky when I moved to rub the tip of my cock round her moist slit, stroking her gently with my cock while her hands were feeling out the roundness of my balls. Once she stopped and whispered, 'If we go on like this, I won't be able to get to the end of my story. Just take it easy.' So I did and she was able to finish the story.

'Benny feels played out and drops off to sleep but he's awake again soon after because Judy's at him again. He struggles to stand up but she's all over him. "It's like I'm counted out," Benny says because this woman's pinned him down, her breasts flattened against him and she's rooting out his cock and pushing it against her quim. "One more round to go. I'm on the ropes. Gimme the knock-out, Benny, please," she says. This makes Benny feel horny again so he stands up and she's got her legs around his waist. Benny's walking around the room while she's moving up and down on him till he can't stand it so he lays her on the sofa and they do it again. If he felt emptied before he feels completely drained now and in two minutes he's dead asleep. Then it's about four in the morning. Judy's traipsing round the flat, picking up her clothes as if she's getting ready to leave. She's got her fur coat on and when she sees Benny's awake, she opens her coat. "Like the outfit?" and she's wearing his shorts, nothing else. "Time for the main event" and she yanks him to his feet, her hands start to rub him up again, trying to get him to push inside the shorts she's wearing. "Come on champ. Get in my pants. I've made them all wet waiting for you. You can wear 'em for the fight today, bring you good luck" and before he knows it, Benny's sticking it to her again. Of course it takes him a long time and he can't squeeze much out of himself. But that stops him cold – he just falls dead to the world on the couch.'

Now I understood why the fight ended the way it did. When the fight started Benny looked good. Christoff couldn't do anything because Benny was just tying him up with fancy footwork and jabs, quick punches before he danced away and Christoff wasn't laying a finger on him; he just tried to lean on Benny to wear him out and, after about six rounds, we were getting a little worried because Benny was slowing down. The fight was like a slow-footed dance. We thought it was because Christoff was doing all this leaning, squeezing Benny in hard clinches and Benny was so slow. By now some of Christoff's punches were beginning to land and Benny was hurting. It didn't look as if Benny was going to make it. There was no steam in his punches so he couldn't knock Christoff out and he looked so weary, we couldn't be sure that Christoff wouldn't connect with some humdinger of a sucker punch and lay Benny flat. At the end of the fight Benny was hanging onto the ropes but he had piled up enough points so the ref raised his hand – Benny was the winner on points.

Teresa finished the story. 'Benny says it came to him about halfway through the fight that Bledsoe had sent Judy to wear him out so he wouldn't last. Benny knows he doesn't have enough power in his punches so he just tries to stay out of Christoff's reach, hanging on, hoping to make it to the end. Well, you know what happened at the end of the fight.'

Benny went over to Christoff's corner. Everyone thought he was going over to shake hands but he walked right past him, climbed through the ropes and made for Bledsoe. By this time the whole place had gone silent and all eyes were on Benny. I was thinking that Benny wasn't that dense – he wasn't going to take on Bledsoe, was he? But he took up a square stance in front of Bledsoe and everyone could hear what he said. 'That's some woman you got. A good fuck. I gave it to her good. So every time you or your big ape Christoff stick it to her, remember who's been there before you.' Then, though he looked really exhausted, he took a quick step to his left, put his hand on Judy's shoulder –

she was standing next to Bledsoe – turned her towards him and flashed out a beautiful right hook on the point of her jaw. Everyone heard the bone crack and she was out cold, flat on her back at Bledsoe's feet.

'Benny got a real kick out of doing that to Judy,' Teresa told me. 'He said, "It was the best punch I threw all afternoon!" '

As soon as she stopped talking Teresa placed her open mouth on mine, her tongue licking at the inside of my lips. Then she slipped a finger in my mouth and that reminded me just how much I liked her mouth on my cock and of course I began to feel harder than ever. She pushed me back on the bed.

'Now you can get into my pants. If Judy can wear Benny's shorts, you can wear mine.'

She picked up her red panties and drew them up my legs, careful to lift the elastic at the waist wide so it could go over my hard-on. It was terrific to feel that silky nylon like a soft skin around my cock, especially when Teresa began to stroke the nylon up and down.

'Maybe I'll toss you off so you make my panties all wet,' she murmured. 'Then when I put them on, I'll feel all your cream on me and I can think about you and your cock and what it does to me.'

I put my hand on her mouth. When she talked like that – and she loved to say things like that – it was difficult to stop myself from letting a flood come out, and after that story I had this great urge to push myself deep into Teresa. And that's what I did. I rolled her over, unleashed my cock from the confines of the panties and sank deep inside her.

Teresa was always talking about those magic moments, those sudden realizations about what is going to happen, and this was one of them. Imagine how I felt, with my cock prodding out of that red nylon, those panties wet with Teresa's juices and my cock just nosing into her very silky, very creamy slit, pushing in till I was feeling that wetness clamping me in its velvety grip and it just made me want to press in deeper and deeper. Teresa and me. If Benny said that hook to Judy's jaw was the best punch he'd thrown, then this leisurely, excruciatingly exciting pleasure, this rich warm soft slipperiness my cock was immersed in, well, when I did this with Teresa, I always thanked my stars I'd met her, for each time I thought it was the best fuck I'd ever had. A knock-out, you might say. And every time we came together, it was a more complete knock-out than ever before.

10. Hoopla and Blind Man's Buff

My Maltese connection was finished. At least that's
what I thought. The eight women had been billeted at
Margo's for about ten days. They were being 'straightened out,' Teresa told me, and then a few days later,
when Gerry had rounded up eight 'helpers', they were
to be married off and so become British citizens. The
men, as payment, were allowed a week's 'honeymoon'
with their brides though this arrangement was a little
different from a normal marriage – the honeymoon
took place before the marriage. That gave Gerry time to
organize all the necessary papers and official business
at the registry offices. I suspected that in fact Gerry
needed the time to provide false papers. After the
honeymoon and the wedding, the women were to
become part of Margo's call-girl service for a year or so,
then they were free to go their own way unless they
took the option of staying on with Margo.

I didn't expect to see any of the women again,
except perhaps for Carmella who had indicated that
she might be interested. But I hadn't had a chance to go
round to Margo's as Gerry kept me busy for a couple of
weeks after I'd come back from Malta, doing deliveries
on my own, though once I went with Helen. I wasn't
seeing much of her now. She was working on her own
and she was still carrying on with Bledsoe, spying on
him for Gerry, I supposed.

On the way back from the delivery I made with her, Helen turned to me as she was driving, still as reckless as ever, and said, 'Don't arrange anything for the day after tomorrow, not for the evening anyhow.'

'Wednesday? Why not?'

'Gerry's throwing a party at the club. He always does that when he brings in new girls. A celebration before they go off on their honeymoons. You'll enjoy it. Gerry throws terrific parties.'

'Who'll be going?'

'Well, the girls of course and their intendeds. Then Gerry normally invites all the people who've helped in the operation over the last few months. I guess Margo will be there. And Teresa. And a few others. Not a lot of people. But we usually whoop it up. Great time. And he asked me to make sure you'd be there.'

'I'll be there. What time?'

'Oh, about nine or so. At the club.'

'This Wednesday?'

'Right!'

When I saw Teresa that night, I asked her if she was going to the party that week. 'Sure I'm going. Tomorrow night, nine o'clock. Got the girls all ready.'

'Tomorrow? Helen told me it's Wednesday.'

'Well, she's got the day wrong. Too strung out on her pills to remember the right day, I suppose.'

'You sure it's tomorrow? Short notice, isn't it? I mean, I didn't learn about it till today.'

'Well, you know Gerry. He likes to keep things quiet. It's a kind of personal thing with him. He's very particular who he invites. We wouldn't want someone like Bledsoe gate-crashing, would we? But he always makes sure all the right people know about it. Haven't you noticed? He's been telling the members that he's having some work done on the club and it's going to be done this week. The club'll be closed to them but that's so we can have the place to ourselves.'

'I'd better tell Helen if I see her, that she's got the wrong day, I mean.'

'Why bother? She'll find out, I suppose, when she comes down from taking her pills.'

So, while I thought my Maltese connection was over, I was going to see the women again – the Maltesers, as I called them to myself. Maltesers – I was sure Margo would turn them all into delectably chocolate-coated delights and they'd just melt in anybody's mouths. I was particularly interested in seeing what Carmella would look like, and also see how Margo had worked on those five who had been so waif-like and forlorn when I had first seen them in the Nissen hut.

I arrived at the club just before nine, not wanting to miss any of the party. I was the first guest there so I sat at the bar and talked to Benny. A musician was strumming rather listlessly at the piano and then two waitresses came in. One of them was Dorothy and she came over to say hello. 'I'm only waiting on for a couple of hours,' she told me.

'Is that all? I'm sorry you're not staying for the party.'

'Oh, but I am. Not as a waitress though. Gerry wants me to do my act, see how it goes over now that Judy's out of commission.' She nudged me with her elbow. 'I've added a few new bits. And once I've done the dance, Gerry says I can stay for the rest of the party. In fact, he made a point of saying I should stay. See you later.'

Soon Gerry came in with three other men. They

were all young like me so I supposed they were errand boys as well. I thought maybe I'd talk to them later in the evening to ask them what kind of things they did. A few more people dribbled in – though Helen had said it would only be a small party, there were more people there than I imagined there'd be. It was becoming more obvious that Gerry's business was a lot bigger than I'd thought at first. After only ten days or so he'd managed to round up eight young men as 'husbands' and I knew he had brought in other consignments of women before so he must have had other men ready to become husbands for those women as well. And if these eight were going to be gone for a week on their honeymoons, he would surely have some others ready to carry on with the deliveries and whatever other jobs he needed doing. Margo also must have had some helpers – I knew Teresa worked for her but there must have been others scattered about in those houses Gerry owned. And Gerry also had people like Margery Nicholson spying for him.

I hinted at this to Teresa soon after I'd come back from Malta but she didn't tell me much: maybe she didn't know any more than I did though she had picked up a few things from Margo. She did, however, pass on an interesting tit-bit. 'Gerry asked me if I thought you'd like to go on a "honeymoon".'

'With one of the Maltesers?'

'Yes. In fact, he said he could arrange it with Carmella for you.'

'Really?'

'That's unusual for Gerry. He doesn't arrange things like that. He likes it to happen sort of spontaneously.'

'How's that?'

'You'll see. Anyhow, it seems Carmella told Margo

she'd been a help to you and she'd liked the way you'd treated the girls, so Gerry suggested maybe you'd like to go with her.' She paused. 'What did you two get up to?'

'Nothing really. She just helped me deal with paying off the bloke at the other end.'

'Well, just watch it! I don't mind the way things happen here at the club. I mean, we all join in but I draw the line at you going on a honeymoon. After all, you can always honeymoon with me.'

'I know that.'

'So I told Gerry you were not available just yet.'

'That's right.'

'Well, you'll see Carmella at the party. And all the others.'

I was looking forward to it. I'd seen what happened at the dances and I'd always liked the nights with the strippers. And I really wanted to see what had happened to the Maltesers.

Other young men ambled in, one or two of them looking thuggish. Gerry talked to them and they sat around and drank beer. I chatted to some of them but it was clear none of us knew much about Gerry's business. I may have seen them in the club some nights but I wasn't sure. In any case, Gerry always liked to keep things under wraps so he never made any introductions unless it was absolutely necessary. I noticed that some of them looked a little anxious and I supposed they were the honeymooners waiting to see what their brides would be like.

Before the Maltesers arrived in walked Margery, slipping off her coat, handing it to Benny and ordering a Brandy Alexander. She waved briefly to two or three men, smiled, sipped her drink, then turned to me and said, 'Done anything indecent recently?'

I shook my head. 'Nothing out of the ordinary, and certainly not in public.'

She smiled again. 'A pity. You're pretty good at it.' Her eyes twinkled over the rim of her glass. 'Maybe we'll be able to fix that tonight.' She was looking fantastic. Her plain but vividly blue dress fitted snugly round her breasts, cinched tightly at the waist, then floating widely down to knee length. She sat on a bar stool and quite deliberately crossed her legs. 'I know you like to look at legs,' she said. 'Pity there isn't a ladder I can climb up for you.'

'The view's terrific from here.'

'I can see you haven't lost your knack of paying compliments.' She sipped her drink, then winked. 'Maybe we'll see whether you still have your knack with . . . other things tonight.'

I asked her how things were going at the tea company especially after the robbery. 'Oh, that threw them into a real tizzy, that did. The police came round. Found nothing of course. They put new locks on. And then they forgot about it. I suppose the insurance paid up. Anyhow, I left last week.'

She took a long sip of her brandy. 'A girl like me. Have to keep on the move if I want to keep drinking these expensive drinks. And Gerry wants me to go to another place soon. He said I needed a rest first so I've been taking it easy. I'm raring to go tonight though.'

The pianist was now playing some slow tunes so I danced with Margery. She was very cosy next to me. At one point she said, 'My! I can feel you're raring to go as well!' Dorothy and the other waitress were also dancing, Gerry was talking to Benny so I imagined the party was about to get under way. I was surprised that

Helen had not come in but I expected she would arrive soon.

But it was Margo and Teresa who arrived next with the Maltesers. They were greeted with a round of applause. What a transformation had taken place! Teresa walked straight over to me and asked, 'What d'you think?'

'I wouldn't think they were the same girls!'

'We've whipped them into shape, haven't we?'

'Shape' was the right word. They all looked in terrific shape, some in tight dresses, some in full skirts and silky blouses with deep necklines, some in short, snug skirts. Most of them had their long hair fluffed out or curled at the shoulder. Most of them still looked a little bewildered and shy but Margo was bustling around, urging the young men to dance with them. Teresa touched my arm briefly, then said, 'I'd best go and help Margo. Then I'll be back for a dance.'

I watched her walk away and as usual admired her from the back. It looked as if her dress was a second skin. As I was watching her, someone tapped me on the shoulder. It was Carmella. Margo had put her in a red dress, filmy and full, that floated around her when she moved but clung to her figure when she stopped.

'Hi!' she said. 'Pussy?'

I didn't know whether she'd seen me watching Teresa or whether she was alluding to herself. Maybe she meant both so I simply replied, 'Yes.'

She laughed. 'OK.' She watched the couples dancing for a few seconds. 'Nice,' she said. 'Dancing like fucking, yes?' She extended her hand to me. 'Can I have the next fuck with you?'

I laughed back at her and took her out onto the floor. She fitted herself against me tightly as she whispered in my ear. 'I bring the money with me. Maybe you want it back. Or you want to get it – in the same place.' She glanced down at her cleavage. 'Margo tell me you had birthday.' She touched herself at the neckline of her dress. 'Maybe I give you present.'

'Why, Carmella, you're almost a married lady.'

'After my honeymoon, you come see me, yes?'

'That would be nice.'

'Very nice. Pussy and suck and fuck.'

'Your English is getting better.'

'Margo give me a few words.'

'I bet she did!'

'But I know some before.'

The dancing went on, the couples in slow, smoochy clinches, the drinking was steady but no one became raucous. The lights were low, the music from the piano dreamy. A few men came in, spiffily dressed wide boys with their gaudy women. One or two I'd seen in the club before but most of them I didn't know. And there was still no sign of Helen.

So the atmosphere was becoming very relaxed. The Maltesers were mingling, Margo keeping an eye on them, the young men were circulating and I was dancing, mostly with Teresa, once or twice more with Margery and things were obviously moving towards that kind of sexy, enticing mood I'd noticed at the dances.

Then Gerry stood up and called for silence. 'I know you don't want to hear me nattering on. But I'd just like to welcome you all. Have a great time tonight – you deserve it. You've all worked hard these past few weeks so you can go to town tonight! And we'll get off to a great start with . . . Dorothy!'

The pianist played a few chords, then broke into a

rolling, insistent boogie beat and Dorothy swayed into the centre of the dance floor. She was in her waitress dress and began the strip she'd danced for me. It started in the same way – she was soon fondling a long, French loaf around her bare breasts, dancing close to one man after another, stroking the loaf on their faces, then pushing it across her breasts. Soon the loaf was poking beneath her dress. She sat on one man's knee, putting the loaf between his thighs near his crotch so it stuck up and she ran her fingers up and down it, finally pushing it under her skirt. It poked up inside the material and her face took on a surprised look. She beat at the loaf with her hands, slapped the man's face gently, then removed the loaf.

Then she somehow managed to place two rolls at the end of the loaf and rubbed all of that arrangement around her body before she opened her mouth to let the end of the loaf slide in, her hands holding the two rolls.

Much of the dance was the same as the one she had performed for me so I was looking out for the new bits she'd told me she'd added.

She danced over to the buffet Gerry had piled with food for us and she took two curled balls of butter. She sashayed back to the centre of the floor with the butter and stuck a ball on each nipple. The music was very slow now and she swayed slowly over to a table, took a breadstick from a basket, scooped a little butter from her breasts, pushed it out and into the mouth of one of the Maltesers sitting at the table, sliding it in, then out, then in deeply. The Malteser bit the end off, Dorothy looking at her in mock horror, looking at the stub of breadstick left, shaking her head, grinning, then throwing it away, taking another and repeating the procedure till all the butter had been wiped off her nipples. They now glistened with a thin film of shiny grease and she began to run her fingers round and round them, her face growing into a happy smile as she did it.

She went on to perform the bottle and cigar routine till eventually, to close her dance, she laid a large tablecloth on the floor and as she writhed around seductively on it, she touched herself all over with rolls and the bottle. Benny brought her a bottle of champagne and when he opened it, the froth gushed out and Dorothy let it pour out over her breasts, rubbing the neck of the bottle between them. She spread whipped cream on herself, letting it dribble down to her triangle of pubic hair where it was mixed with the champagne to become a sticky fluid moistness, slick and slippery. She scooped her fingers in it and licked it lovingly with her tongue, letting it cover her lips.

While the way I've described it makes it sound a messy dance, Dorothy brought it off with a kind of innocent panache. The audience was delighted and gave her a big round of applause. It was just the right performance to set the mood – sexy, not too serious, even funny at times, and altogether enjoyable. So Gerry's announcement after she had finished was just right. 'I hope that has whet your appetites. In a few minutes we're going to have a few party games. We just have to set them up so while we're doing that, why don't you follow Dorothy's example and eat?' Gerry obviously meant everyone should go over to the buffet but a few took Dorothy's example in a different way and began nuzzling each other, stroking, hands slipping inside blouses, one couple feeding each other breadsticks in a suggestive manner.

Benny was setting out two rows of chairs on the dance floor and by the chairs in one row he set packs of cards. Then Gerry asked people to go back to their places – the first game was ready.

'It's a very simple card game. Our new ladies do not know too much English yet but they know something about cards; at least they know the difference between red and black – and that's all they need to know for this game. And as you can see, most of them are dressed in red and black, very appealing colours for ladies. And who knows? Maybe we'll find out if they continue their colour schemes in places we can't see . . . at the moment.'

He signalled to Margo and she collected the Maltesers, sitting them in one row of chairs. Then Gerry's eight 'husbands' came onto the floor and sat in the other row. They all picked up the cards from the floor.

Gerry said, 'We're going to play our version of Strip Jack Naked but the rules are a little simpler.' Then he pointed out to all of us sitting watching. 'And you can join in if you want. You'll see there's a pack of cards on each table. We call our game Strip Jack and Jill Naked, a very easy game to play. Here's how it goes. The girls here have to decide whether the card turned up by the man opposite them is red or black. That's all and that's when the fun begins. If they guess wrong, they have to undo a button, unbuckle a belt, unzip a zipper. And when all the buttons and so on are undone, the next time they guess wrong, off that piece of clothing comes. Of course it's a bit slow to start with – most dresses and blouses have a few buttons but once they're out of the way, the rest of the clothing doesn't have too much to unfasten. Oh, and by the way, our jacks here,' and he pointed to the men in the chairs, 'don't get off scot free. If the girls guess right, they have to do the button and buckle thing. Fair shares for all.' Then he pointed out at us. 'The same goes for you!'

'How about you, Gerry?' someone shouted.

'Don't worry. We'll all join in.' He turned to Dorothy. 'Why don't you go and join Nick? He doesn't want to be left out, I'm sure.' I gestured at Teresa sitting next to me. 'Oh yes, Teresa's joining in. You'll see. Come on up here, Teresa.'

Teresa went onto the floor as Dorothy came over to my table. Gerry went on, 'A card game goes better when there are wild cards and this one will have two wild cards. Teresa here and . . .' He pointed to Margery who was strolling onto the floor, ' . . .Margery.' Teresa and Margery stood opposite each other at the ends of the rows of chairs. 'Here's how the wild cards work. Each pack has two jokers. When a joker turns up, our two wild card ladies join in. That's their cue to do what everyone else is doing.'

'Including you, Gerry!'

'Alright, I haven't forgotten.' He took a pack of cards out of his pocket. 'See. I'm all prepared. Come on up here, Margo.' And she joined him on the small stage. 'I'm onto a good thing here.' He opened his jacket to show his waistcoat. 'Lots of buttons. But look at Margo!' She was wearing a dark green dress, belted at the waist. Gerry turned her around so we could see the back. 'Look there! Just a hook and eye at the top and then one long zipper down the back.' He laughed. 'So, are we all set?' Those of us sitting round the club yelled, 'Yes!' and Gerry said, 'Right! Let the games begin!'

Dorothy handed me the pack of cards. She was

wearing a white blouse with three large buttons and a
skirt with five buttons down the side. 'I'm ready,' she
said. 'I can be the wild card as well, if you like.'

So the cards began to turn and the air was soon
filled with cries of 'red' and 'black' followed by
screeches, cheers and laughs and soon all around men
and women were in various stages of undress. I was
keeping an eye on Teresa even though I was playing
with Dorothy, whose blouse was already off and she
had undone two of my fly buttons with some winking
and nudging, fumbling with her hands so I was very
stiff, as indeed were most of the men. All around the
room dresses and blouses and skirts were shucked.

As there were two jokers in each pack belonging to
the men in the row of chairs, both Teresa and Margery
were in the process of peeling clothes off. Teresa's tight
dress was held in place by only one long zipper so she
was soon standing in her slip and as there were no
buttons on that she was soon down to panties and bra.
With very few buttons left to deal with, she would
soon be completely naked – not that she minded; she
was a thorough exhibitionist. She looked delectable in
her long-legged stance wearing a garter belt, black
stockings and high heels.

Then I heard Margery shout across to her, 'You're
way ahead. I'll take the next few jokers.' And within a
few minutes she was laughingly swirling off her blue
dress to reveal her voluptuous figure in tight-clinging
black knickers (as she called them) and a very filmy
black bra. She was completely immersed in the spirit
of the game, not at all the snooty person I'd first taken
her to be.

Gerry was doing well with Margo. She was already
out of her dress and was strutting seductively around

Gerry in a form-fitting slip of brilliant green. In fact, the
club was a riot of colour, for the Maltesers and the
other women were wearing some of Gerry's most
exotically provocative and highly coloured lingerie —
shimmering blue slips, white see-through camisoles,
black panties with high slits at the sides, tight red
panties, lots of frills and lace. Most of the women had
lost their shyness with their clothes, moving with
sexual motions closer to their men, most of whom
were now with their shirts off, some down to just their
underpants. I had only one button left to unfasten on
my shirt, my trousers were already discarded. Close by
me Dorothy unhooked her bra and was left in deliciously lacy panties.

The whole club was full of that highly charged
sexuality I had noticed during the dances, though this
was infinitely more daring in its openness with everybody involved in the action. It was exactly the kind of
game Helen liked to play and I was a little disappointed that she hadn't arrived in time to take part.
She would have made the most of it but looking round
I couldn't say I really missed her. After all, she had
been acting unreliably and she might have been in a
bitchy mood. In any case, there were too many gorgeous, half-dressed women to look at.

Eventually Gerry shouted that the game was over.
There were moans and groans from everyone but he
shouted over the noise, 'We have some other games to
play yet and they're even more interesting! Everybody
back to your places please!'

When I was back at my table I found myself surrounded by Teresa, Margery and Dorothy, all appeal-
ingly half-dressed — another situation I'd never
dreamed I could have been in just a few months back.

The three young women were all obviously eager to be with me. On my left Teresa, in just her panties, garter belt and stockings, stroked the inside of my thigh, a finger occasionally straying to slide under the elastic high on my thigh. On my right, Dorothy was sitting in her white, almost see-through panties and she was stroking my other thigh. Behind me was Margery. She was pressing her bare breasts along my shoulders, one of her hands fondling my neck and upper back under my shirt, the other tracing my backbone down towards my arse, sometimes slipping her fingers under my underpants to fondle the crack of my arse.

Out on the floor the Maltesers were sitting at ease, enjoying showing themselves off and obviously used to being on display. The men in the chairs were not so comfortable, one or two still a little embarrassed, especially as it was obvious they were very excited by their women looking so enticing. Some were trying to hide the fact that they were excited, though one or two slouched easily in their chairs, their pelvises thrust out, making sure everyone could see just how stimulated they were.

Then Gerry spoke up. He was still dressed, relatively speaking – just his waistcoat was unbuttoned. Margo was at his side. She looked stunning in just her green bra and panties.

'Let's not forget that this is a celebration of weddings,' Gerry announced. 'The brides and grooms are breathless with anticipation.' Lots of cheering and clapping. 'The nuptials start tomorrow – with the honeymoons.' More clapping and shouting. 'Now these ladies from Malta, new here, don't quite know what to expect. Well, they know what happens on honeymoons – don't we all?' Cheering, laughing, whistles. 'But like most ladies, they'd like to know if these gents will measure up to their expectations. So we have a little game for them to help them find out. It's our own version of Blind Man's Bluff, just to see if they can tell by touch just how the men measure up, if you know what I mean. It's also a kind of "Guess Your Weight" game – but it's not weight they'll be guessing.' The audience laughed along with Gerry. 'And if they guess correctly, then that's the way they'll choose their husband. And those who don't guess correctly, they get another chance because we have another game ready for them. So, on your marks, gentlemen.'

The eight men stood up. 'Now, ladies.' The women stood up.

Margo had moved onto the floor and was leading the first woman – it was Carmella – to the first man, the other women in a line behind her. 'Here's your chance to examine each man. Take your time but you have to move on to the next after a minute. Just get to know him . . . with your hands. Only your hands. Then it'll be Blind Man's Bluff. So if you recognize someone then, that'll be the man for you.'

I'm not sure the Maltesers understood much of this but Teresa later told me that she and Margo had instructed them in what they were supposed to do. It was probable that Margo had made certain Carmella would be the first because she knew some English and was the most outgoing. 'Those of you out there can join in and play the game with each other if you want to. And, to make sure you get a proper examination, you're allowed to remove anything that gets in the way. Off you go, Carmella.'

The first man in line was standing with his shirt undone but still with his underpants on and he was showing a noticeable bulge. Carmella, being the ham she was, was rubbing her hands, a great big smile on her face. She stood back from the man and slowly stretched out her hand and with her fingertips she traced the length of the man's shaft through his underpants. Her other hand rose up his thigh and stopped to curl round his balls. She slipped her hand inside his pants then looped her thumb and finger round the base of his prick and slowly slid that loop up the length. She turned to demonstrate to those watching just how thick the man was by holding up the ring her thumb and finger formed. Then she gave the thumbs up sign. Everyone laughed.

Carmella turned back and hooked her fingers in the man's waistband, lifted the band carefully down and out, then quickly tore the underpants down to his ankles. His cock sprang stiffly up. The other men in the line were gazing at this exhibition and it was obvious that what Carmella was doing was having a great effect on them. Two already had their underpants off and both of them were twitching their cocks in appreciation and anticipation.

By now Carmella was stooping down a little and her face was very close to the first man's shaft, her fingers very delicately rolling back skin, fingers circling, other fingers holding his balls. Then she was sliding her fingers down, spreading them wide in his pubic hair, then up, then down again, each time going a little faster, the man now beaming and thrusting his prick hard into Carmella's hands.

'Time's up, Carmella. Move on,' shouted Gerry. Then he said to the man, 'Sorry about that but you've got all the others to come yet!'

Carmella moved on to the next man, this time

grasping the cock firmly in both hands, wrapping many fingers around the length and squeezing. The next Malteser was stroking the first man up and down. 'Keep it moving, ladies. Oh, I can see you are keeping it moving! I mean, keep moving down the line.' And soon the women were passing on from man to man and by the time the sixth and seventh women came to them, they were all in a high state of excitement, and as new fingers came to touch them, they flinched with pleasure. They had to speak out their names as each woman came to them and towards the end their voices occasionally faltered and groaned as they were fondled.

I glanced around and saw a few watching couples in small groups were participating in their own way. One or two women were trying different methods – I saw two women bending low at a man's crotch and in fact now the Maltesers were stooping, faces only inches away from the pulsing cocks they were holding. 'Only hands, please, ladies, much as you might like to sample the measure with something else. Save that for your honeymoons!'

Even Margo was joining in. She had gone back to Gerry and was delving inside his trousers. 'Steady on, Margo. Fair's fair. You've done your measuring down there lots of times. Take someone else's measure!' But she kept on, her hands working inside Gerry's trousers.

While all this was going on, Teresa's hand had moved up my thigh inside my underpants and she had her hands full with my balls, squeezing the thick base of my cock. Dorothy's hand had also crawled up; her fingers slid under my waistband and her fingertips were fluttering around my cock-head and sometimes I could feel one finger prodding carefully at the slit of my cock as if she was trying to induce a little cream there. Margery had found a cushion from somewhere and was now sitting on the floor between my thighs. Both her hands were inside my pants, pushing and pulling at my prick. Teresa whispered in my ear as she held her hand deliciously tightly on me, 'I'd recognize this anywhere.' Even Dorothy murmured, 'Once is not enough. We should try it again.' Margery was simply sitting below me, grinning up at me. Maybe the Brandy Alexanders had made her lose her snootiness. Certainly the way her fingers were working on me gave no indications that she was at all stuck up.

'Alright, alright!' Gerry announced. 'It's pay-off time! Let's see who's remembered what! Who's got the best memory?' Margo and Benny were now walking along the line of Maltesers tying black cloths round the women's eyes. 'I told you it was Blind Man's Bluff. Now, if you guess right, that's your man and you can go off with him to start your honeymoon. Come back for the wedding next week.' The men had been shuffled around into a different order in their line. Then the Maltesers started again, each one being led down the newly formed line. From then on they simply took one step to the side, fumbling their hands out to make a grab for the next knob sticking out. They shouted out names and, whether by chance or by some instinctive memory, three women, including Carmella, guessed the right name. When that happened, Margo pulled the woman out of the line and the man followed. They walked over to Gerry who gave the man a piece of paper. Teresa told me that the paper had the name of a hotel on it where the couple could stay or instructions to go to Margo's or one of the other houses. There was also a reminder about the wedding for the following week – the man was responsible for making sure he knew which registry office he should take his partner to.

I was still being attended to by my three ladies and off in some corners couples were cuddled together, some embracing standing up, leaning against the walls, others leaning back in their chairs with partners bending over them. At this rate I couldn't see how the party would go on much longer as everybody was becoming so involved with each other. But I was wrong.

Once the game of Blind Man's Bluff had finished there were still five couples to be paired off so Gerry introduced the next game. Those left were lined up in their separate rows facing each other.

'It's hoopla time now!' Gerry explained. 'These ladies are going to have a throwing contest to choose their partners. They can throw at any of these men but naturally it'll be easiest for them to throw at the man opposite them. But they can take their chances with others if they want.' Benny had now deposited a pile of large throwing rings near the women. 'Of course there's a catch. The women can take their chances, throwing for any of the men they fancy. But the rings are not free. They have to buy a hoop with any article of clothing they're still wearing.'

Of course the women didn't have much clothing left. Most had stockings and garter belts, two had somehow managed to retain their panties, one still had a bra.

Gerry went on, 'I suppose it's obvious to everyone what they have to throw the rings on to!' Some laughter rang out. 'If the man really wants to be the partner of the one throwing at him, he can help any way he wants. Move himself so the hoop will land on the right . . . place! And if the ladies miss, they can then step one pace closer and buy another ring with another piece of clothing. Ready, ladies?'

There was a rolling down of stockings, an unclipping of a bra, one shoe was kicked off, a garter belt unfastened. The hoops were thrown – two collided in mid-air, the other three clattered to the floor though two of the men frantically danced towards the rings, wagging their cocks in a vain endeavour to catch them.

'Come along, ladies,' Gerry encouraged. 'Buy another one, then step up.' More stockings and shoes and garter belts came off. More hoops were thrown and two floated over cocks. These couples jumped up and down and then ran over to Gerry who gave them their piece of paper. He then spoke to the three couples remaining in the throwing game.

'Now, don't be shy. This looks like your last chance, Helga.' Helga in response took off her garter belt, stepped forward and threw a perfect hoop and so off she went with her man.

Gerry went to the next woman. 'Now, Frankie. Your turn.' She was left with a pair of stockings. She stretched her leg out and rolled a stocking down very carefully showing the shapeliness of her leg. When she threw she missed. 'Take the other one off!' someone yelled and she did, then threw and the ring plopped neatly over the man opposite her. Away they went.

'Well, Maria,' Gerry said, going to her and putting his arm round her, 'you're the last one.' Maria was looking sheepish but beautiful. She had retained a certain shyness throughout the proceedings but she had joined in willingly enough. Now she was centre stage but she was game to continue, in spite of her reticence. I suppose her shyness accounted for the fact that she was still wearing her panties. But that was all she was wearing.

'Just one more chance for you, Maria,' Gerry told her. 'Are you going to try?' Maria nodded timidly, then stepped towards the remaining man.

Gerry tried to pull her back. 'You have to pay first.' She took one more step towards the man, stopping quite close to him.

'Hey! Pay up, Maria!' Gerry was still insisting.

Then Maria broke into a smile and unexpectedly, very tantalisingly, she began to slide her lacy red panties down, showing first one nicely curvaceous buttock, then another, pulling the front down to show a curly-haired mound. Slowly and deliberately she pushed the lacy silk down, lifting her foot out, showing a shapely leg, then pulled the other foot out. She stood still, holding the panties hanging down from the ends of her fingers.

'Want your hoop now?' Gerry asked her, smiling she shook her head. 'Well, what can I say? You have to throw to win, Maria. You have to make it land on him.'

Maria, with one more seductive step forward, stared at the man's stand for a few seconds. She raised the panties high and then let them descend to drape his cock, giving him a gentle stroke with the silk and letting them hang there. Then her hand went out to him again and she placed her fingertips on the panties just at the end of his cock and led him over to Gerry who said, grinning at her, 'That's just as good as a hoop, I guess.' Someone yelled, 'Better! Better!' and Gerry gave the couple their paper.

My ladies had still continued their ministrations while all this was happening and, as the game was

226

now over, I assumed we'd just be concentrating on each other. I thought the party was virtually over so I looked forward to going up to Teresa's flat as I'd arranged with her earlier. Benny and one of the other men were collecting the chairs together and moving them to the side and then they were pushing in a long wide sofa draped with a purple silk throw. I imagined Gerry was installing it there for one of the couples to stay the night and I supposed some of the others would drift upstairs like me to stay in the flats. I presumed Gerry himself would go back to Margo's.

Margo had changed out of her green bra and panties. She was still wearing that vivid green but it was hardly a gown – it was long but more like a full length slip with a wide skirt edged in black lace, the upper part outlining her breasts. It fitted so tightly it was clear she was wearing nothing underneath.

There were only about thirty of us left now. The pianist had gone and so had the other waitress, though Dorothy was still with me. It certainly looked as if the party was winding down and would finish over the next half hour or so. I was contemplating asking Teresa if all three of us should retire to her flat but I never got around to that. Things did not turn out as I had imagined they would. The party was not winding down. I was wrong about that, quite delectably wrong, as I was soon to find out.

Gerry was standing by the ottoman with Margo when he began to speak to those of us remaining. 'Ladies and gentlemen. I hope you've all enjoyed yourselves this evening. You deserve to because you've all worked hard these last few months. But I thought we shouldn't break up tonight before I mentioned something important. What we have been celebrating here tonight is mostly the work of one person and I think we should all give him a big round of applause. I mean Nick.'

He pointed at me and the three ladies pulled me to my feet.

'This is Nick, ladies and gentlemen. Come on out here, Nick.'

I ought to have felt embarrassed. After all, my three ladies had been working me over all along so when I walked out onto the dance floor, I was sticking well out in front in my underpants. The three girls accompanied me and Margo also guided me by the elbow. All four of them obviously knew that this was going to happen for they were all smiling at me.

'Nick did the Malta run safely and soundly.' Gerry announced and applause followed. I was more embarrassed by the applause than by standing there in front of people half-dressed. That didn't matter because nearly everybody else was in the same state of undress. And I'd had a few beers.

'What's more, just a few days ago Nick had a birthday. Now I know Teresa gave him a present that night I'm sure he enjoyed.' There were a few laughs at that. 'But I really wanted to give Nick a special present tonight, from all of us, but particularly from these three delicious ladies who've been looking after him all evening. In fact, these ladies have looked after him at other times as well. And so has Margo. She didn't want to be left out tonight because she was the one who convinced me that Nick was the lad to send to Malta.'

Margo stepped up to me and gave me a lovely, sloppy, tongue-tickling kiss, grabbing my cock very persuasively as she did so. A big round of applause followed. 'So, Nick,' Gerry continued, 'one more game.

Your very special present is one more game of Blind Man's Bluff and, believe me old son, this Blind Man's Bluff is going to be like nothing you ever played when you were a kid.'

Teresa, Dorothy and Margery were all standing near grinning at me. For just a moment I thought I was going to be blindfolded, then let loose to catch one of the three. Whoever I caught, I'd take to the ottoman and find whatever pleasure I wanted with her. But Gerry explained a different game.

'You've had a little experience with these three lovely ladies.' Then Margo whispered in his ear. 'Oh, I nearly forgot. Of course this lovely lady here,' and he indicated Margo, 'is included as well. So what happens is this. We put a blindfold on you, you stretch out on the sofa and the three ladies . . .' He stopped because Margo was looking daggers at him. 'Later, Margo, later for you.' He turned back to me. 'Well, you're blindfolded and then, to begin with, these three ladies will touch you in whatever way they want and with whatever they fancy. As you know them, and their touches, maybe you'll be able to guess just who is touching you. You can go ahead and guess any time you want during the game. And when you've got five right guesses, we take the blindfold off. The game doesn't end with that – now you can see them, you can go after them any way you want. Understood?'

I nodded and grinned foolishly. 'Of course they may try to fool you so save your guesses till you're sure. At first you'll probably just want to lie back and enjoy yourself. That's alright, that's part of the game. But we'll see just how much you remember about these ladies. Sometimes they'll take it in turns, sometimes they'll operate together, or just two of them. You'll never know what's coming next. Are you ladies ready?' The three of them smiled their readiness. Margo whispered in Gerry's ear again. 'Margo's just reminding me she reserves the right to join in any time she wants to – when she gets the urge. And you know what she's like when she gets the urge!'

My back was turned to Gerry as I was looking at the three ladies so I was suddenly surprised when I felt gentle hands slipping my shirt, unbuttoned earlier, from my shoulders. Soon I recognized that it was Margo for she stepped very close to me and I could feel the silky surface of her slip/gown on my skin, her breasts squashed against my back. Her hands moved from my shoulders and she tied a cloth over my eyes, turned me around, kissed me gently and said, 'This isn't a firing squad, you know. These girls are just going to be going for your gun!'

Hands then guided me towards the ottoman, and when I knocked against it with my knees, I was turned and pushed down on it. The purple cloth draped on it was deliciously soft on my back and after a minute or so it was folded over to cover me completely. Hands began to stroke the silkiness all over – my legs, thighs, stomach, chest, shoulders, face. I never knew where the next touch was going to be though the touches deliberately avoided my centre even though my erection was strong and hard, thrusting up inside my underpants.

Then the cover was drawn back and by a movement of air I could tell that two of them were holding the cover up on both sides so I presumed those watching couldn't see what was going on behind the cover. Not that too many would be watching, I felt, they would be too busy playing their own games with their partners by this time in the evening. And that was a further reason why it no longer mattered to me that I was on view: I was merely a part of the sex-drenched mood of all those still in the club.

Then a pair of hands gently slid inside my waistband, carefully lifted it out and over my cock so it sprang free. Lips placed a quick wet kiss on the tip, drew my underpants down and off. There were one or two cheers and desultory clapping – I imagined whoever it was emerged with my underpants, waved them in the air like a flag, then threw them aside.

And so began one of the most memorable, most exhausting, most fulfilling sexual experiences of my life. Since then I have managed to live an active sex life and inveigled myself into some uncommonly kinky, lavishly lascivious, lazily indolent, breathtakingly long-lasting extravaganzas of sex but this one remains the best.

It happened many years ago now but I can still remember many of the details, though of course my memory has blurred the exact order of events. I'll try to describe it as best I can but anything I write here will fall far short of the sexual pleasure those three lavished on me.

It started quietly and gently enough, so much so that I wondered later whether the three had talked things over before. It became apparent they had cooked this up for me: they had stayed with me through the evening and they had led me onto the floor, keeping hold of me. Anyhow, what first occurred was a tongue licking round my ears, flicking inside, a hand on each of my nipples stroking and tweaking. One lady was obviously kneeling by my head, leaning down to put her open mouth on mine, her tongue probing in, circling my teeth, hands sliding down across my stomach.

I suspected the kisser was Margery with her luscious lips though she was not sucking my tongue hard as she had done on our date. She was soft and moist, her lips slowly sliding across mine. I flailed my arms out carefully, searching to touch something and a breast was slotted into my palm and my fingers reached up to feel that rubbery hardness of nipple. The kiss grew deeper and more moist. My other hand encountered a buttock wrapped in flimsy silk and I remembered Dorothy's see-through panties. With my hand on that roundness my fingers traced a path to where the panties stretched snugly inside the crack of her arse and I imagined Dorothy sucking at my ear, circling my nipple with her fingers, bending beside me with her curvaceous arse in those filmy panties.

I thought it was probably Teresa nibbling at my other ear, tweaking my other nipple, her breast fitting its soft roundness into my palm, and then Margery's wide open mouth dribbling on mine – all this sent my cock haywire, the cock-head exposed, foreskin rolled back, my shaft poking up, twitching every now and again. Of course I had no real idea if I had the positions of the three of them correct and in a sense I didn't care. I was just content to lie there floating through this relaxing and attentive nuzzling.

Then the two at my ears let their slippery tongues slide down my arms, their hands holding me down, tongues going to my palms, licking them with wet tongue-tips, and Margery, if it was her at my mouth, moved downwards and I felt her trailing her tongue across the centre of my chest down to my navel. Naturally her breasts were now gently pressing onto my face and I managed to do some licking of my own while I experienced two hands on my knees gliding ever so meticulously up my thighs. I lay there, expecting those hands to arrive at my balls to caress them but they were too maddeningly slow. The tongue on my navel was now sliding lower, nearing my pubic hair.

It was all very tantalising, the three of them obviously aware how close they were to touching my burning centre which was raised up straight expectantly. I found this excruciating, waiting for them to touch me there as I imagined them seeing my cock so stiffly at attention, twitching and pulsing, red and fat. I thought of them bending over me, those watching seeing their arses so shapely, covered in their panties stretched tightly, red, black and white, edged with lace. My hands were held down so I couldn't reach out to smooth those curves and my imagination was beginning to make me boil with desires, with ideas of what would follow.

One of them must have made a sign for suddenly everything stopped – there was no more touching of any kind. A minute passed and nothing happened. I had a fleeting, tormenting moment when I thought all this was a joke – these people had played tricks on me before. I could hear movement around me: two of them were still wearing shoes. I also heard shimmery rustlings and I construed that was their removing whatever clothing they had left – panties, stockings, garter belts.

I was lying there, trying to construct in my mind what was going on and so I was becoming more excited. I have always been one for the visual. Much of my fascination with lingerie is the discovery of what a woman is wearing underneath a frequently very ordinary exterior. One of the most stimulating sights for me is to see a woman whose skirt and slip is bunched up near her waist, my hands having felt the soft slipperiness as I raised her clothing – and then to edge my fingers under her panties to feel the gentle scratch of hair there, then to glide a finger lower to touch her clit or slowly flex to the lips of her quim. Both Margo and Teresa had indulged my visual sense with their use of mirrors and Margery had sensed my interest in the feel of silk and nylon. Dorothy had stripped off her clothes for me. And here they all were and I was waiting for them, imagining them though I couldn't see them. But I discovered that that lack of vision enhanced the sense of touch, giving me an even more rousing experience under their expert hands and what they brought to stroke me with.

That long wait of two minutes or so made me breathless with anticipation, trying to outguess them – where would they touch me next? Would it be a frontal attack? Or some subtle infiltration with a few fingers stroking with soft silk? Or with hands slippery-slick with oil? But I never dreamed they would touch me where they did – my feet! Two pairs of hands lifted my ankles a little and fingers began to intertwine my toes. First one set of toes was coated with thin grease, then the other. Fingers poked between the toes, in and out, sliding in the grease, and of course my mind shifted to think of a cock sliding in and out of a quim. Such massaging of toes may not sound very sensual but in the darkness behind my eyes it made me deliciously excited – two women were treating my extremities in an overtly sexy manner and that pushed me on to fancy just how they would treat my more important sexual parts.

After a time the foot and toe massage stopped. My legs were raised higher and soon I felt a silky shimmering glide of nylon on my feet. I sensed that the two women there had carefully placed a pair of panties on each foot so that my legs were now being wrapped loosely in nylon – each foot had been placed through a leg-opening of the panties. Two hands on each leg let the nylon almost float along my calves, past my knee, the other part of the panties dangling down because my legs were raised.

I imagined how close that material must be to touching the tops of my thighs, eventually to brush softly at my balls, perhaps then lifted to cover my cock. The hands were relentlessly but almost imperceptibly stroking higher, the silkiness now around my thighs, a tickle of lace somewhere in my groin, nylon just tickling my balls. I was breathing heavily now, expecting fingers to take the nylon onto my balls and I was being driven crazy by the insistent stroking of my thighs and my cock was throbbing with a steady pulse.

I was trying to reach out to stroke the girls but, as I tried to sit up a little, hands applied pressure to my shoulders. Those hands then slid silky material onto my chest – a slip, I imagined – and began to rub, feeling out my nipples, then down onto my stomach, agonizingly near the end of my erect cock.

I had those three massaging me in that way for some time. Panties on my legs now briefly fluttered around my balls – one hand bunched nylon around them, feeling them out, stroking first one ball, then the other, finally fondling both. The other hands there were pushing nylon under my balls, behind them. I really couldn't make any guesses about those hands though those fingering their way behind my balls might have been Teresa's searching out my secret place. I didn't think to shout out her name because I was too involved in simply submitting to those extremely sensual touches.

Then I heard a movement at my side. I thought I had placed the three women – Teresa at one leg, Dorothy at the other leg stroking with her filmy white panties and so Margery would be still at my head, leaning onto my chest and stomach, using her black slip to excite me. So who was at my side? Could it be Margo joining in? Perhaps that long, green slip she was wearing had caused me to hear her moving and, given the nylon massage I was undergoing and remembering the one Margo gave me, I now imagined that Margo was orchestrating the whole proceedings. I fully expected her full-skirted slip to float down to enfold my cock but that didn't happen. Somehow I sensed someone striding over me as if she was going to sit on my middle. That really charged me up, for naturally I thought my prick would soon be sliding into softly moist vaginal lips pushing down and down on me to take all my length inside.

But that didn't happen either. I did feel something soft brush against the tip of my cock, then lift away, then touch again. I pushed my pelvis up, wanting my cock inside but all I managed to get was this devastating little flick. Those hands were still wrapping my balls in nylon, fingers inside the silkiness pushing behind, rimming my arsehole. The hands on my body were low down, my cock was flickering constantly now and still I felt only a little light touch on it. Then a hand held my cock – at last! But it was just a finger and thumb and that moved my cock firmly along what seemed a vaginal slit. Now, I thought, I will be taken inside. But no again. The finger and thumb simply moved my cock so that the length of my shaft moved there, not in but along, back and forth. And there was no opening to slide into. Back and forth my cock was moved, then pulled down so that it moved towards the crack of the arse of whoever was doing this to me. My balls and all that area were still in slippery nylon and my cock was being manipulated along the slit of a quim and past and along an arse-crack and then it occurred to me that this must be Margery. The women must have switched places and so it was Margery who was riding me. I remembered her knickers and the way she had held my knob between her legs letting me rub along that silk band over her quim and arse in the doorway. I had imagined all the women were now completely naked but during that pause Margery had obviously put her knickers back on and she was now teasing me with them, moving slowly across my cock.

'That's Margery over me,' I panted out.

A little clapping, a quiet whoop and Gerry's voice said, 'Right first time, Nick. Well done!'

The massaging and riding continued and then my mouth was fixed by someone's warm, open mouth, a tongue searching inside, lips moving lingeringly across mine, one of the most insididiously sexual kisses I had ever experienced. At first I thought it was Teresa but couldn't figure out how she could reach up from below without my knowing it. The same applied to Dorothy. Margo, if it was her, was at my head, I thought, so couldn't twist round to kiss me that way. That left Margery leaning down as she rode me – but the kiss was not like hers: she was an expert with her mouth, I knew, but she also liked to suck hard at my tongue. And this kiss was a lazy but dewy kiss held to an extravagant length. So I just let myself relax into it, the delectable brushing ride of Margery and the soft encasements of nylon.

My hands were now reaching up to stroke Margery's breasts and, as I touched them, I knew she hadn't leaned down to kiss me. Had one of the others moved round to do it? Yet I had felt too many fingers doing their soft massaging under my cock. So the kiss remained a mystery, part of my blindness and strangely exciting, so much so that a little jism escaped from the slit of my cock and that moisture dampened Margery's knickers, now slick with her own juice.

That open-mouthed kiss at last slid away, the mouth moving to my chin. Margery stopped her ride, clambering off me as the wet mouth moved down my chest. I knew where it was heading and I could hardly wait to push my whole stand inside its warm moistness. The two at my balls moved the nylon down my thighs and then I felt two tongues flicker around my balls. Soon those soft lips of the kisser nuzzled at my cock-head. Whoever it was knew exactly what to do. I suspected Margo but I wasn't sure. Whoever it was was now on her knees at the side of my head and she lowered herself to my face. My hands went up to stroke her thighs, my fingers splaying out till I was flicking gently at her lips there, lips softer and more moist than those which had given me the kiss. As she moved her mouth slowly down my cock, she made small, guttural sounds but I couldn't recognize the voice.

My balls were still being lapped but I couldn't figure out where Margery was after her ride on my cock. The mouth at my cock was sliding up and down, I was pushing my pelvis in time with it, my balls were slathered by busy tongues and my tongue was revolving round a juicy quim as my fingers played with a clit. I relaxed into these motions forgetting about Margery's whereabouts till I was certain she took over the flurry of silkiness now suffusing my thighs. There seemed to be four women working on me then – so it must have been Margo with her marvellous mouth and I remembered how it was when she had sucked me that first time. Yet something nagged in my head that it was somehow different. Besides, she was wearing that long slip – she could have taken it off, but then again she seemed to be enjoying floating around in it.

Hands and mouth were now pulling very slowly up my cock as if they were urging come up its length. And when the lips came to the tip they did suck in a little ooze of juice. The fingers pulled at my skin, trying to cover my cock-head, almost like a mother tucking a child into bed but, as I was so stiff, the skin rolled back immediately. Then a final soft kiss finished that part; she moved from my cock and her thighs lifted away from my hands and mouth. The tongues also stopped their licking, the stroking of my thighs came to an end and again I was left untouched. In a way I was thankful for a rest but so suffused with wanting those delicious mouths on me I longed for them to continue. But would what came next surpass all that? Again I was left breathless with anticipation.

They made me wait. They knew the exact moment when to begin again, when to stretch me out to a far sexual edge, making sure I didn't flag, seeming to know how my mind would be filling with ideas, hoping they would fulfil them. It must have been the experienced head of Margo in control and she started the others again with something very gentle. Two pairs of hands again moved those flimsy nylon panties down my legs, down my thighs, leaving one pair just below my knee, the other slid down and off. Then I felt one hand on each ankle and my legs were pulled up very high so that my cock flattened against my stomach. My legs were opened and I could sense someone between them. I knew then what was about to happen and sure enough a fingertip nudged lightly just at the rim of my arsehole. 'Teresa!' I yelled.

'Three cheers for Nick!' But nobody cheered. 'Second one on the nose . . . or some other place!' Gerry blurted out.

Teresa was holding my thighs, fingering the nylon on them. Her two hands worked at my balls, fingers rubbing gently at my secret place, one finger edging into my arse, that lovely mouth of hers spilling wetness behind my balls on that special inch, a little whiskery, her tongue at the rim of the hole, slipping in wetly, a finger probing deeply.

The other two were no longer holding my ankles and as Teresa licked and sucked and prodded at me, some slippery moist fingers softly lifted my cock away from my stomach and a thin veil of silk was folded over the fat shaft – the panties that had been taken off my leg. I guessed that material was so flimsy that it must have been Dorothy's see-through pair so I shouted her name and Gerry announced, 'Number three. You really know these ladies, Nick!'

Dorothy's hand folded the thin nylon round my cock, palm circling the cock-head, fingers spreading down my length, grasping and teasing. Her other hand took mine, sucked my fingers as if they were another prick, then placed them on her pubic mound. She must have been lying next to me – I could feel the warmth of her whole body next to me. I began to massage her wet quim, first sliding one finger in, then two and I kept on with a regular fucking motion. Then I felt another mouth on my other hand. It was Margery, I thought, standing by my head, and she too placed that hand on her pubic mound. And we stayed that way, my hands massaging two quims, Teresa's mouth and fingers doing that incredible secret searching, my cock wrapped and stroked in nylon, and then Margery's other hand rubbing damp, cunt-smelling panties – her black knickers, I supposed – all round my face and neck. It was an ecstatic experience and my voice was hoarse as I said, 'Margery!'

'Right again!' came Gerry's answer. 'One to go.'

Immediately Margery pulled herself away from me as if she wanted to conceal herself after her discovery. She came round to my head, knelt over me and lowered her pelvis to my face. These three were now offering me an extraordinary array of sensuality: I was licking at Margery's juicy quim while one of my hands was caressing her breasts; Dorothy, after the delectable stroking she'd performed, was now busy with her mouth on my cock while my other hand was doodling in and out and around her equally juicy cunt; and Teresa was still doing her excruciating but exquisite manipulation of my secret spot, fingers and mouth wandering in and out of my arse, stroking, squeezing, licking, dribbling her very moist mouth over the whole area. All four of us were caught up in what was turning into a gently heaving rhythm – we were all immersed to an immeasurable degree in complete sex, at least, as complete as it can be without cock plunging into cunt.

And that was soon to happen because one of those panting pauses came again. This time I think we all needed a rest to calm down, catch our breath, regain our sense of ourselves after we had all mingled in stroking and sucking and licking and fondling until we didn't know who was who.

Soon enough we started again. I heard the usual rustlings, the quiet steps, but I had no idea what was going to happen. Someone laid a slip carefully over my thighs, smoothing it softly across me and then one of them sat across me to let herself down on my cock, slowly, savouring the shaft, her inner, slippery muscles fluttering around the length, descending gently till my pubic hairs could feel the wetness of her outer lips. Her hands went behind her and she eased the slip round my thighs, rubbing till I felt that was almost as slippery and enticing as her quim which slid up and down till her wet slit hovered over the tip of my cock, then eased down again. She did this several times and during that time Gerry reminded me I had one more guess to free me from the blindfold. 'And remember, that doesn't mean the end of the game.'

Then I felt her move up the length of my cock and it did not come down again. Another pause and this time it was one of the other cunts sliding down my cock, this time not so slowly, letting my prick jab in fast, hands scrunching the slip into my balls, another hand holding the base of my dick so it stuck straight up. She plunged down as far as she could, my cock right inside, her stickiness slippery on my cock-head. This steady jabbing in and out continued for a while with Gerry urging me to guess who it was but I had no idea. After all, of the three I had only had my cock inside Teresa, unless Margo was also participating in this riding rotation.

They kept at it, varying the strokes, each one doing it just in short spasms, changing the pace, working the silky slip in different ways, each one seeming to know how to stop before I spurted out, my cock waiting for the next one to start. I was in a kind of trance of ecstasy, on the verge of coming time and time again, spots of jism wiped across the head of my cock by fingers before another quim mounted my stand and began yet another different rhythm. Eventually the pace slowed, the pauses between grew longer, the rides shorter. I had been trying to keep track of the changes, seeing if I could guess who the riders were but I had to give up. I am not sure if they kept the same order, I was not even sure if it was just the three of them at it. I imagined Margo might be participating again though, as the riding tailed off, then stopped, we had another pause and that was when I found out about Margo's part in all this.

After lying there expectant, my cock bathed in quim-juice and some of my come, with no action going on, even though I was still blindfolded, I suddenly became aware that I was somehow being covered, almost as if a tent was placed around my head and shoulders. I felt a trickle of lace low down on my stomach, then soft silk smoothed onto my chest by several hands. A warmth descended around my head and a musky smell as wet slipperiness met my face and a long slit, searching for my mouth, settled down on me. My hands were under that tent and I felt the shiver of nylon along my arms as I raised my hand to stroke warm thighs, then open that slit and reach up the tip of my tongue into the taste of soft quim-lips. It was Margo, I was sure, crouching over me, her long green slip spread over my body, the others sliding it around me. The whole of my upper body felt like one gigantic cock sliding into an exquisite quim. My mouth and my tongue felt like the tip of that enormous cock, urging itself inside the warm silkiness of Margo's spread vagina.

'Margo!' I spluttered.

'What's that?' Gerry's voice came to me in a muffled way.

'Margo!' I roared as loud as I could, sending the name with my tongue as deep as I could get it into her cunt.

'The boy's right, Gerry.'

Margo's hands came under her slip and lifted my head. I thought at first she wanted more of my tongue inside her, my mouth squashed in all her juiciness but she was untying my blindfold. She pulled it off and stood up.

I sat up on the ottoman to discover Teresa, Dorothy and Margery standing next to me, all naked. Margo behind me raised my arm and said, 'The winner!' Those who had been watching closely what had been going on had surely been stimulated by it so I thought they had probably followed our example in their own ways. Still, there was some cheering as well as scattered clapping.

Then Teresa reached down to hold my cock, pulled on it and said, 'The winner!' There was some laughter and I glanced around the club, now my eyes had grown accustomed to the dim light, to see how many people were left. And there, near the stage, giving me a flickering wave of the hand was Carmella. She'd been one of the first to leave with her man, I knew, but there she was. She was grinning and waving and it dawned on me that not only Margo had joined in but probably Carmella as well. So there had been five of them altogether, not three. Perhaps that deep kiss, that long and deep suck, and some of the riding of my cock had been done by Carmella. And then I remembered what she had said to me while we danced – pussy, suck and fuck – and so probably that's what she had done. I also remembered the others saying things which may have been clues – Margery had said maybe I'd be publicly indecent, Dorothy said we should try things again.

Though I had been brought repeatedly to a high state of excitement I had not come and I had clambered from the ottoman, still very obviously in a state of excitement with my stiff prick sticking out. While I was surveying the club, Teresa perched herself toward the end of the ottoman, on her knees, her arse shaped invitingly in my direction. The other two turned me around to show me. Teresa smiled and said, 'Come on Nick. I get first go.'

Margo gave me a little push. Margery lay down on the ottoman, her head under Teresa's legs while Dorothy led me by the cock into Teresa's lavishly juicy quim. Dorothy climbed on behind me, snuggling against my arse as I half knelt to push into Teresa. Dorothy rubbed her breasts against me, her nipples jutting out hard. She grabbed at a slip to rub it all over my back and again I had that feeling that the whole of my body was involved in the fucking, as if I was swimming inside a whole soft silkiness of quim as I rammed energetically into Teresa.

Margery leaned up on her elbows, her hands grasping my thighs as she licked and sucked my balls. I slowed a little so I could accommodate her sucking, her very hard pull dragging at my balls, tightening them, her tongue circling them in her mouth. We all fell into a rhythm. After all the foreplay we'd been through – foreplay, of course, is a very inadequate

245

word: it was almost like new ways of encouraging sexual feeling, a fucking beyond fucking though until that riding of my cock no fucking was involved. Anyhow, after that foreplay, I felt the need for release. I was sure I had gathered an enormous flood of come and I pushed and jabbed and slid in deeply, tickling the edges of Teresa's quim, waiting till she wanted to feel the whole length of my cock sliding inside her again.

Soon I felt the pressure begin to build, that sensation of liquefied heat gathering down in my balls, whirling up to the root of my cock, ready to spray out, me wanting to make it last, trying to hold on but dying to let go. Teresa was ready: she was waggling her arse, her quim sucking at me and, remembering how Teresa had told me she sometimes liked come to spill outside, as I felt the surge I let my prick rest at her lips and the come shot out there, flooding her arse-crack, spilling in profusion, dribbling round her arsehole. I pushed my cock along her crack as it throbbed out the last drops, spreading the hot stickiness down and Margery caught some on her tongue.

I fell back as Margery slid from under me and Dorothy held me, her hands reaching for my come-covered dick, reminding me how expertly she'd brought me off in the taxi after she'd danced for me. She wouldn't let my cock go and she made it tingle with her stroking. I was only half-erect but I somehow knew she wouldn't let me go completely limp. She slithered her hands, coated with jism, lightly around my cock, occasionally gripping it hard as if that would make it stiff again. Soon my prick began to swell a little, tingling at the tip as Dorothy smoothed a finger over it.

I felt as if a rod ran right down the centre of my cock, into my balls, iron-hard but making an ache along the length of it. Teresa had moved over me, was nibbling my ear, her tongue like a small snake trailing across my cheek, seeking my lips, flicking at them, making me open them. It squirmed inside my mouth. Margery pulled my hands onto her breasts as she stood in front of me. All these attentions had the desired effect – my cock was now as stiff and hard as that rod I'd imagined.

'Just look at that!' Dorothy murmured as she sank back onto the ottoman. I was ready for her and this time Margery's hand on my cock put me at Dorothy's slit. And in I slid, slowly, hoping I wouldn't lose my stiffness though I knew I'd have very little come to shoot out. My cock was still aching a little but my balls were now neatly balanced in Teresa's hands and that seemed to lift the weight off my prick so the ache didn't feel so bad. Every so often one of Teresa's fingers strayed onto my secret place.

Margery was fussing around us, letting nylon things – slips, panties – fall over our bodies, stuffing them in the crack of my arse, leaning into me to do her hard sucking-of-the-root-of-my-tongue kiss, slavering, smearing wetness all round my mouth. That fierce sucking of my tongue corresponded with the slight ache in my cock and in some way it made it feel harder, made me feel as if the slithering in and out, the drooling moistness of Margery's mouth round my tongue were like another flood of come. That made me speed up my probing inside Dorothy and I increased the pace.

Teresa began to push my arse in rhythm, Dorothy was panting and moaning and I honestly experienced a sense of my prick being bigger and harder than it had ever been. I thought I would bring up a spate of come from somewhere deep in my balls as Teresa's strokings down there became more insistent. Her finger was poking inside my arsehole to the same rhythm as my cock moved in and out of Dorothy. I could hear Teresa panting and Margery's voice spluttered out of her throat though her mouth was still pulling my tongue deeply in.

And so we went on and on and I could sense I was coming to climax again. My dick was pulsing fast and suddenly it seemed to burst through, with nothing to stop it, running free, out and over and deep inside Dorothy. Maybe there was come, maybe not, but I certainly felt that surge of release in a kind of spurting explosion inside her. As I pulled out, Dorothy's hands found my cock and she made it squirm and wriggle in her fingers and it felt as if it was covered with come.

Dorothy then lounged back, still with her hands all over my cock, not letting it rest. Margery had stopped her tongue-sucking to whisper. 'Three, remember. My turn now.'

'I don't think I can. Not for a long time anyhow.'

'Oh, I think I'll be able to fix that.' I remembered that's what she had said when she'd first come into the club after I told her I'd been doing nothing out of the ordinary. I also remembered Margery's take-charge attitude that evening we'd been to the cinema. So it came into my head that Margery was taking control of me right then. I was convinced that I could not help her out at all for at least an hour. Even in those early marathon sessions with Helen I'd had to take a breather but it was clear that Margery had no intention of waiting for very long. The other two lay back and seemed content to let Margery work it out for herself. They stroked my shoulders, my back, Teresa had found Margery's knickers and let them rest around my neck and I think I detected that cunty-come smell on them.

When Margery saw Teresa doing this, she began to talk to me in a low voice. I was sitting up straight and Margery was on a cushion on the floor in front of me. Her fingers were straying all round my limp cock. My balls were aching. Her finger stretched into my pubic hair, touching the base of my cock and that reminded me of the way she kissed as if my tongue would come unglued from its base. As I thought of this, strangely my limp prick twitched a little. Margery's fingers sensed it.

'There! What did I tell you?'

I didn't have the nerve or the strength to pass comment and her hands kept working on me. And she kept talking.

'Remember that night on point?' She touched the slit of my cock, opening it out between two fingers, leaned down to it and pried it open further with the tip of her tongue.

'Remember how my knickers got all wet? You spilling out all over them.'

She sucked a little of my cock into her mouth, letting it rest at her lips as she said, 'We can do it again, Nick. Properly. No knickers. On point.' My cock was remembering that evening for it swelled up a little.

'Such a nice little fellow he is,' she murmured. 'I'll bet he'll soon be growing up.' With that, she sank her mouth onto my cock, going down, her full lips at the base, then further. She began to suck at the loose skin joining the base of my cock, her tongue licking down to my balls.

I didn't really believe it but I was stiffening. She drew her lips back but they stayed at the base and she started her ferociously strong sucking again and I knew, if she ever kissed me again, I would be reminded of how strongly she had sucked my cock, as if it was some bone and she was sucking the marrow out of it. My cock responded and it began to fatten and fill her mouth. Her lips were very full, the insides deliciously soft and she drew them up the shaft, still sucking. She was making me very stiff. Her lips came up to my cock-head, she was making squishy sounds as she sucked there. Her fingers still circled the base hard and her other hand was fondling my balls.

I didn't know whether I was hard enough yet but I felt as if I wanted to fuck again, sink myself into soft juiciness. I believed that the ache and stinging tingle in my cock could be cured only by jabbing inside the wet, squirming, squishy texture of quim. Margery perhaps recognized my feeling and held my cock tightly as if her grip would hold up its stiffness. Then she stood up, placing one leg on mine just above the knee. Teresa and Dorothy held her shoulders steady as she lifted her other leg in the same way, thrusting her pelvis forward, her quim just at the tip of my prick. Her legs rested on mine and my cock slid inside her. And as soon as I felt the velvety touch of her quim it stiffened some more. In fact, though I knew it was impossible, I expected to come immediately.

And then Margery began her ride. Teresa and Dorothy helped by lifting her at the armpits, judging how far to lift so my cock came just to the opening of her slit before they let her down again and she pushed hard onto me. They kept up that steady rhythm and soon my cock was hardening more, my balls tight in their bag, Margery smiling down at me as she pushed and pulled. At one out-stroke she raised one leg high to hook it over my shoulder, then the other one followed and that allowed her to sit way down on my pelvis, my prick as deep as it could go inside her, Teresa and Dorothy pulling her up and letting her down, Margery beginning to pant and moan, me thrusting into her as much as I could from my sitting position.

It was soon apparent that my cock was as hard as it could get and we were riding hard and we weren't far, both of us, from that high plateau reaching up to the peak. If my cock could have spurted out any come, it would have splashed very deep inside Margery and she sensed that from the hard throbbing of my cock for that sent her into wild twistings of her hips and pelvis, pushing even harder against me and letting out a long gush of air that rattled out of her throat.

Then we all collapsed together. Margery tumbled off onto her cushions on the floor and the other three of us lay across each other, an occasional hand straying across my limp dick, my hand on a breast, pubic hair, someone's fingers tweaking my balls but it was just an affectionate pat, nothing that could induce me to action again.

Then, as we lay there, breathless, recovering, oblivious to anyone but ourselves, I heard a quiet voice close by. 'What about me?'

I looked up out of fuzzy eyes and saw Margo in her green.

'Yes, me,' she said. 'I said I'd join in if I felt the urge and you know I did join in. Well, the urge is still there, especially after watching the way you went at it and remembering our afternoon together. So what about it, Nick?'

I stared up at her in disbelief. I struggled to sit up and Teresa and Dorothy moved aside from me. 'I'd love to, Margo, but I honestly don't think I . . .'

'That's what you said to Margery and look what happened. You managed just fine.'

'But Margo . . .'

'No buts, fair shares for all.' I was amazed she was insisting because I knew I would disappoint her. I was worn out and though I remembered my afternoon with her with delight, I knew I could summon nothing up for her. 'After this . . .' and I waved my arms around. 'It's impossible.'

'Nothing's impossible for a strapping young lad like you, Nick.' She nodded her head and Teresa and Dorothy moved off the ottoman – it looked as if Margo was saying to them, 'Just leave this to me.' Margery stood, picked up her cushions and moved away. All three of them sat together at a nearby table.

Margo sat next to me. 'Is the poor boy tired?' she asked me in a soothing voice. 'Used up all his strength? There, there!' She put her arm around my shoulder and pulled my head onto her breasts. 'Rest your weary head.' She cuddled me close to her, giving me little kisses on my head and cheeks, rocking me.

It was very restful sitting there, her breasts very soft but rounding out her slip which was extraordinarily silky – it was probably real silk. My eyes closed every now and again, lulled by Margo's rocking and her voice. I suspect Teresa had learned how to give her running commentary from Margo.

'You've been very busy. No wonder you're tired. Just take it easy.' She lifted part of the skirt of her long slip and let it fall over my legs. It was so shimmeringly soft that I shuddered a little at the pleasure it gave me. Margo's hand lay just above my knee and moved the silk ever so slowly.

'Isn't that nice? It's nice to feel it against you, isn't it? I just love to wear this. It makes me feel as if my skin is just as soft.' She squashed my head in closer to her breasts. 'Does that feel soft to you?' She swayed a little so my cheek rubbed against her round breast. She slipped the strap down from her shoulder and pulled the material away from her bosom. 'Is that silky?' she asked as she set my cheek against her bare breast. 'Does your cheek feel nice there?' I tried to nod so my face rubbed against her. 'Well, that feels nice too.' Her hand was still slowly stroking my thigh with the silk. 'Sleepy head. There! Would you like to suck titty? Most boys do. It calms them down.'

She pushed her large nipple to my lips and I held it there. My tongue flicked onto it and it became a little hard and I rubbed at it. I felt a vague stirring but I certainly wasn't aroused. My penis was still limp but it was decidedly pleasant sitting with Margo, her breast against me, my mouth licking at her. 'Nice mouth on nice titty.' She slipped the other strap from her shoulder and pushed my face across. 'Give this one a little lick.' And I did. 'Touch it with a finger.' I did that. 'Suck the other.' I did, and we sat there with my fingers rolling round her moist nipples, my hand holding the roundness of first one full tit, then the other.

Her hand was very gradually sliding up my thigh, stroking, gripping it. 'Wasn't it lovely this evening? Did you like your present? I loved covering you with this,' and she pressed the silk enticingly against me, 'and then your mouth on me. Making me so wet. I still feel wet there.' She continued to rock me gently, letting me fondle and caress her breasts 'It's so juicy. So easy to slide into. Silky. Like this,' and she was moving the silk closer to my balls, not quite touching them. 'It feels like pussy, doesn't it? That's what Carmella calls it. Pussy, soft to stroke like a pussycat. Pussy.'

Her hand was beautifully circling the silk on my thigh and tired as I was, I felt a little stiffening in my cock, though not much. Margo knew the effect she was having because she pushed me back onto the ottoman and I lifted my legs so I was lying on my side. 'Make room for me,' she said and she lay down facing me, putting her arm round me and pulling me against her. She wriggled her pelvis close to mine and the silk rubbed at my cock.

'Is your little friend tired or is he waking up? He feels nice there. I bet he feels silky, all covered in juice and next to the silk. I could tell you just loved to slip him inside those ladies. And they loved feeling him. And I loved to watch your big prick going in.' Margo seemed to know just how to talk in soft enticing whispers that suddenly broke into sexy words. She was still smoothing her silk-covered pelvis on me and I was certainly growing, painfully but also pleasurably semi-aroused.

'You just lie back now. Maybe you'd like a little snooze. I'll cover you up to keep you warm.' She stood up and shimmied out of her slip. She fluttered it out and let it drop onto the length of my body. Then she began her incredible stroking, just as she had done that afternoon I'd spent with her. Her hands went all over my body, stroking the silk lightly against me, edging at times towards my prick but not touching it.

'Relax, Nick.' I *was* relaxed in the middle of all this

silkiness but Margo could now see I was beginning to show signs of standing up hard. 'Well now. He's waking up, isn't he?'

One hand gently wrapped silk around my cock, the other moved the material up my thighs to cover my balls and she began a captivating massage, as she talked. 'I love to stroke a big cock. It makes me wet. Very wet. I've been wet since you licked me. Does this feel like pussy on your cock? Pussy cunt. Such lovely balls. Full of come. That makes my cunt even wetter. You know what it makes me want? A nice big fuck. I like the way you do that, Nick, and when I feel your cock getting bigger, it makes me want to fuck. It's best to be last. Because I know we will last a long time. And you'll be inside me with your fat hot cock for a long time. I think he's ready. Does he feel ready? Ready to slide inside me, feel me all juicy and silky.'

Her stroking and talking had really got me going. The stroking was delicious though just a little painful because every now and then she gripped me hard and I flinched.

'There, there. Did I hurt him? Is he a little sore? Maybe he needs a soothing bath. A bath in soft pussy juice.' She drew the slip away, straddled me and holding my cock in two fingers she slowly lowered herself down. I was sore when she first touched the tip of my cock – the skin round the head felt painful but, as I slid further in, I forgot my soreness and she began to make slow revolving motions, still talking.

'You are filling me up. The head of your cock is so fat.' And she squeezed her muscles and it felt like wet fur fondling the head of my cock. 'There. I bet he can go deeper, he's so long and fat. Deeper.' I was sure I was still wilting but Margo's movements and her talk made me feel as if I had a very large cock ready for action so I began to bounce up and down on my pelvis, quickening the pace. 'I knew you were a strong boy, Nick. I knew you could do it. Just keep fucking me like that. We'll last a long time.'

Her quim felt like thick velvet, creamy and slippery, juice all over my cock. We kept on jigging up and down, I was fondling her breasts, one of her hands held and stroked my balls and I had broken out in a profuse sweat. I wanted to come, to finish, to rest but I had so little come left I couldn't force anything out and I didn't seem able to drive myself to a climax though I drove as hard as I could. Margo was pushing relentlessly down, making my cock seem even longer.

Without interrupting her incessant plunging up and down, Margo waved her hand and the other three women came over to the ottoman to join us. My cock was even more swollen now, pleasurably painful. Teresa spread the green slip over the length of my legs and crawled under it, one hand hooking out to rub the silk on both my thighs. Her other hand delved beneath the plunging Margo to finger my arsehole at my secret spot; somehow her tongue was licking in there as well. Margery straddled my head, kneeling down so my mouth could lick her quim which was soon slithery with juice as I tongued and fingered her. Her hands were massaging my stomach with a red slip. Dorothy's wide-open legs invited my other hand in and I began a rhythmic probing in time with Margo's now hectic pace.

The women then started to moan and shout, a jumbled chorus of yelps and sighs, saying: 'Yes, yes', 'God, that feels good', 'Fuck me hard', 'Deeper' and other words of endearment and involuntary shouts until we were all fucking and sucking, poking and stroking, plunging and lunging, squealing in delight and gasping out in pain and pleasure.

My cock was now at a point of no return as I began to feel a gathering of pressure somewhere down inside me, perhaps where Teresa's fingers were pressing as if reaching inside me. The exquisite feeling rose into my balls where Margo's hand was squeezing and tweaking. Then from the base of my cock a hard jet started, climbing up my shaft, urged on by Margo's now frantic banging up and down. It shot upwards and out of me in a stream of come I could not believe I possessed.

My orgasmic groans were nearly drowned out by the women's voices and by Margo's vigorous slapping on my pelvis and the rumbling escape of wet snorting sounds from her cunt and her yells of 'I'm nearly there. Keep fucking. It's coming – coming!' and it seemed almost as if we were all trapped and could not stop, trying to find our release. We kept on and on, beyond orgasms, lost in the frenzy of movement, in the creamy sloshing of cock and cunt, with fingers in quim and arse, mouths sucking, slobbery with juice, till all of us, as if with one will, began to slow down. The wild motion faded away with little snatches of pokes and pats, rubbings and lacy strokings till I was criss-crossed with limbs and fleshy parts, lying panting and exhausted after what had seemed the most agonizingly ecstatic and complete fuck I had ever had – a kind of sex that escaped from mere fucking into another realm of body experience, as if I was all cock and the four women were transformed into an all-encompassing liquefaction of cunt.

Gerry was soon leaning over us. 'Good show!' he said, helping Margo up – she had collapsed on top of me. Gerry patted me on the shoulder, saying, 'Many happy returns, Nick. Maybe next year we'll arrange an encore!' He put his arm round Margo. 'Anyhow it's time for bed for us old fogeys. Maybe you youngsters will want to keep going.' I shook my head and I saw the women just smile briefly. 'Well, off you go, Nick. You'll be staying here with Teresa, right? I'll see to these other ladies.'

I was so completely worn out I thought I would just remain on the ottoman and fall asleep. But then I remembered that Carmella had also participated and I half-expected that if I stayed there, she would turn up again and ask to be accommodated. I knew I couldn't possibly deal with her if she were to walk in now and claim her rights!

Teresa bundled our things together and we staggered through the bar, then up the stairs. As we left, I vaguely remember Gerry saying he'd lock up and adding something to Teresa about leaving in time in the morning. But I didn't even want to think about the morning right then. I simply needed to close my eyes and sink into sleep, a sleep even more profound than those last minutes of deep-down sexual ecstasy. I fell into bed, as did Teresa, our arms round each other for innocent comfort, and we were both soon dead to the world.

11. Wedding in White

I was awakened by a flutter of Teresa's fingers trailing down my stomach into my groin as she snuggled next to me.

'Not much life down there this morning, I'm afraid,' I told her.

'Oh, I don't know. Not entirely asleep here,' she answered as her fingers pursued their mischievous way. I lay back and gave myself up to Teresa's caresses.

'What time is it?' I asked her.

'About nine. Time for a quickie.'

'Only a quickie?'

'Just now you said nothing was happening and now you're complaining because you're only going to get a quickie. Men!' She gave me a sudden, hard pinch. 'And it has to be a quickie because I have to have you out of here by eleven or so.'

'Why's that?'

'You have to go and pack your things and get out of your place. Mrs Courtney's car's coming at noon.'

'I was there just four days ago.'

'Maybe your Phillipa wants to give you a birthday present!'

'It'll have to be good if it's better than the one I got last night!' Teresa smiled. 'Well, from what you've told me, who knows what she might dream up? Maybe she's grown a new flower for you!' I had told Teresa about my first escapade with Mrs Courtney.

'How d'you know there's a delivery for her? She usually waits a week or ten days.'

'Gerry gave me something for her last night. Told me to pass it on to you.'

'I usually work through Helen with Mrs Courtney.'

'Well, Helen wasn't around yesterday, was she?'

'No, she wasn't. I wonder why she didn't turn up for the party. You know, I sort of expected she'd be part of the game with me when I was blindfolded. Sneak in without my knowing. I mean, I had a real feeling someone else did join in.'

'Is that so?'

'Yes. But I thought it was Carmella.'

'Really? She went off early with one of the men.'

'Yes, I know, but she came back later. I saw her.'

'Did you?'

I raised myself up on my elbow to look at Teresa. She had a sly smile on her face so it looked as if she was teasing me. But she didn't confirm or deny that Carmella had joined in the game. I suspected she'd asked Carmella to participate. And Teresa had mentioned that Gerry could arrange for me to be with Carmella on a honeymoon. Maybe I'd never know. Maybe the game would retain a little mystery in my mind if I never found out whether Carmella had joined in or not. I'd sort of promised I'd go and see her when she was at Margo's later so maybe she'd tell me then.

'Well, anyhow, I was really surprised Helen didn't turn up. I mean, Blind Man's Bluff is just the kind of game she likes to play!'

'Thank your lucky stars she wasn't there. You know Helen. She'd have taken over. And if she was on her pills, there'd have been no stopping her.'

'What d'you mean?'

'You really don't get it about Helen, do you?'

'I know she gets bitchy but I had some great times with her . . . before I met you, I mean. And you said yourself she's a real sexpot.'

'Sure she is. That's one of the reasons she keeps taking the pills. I mean, she really likes doing it and when she takes the pills it helps to keep her going. Once she's on them, she can do it five or six times a night. But she's getting hung up on them. Keeps wanting more and more. Gerry's known about it for some time now. And that's what makes her so bitchy at times . . . when she doesn't get her pills. So she'd have taken a real dose last night. You'd never have woken up in a month of Sundays and this . . .' she squeezed my cock, 'would have rotted off!'

'Still, she's pretty thick with Gerry so I'm surprised she didn't come. Maybe she thought it was Wednesday.'

'She'll be here tonight, I'm sure.'

'Didn't anybody tell her when the party really was?'

'She's been too strung out these days. And I don't think, in fact I know Gerry didn't want her here.'

'Why? I thought Gerry and her were . . .'

'Yes, they were till two or three weeks ago. Helen was really special for Gerry for quite a time but now he's cutting her loose.'

'I noticed she'd begun hanging around with Bledsoe in the club but I thought Gerry had put her up to that. You know, wiggling stuff out of Bledsoe, finding out what he was up to, why he kept coming to the club, that kind of thing.'

'That was Gerry's idea but it sort of got out of hand. I think Helen saw what Judy was getting out of Bledsoe and that seemed better than what Gerry was giving her. So maybe she started to make a play for Bledsoe.' This time it was Teresa who raised herself up on her elbow to stare at me. 'Didn't you think something weird was going on?'

'Sort of. But I thought, even if she was cosying up to Bledsoe, everyone here could see her, so people would let Gerry know. I just assumed it was a put-up job with Helen spying on Bledsoe for Gerry.'

'That's how it started but Helen got more hooked on the pills. She could never get enough from her regular supplier and she'd lost her contacts at the hospital – a doctor used to give her some – so she started asking Bledsoe for them and that's how he got her to spill the beans about Gerry.'

'Did Gerry ever find out just what she'd told Bledsoe?'

'Well, the Malta women, I know he knew about that. I think Helen told him something about the stuff Gerry smuggled in. But Gerry's clever. He runs a real import business, bringing in things for the restaurant, French cheese and Italian wine, so everything looks above board. But it seems as if Bledsoe found a way to put one over on Gerry. I mean, he's really pissed off about Judy and Benny beating up Christoff.'

'Why doesn't Gerry just ditch Helen?'

'Helen's playing off one against the other. She's slipping Gerry some gen about Bledsoe and his drug dealing. So Gerry's playing tit for tat. That's why he told Helen the party was for Wednesday, not Tuesday. She still thinks it's happening tonight.'

'I don't understand.'

'Gerry knew Helen would tell Bledsoe there'd be a party and the Malta women would be at it. That's

Bledsoe's chance. If Gerry gets caught with these women he's smuggled in, it could land him in jail for some time. But Gerry has his people all over the place and he knows Bledsoe's tipped the cops off. Bledsoe's told them they'll catch Gerry and his women tonight. You'll see. The cops'll come romping in here but all they'll find is an empty club and some walls half-plastered. You know how Gerry's closed the club down, said it was being repaired. Bledsoe thinks once he gets Gerry out of the way, he'll be able to take over.'

'How do you know all this?'

'Margo's told me some of it, Benny knows a little and since I've been working at the club I've heard some other things. And that's why we're getting out of here today. Everyone's to lie low for a while. The Maltese girls have gone off with the men and they won't be around till they come back for the weddings in a couple of weeks. Margo's staying put where she is but her other girls are moving out. So the cops won't trace much and Bledsoe's going to look stupid.'

'But Bledsoe must have learned something about Gerry from Helen. He'll tell the police all about that.'

'It won't matter. I told you Gerry runs a proper import business. He keeps his accounts straight. And his name's only on the restaurant of this place. All his houses are under different names. He's got it arranged so that it looks as if someone else rents the club and these flats from him. If they go round to Margo's, she'll have it looking like it's just a high-class boarding house. I think the cops are suspicious of Gerry but they don't have anything on him. It's all sewn up under different names. And you know how he never tells anyone much about what he's doing so even if the cops round some of us up, we won't be able to tell them a great deal.'

'Well, if we have to get out of here, you'd better come and stay at my place.'

'Oh, no. You've got to move. That's why we're going to Mrs Courtney's.'

'We? Are we both going there?'

'Yes. She's putting us up for a while. Gerry's letting her have all the booze and cigarettes, wine and clothes she wants just so long as we can stay there a few weeks. We're going to work for Mrs Courtney as well.' She gave me a teasing smile. 'You know what a terrific maid I am! And I just know that your Phillipa will love having you around working in the garden and that conservatory. I bet she'll help you look after the flowers!'

'What about Helen? What's going to happen about her?'

'She's finished with Gerry now. She'll chance her arm with Bledsoe, I suppose, but when he finds out that the tips she's been giving him about Gerry's business don't amount to anything, Bledsoe'll look a fool to the police and he'll dump her. He'll think it was a put-up job and that Helen's been working on Gerry's side all along. In any case, Margo told me Gerry's going to leave some papers around in the club that'll seem to relate to Bledsoe, make it difficult for him to explain himself. It should all blow over in a few weeks and Gerry'll be back in business. So I'll go back to Margo's, and you'll be back being a delivery boy again — if I can ever get you out of Mrs Courtney's clutches, that is. Maybe we should have invited her to the party for you last night!'

Teresa was snuggling closer and closer to me as she

was telling me all this and of course she was beginning to make me respond. Her hands were busy, her mouth was nibbling me all over. She was pushing her breasts into my face and surprisingly I found I still had enough energy to make the most of what she was offering.

By the time we'd got out of bed to do Teresa's packing, I was putting things together in my mind. Even though Gerry's business was going under for a while, things didn't look too bad for Teresa and me. In fact, they looked decidedly rosy – and 'rosy' was a good word to use, given Phillipa's predilection for flowers and gallivanting about in the conservatory. I was sure Teresa would play her part well there.

So nothing looked too bleak for me. I had already applied to several universities and I was hoping I'd be accepted at one of them so I could start in October, just a few months ahead. I couldn't decide what I'd do about Teresa then but I didn't have to worry about making that decision now. I decided I'd make the most of living out in the country near St Alban's with Mrs Courtney.

All that Teresa told me about Bledsoe and Helen and Gerry turned out to be true. The morning papers gave full accounts of the police raid at the club, printed reports about Frank Bledsoe – 'the Watford Wide Boy', one paper dubbed him – and they also carried interviews with Gerry who came across as an innocent and slightly bewildered business man, simply concerned with running a nice clean business.

'I hold no truck with gangsters and people like that,' he told one paper. 'I had no idea what was going on in those rooms in the back of the restaurant. I just run the restaurant and I rent the rooms at the back to a Mr Temelini. He seemed a nice man and he always pays his rent on time.' But there was no trace of this mysterious Mr Temelini. The police never found him and there was no one by that name at the address that Gerry gave for him. 'He told me he was going to use it as a games club – chess, draughts, cribbage, that kind of thing. Nothing about girls and gambling. If Mr Bledsoe's been saying that, maybe he knows more about it than I do. Maybe this Mr Temelini is a friend of Mr Bledsoe's. I know I've seen him in the restaurant a few times and I've noticed some evenings he went into the back. And he usually had a friend with him, a big man who looked like a boxer. And he always had his girl friend with him those evenings. He must have met her there, because I've seen him leave with her but he never brought her here into the restaurant.' Gerry became quite effusive in his interviews and it was obvious to me he was enjoying himself hugely.

So it came out in the newspapers that it was Bledsoe who knew more than he was telling and it was implied that the police were going to do a thorough investigation of his business dealings. Gerry even suggested, in his naive way, that he felt Bledsoe was hounding him. 'Maybe he's trying to get the restaurant – it's a solid business. Maybe Mr Temelini is one of his henchmen. And – who knows? – if the police are looking into Mr Bledsoe's business, maybe he's trying to implicate me just to throw them off his scent. I mean, maybe Bledsoe runs the club and Mr Temelini doesn't know anything about it. All I know is, I have nothing to hide. I am a respectable business man running a successful restaurant with a small import business on the side and that's mainly to do with providing a few gourmet items for the restaurant – cheese, wine, that kind of thing. As for Mr Bledsoe's allegations about Malta, I can state without reservation that I have no business connections with Malta.'

Gerry must have covered his tracks well for he soon faded from the pages of the newspapers whereas Bledsoe's name kept cropping up and his involvement in illegal activities was mentioned often, though he too had managed to hide his true operations. He emerged in the newspaper reports as a slimy but essentially petty operator working on the fringes of lawful enterprises. But the police could never pin him down and he eventually disappeared from the newspapers and I never did find out what became of him – or of Helen, for that matter.

But Carmella – I did run across her once more. Well, it was more than just running across her . . . I'd been at Phillipa's for just over two weeks, enjoying myself immensely. Teresa and I were sharing the same room and we took full advantage of that as Phillipa left us to our own devices in the evenings, though a couple of times she did join us. But she was strangely shy and awkward. Teresa with her usual breezy manner tried to put her at ease and that meant letting Phillipa watch us to begin with. So Teresa performed very sexily with me, hoping it would make Phillipa feel she wanted to join in as we both invited her to. Eventually she did and while the three of us found some fascinating combinations, I always felt Phillipa remained uncomfortable with the situation. I found that surprising for with me she was still marvellously uninhibited. I was working as a gardener though she had to tell me exactly what to do and when she told me how to take care of certain plants and shrubs, she nearly always expected me to take care of her.

For instance, it was late morning on the second day

I was there – Phillipa never got out of bed early – she had arranged to meet me in the conservatory. She walked in, dressed immaculately in a bright green dress, her shoes with sensible heels shaping her ankles to slim trimness, her hair shiny, carefully in place without looking as if she had spent hours on it, falling to the nape of her neck and framing her face with soft waves. She looked as if she was dressed to go out for lunch, perhaps with two or three lady friends. She laid her small clutch purse on the table where we had had tea the first time I visited her, and then she walked over to me. 'Good morning, Nicholas,' she said quietly and leaned to brush her lips on my cheek. 'You slept well, I trust.' She paused, smiling. 'You and Teresa. Such a nice girl.'

'Yes she is.'

'And I expect she is very nice to you. So I hope you're feeling refreshed and ready for . . .' She waved her arms around, taking in the flowers and small trees in the conservatory. The smile stayed on her face. 'But then, you're always ready, aren't you, Nicholas?'

She took me by the hand and walked me round the conservatory pointing out what had to be done. 'That will keep you busy for a few days and I'll pop in and see how you're getting on every now and again. Just to make sure you're doing things right.' She turned to me to look directly in my eyes. 'I can always count on you to do things right, isn't that so, Nicholas?'

I nodded and then she raised my hand to her mouth and placed a wet kiss on my palm, the tip of her tongue skimming across the skin smoothly. 'There!' she said. 'Before your hands get too dirty with soil. You have lovely hands, Nicholas, so gentle. I'm sure my plants won't come to any harm with you caring for them. I'm lucky to have you two looking after me. Teresa made me an absolutely scrumptious breakfast and now she's busy making some heavenly dish for dinner. She does keep herself busy so I'm sure she won't disturb you while you get on with your work.'

She licked my hand again. 'You know, I almost envy those plants, having your hands to tend to them.' She pulled my hand down to place it on her dress just below her stomach, sighing a little as she moved it up and down. 'You have such a lovely touch, Nicholas. I think you must have green fingers.'

She smiled lasciviously. 'Green fingers on my green frock.' She continued to press my hand on herself. 'Oh, I can tell you know just how to make things grow.' She slowly led my hand down to her leg till it reached the hem of her dress. 'That moss I asked you to put round those two trees. Your hands will feel just how smooth and soft it is, a little damp as well.'

She was drawing my hand up her thigh under her dress and she let it wander up on its own as her fingers moved to stroke my trousers at the crotch. And of course she felt that I had started to become hard there, listening to her talk, feeling her kisses on my hand, and now with my hand under her dress . . . 'My!' she whispered as her fingers grasped my erection. 'You certainly do know how to make things grow!'

I was growing stiffer and stiffer under the pressure of her gently moving fingers. My hand was now at the top of her thigh and I discovered she was wearing nothing under her dress, just her stockings fastened to her garter belt. I inched a finger upwards and felt a warm dampness.

'Is that soft and mossy, Nicholas?' she murmured. 'I'm sure your spade will be able to dig into it easily,' she continued as her hand stroked my cock. I pushed my finger in and out of her slowly. 'Or maybe your spade will find it a little too hard to dig properly. We'd better see to it that it gets the right kind of watering.' And with that her hand began to pull at my fly buttons and her fingers reached inside. 'Let me see here.' She expertly fished out my cock, then licked her fingers and their slippery wetness ringed the foreskin, easing it back as she bent a finger to rub across the exposed head. 'Perhaps you should have a little rest before you start work so the watering will sink in to make it nice and wet.'

She insisted I lie back on the ground, pulling my trousers down to my knees, bunching my shirt up above my stomach, then leaning down, her hair tickly on my skin, her mouth moistly closing around my cock-head, taking a lot of my stiffness into the silky warmth of her mouth. She had placed herself next to me so I could have both hands under her dress, my fingers working in her creamy centre, sliding easily around while my other hand stroked her behind, fingers edging into the crack of her arse.

After a little while we were so steamed up – she whispered lecherously, 'Nicholas, you bad boy! The windows are misting up, you're making me so hot!' – she stood up, walking away from me, leaned her elbows on the table, thrusting her round buttocks out, her dress over her waist. 'Come on, Nicky,' forgetting my full name for once. 'Come on and plough me with your big, fat blade.'

I stood up and struggled out of my trousers, then ran over to her, stroked the shapely curve of her arse and found my way into the creamy delight of her quim.

And that was the way it was for the first two weeks

or so, with Phillipa visiting me in the conservatory in the morning to tell me what work she wanted me to do and then leading me on. She always acted politely but was quite brazen in her well-mannered way, enticing me into deliciously warm and sensual encounters. She always came down to the conservatory and never invited me into her bedroom. It struck me that while she was infinitely provocative and sexy, she maintained her upper-class poise even as I was undressing and groping her, till finally she would let loose as she neared her orgasmic pleasure.

She made me do the jobs in the conservatory just as she made Teresa work in the kitchen. She didn't give us wages but I was quite happy in the way she 'paid' me. We were also sent money from Gerry whenever he sent deliveries to Phillipa. So, five or six times during those first two or three weeks Phillipa 'paid' me. On the surface she seemed just a rather aristocratic employer but when she walked in to see me, I could always sense that she had some interesting ideas she wanted to act out with me.

She came dressed fashionably, often looking superb. Sometimes when she wanted me to strip her, I discovered she was wearing attractive lingerie. Once she crept into the conservatory without my noticing her – she may even have been hiding there before I arrived. She was naked and had made a ring of flowers which she held ready in one hand as her other hand stroked me to stiffness. Then she gently placed the flowers on my standing prick.

'Now I know how Lady Chatterley felt,' she said.

She knelt down to smell them, at least that's what she said but it was really to tease me with her tongue and lips. I loved to hear her murmuring in her impec-

cable upper-class accent and it really made my cock
tingle and pulse harder when once she said to me in
her faultless enunciation, sticking to gardening imag-
ery she used in her steamiest moments: 'Buzz into my
honeypot. Feel how sticky and juicy it is in there.'

She remained for me the epitome of English upper-
class womanhood and it was exciting for me to know
how wanton she was behind that sophistication and
poise and cool manner. I suspect it was her inbred
attitudes that prevented her from really letting loose
with Teresa and me when she joined us in bed.
Somehow she couldn't rid herself of the notion that a
threesome was not quite right, not really a part of the
upper-crust life, though I tried to explain to her that
she should have seen some of the behaviour at the club
involving some of her own class. Maybe it was the idea
that she would not allow herself to unleash her sensuality in front of two servants. And she still did treat us
as servants though she finally forgot the mistress/
servant relationship when she was with me, and
became a mistress in the other sense.

So that was what happened with Mrs Courtney till
one day, while I was just getting ready to start work in
the conservatory, I heard the usual footsteps. Wondering what kind of delight Phillipa had planned for me, I
turned in the direction of the sound, and was surprised
to see Emily, the maid. She was a pert little thing, and
every now and again I caught what I thought was a
mischievous twinkle in her eye. I was certain that
when she walked away from me sometimes she gave
an attractive wiggle to her bum. I suspected that she
knew what was going on between me and Mrs Courtney and wouldn't have minded having some of her
own fun and games but was a little hesitant because

she wondered whether Mrs Courtney would sack her if she found out. And she may also have been wary of Teresa. I did mention to Teresa in an off-hand way that maybe Emily might like to join us but nothing came of it. Under other circumstances I may have made a move on my own but right then it was all I could do to keep up with Mrs Courtney and Teresa.

'The missus wants to see you in the drawing room but not in them gardening clothes,' Emily said and, after giving me a wicked grin, nonchalantly swayed her way out. This summons was a mystery to me for Phillipa had assiduously avoided inviting me into the rest of the house. I quickly dressed myself in some decent flannels and a sports jacket and went to join Mrs Courtney.

She was dressed to kill in a form-fitting dress with bright floral patterns. 'I was just about to come and see you. This frock,' and she swirled the skirt around, 'would go well with the flowers, don't you think?' She looked so sexy I was sorry she hadn't come to the conservatory. I wondered why she hadn't come and tried to figure out whether I was expected to continue our exploits in this part of the house. She went on, 'I have a visitor' and she waved her hand to a plush high-backed armchair I hadn't looked at, so entranced was I by Phillipa. The visitor leaned forward in the chair – it was Gerry. He waved at me and said, 'Hello, Nick.'

'He says he wants to borrow you for a day or two,' Phillipa said with a pout and a tiny shrug. 'I've been telling him that we had some plans for the garden to work on so I tried to persuade him to let you stay.'

'Sorry, old son. Some special business has cropped up and you're the man for the job.'

'You see how secretive he is. He won't tell me what it is.' She came over to me and laid her hand on my arm. 'And after we're doing so well with the flowers. I don't know how I'll be able to get on without you.'

'Come now, Mrs Courtney. He'll probably be back by tomorrow,' Gerry told her.

'Well, just to make sure, I'll send my car for him at two in the afternoon if you leave me his address.'

'Certainly. I'm sure he'll be able to cope with the business at hand this afternoon.'

'Send him back this evening then.'

'Well, just in case, we'd better say tomorrow. Maybe it'll run over into the evening.'

'Very well. Tomorrow at two then.' She patted my arm, then walked to the door. 'I'll go and sulk now. I'll miss the little tête-à-tête I had planned about the flowers this morning, Nicholas. I'll just have to wait till tomorrow. I'll see you at four in the conservatory. Now I'll leave you two to talk over your business.'

'Thank you, Mrs Courtney.' Gerry stood up and gave her a little bow and I mumbled a quick 'goodbye'.

'Well, my lad,' Gerry said after Phillipa had left us, 'You seem to have got yourself well and truly in here. She's a rare bit of stuff is Mrs Courtney.' I must have looked a little upset. 'You're right, of course. You don't call women like Mrs Courtney bits of stuff. More like high-class princesses, right?' He came over to me and put his arm round my shoulder. 'Sorry to drag you away but you'll be back tomorrow.'

'Is Teresa coming as well?'

'Oh no. Maybe in a couple of weeks or so when Margo's back in full swing.' He began to walk towards the door. 'Come on then. No need to hang around here. I'll tell you about the job as we're driving back.'

Gerry was driving the car Helen had driven me around in so the journey reminded me of those dangerous but sexy rides with her. Gerry didn't say anything about Helen but he did talk about the Maltesers. 'Good name you dreamed up for them, Maltesers. Very tasty, those ladies.'

'How did the weddings go?'

'No problems there. Did 'em at different registry offices. No one any the wiser that way. Most of 'em are rarin' to go now the Bledsoe stuff is just about blown over. Had nice honeymoons, so I hear. Got most of them set up in three different houses. And Margo's taking two of them. Those are the ones I want to tell you about. The job. Bit of trouble with them.'

'What kind of trouble?'

'Soon be able to clear it up. And as you were the one who brought 'em over, I think they trust you to do right by them.' He paused a moment. 'One of them's feelin' her oats a bit, actually fallen in love with the feller we married her to. Doesn't want to leave him yet. I mean, she's not causing too much of a fuss, just wants the honeymoon to go on a bit longer, so she's holed up in the hotel I got 'em for their honeymoon. Margo's been to talk to her to explain the bargain – you know, work with Margo for a year or so, then she's free and clear. I don't want to try any rough stuff with her. It's a classy operation we run. We're not going to turn her out on the streets but that's where she'll finish up if we can't talk sense into her. That's where you come in. Just explain she'll get plenty of free time to spend with her husband, providing she doesn't let it interfere with business. Her husband's keeping an eye on her and we can't really kidnap her out of the hotel. She'll make a hell of a racket if we try to force her out of the hotel.'

'But what can I do?'

'The Maltesers thought you were a nice guy, the way you looked after them on the plane and that. And then there's Margo. She's taken something of a shine to you as well and she thought you'd be the one to deal with this young lady. Talk her out of it.'

'But none of them know much English, except for Carmella maybe. And I don't know any Italian to speak of.'

'But I think you can be very persuasive.' He nudged me with his elbow. 'Look how you got round all those ladies at the club! And Teresa. And Margo.'

'But if she's locked herself in . . .'

'It's a hotel I use a lot. I know the manager. He'll let you in, then it'll be up to you. Drive round there in a taxi,' and he rooted in his inside pocket and passed me a thick envelope. 'Running expenses. Keep the taxi waiting. Bundle her in any way you can and take her round to Margo's and she'll tell you about the other problem.'

'Who's the Malteser in the hotel?'

'I never thought she'd stick up for herself like this. Maria. Remember? The last one to go that night. Sort of shy but then she pulled that trick with her panties. I mean, that was a nice touch, that was. Must have really got that feller ready for action, I'd say, and I must say she seems to be carrying on in the same way, and enjoying herself into the bargain.'

I remembered Maria and how she had approached that last man at the club, refusing to buy a throwing ring with her last article of clothing, her panties, taking them off seductively and dropping them on his upstanding shaft, a neat trick that won her a good round of applause. She had seemed a little quiet and bashful and that trick had taken us all by surprise. No one would think she'd turn out to be stubborn.

'We know she's going to be on her own this afternoon. I've sent her husband out on a job. I'll deal with him. So you just exercise those wily charms of yours, Nick. You'll be able to do it and once she's at Margo's, she'll come round.'

'I don't know, Gerry. I don't want to get into anything rough.'

'Don't worry. Margo's mentioned you and Maria thinks you're nice. We treat the girls right. They have a good life, live in a nice house, get some free time. They can have boyfriends and we vet our clients carefully. Just think – none of 'em would have as comfortable a life if they'd stayed back home and if they'd tried to get another job here. And it's only a year. So don't worry about it, Nick. It'll work out fine.'

In fact, Gerry was right. It was nowhere near as difficult as I anticipated it would be. Maria was living in a small hotel in Russell Square and I went round there, asking the cabbie to park nearby. The manager, a smarmy, oily man, smiling and winking at me, obviously thought I was a client visiting Maria. He had his key out, ready to unlock the door so I could barge in without warning but I stopped him. I tapped on the door and called quietly, 'Maria.' We heard nothing and the manager brandished his key but I shook my head as I tapped and called again. I heard a little cough and then 'Yes?'

'Maria? It's me, Nick. On the plane, remember?'

'Nick. Yes.'

'Can we talk?'

'Talk?'

The manager smirked and I turned to him. 'You can

go now. I don't want her to see you at the door with your key.' He pocketed the key with a flourish, still smirking at me, then strolled along the corridor, looking back before he turned onto the stairs, giving me a big smile and a wave.

I heard Maria unlock the door and it inched open, then swung wider when she saw me. She looked pretty but a little unkempt, a robe pulled tightly around her. She turned away without saying anything and I followed her into the room to sit next to her on the bed. I wasn't sure how much English she knew or how much she might have picked up during her two weeks with the man she'd been married off to. If she really liked him and he'd treated her well, maybe she'd know some simple words. 'Maria. Really nice. Pretty.'

· She smiled briefly, then said, 'Sad.'

'Don't be sad. Not sad.' I tried to comfort her with a big smile, put my hand under her chin and lifted it so she was looking directly at me. 'Margo. Go to Margo now.'

She shook her head. 'Harry.'

I presumed Harry was her husband. 'Alright. You still see him. At Margo's.'

She shook her head again. 'Stay here.'

I stood up in front of her and took both her hands so she stood up too. I nodded at the window. 'Nice. Sunny. We walk.' After a time I convinced her that no harm would come to her if we just walked in the small park across from the hotel.

Then she surprised me. She'd been acting coy, looking demure and sad but she slipped off her robe. I remembered how she looked on that evening at the club and here she was again, standing in front of me in just her panties and bra. I don't think she was inviting

278

me and I didn't want to take a chance, especially as she had agreed to take the walk with me. She smiled a little quizzically, shaking her hair around her head, fluffing it out, then sauntered seductively over to me. She touched her lips briefly on my cheek. 'Nice man. Like my Harry. You help.'

'Sure I will.' She found a blouse in a drawer and slipped it on slowly. I'd become used to seeing women strip for me by now but this was different. She was dressing herself but in such a way as to make it enticing, slowing her pace, stepping into a half-slip daintily, walking to a mirror to apply make-up, her movement showing the outline of her small buttocks. I don't think she was egging me on and it would probably have been a mistake if I'd tried anything with her. It would have put her off, especially if she really loved Harry. But I began to realize that her coyness and shyness were perhaps something she had learned to use to her best advantage. Perhaps she was not quite as innocent as we had all presumed.

As she was at the mirror, she murmured without turning round to look at me though I could see a kind of teasing smile playing round her mouth, 'Good with Harry. Honeymoon very good. I like. Lots.' Then she turned round, held up her hands, made a circle with one thumb and finger and prodded two fingers in and out. 'Very big.' Her hands dropped to smooth her half-slip at her groin. 'What you say? Fuck, yes?' I nodded. 'Much we do it. Harry good.' She said it softly, her eyes wide open and ended with a large smile on her face. She said it so simply she looked almost like an innocent child but it had the effect of making it sound intensely erotic. 'I like very much,' she added.

Eventually she was dressed in her simple blouse

and skirt. She came to me and linked arms with me. 'Walk, yes?' And of course the manager who was hanging about the lobby was surprised to see us but he smiled his smarmy smile, bowed and said, 'Good afternoon, sir. Madame. Lovely sunny day, isn't it? Going for a stroll? See you later.' I ignored him and Maria moved closer to me.

As we walked I tried to explain what she had promised to do in exchange for coming to England. I made it sound as captivating as I could for, in a way, I agreed with Gerry. I didn't think these young Maltesers would be badly treated and their lives would be much more luxurious than any they might have known in Malta. And, given the way Maria had behaved with me a few minutes before, I was certain that she was not as guileless as all that. I told Maria that by comparison, if she ran away, any other work she could find would be only drudgery.

'But I Inglish,' she said.

'Yes. But what work can you do?' She shrugged. 'Harry work.'

I then told her that he worked for Gerry and if she reneged on the deal, he would be out of a job. I don't know whether she completely understood all this but we walked and talked a while and I managed to steer her towards the taxi. I took her arm and gave a gentle push as I opened the door. She gave a little cry but she didn't put up much of a struggle. I gave the driver Margo's address and then Maria squirmed across to me, her head on my shoulder. I put my arm around her and patted her to comfort her all the way to Margo's.

After settling Maria in her room, Margo came into the reception room where I was waiting for her. She was looking her usual stunning self, her black dress very clingy, outlining her thighs as she walked towards me on her very high heels. She placed a lovely warm kiss full on my mouth, her tongue flicking moistly, holding me tight for a moment.

'You're such a good boy, Nick. You deserve a nice reward for bringing Maria here so easily. I knew I could trust you to do it.' She kissed me again, then stepped back a little. 'Remember when we first met here? I thought you looked so shy but let me tell you, you made me feel . . . exquisite.' She put her hand to her cheek. 'Am I blushing? I'm a little ashamed to admit it. I mean, we did play a trick on you but it was worth it, wasn't it? Well, at least it was for me.'

'The feeling was mutual, believe me, Margo.'

She glanced at her wristwatch. 'If it wasn't quite so late . . .' She shook her head. 'There'll be another time. After all, you'll be coming to see Teresa when she's moved back here and I guess we can both entertain you then.' She laughed, then went on, 'Such a good young man. For a woman like me, at my age, the years pass quickly so I try to make the most of it when I find a . . . capable young man. I just like to enjoy his company . . . and it's so easy to make you enjoy yourself as well. But we can't allow ourselves to get sidetracked. This other piece of business is a bit more difficult perhaps but there's no real trouble involved. She's ready to come here. We've done her room up nicely. She wants to stay here and when she's settled in I'm sure she'll be straining at the bit to get to work. And you can bet she'll be good at her work!' She reached into the drawer of a table next to her and pulled out a small piece of paper. 'Here's the address. Take the taxi and pick the lady up. She'll be expecting you, I hope. Her room's all ready here.'

I decided that this job sounded even easier than the last one if the Malteser was willing to come. I couldn't understand what the problem was – why couldn't she just come on her own? So I asked Margo.

'It's a bit complicated. At first it looked as if she was trying to set up on her own but we found she was being put up to it by the man she married. Gerry's going to deal with him and then we thought we'd be able to put pressure on Carmella.'

'Carmella? It's Carmella?'

'That's who it is.'

I collected the address from her. It was somewhere in Whitechapel, not the kind of place I expected Gerry would keep his women in. I must have looked puzzled because Margo said, 'She'll be waiting for you, I'm sure. You know Carmella. She'll have arranged things. They got a thug to keep watch on her but somehow she got a message out to Gerry.'

'What if the thug's still there?'

'Gerry's taken care of him. Carmella will do the rest.'

So it was Carmella. I was surprised. She knew how to take care of herself, I was sure. After all, I suspected she had been a bar girl back in Malta, probably in some low-life dive in the dock area. I couldn't believe she'd want to operate by herself around Whitechapel. It sounded as if she'd been some kind of prisoner so now I began to feel this wasn't going to be as simple as I at first imagined. 'You're sure this is going to be alright?' I asked Margo.

'You'll be in and out of there in no time.' She gave me another brief kiss. 'Off you go.'

The taxi made its way down back streets till we came to a narrow, cobbled street of terraced houses.

The driver pulled the taxi to a quiet stop and almost before it had really stopped, out came Carmella, struggling with what looked like a heavy suitcase and an overstuffed paper carrier bag. I opened the door to climb out to help her but in spite of her cumbersome luggage she was too fast for me. She thumped the case and bag hard in the luggage space next to the driver and then yanked the door I'd opened with such a wrench I thought she'd pull it off its hinges. She clambered in, pushing me back, throwing herself into the corner and pulling her ratty fur coat around her.

I tapped on the glass to tell the driver to start. He had some difficulties turning the taxi around and every now and then it lurched, then stuttered, jerking us a little in the back. I glanced at Carmella and every time the taxi stopped and started, she looked as if it was a personal insult. Once we were underway I leaned towards her. 'How are you, Carmella? Nice to see you again.' She scowled ahead, not turning to look at me, her lips in a tight, straight line. 'Come on, Carmella,' I cajoled her. 'Tell me what's the matter.'

She remained silent until suddenly she snapped her head sideways to look at me. Her stare was almost venomous. 'Why you bring me this place?'

'I didn't bring you here. Besides, you knew what the deal was. Looks like you got yourself in this mess.'

She flailed her arms around and shook her head vigorously. 'You let them.' She sank further into her corner, her chin dropping down as if she was inspecting her shoes. I reached to pat her on her knee but she flinched and moved further away. 'Well, at least tell me what happened and why you're so upset.' I didn't know how good her English was but I knew she was better with it than the others and I tried to put a consoling tone in my voice. She sat up a little but she was still clutching herself tightly. She looked at me: her stare was not quite so vicious, her mouth even twitched towards a smile.

'Sorry. Make me crazy, this.' She gave a shrug. 'Go to Margo, yes?' I nodded. 'Good.' She gestured out to the narrow streets, the houses huddled together between the heaps of waste and rubble where the bombs had fallen. 'I work for Margo. That the deal.' She jerked her head back. 'Not him. Her.'

'Who? What did they do?'

'He take me there. Set me up. He fuck all time, try send me out. His mamma make me clean house, wash floors.' She rambled on like this for some time. As far as I could gather it seemed that the man she had married lived at the house. He had tried to make Carmella go out on the streets for him and during the day she had been little more than a cleaning woman in the house. She wasn't the one who had tried to work for herself; she'd been forced into it and Gerry and Margo had somehow misunderstood. No wonder she was upset. In spite of her spasmodic phrasing, her pronunciation, her still limited knowledge of English I was able to get the gist of her story. She felt she had been betrayed and I was part of the betrayal because I had brought her here. I managed to convince her it was all a mistake and things would be alright now. She'd be at Margo's and she'd have a nice place to live in and a better life. Carmella had seemed such a spirited woman I was staggered she had got herself into this situation without putting up a fight. I mentioned this to her and she replied, 'Ha, you know Carmella. But big guys, big . . . how you say?' and she crooked her arm and felt her muscle.

'Muscles.'

'Yes.'

'They hit you?'

She shook her head. 'No. Not let them.' As she was telling her story, some animation returned to her features and she relaxed a little. She even began to enjoy telling her story, smiling a little when she explained how she'd called the mother up to her room, smashed a vase on her head, got her things out and locked the mother in. 'Margo say car come so I wait. She not say you come. But I happy you come.' She gave my knee an affectionate squeeze.

She was not quite the Carmella I remembered, not yet the woman whose moist mouth I suspected I had experienced that evening in the club. But by the time we arrived at Margo's she was acting a little more comfortably. As the taxi stopped, Margo opened the front door and watched as Carmella flung herself out of the taxi, grabbed her luggage and banged past Margo into the house.

I paid off the taxi driver and went into the house where I saw Carmella blustering her way up the stairs with Margo behind her, trying to calm her down and explain she'd been mistaken, hoping Carmella was not going to hold a grudge against her.

I went into the large reception room but it was quite some time before Margo returned. She came into the room, patted my arm, tousled my hair a little. 'Good boy, Nick. You've done well. She's still upset but you seem to have got round her. She likes her room so she'll soon be feeling alright.'

'I don't know. She's still in a pretty bad mood.'

'I don't blame her. We were wrong. We'll just have to make her feel welcome. I put a bottle of wine in her room for her. And some flowers. She said you'd tried to cheer her up and she says she's sorry she acted the way she did with you to start with. She's got a soft spot for you, you know.' She paused. 'She's still going on about how she'd have liked to go on a honeymoon with you. Did you know about that? Carmella wanting you to do that?'

'Teresa told me.'

'It's all been a bit of a shock to her but at least she was glad to see you again.'

'I'd never have guessed that. Not at first anyhow.'

'Just give her a few minutes. She'll be the same Carmella again. We'll look after her here. You know, she reminds me a bit of how I was when I was her age.'

'I thought that too. And I thought, well, because of that maybe you would be daggers drawn with her.'

'I guess I did jump to conclusions about her. I suppose that's how Gerry and I misunderstood. Anyhow, she's the kind of woman who'll blossom here. I'm sure she'll be a great success. Some of our rich clients will really like her – and she'll respond to that. And she'll get plenty of free time.'

'I hope she's happy here. I didn't like seeing her down and so angry.'

I stood up. 'Well, if there's nothing else for me to do, I'd best be on my way.'

'Oh, don't go yet, Nick. Besides, Gerry told me that Mrs Courtney isn't sending a car for you till tomorrow.'

'I can catch a train.'

'I'm sure Teresa and Mrs Courtney can spare you for an evening.' I began to think that maybe Margo wanted me with her for the night, especially as she had been hinting at it earlier and so, remembering her delectable ways with me on our first meeting, I sat down again.

Then Margo went on, 'Besides, Carmella wants to see you again before you go. She'll be down in a few minutes. In the meantime I've a bottle of champagne ready. To celebrate.'

'Celebrate what?'

'The way you've handled the mission, I suppose. Anyhow, there's Carmella's divorce to celebrate – she won't be seeing her husband any more. And we can celebrate the beginning of Gerry's business again. In any case, any reason's good enough to celebrate and drink champagne. Celebration's good for the soul – and other things.' And she looked lewdly at me, 'As you found out on your birthday at the club, eh, Nick?'

'I certainly did.'

'Well then, don't be in such a rush to miss another celebration.'

Margo seemed to be promising me an entertaining evening so I smiled at her and composed myself for whatever might happen. Then the maid brought in a bottle of champagne – Margo must have had it ready. I had never seen the maid before, a pretty young girl, very pert and obviously one of those who was used to whatever went on in the house. I had a quick flash remembering Margo and Teresa on that first afternoon and I wondered if the maid would be joining in the celebration. Margo saw me watching her appreciatively as she left the room. 'I can see you haven't lost your eye for the ladies, Nick. Shirley's a lovely looking girl, isn't she? I'm sure you'll get on famously with her.'

'I'm sure I would.'

'I'm keeping her on even when Teresa's back with me, so you'll be seeing her again. No rush just now.' That sounded as if Shirley was not part of the plan for

the evening so I wondered just what Margo was up to.
She sipped her champagne and gave me her lewd look
again over the top of the glass. 'Who knows what other
things might crop up this evening?' She raised her
glass. 'Cheers to that.'

We drank the champagne and talked, Margo every
now and again losing track of the conversation. Once
or twice I caught her glancing at the door as though she
half-expected Carmella's husband to come barging in.
After about half an hour of this desultory conversation,
there was a tap at the door. I quickly wondered if I'd
been wrong and that the maid, Shirley, was coming
back to join us.

'Come in,' Margo said when she heard a second tap.
The door opened but it wasn't Shirley. It was Carmella.
And what a transformation! Instead of the frowning,
scowling woman who had scrunched herself inside
her moth-eaten fur coat in the taxi, she was now
looking marvellously cheerful and attractive, her face
beaming. She was wearing a plain white dress she had
buttoned herself into as though it was a smooth second
skin. It showed off every curvaceous inch of her, this
tall young woman made taller by white high heels, her
sheer white stockings glistening snugly on her perfectly shaped legs. Her hair had been brushed so that it
fell down to the top of her backbone in a lustrous black
curtain.

She stood by the door with just the suggestion of a
smile playing around her mouth. She looked incredibly sexy while at the same time she managed to appear
almost demure, a mood created by her standing still
with a bunch of flowers held against her breast. I
remembered how tough she had been with Joe in
Malta, taking charge of the girls, then showing herself

off in the plane. Then that evening at the club with the men, hamming it up, having a great deal of fun while still retaining her glowing sexuality. She seemed able to carry all this off without becoming too brash about it, a manner she could have easily adopted as her days as a bar girl must have put her in pretty rough company. None of that roughness had rubbed off on her appearance – she still looked young and fresh.

She waited at the door till Margo said, 'Come in, Carmella. Feeling better now?' Carmella nodded and strolled slowly into the room.

'Let's all just take it easy for a little while. Champagne?' Margo poured her a glass. Carmella took it, raised it and beamed at me.

'Cheers,' Margo said. 'To you, Carmella.' Carmella sat and there I was again in the presence of two alluring women who sat with me in their black and white dresses, both with their stunning legs crossed, both completely at ease, both sending out a real ambience of sensuality.

Margo sipped at her glass, then turned to me. 'I think we do have something to celebrate now, Nick, and I know Carmella won't mind you joining in.'

'As you said, Margo, any reason's good enough for a celebration.'

'Well, Carmella needs cheering up.' Carmella nodded at me and dazzled me with her bright smile. 'And she's all dressed up for the celebration. With the flowers as well. We had a long talk upstairs and what I found out is that Carmella would like to be a bride, a real bride. Make it proper this time.' I had a slightly queasy feeling that somehow Margo was going to marry me off to Carmella. It had been mentioned before – but of course she was still married, in name at least.

Carmella stood up and came to stand next to my chair. 'White,' she said, smoothing the dress against herself. 'Bride.' Then Margo added, 'She told me I reminded her of a priest, dressed all in black like this.' Anyone less like a priest than Margo I couldn't imagine.

Carmella leaned down to take my hand. It felt warm and soft and I began to have an inkling of what was going on. 'Carmella told me she'd like to start all over. With a wedding. That's why she chose her white dress. In fact, she dressed all in white, didn't you, Carmella?'

Carmella let go of my hand, put the flowers she was holding on my lap, her hand just brushing against my crotch. She stood in front of me and began to unfasten the line of buttons down the front of her dress. When she reached the last one, she pulled the dress open. 'White,' she said again and, indeed, everything she was wearing was white, edged with lace – a white bra which lifted up the roundness of her breasts exquisitely, a garter belt and a pair of panties which were almost see-through, for I could see the full dark bush under them. Carmella fingered the filmy material of her panties and Margo said 'Carmella wanted a veil and that's the only thing we could come up with. And Carmella even suggested that at some point you might want to lift the veil to kiss the bride.'

That seemed like a good idea to me so I stood up next to Carmella, putting the flowers on the chair and starting to reach my hand out towards her. 'Bride and gloom,' she said.

'Groom, Carmella, groom,' Margo said and laughed. 'I'm sure you're not making Nick gloomy.'

'You can say that again!'

'So what d'you think, Nick?'

'About what?'

'The wedding. I'm not explaining this very well, am I? Carmella was disappointed with her wedding. She thought it would be some slap-up do, not just a quick turn at the registry office. She expected flowers and all the trimmings. I suppose it's her Catholic upbringing. So now she thinks she'd like to try it all over again. We cooked up this idea together while we were talking upstairs. Would you, just as a favour to her, go through the motions? And have a quick honeymoon with her afterwards. I'll do the honours as the priest. As Carmella told me, I am dressed for the priest part.' She opened her dress to show the shiny black slip she was wearing. 'So we're all set. Well, almost. I don't know all the words and you don't have a ring but still . . .'

Carmella reached past me to pick up the flowers. 'See,' Margo went on, 'the blushing bride, coming down the aisle with her bouquet. What d'you say, Nick? It won't take too long, then you and Carmella . . . What have you got to lose?'

I was beginning to feel that this whole thing was a comedy but if that's what Carmella wanted, as Margo said, there didn't seem to be any harm in it, so I nodded. 'Good man,' said Margo, grinning at the pair of us. 'We can skip most of the preliminaries, just reel off the essentials and then you two can trip off upstairs for your honeymoon.'

So began what was an odd parody of a wedding ceremony, Carmella arranging herself next to me, still with her dress hanging open, just like Margo who took up her stance as the presiding minister. Both women kept looking at me with a blatant lewdness, then Carmella would be the blushing bride with eyes cast down. Margo tried hard to keep a straight face as she rattled off whatever she remembered of the words of the service. She took our hands and began stroking mine in a distinctly suggestive manner. Already, with these two half-dressed women standing close to me, I was beginning to feel a warm swelling in my groin.

'I guess I don't need to ask if there's anyone here who objects to the marriage, so I won't. Now you can go and get on with it upstairs.'

Carmella pulled at my arm as if she wanted to take me upstairs right away.

'Wait a minute,' Margo said, holding up her hand. 'You have to say something about "love, honour and obey". Say it.'

'Yes,' Carmella shouted out. 'He say something, I do it!'

'There! You can't say fairer than that, can you, Nick?'

Carmella pulled at me again.

'Steady on!' Margo stopped us once more. 'What about your vows?'

'What is this, vows?' Carmella asked.

'It's just, you know, what you say you'll do, what you want.'

'Pussy, suck and fuck!'

When she said that, I knew that the old Carmella was back with us. 'That alright with you, Nick?'

'Too true!'

'So that's it. By the authority vested in me, I now pronounce you man and wife. You may kiss the bride.'

I put my arms round Carmella and placed my mouth gently on hers. As soon as I touched her, I was convinced she had really been involved with my birthday celebration at the club for her kiss was one of those melting kisses, not the aggressive kind like

Margery's. Carmella's was yielding without being too limp, her tongue searching inside my lips, moving slowly, savouring the moistness while letting my tongue probe deep into her mouth. Her body pressed up against me, merging with mine, nestling into the gradually growing hardness in my crotch. One of my hands slid down her back and smoothed the filmy material of her panties round the inviting globes of her buttocks as I pulled her closer to me. We stayed like that for a while, her hands stroking my back, then one descended to the back of my thighs to hold me in place against her.

I heard Margo mutter 'Amen' and so we broke apart. 'I think you're going to be very happy,' Margo continued.

Carmella stood there, beaming, then she looked down at her feet. The flowers were a little trampled as she had let them fall from her hand when we had started our embrace.

'Leave them, Carmella,' Margo said. 'Now you'll be able to tiptoe through the tulips up to your room.'

I'm sure Carmella didn't know what the words meant but she knew what Margo was suggesting as she pulled me by the arm.

Margo grabbed me by my other arm. 'Wait a minute! I have to collect my fee first.' She dropped my arm and reached to fondle my crotch. 'My! I'd say you've got a heavy fee. I'd better let Carmella collect it!' Then she said, 'Come here,' pulling me close, her hand still in its fondling place as she gave me a big, wet kiss, as enticing as Carmella's but in a different way, a little more pushy, as if she was trying to go deeply into me, her hand working at my erection.

'Mmm!' she said as she pulled away from me. 'Save

the fee for me for some other time. This is Carmella's wedding. But remember, Nick, you owe me!' Then she waved her arm as a signal that the ceremony was over and we were free to leave.

If the so-called wedding service was a parody, there was no doubt that the 'honeymoon' I spent with Carmella that evening and through the night was the real thing. Carmella offered a whole new range of delights and pleasures, different in some ways from what I had grown accustomed to and, in others, extensions and elaborations of what I'd come to expect.

She held my hand leading me up the stairs, preceding me but still holding on to me, her other hand pulling the hem of her dress aside so I was given a full view of her long legs. The seam of her stockings followed the line of her slim thighs to disappear under the veil of her panties. At the top of the stairs she turned and, as I came up the last step, her mouth slid moistly onto mine, her deliciously warm body pressing softly into me. I was to discover that while at times Carmella's personality was tough, making me think I'd be having a real rough-and-tumble with her with her taking charge, there was much more of an agreeable and melting softness about her. Her appearance as a bride was not completely a pose – she knew all kinds of sexual tricks, certainly, often looking openly lascivious but much of the time she appeared almost bashful. It was an intriguing ambivalence, both a glorious invitation to deliver myself into her knowing hands while at the same time I still felt she was a woman wanting to be seduced.

Margo had given her a lovely room with a low, long bed and a thick billowy counterpane which Carmella flung back to reveal black satin sheets and fluffy pillows. She sat on the bed, allowing her dress to fall away so I had a full view of her splendidly shapely body, smoothly filling out her bra and panties. She beckoned to me with her finger, waiting there lecherously and when I reached her she began expertly to undress me, slipping my jacket off my shoulders, pulling my shirt out of my trousers, unbuckling my belt and pulling my trousers down. This was the tough Carmella taking control, smiling that lewd smile which widened when she saw my fat and stiff prick straining up towards her face.

She leaned down and placed a delicate wet kiss on the slit, then with one finger she touched me there, tracing the length slowly down the throbbing vein till that finger circled my balls. She reached under them, lingering there, briefly touching the secret place Teresa had discovered for me, rubbing gently before probing a little at my groin, the finger coming back to the root of my cock and sliding upwards to play a flickering touch at the slit again. My cock-head had swollen considerably during this opening gambit, the skin rolling back and my shaft pulsing hard as the finger began a maddening slow tour around that rolled-back skin, round and round, flicking each time at the strand of skin stretched tight. I felt that it might actually snap and the skin would roll all the way down, exposing the whole length of my cock as one throbbing, red rod.

I stood there and let her tickle and tease me, watching her as she looked up at me with that lewd and inviting smile. Then she stopped, lowered her eyes, withdrew her finger and became the shy young lady as if she was almost ashamed of what she had been doing.

I took both her hands and drew her up to me and she pressed against my body. She carefully arranged for the tip of my cock to brush teasingly against those filmy panties. My hands snaked round her back to rest on her arse, feeling that thin silkiness there, stroking her as she swayed her pelvis against mine. She nestled her head next to mine and her shyness suddenly dissipated as she whispered in my ear, 'Pussy, suck and fuck.'

One hand then grabbed at my cock, slipping it under the silky tissue of her panties. Her hand held me there, the cock-head tickled by her bush of hair, her hand stroking the silk along my shaft as her other hand slid down to finger the crack of my arse, pushing me hard against her, her wide open mouth nibbling sloppily against my lips and her tongue licking mine. We stayed like that for some time, my hands now inside her panties, my fingers moving into the creamy moistness of her slit. It was a liquid honeypot and my fingers were lubricated by a rich wetness running all over my hand bathing it in a warm stickiness. The lips of her quim were enticingly soft and Carmella breathed into my ear, 'Pussy juice. Hot for you,' followed by some Italian words sighing out of her.

Soon our movements against each other became more hectic until Carmella's sloppy mouth slid away from mine, her tongue tracing its way across my chin. Her hand moved my cock from inside her panties, letting it stand upright as her tongue travelled down my chest and onto my stomach. She sat on the edge of the bed and then she devoted herself to a long, excruciatingly delicious sucking.

Such oral delight was still relatively new to me as I had only been introduced to it on my visit to Margo's just a few weeks before. Then Teresa had taken charge of my oral education and finally all the women at my birthday celebration had convinced me that mouths could do an infinite variety of tricks – nibbling and sucking, licking and swallowing. I knew now that Carmella had participated in that celebration because, although sexual memories do not stay long, the mind is triggered by repeat performances. I recognized the masterly skill of Carmella as her tongue probed into my pubic hair, flickered at the base of my cock, her hands coming to stroke my balls as that slippery tongue slid slowly up as she made me wait for her mouth to take my cock-head inside, enclosing me in a soft velvety moistness, a warmth that spread down my shaft as she swallowed an incredible amount of my length.

Like Teresa, Carmella was one of those women who knew the delights of cock-sucking depended not simply on the slippery swallowing and tongue-trailing. The pleasure is increased by those pauses when the mouth lingers at the tip and fingers crawl up the length to stroke the wetness over every little stretch of cock, squeezing and teasing. Carmella pumped her mouth up and down, then tapped my prick against her lips, held the length of it nestled at her neck, poked the head in her ear, let it rest on her eye, her eyelashes tickling deliciously, then rubbing the length along her nose. And while she was doing these things, her hands were fondling my balls, rolling them through her fingers. Sometimes her palms held them while her fingers searched behind them, finding that secret place, then one finger reaching to slide into the crack of my arse, carefully penetrating. Sometimes she stopped altogether, smiling lecherously, licking her fingers and then bending over me to dribble strands of saliva onto the head and her fingertips moved to oil that hard fat head, fingers gripping my shaft, pulling the skin further back so her tongue could trace its tip round and round until her mouth opened and she took me deep inside.

All this was steaming me up of course, and I soon had her bra off. I licked my fingers and let their moistness cover her nipples till they stood up, jutting into my hands. I wanted to suck them but I didn't want to bend down to them yet for that would mean that she could not keep sucking me and she seemed content enough to have my hands fondle her breasts with my fingery slippiness. Her mouth became sloppier and I heard wet, gulping noises escape from her as her tongue slithered and slid around me, taking in the length of my cock till I imagined I was nudging at her tonsils.

My hands kept busy at her breasts, pinching hard on those long, upstanding nipples, rolling them between my fingers, their rubbery feel squirming at my touch till finally Carmella, with a long, lip-smacking, lingering dribble let loose my cock from her mouth. She stood up and clamped her musky mouth on mine as I probed my tongue into her. She was slavering and our mouths and chins were damp and sticky. Her hands clasped my stiffness, easing the hardness as her palm stroked the head. I felt I would soon be squirting all over her fingers but she must have sensed that for her hands slowed a little and then it was only her fingertips teasing me.

Somehow she turned me around and I felt the edge of the bed at the back of my knees. She leaned against me so that I fell back on the bed. She loosened my shoes, pulled them off, then my socks. She stood next to me, eyeing my stiff prick as her hands stroked up her thighs, sliding past the tops of her stockings, to insert her fingers just under those flimsy white panties. She moved her legs apart and I could make out, under the thin material, the dark mass of hair and the outline of the hooded lips of her quim. She smiled down at me, her gaze fixed on that rod of mine sticking up iron-hard. Then she said what at first sounded like 'Fucka pussy' and soon I understood she was telling me the name in Italian and translating it into English — 'fica' was 'pussy' in Italian. So I said, 'Fica' to her and added, 'Bella fica.' She pulled one hand away and gave me a jaunty thumbs-up.

Then she hooked her thumbs in the waistband of her panties and drew them slowly down, uncovering her full bush of hair, and then the thick lips of her cunt which she spread a little as her fingers pulled her panties in a tantalising motion along her thighs, right down until she stepped out of them.

'Bella, molto bella fica,' I gasped out, hoping my limited Italian made sense. She raised the panties high above her head, lowering them as she climbed onto the bed. They descended till she touched them at the tip of my cock, then let them fall over my stand and I could see myself in the mirror, poking into that flimsy silk. Her fingers, hardly touching me, stroked along my length and it felt deliciously soft as they travelled, wrapping the silk round my balls, tickling the silk under them. The fingers on her other hand gently squeezed my fat, swollen head inside the silk.

She kept stroking me like this till my cock began an uncontrollable twitching. I was shuddering, moaning, 'Bella, bella, molto bene.' I didn't really know if they were the right words but I didn't care as Carmella crawled up so that I could let her beautiful breasts rub against my face. I nuzzled into their warmth, then lapped at them, touching their roundness with my palms, sucking those hard, jutting nubs, licking my tongue round them as she murmured, 'Tette, tette' and I smothered them with moistness. Her hands continued their fabulous ministrations as she swayed her torso across my face.

I felt we were bathing in a hot glow and I wanted to prod my fingers inside her, slide a finger in and out of her and I shifted myself so I could touch her there, sighing out, 'Fica, fica.' She gripped my cock hard when she heard that and in a voice that seemed somehow to describe my hardness, she said, 'Cazzo,' with a fierce squeeze. 'Bel cazzo,' she whispered.

I slowly slid my finger into her deliciously creamy quim in an easy slide. I was in deep, circling my finger, then slowly pulling it out to feel those wet lips with my fingertips till they were dripping with slippery warmth. My touch circled her clit, round and round, before I let my finger prod inside again, moving it in gentle motions, gasping 'Bella fica' as her hands became dextrously insistent. A whole flood of come was gathering in my balls squirming in her hands, pumping up the length of my cock as she wriggled herself on my hand to draw my fingers into her, moaning in her throat till I caught what she was saying, all as one word, 'Ficacazzo,' over and over, till she gasped out what I thought was 'Si.' But she swivelled her head round towards the mirror. She wanted me to watch, to 'see'.

I managed to raise my head a little and saw the captivating sight of her arse swaying on my fingers and my arm probing between her legs. She moved aside a little so I could watch her busy hands on my shaft which she squeezed so that it became fatter and longer. But however engrossed Carmella was in this mutual stroking and teasing, she knew, as I did, that we were both on the verge of tipping over into a climax we wouldn't be able to stop so, with a last little trill along my length, she took her hands away and knelt up which caused my head to slide away from her. She was still chanting almost hypnotically in a throaty whisper, 'Ficacazzo' so I joined in with her. Somehow that chant made us feel even closer together, ready to submit to each other's every whim.

She indicated she wanted me to roll onto my stomach, and, remembering Teresa's hands wakening me to the extraordinary pleasure of my secret place, I complied with Carmella's request. As I rolled, she removed her silky panties from my cock and, when I was comfortable, my prick long and hard and hot on my stomach, Carmella straddled me, sitting on the back of my thighs, her behind spreading a lovely warm softness over them.

I felt the lightest trail of caresses wandering all over my body. I gasped at this touch and then she leaned down and I felt two trails barely touching my skin and then the silk of her panties was spread over my lower back. I turned my head and saw Carmella in the mirror leaning over me so that those nipples I had stroked to hardness were tracing a pattern of touches all over my back. Her hand crept up to slide along my neck, a finger reaching out to feel the corner of my mouth so that I dribbled onto the finger to make it wet. Carmella's other hand was now stuffing her panties into the crack of my arse.

Though these caresses were not part of any direct genital stimulation, they were driving me crazy, filling me with an almost feverish desire. I wanted to touch and stroke her, to make her feel the same urges but of course she was still straddling me, making me a virtual if willing prisoner. I could feel my hot prick twitching against my stomach and I gripped the black satin sheet in my teeth hoping that would stop me from releasing my load.

The skilful ministrations of Carmella's hand and breasts continued, driving me on but once again she knew when to stop. She climbed off and quite roughly rolled me over, one hand suddenly diving between my legs. Then she delicately pulled her panties out of my arse till they dangled again on my balls and cock. She straddled me once more and her trailing fingers and nipples moved all over me. I could feel my cock twitching against her arse and one hand snaked back to press that stiffness against her till slowly, one knee on each side of my body, she crawled up till she was straddled over my face. I could see her glistening slit, those loose lips like two hooded flaps. I gripped her thighs to spread her open and she let herself down, murmuring, 'Fica.'

How can anyone describe the exquisite sensation of taste and touch, entailed in licking and kissing and sucking a quim like Carmella's? Think of a slightly over-ripe fruit, an orange or, better still, a peach, and imagine inserting a finger into that squelchy, juicy texture. The smooth slither of juice around the finger gives something of the feel of the moistness, the flesh of the fruit something of the soft smoothness. I can only approximate my sense of the experience with Carmella. First I placed a gentle kiss on her exposed lips, letting my tongue venture a little inside. The taste was not really sweet. It was slightly – what? Muddy, a little earthy, but not as strong as that, a little like the taste of mussel, slightly salty, a little like a whiff of sea wind. And then, just as cock-sucking is helped by finger touches, so I moved my fingers to stroke those lips, curling my tongue in on itself, using it like a small, wet cock to prod inside, my lips on her quim-lips. I flicked my tongue into her, then drew it out. I lapped along those slithery lips, one finger easing in and out, till my tongue rested on her clitoris, flicking at it in gentle, butterfly kisses. I heard Carmella gasp and she breathed out rapidly in one word, 'Ficaficaficafi-cafica,' wriggling round to grasp my cock as if she would wrench it off, rubbing it hard and fast, fingers at the base moving to slide her silky panties up and down the shaft.

This made me agitate my fingers more insistently in and out of her, quickening the pace, my mouth now milking her juicy wet pussy, my saliva dribbling into her. Her juice was almost frothy as she squirmed on me, pressing herself down as if she wanted my whole hand inside her and my mouth to swallow all that soft flesh and all those dribbling juices. My nose breathed in that musky sea-smell as my finger drove into her quickly and somehow she wiggled round me, leaning down to my cock, her mouth wetter and wider and deeper than ever, taking me inside, her hands brushing silk on my balls and thighs.

I was content to lie back and slide my fingers all round her quim, my tongue now licking, my fingers plunging deep. Her mouth was making sloppy, slapping noises as she sucked at me and I knew that both of us now could not stop. We were driving each other on

303

till, with Carmella's mouth slurping and sloshing all over my cock and with my lips guzzling at her, her arse moving with my rhythm, both of us squirming and moaning, she brought me off, letting me pump myself into her mouth. Her tongue flicked at the slit while the jism poured out and, as her mouth gulped it down, a strangled, loud grunt came out of her washed throat and I tasted an extra gush of her juices from her leaping thrashing body.

Amazingly Carmella kept me in her mouth, bathing me in that oozy liquid inside. Of course the feeling was intense for a minute, an almost unbearable tingling all along the length of my prick, till gradually I lost my stiffness. But Carmella persisted, sucking gently so that I was reduced to a somewhat limp but fat stand, if that's not too much of a contradiction. Carmella's hands were still busy, caressing my thighs and my balls. It was a gentle flow of stroking and sucking and I lay back letting a flood of sensual warmth envelop me. Gradually I felt a small ache begin to grow deep in my scrotum. I began to twitch a little against Carmella's tongue and I returned to kissing her slippery lips, tasting that salty juice again, sliding my fingers inside.

Soon her mouth was taking me over. My cock grew stiffer, not to a full stand but pleasantly full. Carmella nibbled her way along its length, her fingers tight around it and she trailed the shaft along her breasts, then down her stomach. By now she was over me and her mouth descended on mine, opening to let me taste myself, a trace of saltiness diluted by the full wetness of her lips and tongue. She held my prick between a finger and thumb and she used it like a paintbrush to paint her quim lips, shuddering and whimpering a little – I could feel the sound vibrating on her lips as they touched mine. That touch of her moistness on me strengthened my cock and I was now fully erect. Carmella mumbled, 'Bel cazzo' as she slipped it inside her, pressing down to take me in, her hand pushing my balls against herself as if she was trying to take as much of me inside her as she could.

And then she began to ride me in a teasing canter, pulling herself up till the tip of my cock felt as if it would slide out of that liquid slit but then she wriggled down, incredible muscles inside her twitching around me like velvet claws, swelling my cock to a thick fatness. Each time she pushed down, feeling me thrust deeply inside, she sighed and mumbled Italian words fast, then fell silent, gripping her bottom lip with her teeth as she concentrated on levering herself up, wiggling to let my cock-head nudge at her clit before her quim lips clutched it again and there was that astonishing long-drawn-out pressure on my cock – astonishing because she was making me thicker and longer, at least that's what it felt like, my prick extending up inside her, hearing her gasp out her delight till she was unable to keep these slow motions going.

Now she was being overtaken by her own drive to orgasm and she quickened, pressing her whole body down on me, her mouth sucking at me as her pelvis jerked and jogged faster. Her voice mumbled, squashed against my mouth till at one enormous plunge down on me, she raised her body off me, threw her head back and let out a wail like a delirious banshee. That, and the sense of my cock so deep in her, my whole body feeling as if it was all concentrated down there in one gigantic stiffness, made me release a hot stream into her. I don't know how I managed it so soon after that first release but Carmella sensed it, went plunging on, riding me hard, making the most of my stiff shaft before it wilted. She went on yelling, mounting into several orgasms, her face wrenched into contortions of pain and pleasure, till the riding slowed and her pelvic movements became gentler, trying to keep my cock from becoming too limp for her to hold inside her. Finally she fell against me, rolled to the side, her fingers pushing at me to keep me inside her till at last my cock slipped out and her hands rubbed the juice up and down my dwindling member, muttering soft Italian words in my ear.

And that was only the beginning of my honeymoon night with Carmella. Bride and groom tasted all kinds of delights through to the dawn. Carmella cuddled against me, the smell of my come mingling with her perfume, her fingers playing with my half-erect cock, her panties stroking me, till I hardened in her hand and she slipped me inside her yet again. 'Fica full. Come. Come,' she said fiercely as she rammed me home. After each bout Carmella seemed able to start me again, never letting me rest, insisting on holding my cock which was getting more and more sensitive as the night wore on. And somehow I lasted. I lost count until finally we both lay back, exhausted.

The last thing I remember as Carmella flopped back to her side of the bed was her voice, husky and seductively soft, muttering that word we had chanted together, 'Ficacazzo.' Then she said, 'Goodnight' though it was really about five o'clock in the morning.

Epilogue

After about six weeks at Mrs Courtney's, Teresa and I moved back to the city as Gerry's business got fully underway again. I had enjoyed my stay at Mrs Courtney's. During that time she seemed to enjoy my company in the conservatory though I had the feeling that we would never get over the fact that she was upper class and I was only from a working-class background. She sometimes forgot about that class difference when I talked about going to university. I suppose that made her think I would eventually become part of a class closer to hers because of my university education. That difference between us didn't mean we stopped being together two or three times a week though towards the end I had the impression she was becoming a little condescending towards me, even a little bossy, though I always enjoyed our encounters – after all, I have always enjoyed it when the woman takes charge.

Eventually she heard that her husband was going to be demobbed in the near future. 'And, my dear Nicholas, while I could keep you on as gardener, I'd better not.' We were lying naked in the conservatory. She had sprinkled petals all over me, crushed them against me and then she had nuzzled every inch of me, claiming she was smelling their scent. 'Though I must say,' she told me in that precisely modulated accent of hers, 'it's *this* scent,' sliding her fingers around my cock which was squirmy with come, 'I prefer.' Then she bent down to sniff at it, her tongue lapping at the slippery skin. 'So you see, if he's around, it'd be difficult for us. How could I possibly keep my hands off you? Or my nose' she added, prodding her nose at my pubic hair. 'Or my mouth,' and she started again to lick at me.

She made me promise to keep in touch. 'And I do mean, in touch.' She promised she'd come to visit me to spend 'a naughty little weekend', as she called it, when I settled into my studies at university.

Teresa and I went back to work for Gerry, Teresa then returned to Margo to help her though she sometimes also did something with the accounts at the restaurant and the club. I used to see her two or three times a week, usually at the club and it was always delectably captivating with her. I tried to convince her to come and live with me in the city where I eventually went to university but she told me that the kind of life I would lead there as a student was not for her. 'But there'll always be a place here for you to sleep . . . and other things . . . when you come back here,' she told me. In fact when I came home on vacations I did see Teresa but after about a year or so we drifted apart and finally I lost contact with her. I knew it wouldn't help matters between us with my being so far away. She was so sexually alive, I couldn't expect her to keep herself for me. I missed her very much to begin with but I did get over her.

In any case Teresa felt I'd be moving in a new circle with new 'intellectual women' as she called them though I could tell she believed they could never be as good as she was in sexual matters. To some extent that was true though I soon discovered at university that the interests of 'intellectual women' were not always intellectual!

While I kept in contact with Teresa for a time, I found I couldn't see Carmella again. Margo had discovered that she was her most popular girl. She was a great success and Margo kept her fees high and treated her very well. I tried to go round to Margo's once to see Carmella but Margo put me off. She indicated it would not be good for the business if Carmella was seen with one of the help. 'You know I like you, Nick, but . . . I tell you what – ring me up some time and you can spend some time with me.' I liked Margo but at this time I resented her attitude about Carmella so I never did go round to see her again. And I heard that after her year was up, Carmella left Margo's and set up what she called her Italian salon, bringing over twin sisters from Italy to work with her. I always fancied that I'd pay her a visit there but by the time I got around to it she had moved. Besides, my life really changed at university and while I missed that free and easy sexual life I lived for those few months, there were other compensations at university – and as I say, the women I met there did not always stay stuck in their intellectual ways.

I also saw Dorothy occasionally at the club but she had moved up in the world. She was now the star attraction at the club because of course Judy had gone. And I never went on point with Margery again though we did have a few boisterously hectic meetings. Eventually I got tired of her because in her own way she was a little like Mrs Courtney in her bossy ways.

Eventually I drifted away from that life. Naturally I'll never forget the good times I had – those weeks with Teresa, those mad escapades with Helen and Margo, my birthday celebration, Carmella and Mrs

Courtney's horticultural delights all packed into a few months. My years at university were a separate chapter of my life and I never again lived that invigorating but adventurous time I spent as an errand boy for Gerry.

More Erotic Fiction from Headline:

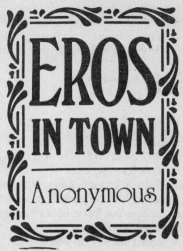

EROS IN TOWN

Anonymous

When the aristocratic Sir Franklin Franklyn and his half-brother Andy arrive in London to claim their inheritance, they find not the respectable family home they expected but the most lascivious of brothels. Frank takes things into his own hands and transforms the town-house into the most luxurious, romantic house of pleasure in all London. Here, every desire is catered for, any amorous wish met.

Not to be outdone, Frank's saucy sister Sophie declares that women are as much slaves to desire as men, and to prove her point she establishes a stable of lusty lovers patronised by the most elegant ladies in the land.

Thus both brother and sister indulge themselves in an orgy of sensuality that surpasses even the wildest flights of erotic fantasy . . .

Also available from Headline – EROS IN THE COUNTRY – the first volume in the sensual adventures of a lady and gentleman of leisure.

FICTION/EROTICA   0 7472 3199 0

Headline Delta Erotic Survey

In order to provide the kind of books you like to read - and to qualify for a free erotic novel of the Editor's choice - we would appreciate it if you would complete the following survey and send your answers, together with any further comments, to:

> Headline Book Publishing
> FREEPOST (WD 4984)
> London
> NW1 0YR

1. Are you male or female?
2. Age? Under 20 / 20 to 30 / 30 to 40 / 40 to 50 / 50 to 60 / 60 to 70 / over
3. At what age did you leave full-time education?
4. Where do you live? (Main geographical area)
5. Are you a regular erotic book buyer / a regular book buyer in general / both?
6. How much approximately do you spend a year on erotic books / on books in general?
7. How did you come by this book?
7a. If you bought it, did you purchase from:
    a national bookchain / a high street store / a newsagent / a motorway station / an airport / a railway station / other........
8. Do you find erotic books easy / hard to come by?
8a. Do you find Headline Delta erotic books easy / hard to come by?
9. Which are the best / worst erotic books you have ever read?
9a. Which are the best / worst Headline Delta erotic books you have ever read?
10. Within the erotic genre there are many periods, subjects and literary styles. Which of the following do you prefer:
10a. (period) historical / Victorian / C20th / contemporary / future?
10b. (subject) nuns / whores & whorehouses / Continental frolics / s&m / vampires / modern realism / escapist fantasy / science fiction?

10c. (styles) hardboiled / humorous / hardcore / ironic / romantic / realistic?

10d. Are there any other ingredients that particularly appeal to you?

11. We try to create a cover appearance that is suitable for each title. Do you consider them to be successful?

12. Would you prefer them to be less explicit / more explicit?

13. We would be interested to hear of your other reading habits. What other types of books do you read?

14. Who are your favourite authors?

15. Which newspapers do you read?

16. Which magazines?

17. Do you have any other comments or suggestions to make?

If you would like to receive a free erotic novel of the Editor's choice (available only to UK residents), together with an up-to-date listing of Headline Delta titles, please supply your name and address. Please allow 28 days for delivery.

Name..

Address..

....

....

A selection of Erotica from Headline